1

The smoke-stained rafters were slo~~ly~~ beginning to take shape above Winfri~~th~~ ......~~n~~g would ever make winter daylight come faster, however much she wished it. She lowered her feet to the floor, lifting her shoulders and arching her back, stretching away the stiffness of a night on a hard sleeping platform with too few blankets. Doing her best to avoid the worst creaks in the planks underfoot, she felt her way across the floor to the corner where the ale bucket stood. She slid the dry leather lid gently aside and scooped some of the ale into a cup. No-one had bothered to refill the bucket and she felt the cup scrape the bottom before it was even half full. She screwed up her face as she took the first mouthful, more sour sludge than thirst-quenching liquid.

She glanced across to where Olwen and Ourdilic were sleeping. Two girls, not-quite-women, striking enough to draw looks from Alfred's thegns...both expecting to be waited on hand and foot. She could wake them of course...remind them there was kindling to be gathered, logs to be cut, water to be fetched, onions to slice, soup to cook ...but that would mean listening to their complaints, arguing, putting up with their muttering and sour looks. No, better to leave them to stir in their own time. Perhaps they might even wake while she was on her way to the spring and discover there was no-one about to find their clothes or fetch their food.

Winfrith picked up the ale bucket and stepped outside into the damp morning air. Heavy grey clouds hung motionless above the trees and rooftops and a few thin spirals of woodsmoke curled listlessly up towards them. She kicked impatiently at the dead leaves around the door. What on earth had persuaded her to agree to look after both girls? It wasn't as if either one of them was hers. She ought not to complain about Olwen. That was largely her own doing and at least she could feel satisfied at having freed a slave from a harsh master. Ourdilic on the other hand was a different matter altogether. Only such an unworldly man as Alfred would expect the wilful daughter of a dead Cornish king to settle peaceably into a Saxon household. Just because Winfrith had ensured Olwen conducted herself meekly in the king's presence,

Alfred assumed she was just the woman to teach Ourdilic similar ways. He'd clearly had no experience of trying to offer her advice!

It wasn't that Ourdilic resented being brought to Chippenham…quite the opposite in fact. She reveled in it. To her the royal vill was the natural place for a king's daughter. The fact that her father's kingdom had been Cornwall and that most Saxons thought all who dwelt there were either witches, monsters or traitors didn't seem to trouble her at all. She walked the streets with her head held high, assuming even poor Wiltshire folk owed her respect.

Winfrith kicked a loose stone across the rutted, muddy track that separated the house from the strip fields opposite. The track passed around the edge of the house before climbing a slight rise and heading out across the moor beyond. She'd had no time to explore it but now she began to follow it, wondering about the other houses which might lie further along its way. Even at this early hour would there be other people waking and stretching, grumbling about how stiff and hungry they were, and railing at the laziness of those still asleep? The thought cheered her up a little. Others had worse lives…had more to complain about probably. Olwen might be at her side for a few years yet but not for ever. If most men were wary of taking freed slaves as wives, Olwen's blue eyes and slender waist would overcome someone's hesitancy one day. Ourdilic would surely be off her hands sooner though. Those high cheekbones, the black eyes, the easy long-limbed stride…some thegn or other would be charmed by them before too long. She had land too, enough to encourage even the most suspicious of Saxon thegns to put aside his doubts about the Cornish. She'd have Alfred's help in finding a suitable husband as well. Why else had he insisted she be given a safe haven in Chippenham? He had to be counting on her one day marrying someone who would bring added power and strength to the kingdom of Wessex.

Winfrith had seen hopeful signs too, though perhaps not ones Alfred himself would encourage if he got to hear of them. Ourdilic seemed to have developed an ability to know precisely the moment Alfred's nephew, Aethelwold, would emerge from the noisy companionship of the king's hall. She would tie back her thick, wavy hair, demand that someone found her favourite necklace or bracelet for her, and dash outside to make sure he could not pass without setting eyes on her and perhaps even exchanging a few words. And if Winfrith still saw her as a child, even as shy and awkward a man as Aethelwold could surely see the woman she would soon become. Few Chippenham wives would give Aethelwold a second look, despite his rank, but Ourdilic seemed quite unworried by his unimpressive appearance or manner and no doubt he was grateful for any attention at all, even if it did come from a twelve-year-old girl.

Unable to get the two girls out her mind Winfrith turned round and headed back towards the house, intending to insist they fetch water before she would serve up breakfast. On re-entering the house she was surprised to find that the wattle panel which divided the room, allowing the girls a private area to sleep in, had already been moved aside. An untidy pile of clothes and blankets suggested the two of them had made a hurried exit. As she bent down to pick up the discarded heap from the floor she heard the unmistakable crunch of horses' hooves crossing the stony track outside. She moved to the doorway, taking care to keep in the shadows.

She was just in time to see Olwen and Ourdilic emerge from between two neighbouring houses as three horsemen were passing. Ourdilic called out a greeting and while two of the riders appeared to take little notice the third hung back, leaning down to say something to the girls. Winfrith had no difficulty in recognising Aethelwold with his lank reddish hair, small eyes and pointed chin. He looked in need of a good meal too, his clothes hanging loosely off his shoulders. Not that his looks appeared to trouble Ourdilic. Whatever he said was enough to cause her to her to throw back her head with laughter and even from the shelter of the doorway Winfrith could see Aethelwold blush with pleasure.

Winfrith watched as Ourdilic answered him, reluctant to interfere. It was hard to see what harm could come of a few words exchanged at the roadside. In any case offering Ourdilic advice was generally a fruitless pursuit and if Aethelwold was flattered enough to return Ourdilic's interest there was little Winfrith could do about it. Alfred would probably see it differently of course. He would no doubt blame Winfrith for not keeping the girl on a tighter rein, but there was also just the smallest chance he might raise no objection to his nephew's interest. He must know Aethelwold well enough…petulant, wavering, spiteful, plain…not the most marriageable man in Wessex. He might even see Ourdilic as a potential wife for his nephew…if he thought it would bring him the support of the Cornish. Winfrith smiled at her own wishful thinking. No-one knew the minds of Cornishmen and a shared joke and a betrothal were a thousand miles apart.

Whatever Ourdilic had said, it was clearly enough to coax Aethelwold down from his horse. The moment his feet touched the ground, she took his arm and began to shepherd him towards the house. Winfrith stepped back from the doorway, hoping she hadn't been seen, and snatched up an abandoned piece of tablet weave as she crossed to the wall bench. The wooden tablets had been hastily made, the holes drilled unevenly, and what had begun as a simple braid of blue and green threads now looked little better than a tangle of wool. Patience would be needed to rescue it but the task would allow her to observe Ourdilic and Aethelwold without it seeming too obvious.

Winfrith began to unpick the braid, expecting to see Ourdilic come through the door at any moment, but if the girl had planned to lure Aethelwold inside, she had clearly thought better of it. The sound of voices suggested they had halted outside, not far from the door. Winfrith found that if she gave up the pretence of weaving and listened hard she could just make out their words.

"I thought Olwen would never take the hint," Ourdilic was saying. "It's impossible to talk round here without someone's ears flapping. We could step inside except that Winfrith would be watching us like a hawk."

"I should be getting back…"

"You don't have to go yet. We've hardly had a minute."

"There's much to do."

"But you've just spent the whole day watching out for Danes. You must be allowed some time off for pleasure, surely?"

"Not much. We…we have to be wary…all the time. There's not much room for…for, you know…pleasure." Aethelwold's voice lurched so uncertainly from high notes to low that Winfrith was forced to suppress a giggle.

"Well you must be able to think of better things to look at than forest tracks and horses' backsides, whatever your precious King Alfred thinks. Wouldn't you rather rest your eyes on a beautiful woman?" There was a long pause, followed by an awkward clearing of the throat.

"I suppose so...all in good time. One day perhaps."

"But why not now? What about the beautiful woman you see before you?"

"But you're not...a woman, I mean...though I'm sure you'll become one soon." Winfrith smiled to herself. Perhaps there was hope for the Aethelwold yet.

"What's the matter with you Wessex men? Something in the air gets in your eyes and blinds you? In Cornwall there are girls my age been married for a twelvemonth or more. There's no-one else you'd rather have, is there?"

Winfrith never learned what Aethelwold might have said in answer to that for the weaving tablets slipped from her lap and fell noisily against the floorboards. All she did hear was a curse from Ourdilic and the sound of the girl protesting as Aethelwold made a swift getaway. Winfrith laughed as she picked the tablets up. Ourdilic's weaving had been about as successful as her own!

Winfrith rarely allowed herself to fret over Ourdilic for long. It was really her own fault that she'd been lumbered with the girl. She had chosen to accept the protection of a thegn like Cuthbert and, despite everything that had happened since then, she didn't regret it. He'd provided protection and a home when she'd most needed it and even a husband, albeit briefly, from among his thegns. He wanted something in return of course, especially if it would win him favour with Alfred. With no wife of his own he expected Winfrith to keep an eye on the affairs of his hall and his servants, trusting her to make sure the lazy, overfed steward he employed earned his keep. When he was required to travel Wessex with the king she went too and despite its hardships it was a far better life than scraping a living in some remote hamlet. Keeping an eye on Ourdilic was a small price to pay.

Pleased she had shrugged off her irritation, Winfrith gave up the attempt to untangle the tablet weave and stepped outside. Olwen and Ourdilic had disappeared again and she began to stroll towards the king's hall. There were other gains from travelling with the king's household and the one Winfrith valued most was her friendship with King Alfred's oldest adviser, Milred, and he was more than due a visit. The old man's sight was far from good in the middle of the day but by nightfall he could make out very little at all. There was nothing wrong with his wits though and, unlike Olwen and Ourdilic, he was always glad to see her. She had welcomed his company too, especially when her husband Leofranc had not survived his battle wounds. She had needed a friend then and was happy that she was now able to repay him for his kindness. Few others in Chippenham could read and, while Winfrith sometimes struggled to make out what some of the more clumsy scribes had intended, she knew enough to help Milred make sense of the charters and reeve's accounts he was asked to pass judgement on.

Milred's room was at the far end of the king's hall and to reach it Winfrith had to pass the main entrance, guarded by two bored sentries, and turn into an alleyway which ran alongside it. The kings of Wessex had maintained their own hall in Chippenham for many years and the long, low building was beginning to show signs of neglect. The walls were planked with uneven, mud-stained timbers. In several places the wood had warped, leaving gaps which had been plugged with straw, twigs and even rags. The corner post marking the entrance to the alley leaned outwards at a sharp angle, looking as though it might fall any time a high wind got up. An equally ramshackle building flanked the alley on the opposite side. Formerly used as a store for winter animal feed, in these difficult times it had now been pressed into service as sleeping quarters for the newly arrived Somerset force.

The alley itself was gloomy and narrow, allowing two people to pass each other only if they turned sideways. It was usually deserted but on this occasion Winfrith was aware of a tall broad-shouldered figure entering the alley from the far end and advancing swiftly towards her. She fixed her face into a smile and prepared to edge past him but as the figure came closer it became clear he didn't mean to let her pass easily. They came to an awkward stop, facing each other. A quick glance at his face suggested he offered no threat to her, though Winfrith would not have said he looked exactly happy either. A shame really…but for a flattened, crooked nose, she would have described him as handsome.

"What are you doing here?" he demanded, as if the alley belonged to him.

"Minding my own affairs," Winfrith replied. "And you?"

"Minding the affairs of a bunch of sheep watchers and plough boys…making sure they don't get into any mischief with the likes of you."

Winfrith laughed. "What would I want with plough boys? I wouldn't waste my time on anyone poorer than a thegn, and then only if his nose was straight."

The man's stare hardened for a second before his face suddenly relaxed into a grin. "You look as though you've been in the wars yourself. We should think ourselves lucky. Better a scar or a smashed nose than a dented skull, eh? So you're not here to bother my Somerset lads after all. In that case, I suppose some other lucky fellow must be expecting you."

"He is…more than sixty years old and half blind. Walks slower than a pig with piles. He's good company though and he's better manners than to block a woman's path without at least revealing his name."

The man flattened himself against the wall, waving her past with an exaggerated sweep of his hand. "He's a very fortunate old man then…and my name is Aethelnoth, ealdorman of Somerset, stuck in this miserable hole until either Alfred or the ploughboys tire of it. Hard to say who'll be first. And your name, just in case we should meet again?"

"Winfrith, widow of Leofranc, of the household of Cuthbert, on my way to lend a hand to Milred, the king's most trusted adviser. So not someone to be treated lightly, you see, even by the ealdorman of Somerset."

Without waiting for a reply Winfrith pushed past Aethelnoth and headed for the small side door which opened directly into Milred's tiny, overheated room.

She found him wrapped in a thick blanket which he hugged to his chest even though he sat close to the comfortable glow of a well built peat fire. He lifted his head as she entered and, despite his frequent claims that he struggled to see clearly now, greeted her by name.

"Come in, Winfrith. Make yourself comfortable. It's not the time of year to be wandering about outside. It's not just us old folk who feel it. You're probably too young to remember but Yuletide used to be a time of feasting and laughter. Now all anyone wants to do is either pray all day and night or drink so much strong ale they pass out. The king's as pious a man as you could meet and even he admits we could do with something to lift our spirits."

"What had you in mind, Milred? Walking round Chippenham on your hands maybe? Or tying Alfred's legs together while he's at prayer? That would cheer me up."

Milred smiled. "Easy to mock, my girl, but as it happens I do have an idea. I heard news this morning of a scop passing through Frome. He goes by the name of Raedwald. I'm told he promises a seasonal entertainment Christian enough to please our king but with enough humour in it to satisfy the rest of us. He's supposed to be able to remind us of the holy texts without sending us to sleep. We could do with a bit of laughter, don't you think?"

Winfrith did not answer straight away. It was not the idea of an entertainer but the mention of Raedwald's name that unsettled her. There surely couldn't be many scops of that name and the Raedwald she remembered had been a master of leading his listeners to both laughter and sadness. She had met him briefly after her father had been killed. The story-teller had invited her into his home on the banks of the Itchen and she had listened all evening to his songs and stories, glad to be able to forget her troubles. In the end she had fallen asleep and passed her first peaceful night since the murder. Raedwald had waved her off the next morning and she had not expected to see him again. Milred's polite cough interrupted her recollections.

"Sorry, Milred. I was miles away. Of course it would be welcome."

"Good. Cuthbert has offered to go and find this fellow. Perhaps you'd like to go with him? He can ensure that you get there and back safely and you can ensure that this Raedwald will present something worth listening to and likely to meet with Alfred's approval. Just between you and me, Winfrith, I can't summon much enthusiasm for all this Christmas praying. When I do manage to get down onto my knees without banging or scraping anything, I generally find I can't get up again. Prayer's a young man's pastime."

"I'm sure your soul is safe enough already, Milred. As for me, I'll be very happy to fetch Raedwald. A day or two away from Ourdilic will be a blessing in itself. When do we leave?"

"Not for a day or two, I'm afraid. Some thegns are agitating for a meeting of the witan and, though Alfred thinks it can wait, their mood is restless enough to make it likely he'll reconsider. I'll be glad of your help again if it does happen…to keep me awake as much as to mark down what's said. As soon as that's settled, you can be off. Anyway, that's enough of lighter matters. Let's get on to more important things. What's happened to that soup you promised yesterday? I swear the cooking pot in the king's hall this morning contained nothing but boiled nettles. Even an old man needs something tastier than that."

2

As usual Milred's judgement of the mood among Alfred's thegns proved accurate. The following afternoon he summoned Winfrith to tell her Alfred had reluctantly agreed to call a meeting of his witan. She took his elbow as he moved a little unsteadily through the narrow doorway separating his own room from the king's hall. A long table had been set down the centre of the hall and most places along it had already been taken. Some of those seated around it were deep in whispered conversations, but others waited in silence, casting wary glances around the room. There was little sign of the usual banter and laughter and many of the faces looked as though trouble was expected.

Several heads turned to watch as Winfrith hurried Milred towards the end of a bench, close enough to the wall for him to lean back against it, and rescued an unclaimed stool for herself. She quickly discovered why no-one had made use of it. The surface was rough and the legs uneven, cut by a craftsman with worse eyesight even than Milred. While Winfrith was edging the stool nearer the table, searching for a position with less chance of tipping her to the floor, she heard the first argument begin. A heavy set man with a bushy black beard which he pulled at fiercely from time to time was on his feet. She looked up, all concerns about the stool gone. Wulfhere was ealdorman of Wiltshire and two years back a key figure in the very first task in which Milred had sought her help. She remembered him well, happy to use all the cunning he had to deliver up as little food and men as he could get away with. She'd since learned he rarely missed a chance to stir up the witan either. In fact he seemed to take great delight in it.

"Look at you all…struck dumb. We don't need to sit round a table for hours to know what's wrong. Guthrum's sitting comfortably in Wessex while we talk endlessly with no idea what to do about it. Well the answer is staring you all in the face. Settle with him. Give yourselves some hope of a comfortable winter…"

Growls of protests rose until they threatened to drown him out but he ignored them, hammering a heavy fist against the table and raising his voice to a raucous shout.

"What's wrong with sharing the kingdom with Guthrum? At least we get to keep some of it that way. What else are you going to do? Hide in Chippenham until you all starve?"

"What's the matter...Wiltshire not big enough for you?" an angry voice called from somewhere lower down the hall and others quickly took up the theme.

"What're you after then? Think Guthrum'll give you all of Wessex?"

"Look at him...too fat to fight..."

"Lost his nerve...and too fat to run away more like."

This last remark provoked some laughter but it swiftly subsided. It was obvious to Winfrith that there were still many in the room who were intent on keeping their thoughts to themselves. Forgetting what she'd chosen to sit on, she leaned forward to get a better view down the table, curious as to why Alfred himself had not answered Wulfhere. The stool tipped sideways, throwing her against the firm shoulder of the thegn to her left. She struggled to push herself upright but not before she had taken in Aethelnoth's grinning face looking down at her. Nor was he the only one amused by her plight.

"Look at her," Wulfhere shouted, pointing triumphantly at Winfrith. "She understands the state we're in. She hasn't the strength to sit up. She knows we're close to starvation."

"So what do you suggest we do?" a familiar voice demanded from further down the table. Cuthbert had little patience with the affairs of the witan and often sat in silence but every now and again Winfrith had heard him needled into speaking, especially when it was a matter of defending the things he valued...Wessex, its kings, or members of his own household. "Invite him to dine with us? I won't be staying to watch you have your throat cut. Look around you. There are plenty at this table who'll never agree to share it with a murderous heathen like Guthrum." Several murmured their agreement but others merely looked expectantly towards Wulfhere or Alfred, sitting impassively at the top end of the table. Wulfhere at least did not disappoint them.

"Then they'd better get moving. Guthrum won't stay in Gloucester for ever. You can shout as much as you like. That won't stop him. Someone needs to do something. It's obvious this sickly king of ours has no ideas. Others have made peace with

Guthrum and thrived. Look at Ceolwulf…once a thegn; now lord of half Mercia."

The mention of Ceolwulf was greeted with a fresh outbreak of abuse and it was only Alfred getting to his feet and holding up his hands for silence that gradually restored some order. He stared across the table at Wulfhere, his face impassive and his body strangely still amid all the tension.

"So you think Guthrum will break his agreement to stay in Gloucester and will soon be on his way here. Perhaps you're right. Only a fool would count on such a man keeping his word. What surprises me, Wulfhere, is that you think I'm not ready for that. Perhaps you've been away from the heart of Wessex too long. You must have grown too used to having Guthrum as your neighbour."

It was easy to see what Alfred was hinting at and a young thegn on Wulfhere's left jumped to his feet, waving a fist in Wulfhere's face. The ealdorman stood, grabbing the younger man's wrist and pushing him away. Despite a few shouts of encouragement, others were quick to intervene, coming between the two men and escorting the young thegn to a seat further down the table.

"That would please Guthrum," Alfred said, once the room had settled down. "He'd be glad to see us fighting among ourselves. We can do better than that…all of us. Wulfhere thinks we should offer Guthrum peace. I say he has a short memory. Less than two years ago we entrusted Saxon hostages to Guthrum at Wareham. In case you've forgotten, he cut all their throats. The dogs and ravens fed well that winter."

There was an awkward silence. How could they have forgotten? Winfrith gripped the edge of the table…memories flooding back. All those young men promised life…and all of them slaughtered, including her husband Leofranc. She'd had him for such a short time and much of that he'd been away fighting Danes. She looked across at Alfred but he seemed in no hurry to continue. He stared at Wulfhere, challenging him to respond, but the ealdorman appeared to recognise he had been outwitted and it was Alfred who finally resumed his attack.

"Don't you recall it, Wulfhere, how your generous Guthrum swore great oaths on his precious gold arm bands to respect the lives of our brothers and sons? Well, let him come here. Stay and embrace him if you will. See how such loyalty will be rewarded.

But I won't be standing alongside you or to surrendering the kingship of Wessex to Guthrum or anyone in this hall. I think you'll find all true Wessex men will follow me. You see me as a man with no ideas? I see you as a man I no longer trust enough to tell what I have planned...until now that is. Guthrum may or may not be on his way here but as for us, we leave tomorrow at first light. Guthrum can't make false promises to someone he can't find."

Milred slapped his palm gently against the table in approval and others followed suit so that soon the hall echoed to the regular beat of fists on wood, drowning out Wulfhere's half-hearted attempts to defend himself. Alfred stepped behind his chair and made his way slowly down the hall towards the main door. Thegns stood as he passed and, despite the prospect of a dawn summons and a midwinter journey to follow, most looked happy at the outcome. It was an exit worthy of a king, one that suggested to anyone watching closely that beneath his unhealthy pallor and slight frame there lay an unshakeable resolve. As for Wulfhere, he hurried away through a side door, a hail of insults echoing after him.

Once Alfred had gone the clamour of excited voices quickly resumed. The decision to leave had clearly taken most by surprise. From what Winfrith could see even Milred had been given no hint of it, else he would surely not have proposed fetching the scop Raedwald in a bid to cheer everyone up. He was still looking mildly surprised when Cuthbert came over to join them.

"No need to look quite so worried," he said, helping Milred to his feet. "The roads are watched. Even if Guthrum was already on his way he'd not be here before mid-morning tomorrow, by which time we'll be long gone. You might need a bit of help getting things together though. Why don't Winfrith and I give you a hand? Better make good use of the last hour or two of daylight."

Winfrith followed the two men out. She wouldn't regret leaving Chippenham...food which rarely stretched beyond thin soup and gritty bread; no wool to weave or cloth to cut and sew; no-one who remembered the endings of tales or riddles; barely enough firewood to keep anyone except thegns warm; Olwen and Ourdilic expecting her to fetch and carry for them. As far as she was concerned it didn't much matter where Alfred was heading.

Almost anywhere would be an improvement. Olwen and Ourdilic would have to be dragged along of course. She couldn't abandon them, however tempting that might seem, and it ought not to surprise her if they found being uprooted again less appealing than she did. Both had seen more hardship already than many women met in a lifetime and in all likelihood they were about to encounter more. Not for the first time Winfrith promised herself she would try and be more patient with them. Keeping that thought uppermost in her mind, Winfrith left Cuthbert helping Milred to gather together his few possessions and set off with the intention of preparing Olwen and Ourdilic for a swift departure.

They left just before dawn, in surprisingly good order considering the haste and the uncertainty about who would go with Alfred and who would stay behind. Now that they were on the move Winfrith found herself quietly looking forward to the journey. She hadn't enjoyed exchanging the warmth of a fire for the chill morning air, and no-one appeared to know where Alfred planned to take them. Even so there was clearly a feeling among those who had left Chippenham that something good would come of the journey.

It was difficult to judge their number exactly, perhaps fifty at most, but one thing Winfrith was sure of was that very few of them were women. She had caught sight of two thegns' wives at the head of the column heading out of the settlement and shortly afterwards two older women had bustled past, both of whom she had seen working in Alfred's kitchens. Assuming that the thegns' wives were faithful to their husbands and that the cooks' short supply of teeth and hair would discourage all but the most desperate of men, it looked likely that Ourdilic and Olwen would not go short of attention once they were clear of Chippenham.

The two girls had protested loudly about the upheaval of course. Yet as soon as they realised most of Alfred's thegns, Aethelwold among them, had no intention of staying, they readied themselves quickly enough. They even appeared to be enjoying themselves, once everyone got moving, despite the low, pale clouds and the thin, drifting rain which seemed determined to follow them all day. Winfrith caught occasional glances of them up ahead, trailing behind a small band of thegns which included Alfred's older nephew, Aethelwold.

Alfred himself looked in far better spirits than his situation merited. It seemed to Winfrith that he ought to be close to despair. His kingdom of Wessex had been reduced to fifty wanderers with no home to call their own. His most powerful ealdorman was suggesting he should offer Guthrum half his kingdom and, however much he had cloaked this journey with fine words, he must be feeling he was running away. Yet, whatever he was thinking, for the first few miles he passed up and down the line of marchers, offering both encouragement and thanks to all who had joined him. Gradually his determination took hold, and complaints about the early departure and the steady drizzle were replaced by questions about their possible destination. Alfred himself gave little away, merely pointing westwards and assuring them that he had come this way as a boy, taken by his brothers to learn the craft of the hunter.

At the end of the first day they spent an uncomfortable night under a copse of dripping trees. Few attempted sleep, with most preferring to lean against tree trunks rather than risking the wet ground and hope that idle talk would help speed the arrival of daylight. At dawn they set off again. Alfred had gone as far as naming Frome as the next place they would pass through and once it was light enough pointed out the dark line of the Mendip Hills ahead of them. Winfrith, as well as trying to keep an eye on Olwen and Ourdilic, was keeping Milred company, walking alongside him wherever the track allowed it. Alfred had insisted that Milred should ride one of the few horses not being used to pull carts or carry goods rescued from Chippenham. The animal's ribs suggesting it had been some time since its last good feed but it was sure-footed and seemed not to mind that Milred sat awkwardly and made little effort to guide it.

Towards mid morning Cuthbert moved up to join them, relieved that his turn at keeping any stragglers moving was over. Even so he seemed irritated by their slow progress and in need of distraction. Winfrith suggested they pass the time setting each other riddles to solve. She was feeling particularly pleased with her first effort – *Water I carry far better than any bucket, yet try to carry me and your hand will pass through my skin. Though I may lie over your head, you will feel no weight and, when I come and go, no man can say* – even though Milred's upward glance suggested he had the answer straight away. Yet before he could speak, someone ahead of them shouted Winfrith's name and a dishevelled-looking Olwen pushed her way past two of the men from Aethelnoth's Somerset fyrd, stopping the moment she caught sight of Winfrith.

"Have you seen Ourdilic?" she said breathlessly. "I can't find her. She's gone."

Winfrith glanced hurriedly behind them, slipping a reassuring arm around Olwen's shoulder and hoping her face did not betray her lack of concern.

"She won't have gone far, I'm sure. She's not foolish enough to have wandered off on her own."

Olwen pushed Winfrith's arm away. "I know that. I don't think she is on her own. I think Aethelwold might be with her."

"Well that explains it. It won't be the first time she's tried to separate him from his fellows, will it? Why worry…unless you think Aethelwold should have taken you along instead of course."

This was clearly not what was troubling Olwen. Her eyes widened and she looked up at the sky, as if only those on earth were capable of thinking such a thing.

"Me and Aethelwold? No thank you…a face like a fox and usually as slow on the uptake as a man asleep. But him and Ourdilic…it's like trying to make a dog eat acorns…"

"Perhaps he's not slow…just has his eyes on someone nearer his own age," Cuthbert suggested, circling his arms to suggest they should get moving again.

Olwen was quick to deny the possibility. "No, he likes her well enough, but as soon as they come close something ties his tongue in knots."

"They're unlikely to have gone off together then, aren't they?" Cuthbert said. "I don't remember seeing them among the stragglers at the back but they're bound to turn up soon enough." He stepped past Olwen, waving to them to follow, but Winfrith hesitated. There was probably nothing to be concerned about but Ourdilic was still meant to be in her care and it was rare for her to be separated from Olwen. Aethelwold was probably harmless enough but it was better to be safe than sorry.

"Wait. All right, Olwen. Maybe we should make sure they've not been left behind. I'm sure Cuthbert won't mind pushing on ahead and informing Alfred. Aethelwold is his nephew after all and he can't afford to lose any more thegns. We'll stop here and ask anyone behind us if they've seen Ourdilic. If I know her, she won't be lost. She'll happen along soon and enjoy any kind of fuss she's stirred up."

Cuthbert set off again with a sad shake of his head and Milred's horse clearly decided it was wise to amble after him, leaving Winfrith and Olwen to climb a slight rise which gave a better view of the track behind them.

There was little to see at first. The track meandered alongside a small stream before disappearing into a ragged clump of trees. The cloud had lifted slightly so that the distant outlines of hills and woods were clearer than they had been earlier. They were still waiting for the first stragglers to appear when Cuthbert returned, accompanied on foot by Alfred and a rider Winfrith recognised as the Somerset ealdorman, Aethelnoth.

"No sign of them yet then?" Alfred asked, scanning the ground to either side of the track.

Winfrith shook her head. "We haven't had a single man or girl pass us."

"They probably took a side track somewhere…that's if they did go off together. They'll soon realise they're no longer following us. Aethelnoth is going to ride back and take a look. I've told the others to wait if we haven't caught up with them by midday."

"Olwen didn't see them together," Winfrith said, "but neither of them seems to be with us now."

Alfred glanced at the girl, nodding slowly. "It wouldn't be the first time my nephew has lost his way. He'd better turn up soon though if he doesn't want his fellows to question what he's been up to. And as for Ourdilic, you were entrusted with her care, Winfrith. Give you the slip, did she?"

"I'm sorry," Winfrith said. "I thought she was with Olwen."

"She's not the easiest to keep in order," Cuthbert said, coming quickly to Winfrith's defence. "Too used to getting her own way."

"Perhaps," Alfred replied. "When she appears, and I'm sure they can't have gone far, it might be time to sort out what's to be done with her. I'll speak to her."

Alfred's belief Ourdilic would soon turn up proved well founded. They had not been waiting long when a rider pulled clear of the trees and began to move steadily along the stream side towards them. There was no doubting who it was…the rider sitting tall and straight and a smaller figure nestling comfortably in front of him. They seemed in no hurry and Ourdilic gave a casual wave as they drew nearer. If Olwen was glad of her friend's safe return she did not show it, standing silently behind Winfrith as Alfred stepped forward to help Ourdilic down. The girl cast a swift glance over her shoulder before swinging a leg over the horse's neck, resting her hands on Alfred's shoulders and sliding lightly to the ground. Winfrith watched with interest, sure that Ourdilic lingered with Alfred's hands on her waist a moment longer than she needed to.

"Well, Ourdilic, you're back with no harm done it seems," Alfred said, patting her shoulder as if to prove it. "What have you done with my nephew? I was told he was the one leading you astray. You haven't lost him I hope…or lost anything else a girl shouldn't lose?"

Ourdilic gave no sign that anything was amiss. She smiled at Alfred, ignoring his heavy hint and glancing quickly up at Aethelnoth before replying. Winfrith fought back the urge to scold the girl even though it was obvious Ourdilic was determined to make the most of the attention she was getting.

"I'm not to blame for your nephew's behaviour, sir. As everyone keeps telling me, I'm still a child. I can't help it if some of your thegns admire me."

"So where is he, if he's not with you?"

"I couldn't say. For once he wasn't following me everywhere. The last time I saw him he was with two of his cronies, going on and on about goshawks and wild pigs and deer. Much too dull to listen to for long. He didn't have anything to do with me getting lost anyway. I mistook the way alone. I don't suppose anyone would have even missed me if it hadn't been for Aethelnoth. I was sure I'd never see another living soul until he came suddenly upon me. At least one your thegns doesn't spend all day talking."

She looked up at Aethelnoth but he avoided meeting her gaze. Winfrith could see he was eager to get moving again. Whether it was Ourdilic or something else which was making him uncomfortable wasn't clear but he shifted in his saddle and urged his horse forward a couple of steps, coming between Alfred and the girl.

"No sign of your nephew," he said curtly. "We must somehow have missed him. I'll ride forward again and make sure he's still with us." Without waiting for an answer he rode away at a brisk trot, leaving Alfred watching his retreating back. Ourdilic smiled sweetly, before turning and setting off after him.

"That girl is too clever for her own good," Alfred said, loudly enough for the retreating Ourdilic to hear, "unlike my nephew who could do with getting a lot more wisdom. If he is as charmed by her as she thinks he is, perhaps it might not be such a bad thing. Some of her sharpness might rub off on him."

"She'd keep him in order," Cuthbert said. "And stop the rest of us wondering where he is."

Alfred looked along the path where the now tiny figure of Ourdilic was about to disappear over the brow of a hill. "Well if he does have a mind to free her of her maidenhood and she's willing, I expect there to be a betrothal first. The pair of them better not be out of our sight from now on. So let's get after her. Start as we mean to go on."

Winfrith caught Cuthbert's eye. He raised his eyebrows and looked briefly skywards. At least someone recognised that keeping a tight rein on Ourdilic was easier said than done.

"If she sets her mind on something she's hard to dissuade," Winfrith said, hurrying to keep up with Alfred and Cuthbert. "She probably took a wrong turn deliberately, hoping your nephew would come after her."

Alfred didn't appear to find the suggestion improbable. "Then perhaps some swift action is needed. I saw the way she looked at Aethelnoth too. The last thing we need just now is to have my thegns at each other's throats over a girl. A betrothal between them wouldn't be the worst thing that could happen, even if a marriage might have to wait a year or two. A morning gift would seal it…not that Ourdilic has any parents alive to receive it."

"I'm sure she'd be delighted," Winfrith said, "but could the same be said for your nephew? He's flattered by her interest but he's scared of her too. From what I've seen of him he's not ready to take a wife for a few years yet."

"Well, we'll soon see. Assuming we haven't lost him too, I shall have a quiet word in his ear. Scared or not, he can speak for himself. If he wants to be the man to bind the kingdoms of Wessex and Cornwall more closely, I'll make sure Ourdilic is named as his betrothed. In fact, the more I think about it, the more the idea pleases me."

Alfred quickened his pace, almost breaking into a run. "Come on. We need to make up for lost time to get to Frome before dark. No-one will want another damp night under the trees."

3

They reached Frome just as the rain was starting again. It was heavier now, splattering against the tightly thatched roofs and bouncing off the yellowish stones lining the way into the settlement. Winfrith had expected somewhere bigger, but she could count no more than fifteen houses. News of Alfred's imminent arrival had obviously travelled ahead of them and space had been made in the largest house for all but Aethelnoth's Somerset men. Perhaps space was not the best word Winfrith thought as she squeezed between Ourdilic and Cuthbert on a bench running the length of the house. Those sitting opposite were packed equally tightly and there was much nudging and grumbling before everyone was settled. Only Alfred was accorded the honour of his own chair, heavy enough to require four men to carry it inside. Despite its solid legs and the elaborate carvings decorating the back and arms, it looked if anything less comfortable than the benches.

A white-haired old man appeared to be directing the arrangements and once Alfred was seated he turned to look down the room, raising his arms for silence before addressing his visitors.

"Welcome…welcome to Frome." He paused, clearing his throat before continuing. "I'm Ceolstan…the head man here. It's not often we're honoured by a visit from the king himself. We are all poor men here, but it will never be said that when the King of Wessex calls we don't know what's expected of us." He turned to face Alfred. "We'll do our best to supply food and entertainment, though both are in short supply here. And when that's done we'll try and make your night here as comfortable as it can be."

He looked around a little vaguely, unsure how to go on, and Alfred took the opportunity to rise from his chair, stretching his back as he did so. "We're very grateful, Ceolstan. I know this damp winter and the closeness of Guthrum mean there's little food to spare. Your kindness will not be forgotten."

Ceolstan gave an awkward bow, glancing uncomfortably around the faces before him, as if checking how many mouths there were to feed.

"It's not kindness, sir, but the duty of all true Saxons. A pot of stew is being heated, though I hope you won't all expect to be stuffed to the ears before it's empty. As for passing the time, our best scop has left just us I'm afraid, so there'll be no gripping tales of battles or monsters."

Winfrith had been looking up and down the line of faces opposite, aware that their arrival under a warm roof had put Aethelwold out of her mind. She was wondering whether he had arrived and it was only hearing Ceolstan's mention a scop that drew her attention back to what he was saying. She had forgotten all about her old friend Raedwald. Milred had said he was in Frome but the speedy departure from Chippenham had prevented them fetching him there. Now she had actually made her way to Frome it seemed he had gone. Such a shame. She would have enjoyed talking over old times and there was no doubt he would have lifted all their spirits.

Ceolstan cleared his throat before continuing. "There may not be a scop but I'm sure we can find something else pleasant to fill the time. We're poor folk, as I said, but we're not without our talents." He looked towards Alfred. "You may not know, sire, that some of the finest jewels ever seen in Wessex are made here by a wonderful craftsman called Waergar. Perhaps you would like to hear how he turns earthbound stones into things of rare beauty?"

"Waergar?" Alfred repeated the name slowly as he resumed his seat. "Waergar the jewel-maker. That sounds familiar. Though I was only a child, I'm sure I remember my mother speaking the name. She was fond of brooches and bracelets and I expect I was curious about them. Could it be the same man who made them?"

Ceolstan nodded vigorously, stroking his white beard and beaming with delight. "It could…it most certainly could. He has worked his magic for many years. He came here from the west as a young man. I was a mere boy so he's even more ancient than I am." He paused, perhaps expecting laughter, but there was no response apart from a few nods of agreement. "His father had taught him the skills and he has used them ever since to make jewels men marvel at. He's always glad to show off his knowledge to strangers. If you wish, just as soon as I have checked that the stew is heating up, I'll summon him."

"We'd be pleased to hear what he has to say," Alfred replied. "I'm sure it will help to take our minds off present troubles and use up a little of the long evening ahead."

"You'll not be disappointed." Ceolstan said, rubbing his hands together and turning towards the door. "He'll tell you the shapes and colours of every stone and how to set them in silver and gold. There's nothing he doesn't know. You'll be amazed at how so much learning can rest in one man's head. Get him started and he can talk all night."

Ceolstan's promise drew several audible groans and mumbled complaints about having to listen to the voluble jewel-maker, but Alfred chose to ignore them and Ceolstan had already made a hasty exit to check on the stew. Winfrith stretched her legs, trying to make herself more comfortable. They had little choice in the matter. The men of Frome might be as poor and simple as they claimed, but they were hosts and must be accorded due respect. If they wanted to show off their skills, there was nothing to be done but listen patiently.

Winfrith came suddenly awake, roused by Cuthbert jabbing his elbow into her ribs.

"For you see," Waergar was saying, "most women, though obviously not this sleepy one here, hold such adornments in high esteem…and rightly so, for they're not easily wrought. Take garnet, for example. Who would have thought these plain stones could be transformed into the thinnest slices of shiny blood-red beauty, bright enough to dazzle the eyes and make even gold humble. Or what of niello…blended to become blacker than the night sky so that silver cannot but sparkle beside it. How is it done, you may ask? Not by magic, or charms, or spells…though you would think so to look at the brooches and bracelets our thegns' wives wear. Yet there is no magic in it at all. None whatsoever. No, the secrets are the jewel-makers themselves, and I would not tell you how they work their wonders now, were it not for the presence here of the king himself."

Winfrith leaned forward an inch or two to get a better look at Waergar. He was, to judge from his sunken eyes and wrinkled face, as old as Ceolstan had suggested. His pronounced stoop perhaps meant that he was taller than he appeared and his large, gnarled hands, with which he constantly gestured as he spoke, suggested a lifetime spent trying to shape reluctant materials. Despite his age he had declined the offer of a chair and rarely kept still as he spoke, stepping first forward and back, then from side to side, as if to halt might dry up the flow of words. Most of what he had to say was addressed to Alfred, sitting stiffly in his carved chair. The king looked to be following his every word but Winfrith was relieved to note that several others, their eyes half-closed and their heads leaning back against the walls, were finding it no easier than she was to stay awake.

"Now here's something which may surprise you. Niello is most commonly used by Cornish brooch-makers. It was much favoured by their kings and queens…"

Ourdilic, who had seemed tired and had been doing her best to lean her head against Winfrith's unwilling shoulder, suddenly sat up straight, fixing her gaze on the old jewel-maker. Winfrith thought it unlikely Waergar would be aware a daughter of the last King of Cornwall was among the company, but he did seem to be looking more frequently in Ourdilic and Winfrith's direction than elsewhere. It probably meant nothing. With Olwen seated on Ourdilic's other side he had in all likelihood just assumed that three women would be more eager listeners than a roomful of weary thegns.

"But it was far from simple to make. First of all there must be fires five times hotter than you've ever seen…so a man would break into a sweat fifty paces away. Then there must be two bowls to mix in… two, mind, not one. Of course they have to be strong enough not to crack in pieces, even though the heat comes near that of the flames of Hell. Copper and silver and sulphur must be mixed, but not altogether. Exactly how it's done must remain the jeweller's secret for now. It has to be done exactly right but I think it would take longer to explain than we have time for now. The next step is to tip everything into an iron mould…not as easy as when I was a young man. Even then, more remains to be done. Before the mixture cools it must be beaten into a thin sheet…"

"The old fellow should be beaten into a thin sheet." The remark came from the lower end of the room and was greeted with laughter and one or two murmurs of agreement. Winfrith doubted if the comment had been meant for Alfred's ears and as far she could tell Waergar appeared not to have heard it. If he had, he was clearly enjoying himself too much to be put off by a little banter.

"After that of course, it must be ground into a powder ready to use or, more likely, to be stored until later. And that's all there is to it." Waergar rubbed his hands together in a grinding motion and was about to continue when there was a sudden interruption.

"There must be more to it than that." Winfrith felt Ourdilic knock against her shoulder as she stood up. There was a sudden stirring of interest, as if a good argument might be brewing. "Cornish women aren't fools. They wouldn't wear brooches decorated with powder. The first bit of breeze and it would be all gone."

"Of course it would," Waergar replied, smiling. "It's good to see someone is paying attention. When I said that's all there is to it, I only meant insofar as making the powder is concerned. It takes more work to set it in a brooch. First the brooch-maker needs to cut shapes in the silver, where the niello is to go. Then he mixes the powder with water and carefully places it into the gaps he has made. Once that's done the brooch goes back into the fire. As long as the embers are hot enough, the niello will melt and stick to the silver. The jewel-maker then has to wait for it to cool, before scraping away any unwanted specks until, God willing, he is left with a beautiful brooch."

Waergar paused, glancing round the room as if expecting questions. Several of Alfred's thegns had their eyes shut and none of the others looked inclined to prolong Waergar's explanation. He looked towards the door, as if expecting the stew might appear at any moment, though Winfrith decided he was very glad of the chance to continue.

"Now niello is not the only trick we jewel-makers have. No doubt all of you have seen glass…"

"Seen it…and found a better use for it than making jewels." It was the same voice from the far end of the room, but much louder this time. The laughter and the agreements were louder too, but Waergar refused to be put off.

"Indeed…we all enjoy a glass of wine, when we can afford it. But think of it this way, a glass of wine is gone in a moment while a brightly coloured necklace can be enjoyed for ever. That's the secret of using glass…so many shades can be captured in one jewel. It's simply a matter of grinding up the glass with water and placing it on the metal you're decorating. Fierce heat melts the mixture and, once cooled, it's stuck fast. If you have a good eye the glass paste can be shaped into plants or animals…people even. In fact I am half way through completing a piece now. The paste represents a figure and despite my poor eyes I'm pleased with his looks. It's ready for firing now." He turned towards Alfred, stretching his open palms towards the king. "Perhaps you would like to see it?"

Alfred glanced around the weary faces of his followers, before smiling up at Waergar.

"It would please me greatly," he said, rising from his chair. "We might all benefit from a good stretch before eating. Tell me, Waergar, does this figure of yours represent anyone in particular…a man of Frome perhaps?"

Waergar seemed greatly amused by this. "Good Lord no. For the most part we men of Frome are a poor, misshapen lot. This is someone far nobler in looks, though I haven't yet decided what he will stand for. I thought perhaps the sense of sight itself, or maybe he could even stand as a reminder to the wearer of the wisdom of God…that's if He allows the firing to preserve what's best in my work."

"Well whoever it turns out to be, I'd be honoured to see it," Alfred said, half turning towards the door. " I'm sure someone will fetch us when Ceolstan's promised stew arrives. Shall we go?"

Waergar held up a hand. "In just a moment, sir, if it pleases you. There's one other skill I haven't talked of…one that merits at least a few more words. I haven't told you about garnets yet. It won't take long. Now you might think something as common as a garnet stone would present no difficulty. But you'd be quite wrong. The stone has to be ground into pieces thin as a horse's hair. Just think of that…a horse's hair. Many more pieces are broken than are ever set in brooches. You need to buy your stones first of course. There are none of good enough quality anywhere in Wessex…in fact anywhere this side of the narrow sea. They have to be bought from merchants who come on trading ships. And you know what merchants are like…always raising their prices."

"So it's very hard for poor men of Frome to afford them," Alfred said, putting an arm round Waergar's shoulder and, before he had time to say anything more, guiding him gently towards the door. "I think my thegns are looking hungry. Perhaps their minds are more on stew than garnets. Why don't you and I go and look at your unfinished piece while a little light remains? You might even find that kings of Wessex reward fine workmanship better than your usual buyers."

He took the old man's arm and, to the clear relief of many along the benches, ushered the old man out into the rain.

Despite Waergar's efforts to help pass the time there was a marked uneasiness in the room as the evening advanced. Even the appearance of a large iron cauldron, swinging alarmingly from side to side as two gloomy-looking ceorls struggled under its weight, failed to lighten the mood. At first Winfrith put it down to a sense of shame at having run away, leaving Guthrum to do as he pleased with Chippenham…and perhaps the rest of Wessex too. No-one expected him to pursue them this far but the thought that they might be safe provided little satisfaction. An evening gathering of thegns around a fire would usually give rise to a certain amount of laughter, raised voices, horseplay even, but tonight there was none. Cuthbert returned from a swift visit to check that the Somerset fyrd were up to no mischief and reported that they too seemed strangely quiet. Perhaps that was not such a surprise. They had more reason than most to be thoughtful. Many were quite close to home now and the lure of their own hearths must be making the king's service seem less attractive as each hour passed.

Ourdilic and Olwen seemed out of sorts too. They had barely exchanged a word since arriving in Frome. There could be any number of reasons for that of course. As Winfrith knew well, they had a habit of falling out, sulking and making up again, though the sulking part of the process could sometimes last a whole morning. Whatever the cause this time, both girls looked determined not to make the first move to restore peace between them. Winfrith wondered if the cause might be that Olwen had overheard Alfred's talk of a possible betrothal. That would surely have been enough to spark an argument. Yet it seemed unlikely. Olwen had been standing some way off when Alfred spoke of it and if she had heard she would have rushed after Ourdilic to tell her the news. By now Ourdilic would be strolling haughtily round the room, telling everyone. No, it had to be something else. Perhaps Cuthbert had hit on the truth when he'd hinted that Olwen might be jealous of Ourdilic receiving so much interest from Aethelwold. Or could it even have been seeing her astride Aethelnoth's horse that had driven a wedge between the girls?

Winfrith considered the two thegns for a moment. The two men had such similar names and yet they could hardly have been more different. Aethelnoth was powerful, handsome, a leader of men and a charmer of women, though it was Winfrith's impression that any wife he took would never be sure of him. Aethelwold on the other hand was gangly and hesitant, while his face rarely seemed to show anything but slyness or irritation. Without his kinship to Alfred he would surely have few friends. She sighed at the short-sightedness of the young. At that age she wouldn't have given either man a second glance. Still, with half the evening ahead, she determined to make one last effort to restore friendship between the two girls. It had to better than watching them sulk.

"I've never known the two of you so quiet. What's troubling you?"

Olwen turned away, staring hard at the far side of the room, as if something there had deeply offended her. Ourdilic shrugged, pulling her arms more tightly around her chest. For once she seemed unsure of herself but she did at least offer up an answer.

"Nothing. Nothing you can do anything about. You can't change what's already happened."

"It can't be something bad enough to stop you speaking for ever. When I was your age I was often reminded that friends are long in the making and swift in the losing. You need your friends."

"Friends stand by you when you need them. They don't resent what fate brings you."

This was too much for Olwen. She turned to face Ourdilic, her cheeks flushed and her hands trembling, almost spitting out her words.

"Fate had nothing do with it. You planned it all. You knew someone would come looking for you. I doubt if you even cared who it was, as long as it was one of Alfred's thegns. So pleased with yourself, up there on Aethelnoth's horse, leaning all over him. What a pity Aethelwold wasn't there to see it. If you hoped to make him jealous, that part of your plan failed, didn't it?"

Winfrith watched Ourdilic, ready to put herself between the two of them if tempers rose any higher. Ourdilic might be younger by three years or more but she was much the more wilful of the two and yet there was no sign of the angry response Winfrith was expecting. Ourdilic looked defiant, but she did not leap to her own defence. If she was pleased with herself she was no longer showing it. When she did reply she spoke in a low voice and had it been anyone but Ourdilic, Winfrith would have said she looked close to tears.

"I didn't know it was going to be Aethelnoth who would come by. How could I? It could have been anyone. You can't blame me for that...just because you spend all day dreaming about him. You shouldn't waste your time anyway. He's no better than any other man."

"What do you mean 'no better'? How would you know? Did he say something to you?"

"It doesn't matter. It's not important now. You're old enough to know all thegns are the same. Ask Winfrith."

Something was plainly wrong. Winfrith couldn't remember the last time Ourdilic had asked for her opinion about anything. Not only that, it was only hours ago she had looked to be revelling in the close attention of Aethelnoth. Now she turned away from Olwen and Winfrith and stared down at the floor. Whatever had upset Ourdilic would not be easy to prise out of her and Winfrith was too tired to keep on pressing her. The only way to find out would probably be for Winfrith to tackle Aethelnoth herself.

"You can ask me what you like about thegns," she replied, more sharply than she had intended, "but there's only one thing that interests me at the moment. This foolish argument needs putting to rest and, if you won't sort it out between you, then I'll go and have a quiet word with Aethelnoth. By the time I get back I expect the pair of you to be speaking more gently to each other."

As soon as she stepped outside Winfrith cursed her impulsiveness. Aethelnoth might be no more forthcoming than Ourdilic had been. Besides, she didn't even know where to find him and his Somerset men. To make matters worse the night air felt damp and chilly and she would not be able to see her way without a torch. She was about to give up the idea when a door opposite was pushed open and the outline of a grey head peered round it. The familiar voice of the head man, Ceolstan, called across to her.

"Is all well in there? Did you wish for something? The stew was to your liking, I hope?"

"It was fine, thank you. I was looking for Aethelnoth…the Somerset ealdorman. I have a message for him."

"Of course," Ceolstan replied, his relief obvious. "Wait just a moment. I'll light a torch and guide you there."

Flickering light filtered through the doorway as he returned, torch held aloft, and Winfrith followed as he set off down a narrow path between tightly packed dwellings. Ceolstan listed the inhabitants of each shadowy house they passed, proudly naming their ages and occupations. He paused in front of the last house, a rickety affair whose roof of bound rushes looked even in the flickering torchlight too bulky for its walls to support. Several of its upright posts leaned alarmingly into the street and a broad, murky puddle had collected around the front door.

Ceolstan, perhaps hearing Winfrith catch her breath, was quick to apologise.

"It's the only space we had left, I'm afraid. Better than a night out in the rain anyway. Don't forget they're Somerset men in there. Most of them have seen and lived in a lot worse. If you wait here, I'll see if I can bring Aethelnoth out here to you."

He lifted his trousers and stepped cautiously into the water around the door. It quickly rose over his shoes and the squelch of mud sounded each time he lifted a foot. He entered without knocking, leaving Winfrith in the dark. From inside she could hear snoring, someone coughing and then an angry growl, as if someone had been stepped on. Ceolstan reappeared after several minutes, followed by a clearly reluctant Aethelnoth. Even in the wavering light cast by Ceolstan's torch Somerset's ealdorman looked a little the worse for wear. His hair was tousled and his clothes rumpled while his grim expression suggested he was much less pleased to see Winfrith than during their first encounter in the narrow alley. His mood was not improved by Ceolstan's reminder of the flooded doorway…too late to avoid further muddy splashes to his own and Ceolstan's clothes.

"I thought you'd no interest in thegns," he said, kicking a lump of mud from his shoe. "What's so important you have to drag me from an early bed?"

Winfrith pulled her cloak more tightly around her shoulders. This probably wasn't the best time or place to encourage Aethelnoth to talk freely but it was too late to give up the attempt now.

"It's about Ourdilic…the girl whose aid you came to earlier."

Aethelnoth growled dismissively. "No need to tell me who she is. What's she done now? And what's it got to do with me anyway?" He sounded unconcerned, perhaps too much so. Winfrith was sure he hadn't been so unmoved by Ourdilic's charms when she rode back with him earlier in the day.

"She's upset. I think it's something to do with you going back to find her this morning."

"She should be grateful. She wouldn't have survived long otherwise. She's like all girls. They get upset as easily as they breathe."

"This isn't just one of her moods. Usually there's almost nothing that troubles her. Are you quite sure nothing happened when you found her? You didn't say anything? You must have seen how she likes attention from Alfred's thegns."

Aethelnoth sighed. "She's just a girl…even if she thinks she's a woman already. It must be how they bring them up in Cornwall. She needs watching, that's all I'd say. If she keeps wandering off like that, someone will take advantage of her sooner or later."

"As long as you haven't already tried it," Winfrith said, aware she had taken a step back as she spoke. "It's at the request of the king himself that I'm trying to keep an eye on her."

"Then you must have been neglecting your duty this morning. Fortunate for you and Alfred that I found her. As for trying it on, the girl would probably encourage it but I'd rather have the fish than the sprat any day. A nice widow woman, now that's more like it."

"Well this widow woman is more interested in the safety of a young girl than any Somerset thegn, especially one who looks as though he's been sleeping in a pig pen."

Ceolstan switched the torch from right hand to left, as if not liking this turn in the conversation and restless to be going.

Aethelnoth cast an eye over his clothes and ran his hand briskly through his hair.

"We all need sleep. An ealdorman not good enough for you then?"

"If was looking for another man, but as I'm not…"

"Women are always looking."

"And men always flatter themselves that women are looking at them. All I want from you is your promise to steer clear of Ourdilic."

Aethelnoth threw up his arms, appealing to Ceolstan. "She sounds like my wife already, doesn't she? Telling me what do. Well for once I'm happy to obey. I've seen enough of Ourdilic to last me a lifetime. As you say, she's just a girl and so if that's all you came to say I'm going back to my sleep. Pig pen it may be, but it's more comfortable than standing out here."

He splashed his way back to the door and disappeared inside without a backward look. Ceolstan raised the torch higher, showing his readiness to accompany Winfrith back up the street.

"Don't mind Aethelnoth," he said, edging past her. "It's a hard job trying to keep these Somerset men in order. Mind you, there's no-one could do it better. He knows the hills and marshes like the back of his hand and he understands the folk who eke out a living among them. Being ealdorman in a place like this means he has to be always on the move. He has a wife in Glastonbury but the poor woman hardly sees him."

"He doesn't act as if he had a wife."

Ceolstan sighed. "Sadly, that's true…though few here will say so to his face. They might repeat tales of a child or two he's said to have fathered in Frome…but only when his back's turned."

"Did you think he told the truth about the girl Ourdilic then? Might he have laid a hand on her?"

They had almost reached the house where Alfred's followers had been given shelter and Ceolstan stopped, giving himself a moment to consider.

"I hope he didn't," he said, weighing his words carefully. "He denied it firmly enough. It would be a surprising way to treat one of the king's guests. Best to make sure the two are kept apart until you move on."

"Keeping Ourdilic under control is probably as hard as keeping all of Somerset in line, but I'll be doing my best. If Aethelnoth should change his story, I'd be grateful to be told. Anyway, thanks for lighting my way, Ceolstan. I'd better get inside and see if Ourdilic has started to get back to her usual self yet."

As Winfrith turned towards the door, Ceolstan caught her sleeve.

"Not all men in Frome are like Aethelnoth," he said. Even in the flickering torchlight Winfrith could see his eagerness to leave a better impression. "Why don't you come and meet Waergar? He'll show you what a Frome welcome should be. Aside from showing off his wonderful skills, his house must be the warmest place in Somerset and he's bound to offer visitors a cup of ale. You go in and I'll wait here while you check on Ourdilic."

4

Winfrith was not sure more of Waergar's company was really what she needed but when she found Ourdilic and Olwen asleep on opposite ends of a wall bench and one of Alfred's thegns instructed to make sure that was where they stayed she returned to where Ceolstan was waiting. Listening to Waergar for a little longer was a small price to pay for Ceolstan's kindness and eagerness to please.

Waergar's dwelling was only a short walk away and Ceolstan's torch gave off just enough light to show immediately what a fine craftsman he was. Both doorposts were covered from floor to roof with carvings of weavers, ploughmen, shepherds, hunters and cooks, all shaped in such detail that Winfrith half expected them to begin moving. On either side each wall plank nestled tight against the next and the oak door, slightly ajar, had been polished to a light golden shade.

"Such a gifted man," Ceolstan said, pausing in front of the carvings. "He only has to look once at a thing and he's able to create its likeness. There will never be another as good." He shook his head sadly, pushing the door wider and ushering Winfrith inside. She felt a sudden gush of hot air against her face. It didn't take long to see the cause…a charcoal fire burned fiercely in the centre of the room. A small boy, seated behind a wooden screen, kept a pair of bellows fanning the fire, setting up a pleasing roar and glow each time air was exhaled. Waergar, who had been using a long rod to move a small bowl resting above the heat, turned to greet them.

"Come in, come in. I've one visitor already but there's plenty of room for more," he said, beaming and pointing towards the far end of the room where the shadowy outline of Alfred was visible, seated at a small table. "It's not often I get three at one time. It will certainly make it a day to remember. As you see, I've already cast a spell over Alfred…so much so he insists I make him an example of my finest art this very night. He's fortunate I have some pieces already to hand. It will simply be a matter of binding together things he likes." Waergar rubbed his hands together at the thought and, lifting an oil lamp from a shelf near the door, led them towards the far end of the room.

The extra light from the lamp was enough to make Alfred look up briefly but he quickly resumed his study of several small objects which Waergar had provided. He picked one of them up from the table and held it towards the lamp.

"Look at that...a perfect crystal. Does it not suggest both purity and light? Very suitable for what I have in mind. And this gold pin, Waergar, this would be a useful reminder too. It would serve to point to the wisdom of well written words." Alfred returned the crystal and the pin to the table before gently turning a small oval of coloured glass until the image on it faced him. "This is the piece which should be the heart of the jewel though. The face is gentle, full of care and compassion. Framed in gold with the crystal set above and the pin below, it would make a perfect morning gift for Ourdilic. It should prompt her to strive for both purity and wisdom, don't you think?"

"Has your nephew agreed to a betrothal then?" Winfrith asked. "Ourdilic certainly seems unaware of it."

Alfred looked up at her, as if surprised by the question. "I have suggested it's time he began thinking about a suitable wife. I wouldn't name Ourdilic as a possible choice until I've spoken with her."

"It's very beautiful," Ceolstan said, drawing their attention back to the coloured glass. "She would be the envy of many." Waergar moved the lamp nearer to the table so that they could see it more clearly.

"She might agree to many things to get her hands on a brooch made from these,"
Winfrith said.

"It won't be a brooch. The gold pin is too long for that," Alfred said, pushing the three chosen items closer together. "What I'd like you to make, Waergar, is an aestel. Ourdilic has a gift for learning when she puts her mind to it. A beautifully made aestel might encourage her to read. Much easier to follow a poorly written hand with an aestel to point to each letter."

"I shall begin at once," Waergar said, picking up the gold pin from the table. "I'll start by fixing a gold frame to the pin. While I get going, perhaps you'd like to help yourselves to a cup of ale. It's warm work, making jewellery, but I can talk as I go."

"That's kind," Alfred said, rising from his seat, "but I think we should leave you to get on with it. We've an early start in the morning and I think we're all in need of sleep."

Ceolstan and Winfrith followed him to the door. Winfrith would have been grateful for the cup of ale, but Alfred was right. Accepting Waergar's offer would have set him off on further explanations of his craft and she was happy enough to have an excuse to avoid that.

As it turned out Waergar was unable to finish Alfred's commission by the following morning. He was unwilling to risk spoiling the work by hurrying and as Winfrith emerged into a still, grey morning she almost collided with Waergar and Alfred deep in conversation.

"If you wait here another day it will be done to your satisfaction. There's only the frame to be finished but it's detailed work and my eyes are not what they were."

"Frome hospitality has been generous," Alfred replied, "but I don't want to exhaust the goodwill. More than that though, I want to put as much distance as possible between us and Guthrum before he has chance to realise what we're up to. We can't wait any longer I'm afraid."

Waergar looked disappointed, but suddenly his face lit up. "That's it…there is a solution. Take the unfinished jewel with you. Heading west you will pass through Wells and from there you can send it on with someone you trust to Cheddar. There's a fellow there called Eadbald." Waergar chuckled to himself. "He's known to everyone as Long-tongue. He talks twice as much even as I do. But he's a good craftsman. He's certainly got the skills to finish what I've begun. I'd offer to take the jewel there myself but, like my eyes, my legs are not what they were…"

"I wouldn't expect you to," Alfred replied, "but it does sound a good idea. The kings of Wessex have had a hall and land in Cheddar for many years so I know it well. I'm sure one of my retainers will know of this Eadbald. Why don't I bring the payment we agreed for the aestel to your workshop straight away? Then we can pack it up with the unfinished frame ready for us to leave."

Alfred took the old man's arm and they set off for his workshop, leaving Winfrith to wonder how long it would be before Ourdilic got to hear of the jewel and its intended purpose.

Unsurprisingly there was little enthusiasm next morning for the early start. If Frome fell some way short of the comforts of a royal palace, it had at least offered shelter from the rain and somewhere to sleep. There was much grumbling and cursing as the two carts that accompanied Alfred's loyal band were loaded up again . Once he was satisfied everything was ready Alfred took both Ceolstan's hands in his own.

"Thank you for your hospitality, Ceolstan. It will not be forgotten. The next time we pass this way Wessex will be on the rise again and I'm sure Frome will prosper with it."

"God speed you," Ceolstan answered, nodding his head. "Should Guthrum ever venture this far, no-one in Frome has ever seen Alfred, never mind knowing where he might have gone."

Alfred's thegns began to move off slowly, having given instructions for the Somerset band to join the back of the line heading west down a gentle slope. Aethelnoth was standing at the head of his Somerset men and only the slightest bow of his head suggested he had noticed Winfrith, Ourdilic and Olwen as they passed. Neither girl so much as looked in his direction, leaving Winfrith at least able to hope that the girls had for the moment put him out of their minds.

Once they emerged beyond the last house Alfred waited by the roadside, urging everyone who went by to keep up a good pace. Yet even after a night's rest this proved difficult. The previous day's heavy showers had left the ground sodden and several times they were forced to clamber up the banks which flanked the road to avoid the worst of the churned up mud. At least the rain had abated, with even an occasional pale glimmer of sun showing through the drifting cloud. They walked without stopping well into the afternoon, sustained only by hard bread and cheese passed down the line around midday. As the day advanced, the road became hillier until the dark outline of the Mendip Hills appeared ahead of them. The possibility of a long climb encouraged more persistent questions about where they were heading, so much so that Alfred relented enough to say they would pass around Wells, cross Sedge Moor and reach Glastonbury before nightfall. It was not received with as much enthusiasm as he might have hoped. Some, including Winfrith, were curious to see these western settlements for the first time but many shared Olwen and Ourdilic's view that they'd walked far enough already and ought to stop as soon as they reached anything that promised shelter.

Wells proved a disappointment…no more than a cluster of thatched roofs in the distance. A number of Aethelnoth's fyrd hailed from Wells and Alfred was eager not to give them an excuse to slip away to their homes. They hurried past, heading towards Glastonbury in fading afternoon light. Torches were lit and Aethelnoth and his men, more familiar with the route across the moor, moved to the front of the line. The route followed a narrow causeway, forcing them to walk in single file. Despite this and the uncertain torchlight they kept up a steady pace so that Winfrith was startled when those in front of her came to a sudden halt. She waited, listening for any sign of what was holding them up. An explanation was not long in coming. She could see Alfred, carrying one of the torches just ahead of her, and Aethelnoth, who must have made his way back from the front, suddenly called back to him.

"We're less than a mile off Glastonbury now. Something odd's going on. There are no fires or lights burning. Usually you'd see some signs of life from here."

Winfrith recognised Cuthbert's voice shouting back. "They must know we're coming. They're all indoors getting ready…roasting pigs and pouring ale."

"No hope," Aethelnoth shouted back. "They'd grudge a grain of corn to a dying man. No, it doesn't feel right to me. Something's wrong."

"There's no choice. Keep going anyway." It was Alfred's voice this time. "But draw your weapons and cut the talking. We'll try and stay as close together as we can."

For fifteen minutes or so the precautions seemed unnecessary, only making every cracking twig and gust of wind in the trees more alarming than they would otherwise have been. The causeway gradually opened out into a grassy track, allowing them to travel three abreast and keep closer to the torchlight. The torch-bearers leading the way appeared to drift slightly to the right, picking out the shadow of a bramble-covered bank rising alongside them. The path followed the line of the bank, dropping down into a muddy culvert. The only sounds were the occasional scraping of feet on gravel and the swishing of tree branches somewhere overhead.

Winfrith was too busy taking care not to stumble to be looking out for danger so that the sudden chorus of yells and screams coming from the top of the bank took her completely by surprise. She was not alone. Straight away stones and rocks began to hail down onto the path, scattering the walkers in all directions. The torches were waved madly in all directions and confused shouting filled the air. She heard a heavy thud and a cry of pain somewhere just ahead of her and immediately dropped to her knees, pulling Olwen and Ourdilic with her, tight against the base of the bank.

"Keep down," she hissed, though the warning was clearly not needed. Despite the thick mud, the two girls lay flat and still on the ground without even the hint of a complaint. The sounds of lumps of rock hitting the ground soon became less frequent but it was still unnerving not being able to tell when or where the next missile might land. Slowly the clattering of stone against earth and trees lessened until finally it ceased altogether. Winfrith whispered to the girls to stay where they were in case the stone-throwers hadn't yet finished with them. After the din of the attack the silence which followed was unsettling and it came as a relief to hear Cuthbert's familiar voice calling out.

"It's all right…they've gone. We ought to have expected it. Half the witches and spirits in Wessex were born in Glastonbury. Why would you trust anyone who lives there?"

Winfrith helped the girls to their feet, urging them forward towards where Cuthbert's voice had come from. They had only gone a few steps when a sudden movement on the bank above them made them stop. Cuthbert appeared straight away at Winfrith's side, holding up a flickering torch to reveal Aethelwold peering through a gap in the brambles.

"There's no-one up here. We should go after them…teach the cowards a lesson."

"And risk getting lost?" Cuthbert said, making no effort to disguise his contempt. "It's dark and they'll know their way about their own shire far better than you."

Aethelwold kicked at the ground, sending a few loose stones rolling down the bank. "It's treason to attack the king. They should hang."

Cuthbert shrugged and turned away, only to find himself face to face with Alfred.

"And so they might," he said, glancing up at his nephew, "if anyone had seen their faces. Since we didn't, we'll head for Glastonbury, taking care not to be taken by surprise again. If there's a hostile welcome, we won't fight our way in…not after a long day's walk. We'll turn back to the Axe river and follow it to Cheddar. A royal vill is bound to ensure we're well received."

"So you'll let these Glastonbury folk get away with it?" Aethelwold asked, tearing himself free of a thorny branch and scrambling down the bank.

"They'll have their reasons," Alfred said, laying his hand on his nephew's shoulder. "They probably have no food to give us and feared losing face if we arrived. Trying to scare us off in the dark was the obvious thing to do and it doesn't seem as if we've come to much harm."

Aethelwold brushed the hand away. "You wouldn't have said that if a rock had split your head open."

"Perhaps…then we should thank God their aim was poor. Now, let's get moving. You and I have more important things to discuss than stone-throwing. You remember I asked you to think about a betrothal. If you should decide Ourdilic would one day make a suitable wife then my father's old palace at Cheddar would be a good place to settle the matter."

Winfrith glanced behind her to see if Ourdilic was listening but it was too dark to tell. From the way he had spoken she guessed Alfred was unaware the girl might be close enough to overhear. Aethelwold himself seemed in no hurry to reply, turning away so that Winfrith was unable to see whether raising the matter had pleased or annoyed him. He had only taken a couple of steps when Winfrith felt someone push past her, running to catch hold of Aethelwold's sleeve. The slight figure was surely a girl but it was only when Winfrith heard the girl's voice that she realised it was Olwen and not Ourdilic with something urgent to say to Aethelwold.

"If you're going to do it, you better take her now," she said, rushing her words as if she expected to be dragged away at any moment. "Otherwise someone else will. Lots of them follow her with their eyes. She smiles back at them all, whoever they are."

Winfrith stuck out an arm, sure that Ourdilic would not let the accusation pass without confronting Olwen but to her surprise Ourdilic contented herself with coming to stand at her shoulder and watching to see what Aethelwold or Alfred would do. Aethelwold stood open-mouthed for a moment, then roughly tugged his sleeve free of Olwen's clutch. He turned his face from Olwen towards Ourdilic but quickly looked away again and it was Alfred who finally broke the awkward silence, shepherding his nephew away from Olwen as he did so.

"I'm sure your advice is well meant, girl, but Aethelwold and Ourdilic will make up their own minds whether or not they should betrothed. And it will only happen when the time's right. If Ourdilic has her eyes on another, no-one will insist she takes my nephew."

"I don't." Ourdilic stepped past Winfrith, approaching Alfred with her head bowed. "Ignore Olwen. She's only jealous because thegns look more at me than her. I'd agree to a betrothal...if Aethelwold was willing of course."

Alfred sighed impatiently. "It's hardly the best time or place to settle this. I need to talk first with Aethelwold and a warm room in Cheddar might help us think more clearly."

"Watch she doesn't go off with another of your thegns before you get there then," Olwen said, taking care to keep out of Ourdilic's reach.

If Alfred was surprised at being spoken to so forcefully by a young girl, he didn't show it. Instead he turned again to his nephew.

"Well, what about you, Aethelwold? We've spoken about taking a wife. Is betrothal to this girl what you want?"

"Maybe...I'm not sure. It's hard..." His voice trailed off and he cleared his throat, as if preparing to go on, but the task proved beyond him. He didn't sound convinced and Winfrith decided that if a betrothal was forthcoming he'd make a graceless husband. Not that Ourdilic would worry. As long as her position commanded attention among Alfred's closest followers she would be happy enough.

"What's hard about it?" Alfred asked, sounding as though he was close to losing patience with his nephew. "If you like the girl, there's no problem. She's willing to take you. She's clever, good-looking and a king's daughter. If you don't like her…"

"It's…it's not that," Aethelwold replied, stumbling over his words. "J…just she's so young. She might think differently in a year or two."

"I won't," Ourdilic said. "Not once I'm properly betrothed."

Alfred looked from one to the other, shaking his head. "Well we clearly aren't going to settle this here and now. There's half a night's walking still to do if we're forced to press on to Cheddar. Plenty of witnesses have heard what's been said between you and I'm sure they'll want to know the outcome in the next day or two." He put a reassuring arm around Aethelwold's shoulder. "You're right. Ourdilic is still a girl…but it does seem she's one who knows her own mind. That leaves only you to decide. It will give you something to think about and take your mind off the cold and the tired limbs."

Torches were lifted higher and they set off again along the bank, meeting no stone-throwing this time. Winfrith slipped an arm round Olwen's waist, sensing that the girl needed comforting and wanting to keep her and Ourdilic apart. It was hard to believe the talk of betrothal had come out into the open in the way it had. Despite Aethelwold's reluctance there was surely a good chance Ourdilic would eventually get her own way. And if she was betrothed to Aethelwold that would no doubt make her even more insufferable than usual. In the hours and days ahead, Winfrith and Olwen would be sure to need all the patience they could muster.

5

Travelling in the dark wasn't what anyone would have chosen. Aside from the difficulty of seeing the way ahead, there was always the fear of what might be lurking among the trees and bushes that often lined the track. It wasn't as if this was familiar land either. Who knew whether there were outlaws, forest spirits or treacherous swamps round the next bend? Winfrith was sure she wasn't alone in wishing for a warm blanket and a soft bed, preferably behind a stout oak wall and a locked door. Of course once Alfred and the few thegns carrying torches set off, the rest had little choice but to follow. Olwen trudged silently alongside Winfrith, her resentment obvious from every dragging step. Now and again they were forced to speed up for fear of losing sight of the torches ahead, but for the most part it was a steady, tedious tramp through the darkness, accompanied always by the slurps and gurgles of the shifting river water at their side.

Exchanging a few words might have offered some reassurance but no-one seemed to have much to say. No doubt they were all feeling the effects of fatigue and hunger and even when the first faint light of dawn began to show it brought little joy. Slowly the shapes of bushes, trees and low hills emerged from the shadows. Winfrith took little notice of them, more concerned to avoid the growing number of ruts and sharp stones under foot. Only at the last moment did she realise that those ahead had come to a halt, dropping bags to the ground and looking for somewhere to sit.

"If this is Cheddar, don't think much of it," someone grumbled. "A long way to come for such a God-forsaken hole. I've seen smarter pig pens."

Winfrith wasn't inclined to disagree. Cheddar might have royal connections but at first glance both its land and buildings appeared to be in a sadly neglected state. Alfred had said this was his first visit since his childhood, but even so there ought to be a reeve on hand to see that his affairs here were being properly managed. They had stopped in a broad grassless square, bordered on one side by what turned out to be the king's hall and on the other by an uneven row of ramshackle houses. Once it became clear no-one was coming out to greet them, Alfred signalled to two of his thegns to hammer on the hall door with their spear butts. Just when it was beginning to look as though they might have to force their way in, the scraping sound of a heavy bar being lifted came from inside and the door swung slowly open.

The two thegns stepped back as a fat, red-faced figure in a leather jerkin emerged, holding a heavy wooden club above his head, ready to strike.

"Clear off," he shouted. "There's nothing here worth stealing…" He caught sight of the spears and looked around the yard, his eyes widening as he slowly took in the extent of the numbers gathered there. He hesitated, lowering the club to his side, and as he did so Alfred stepped forward.

"You must be Gilberht, the king's reeve here in Cheddar. I heard he'd a foul temper."

"What if I am? What's it to you?" Someone behind Winfrith laughed and Gilberht began, for the first time, to look a little uneasy. It wasn't really surprising that he didn't recognise a king he'd never seen before. Two days' walking, the last ten hours in the dark along often muddy tracks, meant even those who knew him would be hard pressed to tell Alfred apart from his thegns, or even from the men of the Somerset fyrd come to that.

"What it is to me," Alfred replied slowly and deliberately and yet, Winfrith decided, not without some enjoyment, "is that it shows my father did not always devote enough wisdom and care to the appointment of his reeves. Why I'm interested in who is the king's reeve here is because I am Alfred, your king…a position I will almost certainly retain longer than the one you hold."

Gilberht's mouth fell open. He dropped the club to the floor and hurriedly straightened the jerkin which had been falling off his shoulders. He looked swiftly behind him, as if suddenly as much afraid of what lay inside as of what faced him at the door. Nor did it take long to discover why. Alfred and two of his thegns pushed their way past him and seconds later a riot of competing sounds broke out…blows, yells of protest, shouts, and even the squawk of disturbed hens and the insistent bleating of a goat.

Winfrith needed no invitation to join those nearest the door in squeezing inside to see what was going on. Though the hall was long there was enough light from lamps hung from the rafters to make out most of what was happening. The solid, timbered walls and the glowing embers on the broad flat-stoned hearth ensured the room stayed warm, even on the coldest nights, and it looked as though half the residents of Cheddar, as well as several hens and a goat, had been taking advantage of this. The two thegns made short work of getting the sleepers outside, leaving Alfred staring and shaking his head at a black and white goat tethered to the rafters while several hens stalked restlessly around his feet.

"Times may be hard," he said, looking from the goat to Gilberht, "but not hard enough to share my hall with that. Get it out of here…and the hens. I'll give you an hour to get this place fit for a king. Fail, and you'll find yourself sharing a field with the goat. And while you're about it, make some space in the houses across the way for thirty of ealdorman Aethelnoth's men."

Gilberht nodded, hurrying past Alfred to untether the goat and Winfrith stepped outside to look for Olwen and Ourdilic, sure that they would welcome a closer look at a warm fire.

Daylight did little to improve Winfrith's first impression of Cheddar. The king's hall looked sound enough but many of the smaller houses were not wearing well. Corner posts leaned at odd angles, doors hung loose and roofs had been hastily patched up with rags, straw and bundles of twigs. She was grateful not to have to spend long looking for Olwen and Ourdilic and they took little persuading to return with her to the king's hall, already being swept and tidied under Gilberht's watchful eye. After an hour or so warming themselves in the king's hall Winfrith heard her name called from the door at looked up to see Cuthbert beckoning her over.

"We've found a house for you and those two," he said as she joined him. "Alfred's sent me to collect you. He wants to talk about this betrothal without half of Wessex listening."

"I hope it's got a roof on," Winfrith said. "Most of them look unfit for pigs."

"Come and see it. There's a roof, and a fire going already. It's up at the top end of the village, well away from where both Aethelwold and Aethelnoth will be lodged. Why Alfred chose it I expect."

There were brief protests from Olwen and Ourdilic - after all, they were still barely speaking to each other - about having to move from the fire but once they saw the house Alfred had made ready for them, they fell silent again. The small house, clearly newer and better built than those opposite the king's hall, stood alongside a deep ditch which ran between the line of houses marking the top of the village and the steep, tree-covered slopes beyond. A pitted reddish cliff was just visible above the line of trees. Inside a freshly lit fire burned on the hearth and an old woman was arranging straw-filled mattresses on the floor. Ourdilic and Olwen were quick to claim one each and drag them into separate corners of the room, leaving Winfrith to choose the most comfortable looking of the three oak chairs to settle down in.

Once he was satisfied everything was as it should be, Cuthbert moved to the doorway from where he could both talk to Winfrith and keep an eye out for Alfred. He shifted his weight restlessly from one foot to the other, clearly irritated about something more than where Alfred had got to. Winfrith said nothing, sure he would not be able to keep it to himself for long, and he soon proved her right.

"What does he need Aelfstan and Cuthred in there for? Haven't they got their own shires to worry about? Talk…and counting sacks of barley…that's all they're good for."

Winfrith smiled. Cuthbert was not usually an envious man. He didn't share the greed for power that drove many of Alfred's thegns. In any case, he would make a very unsatisfactory ealdorman…no patience with the slow-witted and too much sympathy for anyone claiming they couldn't afford what was due. He still didn't like his own loyalty to go unnoticed though.

"I expect they're discussing…you know, the betrothal." She whispered the last words in case Ourdilic was listening. A quick glance revealed she was lying still on the mattress, breathing steadily enough to suggest she might even be asleep. Winfrith eased herself out of her chair and moved quietly to join Cuthbert in the doorway. "Why waste your time listening to that? Leave it to Alfred and his ealdormen. Beating off the Danes is more interesting work, isn't it?"

"It needs doing, whether I do it or not...like you trying to rule Ourdilic. At least she'll be off your hands if Aethelwold agrees to a betrothal."

Winfrith shrugged. "She's still a girl, remember. Even if the thing's agreed, it'll be two years at least before she leaves to share his bed. Two more years of trying to keep the peace between her and Olwen. I'm not sure I can stand it."

"Not like you to give up though," Cuthbert replied, looking suddenly more cheerful. "You're surely not going to let a slip of a girl get the better of you?"

"Like toothache or a bee sting, she'll go away eventually...that's if we don't lose her on another of Alfred's night marches."

"I wouldn't worry too much about that. You won't be the only one keeping an eye on her next time...Alfred will be, for one. He won't want his nephew's future wife disappearing before they're even betrothed. Mind you, he's not doing much to look out for her at the moment. He was supposed to be coming to talk to her."

"I'm sure he trusts you to watch her for him, just as he trusts his ealdormen to discuss the wisdom or otherwise of this betrothal."

"Then the sooner it's done with the better. Without Aelfstan and Cuthred butting in he could have made his mind up in half the time. Let's hope they've decided it should go ahead. Then Alfred can find some thegns' wives to prepare Ourdilic for it and leave you in peace and me to get on with making sure the Danes don't take us by surprise."

Winfrith wasn't going to argue with that and returned to her chair, hoping that Alfred would not be long in bringing good news.

Whether the cause was the unfamiliarity of her surroundings or the pot of lumpy pottage eaten late in the evening, Winfrith passed a restless first night in Cheddar. Each time she felt herself drifting off to sleep, some small sound or movement woke her again. She would stare anxiously across the room in case Ourdilic was no longer there. It was too dark to make out any clear shapes of course, but she would not try and get back to sleep until she could hear the distinctive sounds of two sets of slow, rhythmic breathing. By then she would be wide awake, listening to the sounds outside...a gust of wind, a creaking branch, the patter of a raindrops against the wall, the hoot of an owl… nothing she hadn't heard a hundred times before.

Eventually a deeper sleep must have come. She dreamt Ourdilic was running away and each time she closed in on the girl, clutching at her skirt, a burst of speed took her away again. She was on the point of giving up the chase when Ourdilic suddenly fell to the ground, crying out in pain. Winfrith woke with a start, aware straight away that she had not dreamt the cry. The room was no longer pitch black. A patch of dull grey light showed through the half open door and the unmistakeable outline of Ourdilic's head and shoulders showed against it. Winfrith threw off the coarse blankets Gilberht had grudgingly provided and crossed quickly to Ourdilic's side.

"What is it? Are you hurt?"

Ourdilic did not answer. Her face was pale and her arm shook as she raised it and pointed at something beyond the door. Winfrith followed her gaze. She breathed in sharply, her fists clenched and her pulse racing. Little wonder Ourdilic had cried out.

At first sight the shape that loomed over them could have been taken for a giant, feet planted firmly on the bank beyond the rainwater ditch and body leaning menacingly over the house. A roughly carved face leered over the doorway, half hidden by a bunched cloth held up to its mouth. Loose, boneless arms and legs flapped in the wind and even in the half-light before dawn dark stains were visible around the mouth and along one of the arms. Both Winfrith and Ourdilic jumped back as a sudden gust made the whole thing sway, so that it seemed for a moment as if the grinning face was about to descend on them.

Yet relief quickly followed. Perhaps it was the breeze, showing up the fragility of the thing, or maybe it was simply having time to look more closely at it. The face, its deep-set eyes and gaping mouth carved well enough to scare in poor light, was surely cut from nothing more than a turnip. The body was a straight tree trunk, its lopped off branches leaving torn white scars, and the limbs were nothing more than long strips of dirty woollen cloth. The only feature which remained unsettling was the bundle held to its mouth. It had been hastily assembled, no more than a tunic stuffed with straw, but the stains around the mouth and arm were wet enough to allow an occasional drip to fall. It was this which still held Ourdilic's gaze.

"It's mine," she said quietly. "The tunic...I thought I'd forgotten it in the hurry to leave Chippenham. Whoever did this thinks anyone from Cornwall must be afraid of Bolster."

Winfrith put an arm round Ourdilic's shoulder, guiding her gently away from the door and into a chair and kneeling beside her.

"Who's Bolster, Ourdilic...and why would you be afraid of him?" She spoke softly, hoping not to wake Olwen.

Ourdilic glanced towards the door, though she already seemed have put her fright behind her.

"Every child in Cornwall knows the story. Bolster was who giant who lived long ago. Old folk used to frighten bad children by saying he'd come and eat them in the night if they carried on that way. Whoever put that thing outside knows the story. The blood on the arm is how Bolster was killed. He fell in love with a maid called Agnes but she wouldn't marry him. He wouldn't leave her alone so she said she would marry him if he would fill a cliff top hole with his blood. He was too big a fool to see what she was up to. He thought giants had more than enough blood to fill such a small hole, so he cut his arm and lay down by the hole. Agnes had chosen a bottomless hole of course, so his blood just drained into the sea and he bled to death. That's it...just a story. If anyone thinks that thing out there will scare me, they're wrong. It doesn't frighten me any more than Bolster frightened Agnes."

Winfrith put an arm round Ourdilic's shoulder, feeling a sudden, unexpected tenderness for the girl. It was easy to forget she was still young and a long way from home. Her mother had died shortly after her birth and battle had put an end to her father before she had much time with him. Perhaps some of her awkwardness could be forgiven.

"It's probably just some young men with too much time on their hands. I expect they thought it was funny."

"It doesn't worry me," Ourdilic said, raising her head and shoulders so that Winfrith's arm slipped away. "Most of them don't like anyone who was born more than twelve miles from Wintanceaster...let alone a girl from Cornwall. They should try going there. Cornish folk aren't much different from them."

"Best to ignore it," Winfrith said. "I'll get Cuthbert to have it removed as soon as it's light."

Ourdilic seemed content with this, returning to her own sleeping place without saying anything more. Winfrith watched her settle down before stepping outside to look again at the giant. The more she looked at it, the more she became it convinced it was something more than a harmless jest. Assembling it and erecting it so that it hung over the house must have required time and thought, not to mention strength and skill. The carving of the grotesque face, the finding and moving of a tree trunk three times the height of a man, the soundless positioning of the whole thing in the middle of the night…all of that suggested careful planning. It had to be someone who knew the old Cornish story too. She looked more closely at the dark stains. They could easily be fresh blood, so that some creature would have had to be caught and killed just for that. The whole thing was meant to do more than just startle Ourdilic. It was meant to terrify her…perhaps enough to make her run away.

Yet it didn't really make sense to go to so much trouble just to just to try and scare away a young girl. She could hardly be much of a threat to anyone. The attempt had followed straight after the first talk of a betrothal to Aethelwold but, try as she might, Winfrith couldn't see who might be so against the idea they would do something like this. Perhaps the arrival of daylight and the obvious fact that Ourdilic was still in Cheddar might be enough for the disappointment on someone's face to give them away. She would certainly be studying Alfred's thegns very carefully as soon as she got the chance.

The news that Winfrith had been hoping for was not long in coming. Alfred appeared at the door shortly before midday, inviting Ourdilic and Winfrith to accompany him back to the king's hall.

"I want you to meet someone," he said. "Her name is Eanflaed. She's come here from Chippenham to be with her husband, Beorhtric. My nephew has agreed to a betrothal, Ourdilic, but we both think you could learn from someone like Eanflaed. Being a thegn's wife isn't as easy as you might think."

"My father was King of Cornwall. I was brought up among powerful men," Ourdilic replied. The scare in the night clearly hadn't shaken her confidence. Irritation showed in Alfred's face, but his voice remained calm.

"Aethelwold thinks you're still young to be his wife for a year or two, so there's plenty of time to prepare yourself. Winfrith has done much to look after you, but you could learn things from Eanflaed too."

"I'm sure she'll be glad to meet Eanflaed," Winfrith said, nudging Ourdilic towards the door. "She's probably had enough of me by now."

Ourdilic made no effort to deny this and Winfrith found herself wishing Eanflaed luck in trying to offer advice to the girl. She certainly felt no envy that the task of guiding Ourdilic in the duties of a wife had been entrusted to someone else. If it was a slight on her own short time married to Leofranc, it was one she was happy to overlook.

The short walk to the hall allowed Winfrith a few moments' thought about the betrothal. Alfred appeared very eager to have the matter settled. Aethelwold was his nephew of course, but he'd young sons of his own who were closer kin. She wondered if he'd heard about the gruesome trick played on Ourdilic in the night and whether that would have prompted him to act swiftly. Cuthbert had made sure the giant was quickly dismantled and burned so it was possible the story hadn't reached Alfred's ears.

As soon as she caught side of Eanflaed, waiting for them outside the south door of the hall, Winfrith realised she had seen the tall, willowy woman with fine fair hair before. It was just before they left Chippenham. She had walked behind her down the main street and it would not have stuck in mind but for the behaviour of the man alongside her. He had stopped suddenly and caught Eanflaed's shoulders, dragging her round to face him. He was shorter than his wife, with muscular arms and a barrel chest, and he was clearly in a foul temper. Winfrith had hung back, ready to shout if he struck her. They'd exchanged angry words but in the end he'd pushed her roughly away and walked on without looking back. Winfrith remembered how at the time she had thought marrying a thegn didn't always result in a pleasanter life.

The south door, a small entrance put in so that servants did not carry full cauldrons and pots through the main doors, was open. Raised voices could be heard coming from inside and as they approached Eanflaed a burly figure stormed out, pushing past them and disappearing round the corner of the building. The briefest glimpse of his face, red with anger, was enough for Winfrith to recognize the man who had grabbed Eanflaed's shoulders on the road in Chippenham…her husband, she supposed.

Eanflaed offered a fleeting glance in the direction of the departing figure. When she looked round and smiled at Ourdilic, though she tried hard, she was unable to hide her embarrassment.

"How upset men get by small things," she said. "A fit of temper just because the stew isn't hot enough. There's a first lesson for you, Ourdilic."

Ourdilic nodded politely and Winfrith smiled to herself. The girl was quite capable of complaining loudly about cold food herself.

"I must go," Alfred said, heading inside. "I'll leave you in Eanflaed's safe hands and we'll talk of the betrothal again at the end of the day."

Eanflaed indicated they should follow and, once inside, led them to a corner where the side and end walls met. She ushered Winfrith and Ourdilic towards a wall bench and sat half-facing them. Eanflaed sat quite still. She took her time, looking Ourdilic over from head to toe, as if that might tell her if the girl was ready yet for betrothal. Ourdilic stared back, unworried by the careful inspection.

"Was that your husband?" she said, breaking the silence.

Eanflaed smiled, a little uneasily. "It was… Beorhtric."

"He looked very angry."

"He has a lot on his mind. He's not very happy that I'm speaking to you, even though his king commanded I should do it."

"What has your husband got against Ourdilic?" Winfrith asked, thinking suddenly of the attempt to scare Ourdilic in the night. "He doesn't even know her."

"He knows where she's from. That's enough for him. All Cornish folk are the same to him. He blames them for his brother's death."

"I've never seen him before…or his brother," Ourdilic protested. "What does he know about Cornish folk anyway?"

Eanflaed was quick to defend her husband, despite his ill temper. "Enough to know some of them guided Guthrum into Wareham, where my husband's brother was taken hostage and later had his throat cut."

The mention of Wareham caught Winfrith by surprise. The killing of hostages there wasn't something she wanted to be reminded of. Her husband Leofranc had died there as well. She too had struggled to put the grief and anger behind her, even if, unlike Beorhtric, she had not blamed the Cornish men said to be on board Guthrum's ships. Ourdilic on the other hand clearly had no sympathy for Eanflaed's husband. She leapt up, planting her feet squarely in front of the thegn's wife.

"It wasn't Cornishmen cut his throat. My father was on one of those ships and drowned before it could reach land. How could what happened have been his fault? He wasn't a Dane. He was king of Cornwall. Neither he nor any other Cornishman would have chosen to be there. Guthrum took them captive and no-one from Wessex came to help."

Eanflaed got up slowly, drawing herself up to her full height until she towered over Ourdilic. There was no longer any sign of the uncertainty she'd shown in the presence of her husband and she was clearly in no mood to be intimidated by a mere girl.

"Believe what you like," she said. "It was Wessex hostages who were killed."

The two stood face to face, neither giving an inch, and Winfrith knew that she ought to do something to calm them. Yet the mention of the murdered hostages at Wareham had flooded her mind with bitter memories, leaving her unable to find any suitable words. She told herself yet again Leofranc was gone. Nothing could change that. She took a deep breath and forced herself to look at the living Ourdilic and Eanflaed, taking in every detail of their hair, their faces, their clothes. Eventually, despite the dryness in her throat, she forced out the words she hadn't spoken for almost two years.

"Many folk lost loved ones at Wareham. My husband was also one of those killed."

Eanflaed turned to look at Winfrith. The admission had clearly taken her by surprise but there was a hint of concern in her face too.

"Then you must undertand how Beorhtric feels. He wants somebody to blame, and anyone he thinks helped Guthrum is, for him, not fit to live. Your father might have been innocent but that won't stop my husband taking a dislike to you. We'll just have to keep you out of his way until you're betrothed. He won't say anything against someone so close to King Alfred."

Ourdilic gave a contemptuous nod in the direction Beorhtric had headed. "I'm not scared of him. He's not the first thegn to show he despises anyone born in Cornwall. It shows how little they know. They ought to go there. They might learn some better manners."

Eanflaed smiled and Winfrith breathed more easily, seeing that the tension between the two was easing. Eanflaed spoke more gently, as if Ourdilic's spirited defence of her father had won her over.

"As it happens, Beorhtric has been to Cornwall. He was sent three years ago, before Wareham, to look for sites where forts might be built. It was a cold spring and food was short. Perhaps that's why he didn't like the place. He found folk hard to understand and I think they enjoyed spinning yarns to him and his companions. If he came back with a poor opinion of them, his brother's death at Wareham only made it worse."

Now that it seemed Eanflaed and Ourdilic might find a way of getting on Winfrith began to think about Beorhtric's hatred of the Cornish and his visit to Cornwall and the tales he'd heard there. Had he come across the tale of Agnes's cunning and Bolster's bloody end? She'd like to ask him, though from what she'd seen of his temper it was unlikely she'd get a polite answer. All the same it was somewhere to start and he'd probably had help in setting up the giant. One of Alfred's thegns might have thought it clever enough to boast about.

"Let's find somewhere comfortable to sit," Eanflaed said, taking Ourdilic's arm. "We've spent enough time talking about Beorhtric. You heard Winfrith too. Getting a thegn to wed you is one thing; living as a thegn's wife is quite another. I can't see someone with your spirit finding it easy to do Aethelwold's bidding, but that's what he'll expect."

Ourdilic looked bemused, as though she couldn't believe anyone would expect her to bow to Aethelwold's wishes. Eanflaed clearly saw Ourdilic's surprise but didn't wait for her to say anything.

"What my mother told me, before I was betrothed Beorhtric, was this. You must bow and smile and fill his cup in the hall, lie willing in his bed at night and save what's in your head and your heart for when you are alone."

As she was speaking, Eanflaed led them around the corner of the hall and into the shelter of a wood store which ran along the back wall. It took a few moments to brush sawdust and chippings off a roughly hewn bench so that by the time they sat down they'd all had time to reflect on Eanflaed's mother's advice. Winfrith, surprised Ourdilic hadn't immediately protested, offered her own view.

"The duties Eanflead talks of are expected. Others will be watching you, especially if you marry the king's nephew. It doesn't mean you can't think for yourself. Even thegns may be persuaded by their wives, but usually only when they're not surrounded by their companions."

"That depends on the thegn," Eaflaed replied, looking as though she had more to add but then clamping her lips tightly shut.

"I can already make Aethelwold do what I want…most of the time," Ourdilic said.

"That might change, if you ever become his wife," Winfrith said without much conviction. From what she'd seen of Aethelwold, he'd be no match for Ourdilic.

"Much will be expected of him too," Eanflaed said. "He'll have more important things than you to deal with. Battling the Danes for one thing. Fighting for power and position for another. He won't always be the meek plaything you seem to consider him now."

Ourdilic nodded, as if she knew the truth of this, though Winfrith had seen her feigning interest often enough to think she wasn't taking Eanflaed's advice very seriously. Despite this Eanflaed continued to talk to the girl for a short while. Much of it was to do with how a thegn's wife should host feasting and welcome guests. Ourdilic appeared to be listening, though Winfrith was sure she looked relieved when Eanflaed finally got up to leave. As she did so a movement in among the twisted branches of an ancient holly tree some thirty paces away to her left caught Winfrith's eye. A stocky figure emerged from the shelter of the tree and disappeared swiftly around the corner of the hall. She got only the briefest glimpse of him but it was enough to convince her it had been Eanflaed's husband, Beorhtric.

6

What few servants there were remaining in Cheddar had done their best to make the hall fit for a special occasion. Holly branches decorated the rafters and candles had been lit along the length of the dining tables. The hearth fire was stacked high with logs, smoking slowly now but looking set to produce a mountain of comforting flames later. A royal betrothal would usually demand generous feasting too but grain supplies were low and the few remaining pigs would be needed to breed in the spring. Alfred had sent out several hunting trips across the flat lands beyond Axebridge but they had returned with nothing more than a few waterfowl. At least the ale was plentiful, though those who had already tasted it complained of an unpleasant sourness on the tongue. Winfrith didn't doubt they would conquer their distaste after a few cups.

Ourdilic had spent much of the afternoon combing her hair, tying and retying the braid which held it in place and adjusting the position of the small silver brooch her father had given her. Eanflaed had reluctantly agreed to stand alongside Ourdilic at her betrothal and, in the absence of any other kin, take the place of a parent. Winfrith was fleetingly upset that Alfred had not asked her. She was a thegn's widow after all, but she soon warmed to the idea of someone else taking more responsibility for Ourdilic. Not that there would be much for Eanflaed to do. She'd have to stand with the girl, listen to what Aethelwold said and then make her mark on the document Milred had been busy preparing. Alfred had provided a list of witnesses who were also to sign though, as Milred had remarked, he would have to write their names for them and, for all they knew, they might be signing a pact with the devil or promising to provide Ourdilic with a lifetime's supply of honey cakes.

The ceremony had been arranged for sunset, leaving a long enough evening for those who felt inclined to celebrate. No doubt many would feel Ourdilic's rise was not a cause for celebration, but the presence of ale would probably help them overcome any resentment. No-one would protest too loudly. Winfrith reassured herself with the thought that Ourdilic should be safe from any further scares or threats. There was a heavy punishment for anyone committing violence in the king's hall and Alfred's presence should ensure that the evening passed peaceably.

Almost as soon as they arrived, Winfrith, Ourdilic and Eanflaed were summoned to the north end of the hall, where Alfred and those who were to be witnesses had gathered. Alfred had laid out the finished aestel on a table in front of Aethelwold. All eyes were drawn to it. The crystal twinkled in the candlelight and the bright gold frame drew attention to the serenity of the enamel figure within it. Ourdilic could not take her eyes off it and the satisfaction on her face was unmistakeable. Aethelwold seemed to be the only person in the hall not spellbound by it. In fact he appeared unwilling to face either the aestel or Ourdilic. It occurred to Winfrith that he had more the look of a man facing the gallows than one about to be betrothed. He looked relieved when Alfred cleared his throat and looked around the group of faces, checking he had their full attention.

"Friends, you're here tonight to witness a contract between my nephew, Aethelwold, and Eanflaed who stands in place of Ourdilic's kin."

Winfrith wondered what Beohrtric thought of his wife being linked with the Cornish in this way and she glanced down the hall, trying to spot him. He was not among the witnesses and, despite the candles and oil lamps fixed along the walls, it was difficult to make out the faces of those further away.

"Betrothal is not something to be entered into lightly," Alfred continued, "and, once done, the contract should be binding until death. Anyone who seeks to lie with you afterwards, Ourdilic, will pay a heavy price, but the rewards for your faithfulness are high too…a place in the king's hall and a share of your husband's household goods. You understand what it means to become betrothed?"

Ourdilic nodded.

"In that case, Aethelwold it is time for you to speak. Ourdilic has no living kin here but Eanflaed has agreed to stand in place of a mother and father. What you promise here, should be as seriously considered as anything you would have said to them. Remember, these witnesses are here to mark your words."

Aethelwold stared down the hall, resting his hands on the table to steady himself. "Before all these witnesses..." He paused, taking a hasty sip from a cup beside him before going on. "I ask that Ourdilic become my wife." He stopped again, as if waiting for someone to object, but there was no reaction apart from the occasional cough and clearing of the throat from those restless to get on with whatever feasting was to be had. "I bring her this morning gift...a richly jewelled aestel...and fifty hides of land at Stanton and Overton in Wiltshire to hold in her own right." He pushed the aestel towards Eanflaed, offering it for her inspection, although of course everyone knew she was bound to accept it.

"On behalf of Ourdilic's kin I accept the gift," Eanflaed said quietly. "In return I am told to ask all here to bear witness that she will not live with you as your wife until another twelvemonth is gone. That is the wish of the king, whose wisdom we should all respect."

And that was it. The deed was done. All that remained was for Alfred and Milred to sign their names and for the other witnesses to make their marks where Milred indicated. No-one seemed eager to offer encouragement or congratulation and only Ourdilic looked determined to make something of the occasion. She picked up the jewelled aestel and stood admiring it while Eanflaed headed for the door without another word. Aethelwold retired to the far end of the hall, joining a table of noisy thegns dividing their attention between a plate of roasted fowl and a game which appeared to involve lobbing stones into the rafters. Winfrith settled down next to Milred, hoping that his company might enliven what promised to be a long evening.

They chatted idly for a while, about betrothals, morning gifts and the weaknesses of thegns. He looked around the hall, his eyes settling on the holly branches above their heads.

"A shortage of berries on them," he said, scratching his chin. "Not that it's such a bad thing. A multitude of berries was always thought to bring bad weather...not that the last month could be called good. At least this lot won't go to waste. Eadbald Long-tongue tells me the sheep round here are hardy enough to eat the stuff."

It was not too difficult to listen to Milred and keep an eye on Ourdilic at the same time. She had found a seat a little further down the hall, as if this betrothal had already set her apart from the likes of Winfrith. No one came to speak to her but she looked unconcerned. The nearest she had to a friend was Olwen and the betrothal was unlikely to go down well with her either. Olwen had not been invited of course. Despite being a part of Winfrith's household she was still a freed slave, something Ourdilic had reminded her of on more than one occasion. Now that Ourdilic was almost kin to King Alfred the rift between the two girls could only grow wider.

Milred stretched his arms and yawned, lifting himself slowly to his feet. "The heat and ale are sending me to sleep. I think a bit of fresh air will do me no harm."

"I'd join you," Winfrith answered, "but I don't think Ourdilic will be persuaded to leave the scene of her triumph just yet. I'd better not let her or that precious jewel of hers out of my sight. Don't be too long out in the cold."

It was true the air in the hall was growing hotter by the minute. The fire had become a roaring, crackling blaze and the lower end of the hall was now far more crowded than it had been earlier. The noise was increasing too…shouts of encouragement, laughter, curses, and then a sudden scream of pain. All heads turned in an instant towards the fire. Winfrith caught a glimpse of a body flying backwards, tripping on the hearth edge and tumbling backwards into the fire. Two men leapt forward to pull him clear, beating the back of the man's tunic before flames could take hold. His attacker, a tall broad-shouldered figure with fair hair and narrow, deep-set eyes, stood facing him, hands defiantly on his hips, looking more than ready to resume their disagreement. As the victim of the attack straightened up and took his hand away from the blood around his mouth Winfrith could see that it was Aethelwold. Ourdilic leapt up, running towards him, and Winfrith wasted no time in following.

They arrived at Aethelwold's side just as the fair-haired man stepped towards him. He stopped at the sight of Ourdilic, but he clearly hadn't finished yet with Aethelwold. Ignoring the two thegns who had come to his rescue, he prodded a finger into Aethelwold's chest.

"Say that again and I'll loosen a few more of your teeth. Wulfhere may have stayed in Chippenham but he's no coward. He's worth ten of you, you skinny stream of cow shit. If it's treachery you want, look closer to home. This Cornish child bride of yours would happily sell us all to the heathens."

Aethelwold brushed his hand aside, before wiping his sleeve across his jaw and spitting on the ground just short of his assailant's feet. "It only takes a few cups of ale, Raedberht, doesn't it…to remind us where your loyalties lie? You should have stayed with your Uncle Wulfhere. He could even have found you an old Danish hag to lie with by now…if the bastards hadn't done the wise thing and cut your throat first."

Raedberht raised his arm to strike and Aethelwold flinched but the expected blow never came. Instead a commanding shout came from immediately behind the circle of thegns who had gathered round them. Both men froze and Ourdilic, who was about to grab Raedberht's sleeve, swiftly pulled back her arm. If Alfred had been staying out of the way up until now, he had clearly been keeping a keen eye out for the first sign of trouble.

"Enough! Don't move another inch." He pushed his way through the circle of watchers until he faced Raedberht. "Have you forgotten where you are? This may not be the heart of Wessex but it's still the king's hall. Dishonour this place and you dishonour me."

It was difficult to tell from his hard stare whether or not the possibility of dishonouring his king had occurred to Raedberht but he was clearly in no mood to back down.

"Any dishonour was your nephew's, not mine. He saw fit to abuse my uncle while sheltering behind the protection of his own."

Alfred looked briefly behind him, taking in Aethelwold's cut face and the simmering resentment in his eyes. "My nephew speaks rashly sometimes, but the blood on his face didn't come there by chance. Your uncle was once my loyal ealdorman. He chose to stay in Chippenham and put his fate in Danish hands. It's hardly surprising that he's not popular here. You showed your own mistrust of Guthrum by coming with us and I'm grateful for that, but it means you abide by my laws. I can ill afford to be punishing my own thegns. There are too few of you, so get yourself outside and sleep off the ale somewhere. You too, Aethelwold."

Raedberht looked disinclined to leave, staring hard at Aethelwold. Alfred nodded towards Cuthbert.

"It looks as though Raedberht needs help in finding the door. Perhaps you'd see him on his way." Raedberht didn't wait for Cuthbert to take his arm. He turned briskly away, shouting over his shoulder as he headed outside, "Maybe my uncle was right. Perhaps he knew a loser when he saw one."

Winfrith looked down at Ourdilic, wondering what the girl made of this assault on her future husband. She didn't look particularly concerned. Alfred had intervened before she could add her efforts to Aethelwold's defence and no doubt, with other thegns looking on, he was glad of that. Ourdilic watched him for a moment, as Alfred waved him away and he turned to follow Raedwald out of the hall. Once he had gone she looked lovingly down at the aestel, still clutched tightly in her left hand, and her mouth curled into a contented smile.

7

The days which followed the betrothal passed without further incident. Much to Winfrith's surprise there was even a slight warming of relations between Olwen and Ourdilic. They did not spend every waking hour in each other's company, as they had once done, but at least they spoke from time to time without it ending in tears or insults. It was not just the peace Winfrith was glad of. It meant she could leave them together without fear of Ourdilic storming off. Despite her new status, few of Alfred's thegns made any attempt to hide their mistrust of her and she seemed happy to pass most of the day inside, admiring her morning gift. There were no more scares in the night, which confirmed Winfrith's belief that someone had wished to put a stop to the betrothal. Whoever it was, their plan had failed, but not before Eanflaed's husband, Beorhtric, had established himself in Winfrith's mind as a likely suspect.

The betrothal had little impact on Aethelwold. He was clearly in no hurry to get to know his bride-to-be better. For the most part he ignored her altogether, preferring to spend his time on often fruitless hunting trips and attempts to prise food from the small settlements along the Axe. Ourdilic showed no sign of being worried by this neglect and Winfrith thought perhaps she even welcomed it. After all, the betrothal was known to everyone now and there was no longer any need to pretend that Aethelwold was charming or interesting. It didn't bode well for their marriage, but then as far as Winfrith could see few thegns' wives saw much of their husbands, especially those who chose to follow their king's fortunes as closely as Aethelwold.

The peace between the girls did not extend to offering to collect firewood and, rather than disturb it, Winfrith set off across the storm water ditch in search of a fresh supply. The bank on the far side was steep and each foothold needed watching to avoid slipping back into the ditch. Only when she reached the top did she become aware of two feet planted firmly in her path. She glanced up, silently cursing herself for not being more on her guard. The face looking down at her was Aethelnoth's and his stance suggested he had been watching her for some minutes. For some reason Ceolstan's mention of his having a wife in Frome but children in all corners of Somerset came into her head. Did Aethelnoth think she might be willing to assist him in adding to them? The thought was enough to get her scrambling to her feet.

"Sorry…I wasn't looking where I was going. I didn't see you there."

"Or you would have turned aside earlier, I suppose." Aethelnoth swept back a lock of black hair which had fallen across his forehead and grinned. "Why always so keen to be rid of my company…especially when fate seems determined to throw us together?"

"Not fate…firewood." Winfrith went to step round him but he caught her arm before she could cross to the far side of the bank.

"What's the hurry?" he asked, as she brushed his hand away. "Firewood will still be there an hour from now."

"But the fire will have gone out by then and Olwen and Ourdilic will be complaining of the cold. There's wood not far away. Old floodwater has washed up a good supply just down the other side of the bank."

Aethelnoth turned to look. "So it has. Since it seems so urgent, why don't I help you gather some? You can tell me all about how Ourdilic's getting on. I've heard my little riding companion is to marry Aethelwold after all. I hope he knows what he's letting himself in for. She's got a mind of her own, that girl."

"And one that should be thinking only of her future husband now. You haven't forgotten you promised to keep away from her?"

Aethelnoth threw up his hands in protest. "Of course not. Aethelwold is welcome to her. I prefer the company of women to girls. Now, how about this wood gathering? I presume Ourdilic is unlikely to join us for that?"

Winfrith glanced back at the house. The roof was still visible. If Aethelnoth laid so much as hand on her it was close enough for a shout for help to bring someone running. A bit of help was not unwelcome either and between them they ought to be able to carry enough to save a second journey.

"If you're not wanted elsewhere, I'd be glad of the help," Winfrith said, crossing the bank and dropping down into the ditch beyond. A ragged line of dead leaves, twisted roots and flattened reed stems marked the edge of recent floodwater and where the ditch turned sharply to the left a dense pile of uprooted bushes and broken branches had formed. She stopped, scanning the tangled mass for the most suitable wood.

"So, is Ourdilic happy with her betrothal?" Aethelnoth asked, leaning forward to drag a thick branch clear. "She looked to me to have eyes for several better-looking thegns."

"That was before her betrothal. I'm sure she'll save her smiles for Aethelwold now." Winfrith set about sorting smaller sticks into a pile for kindling and for a minute or two the only sounds were the scrape and rustle of sticks and branches being added to two rapidly growing heaps. Aethelnoth was the first to pause, sighing with satisfaction at his own handiwork. He turned to face Winfrith, spreading his arms wide, as if expecting her approval.

"There...how's that? Should be enough to keep you all warm for a bit. I think that deserves a show of gratitude, don't you? It's not every day an ealdorman stoops to such lowly work. But then you knew that when you brought me here."

He advanced a couple of paces towards her but, despite a voice in her head telling her to run, Winfrith stood firm. "I didn't bring you here. You offered. And your wife wouldn't like you forcing yourself on another woman."

Aethelnoth looked surprised...perhaps he hadn't expected any resistance at all...but surprise turned quickly to anger.

"Look around you. My wife isn't here, thank God. I didn't take you for the same kind... all smiles one minute; cold as ice the next. You need warming up, reminding what a widow's missing."

"I wouldn't miss a randy old goat like you..." The words were out before she'd had time to think whether or not they were wise. Aethelnoth stepped to his right, blocking Winfrith's way back up the bank. She glared up at him, not giving an inch. "I'm not just any widow. My husband, Leofranc, was one Alfred's loyal thegns. Harm me and you'll..."

"I'll what? Have to pay wergild?" Aethelnoth thrust his head forward so that she could feel the heat of his breath on her face. "How much is a widow worth these days...a hundred shillings? I think I can raise that."

Winfrith cursed her own foolishness, even while she was searching for a way to escape Aethelnoth. A bit late now to be heeding Ceolstan's advice! She ought to shout for help, but the thought of Olwen and Ourdilic seeing her like this, after all the warnings she'd given them about the company they kept, held her back. Aethelnoth stepped closer, sliding his hands down her back and pulling her towards him. She pressed her palm gently against his chest.

"Wait. Just let me think a minute. It's not right here. Anyone might see us."

She looked up at him, thinking her change of heart hardly sounded convincing. His face relaxed into a grin, enough to tell her she had to take her chance now. As he leaned back to get a better look at her, she drew back her leg and kicked out with all the force she could muster. She felt her knee crash into his groin, heard him cry out in pain and saw him fall backwards. She turned and ran, scrambling up the bank, grabbing at clumps of grass to stop herself slipping back. At any moment she expected to feel his hands catch hold of her but she didn't look back until she reached the top. He had got to his feet and was looking as though he intended to follow her when a high-pitched shout rang out from the other side of the bank. Winfrith looked down to see Olwen crossing the ditch below.

"Where have you been?" she called. "The fire's gone out."

She began to climb towards where Winfrith waited, looking slightly bewildered by the relieved laugh which greeted her arrival at the top of the bank.

"Fires do go out when there's no wood," Winfrith said. "And wood doesn't bring itself to the door." She might have enjoyed teasing Olwen longer if a slightly dishevelled looking Aethelnoth hadn't appeared out of a thicket of waist-high bushes twenty paces further along the bank. Even from that distance Winfrith could pick out the unmistakeable glint of a knife blade in his hand. Perhaps he had needed it to cut his way through the bushes but, whatever the reason, when he caught sight of Olwen standing with her, he slid it swiftly back under his belt.

"Not another female following me about," he said, taking a few steps towards them. "You can't keep away, can you? A pity you women can't finish what you start."

Olwen glanced at Winfrith, eyebrows raised, seeking an explanation of what Aethelnoth was hinting at. Winfrith hesitated. Should she tell her the truth? It might cure the girl of some of her illusions about thegns, but it would make offering advice about how to deal with them in the future more difficult. Who would listen to someone who couldn't follow their own words of wisdom? Counting on Aethelnoth not wanting Olwen to hear he'd tried to force himself on Winfrith, she decided a half-truth would have to do.

"You see, Olwen…that's thegns for you. Offer to help collecting firewood, then forget to bring the pile you've gathered back with you. Was the burden too heavy, Aethelnoth, or did you start to worry about the state of your jerkin?"

Aethelnoth looked down, brushing a few strands of dead grass from his clothes. Winfrith watched him, sure he was giving himself time to find an answer which would not make him look foolish.

"Be grateful the harder half of the job is done," he said at length, directing a hard stare at Winfrith. "I could always go back with you to finish it."

"Thank you, but there's no need," Winfrith said quickly. "Now Olwen's here the two of us can manage."

Aethelnoth shook his head. "If that's what you want," he said, stepping off the top of the bank and slithering rapidly down it. He had disappeared down a narrow alley before Olwen realised she had been left with little choice but to help Winfrith collect the firewood.

Shortly after Winfrith and Olwen had struggled back with armfuls of wood and while they were still stacking it out of the way there was a hesitant knock at the door, as if someone outside was unsure of a welcome. Ourdilic, the only one whose hands were free, reluctantly got up from her chair to see who it was. As the door swung open Winfrith looked up. Behind Ourdilic stood a slender figure in a dark cloak, the hood of which was pulled down to cover the top half of the face. It was only when she spoke, softly as if someone outside might overhear, that Winfrith realised their visitor was Eanflaed.

"Can I come in?" Ourdilic did not answer, but stepped aside for her to pass. "I can't stay long," Eanflaed said, uncovering her face and taking the chair Winfrith offered. "I've been thinking about what might be done to make people accept you, Ourdilic. Having a wife who's widely disliked won't help Aethelwold. Reminding

Alfred's followers you come from Cornwall and your father was its king is never going to change anyone's mind about you either."

"And you think I'll just forget where I come from?" Ourdilic said, retreating to a table at the far end of the room where she had placed Alfred's aestel. "Why should I take advice from a woman whose husband beats her?"

"He's not a bad man…and I know all too well we can't forget where we come from. Each wife finds her own way to get along with her husband. You think mine's difficult but Aethelwold will be no easier. All Alfred's men think Cornwall is the devil's own land."

"Shows how ignorant they are," Ourdilic said, picking up the aestel and turning it from side to side so that the enamel caught the light from the fire. Winfrith decided it was time to try and coax Ourdilic into a less hostile mood.

"You'll not be the first girl that wasn't thought good enough. My father sold oysters for a living. No-one expected a thegn like Leofranc to take me as his wife and plenty said as much to my face. Eanflaed's not finding fault with you, just preparing you for what to expect."

Ourdilic sighed and for the first time in weeks Winfrith caught her and Olwen exchanging sympathetic glances.

"Winfrith's right," Eanflaed said, getting up and crossing to where Ourdilic was making a great show of admiring the aestel. "And so are you. People here are ignorant about Cornwall. I ought to know. It's where I met Beorhtric. He'd been sent there to look for sites where hill forts might be built."

Ourdilic stared at Eanflaed in disbelief. "You met your husband in Cornwall? What were you doing there?"

"Living with my father. He married a Cornish woman so you could say I was half-Cornish myself."

"So you keep quiet about it in case a few thegns hate you for it? And why did you marry a man like Beorhtric who hates Cornwall? And, knowing where I was from, why did you treat me like something you'd stepped in?"

"I'm sorry for that," Eanflaed said, resting a hand on Ourdilic's shoulder. "Beorhtric was angry that Alfred had asked me to talk to you. He doesn't seem able to win the king's favour himself and I wasn't going to provoke him further by offering friendship to you.

I can see you must find it strange that I ever agreed to be Beorhtric's wife, but you have to remember I was young, like you. What did I know? I'd had enough of my father's strictness and thought the world beyond Cornwall must be an exciting place. My father thought a Saxon thegn was a good catch. He barely knew Beorhtric or cared to find out what he was like. He thought every Wessex thegn must be wealthy. Poor Beorhtric… away from home for months, hating the food and the people, carrying out a task for which he expected little reward. You see, Ourdilic, he might have been a thegn but he knew no more about the world or himself than I did."

"What about your mother? She'd have seen he didn't like Cornish folk."

"She might have warned me against him if she hadn't died having me. I never knew her." Strangely, the recollection brought a smile to Eanflaed's face. "At that age, like you, I don't expect I'd have taken much notice."

Winfrith watched Ourdilic take in Eanflaed's words. The girl gave no sign of resenting the criticism. She carefully placed the aestel back on the table, alongside a necklace of black stones and a silver ring. Eanflaed leaned forward to get a closer look at the carefully arranged jewels.

"My past and my future," Ourdilic said. "Those to remind me of the cliffs and waves and the call of the gulls in Cornwall; this as a sign of what I shall become, a wife who sits at the king's table."

Eanflaed carefully picked up the aestel, laying it across her palm and holding it towards the light from the doorway.

"It's beautiful," she said." Do you know what my father received from Beorhtric as a morning gift? A stolen pig and a promise he'd never see his daughter again. Make sure you take good care it. There are plenty of people who'd give their right arm for a jewel like this."

"I keep telling her it ought to be locked away," Winfrith said, "but she won't have it of course."

"No-one would dare steal it." Ourdilic said, taking it back from Eanflaed and returning it to the table. "It was the king's gift. Alfred would see anyone who dared to take it hang."

"If they were caught," Winfrith said, not really expecting to convince Ourdilic. "Sitting there on the table, it would only take a second for someone to slip it into their pocket."

Eanflaed stood admiring the aestel for a moment longer before turning away and pulling her hood low over her brow again.

"I should go. Beorhtric will wonder where I am. Think about what I've said, Ourdilic. I do know what it's like to leave your home and find yourself amid strangers. Your marriage is some time off yet and Aethelwold is a man you hardly know. You're sure you have everything worked out, but don't forget you can talk to me whenever you're ready. Goodbye to you both."

Eanflaed slipped out of the door without looking back. Ourdilic went back to her collection of jewels, passing a square of red cloth over the surface of the aestel for perhaps the fiftieth time that day. Winfrith returned to her chair, curious about Eanflaed's efforts to befriend the girl and the unexpected glimpses into her early life. Her Cornish blood had come as a surprise, yet it was natural that in Wessex she would have kept it to herself. She had been very taken with the aestel too. Had that been the real purpose of her visit…to get a closer look at it? She was surely not the only person who would like to feel such a jewel nestling in their palm. And that must mean that, whatever Ourdilic's objections, Alfred had to be persuaded to order that the aestel be removed to the heaviest lockable chest in the king's hall. She wouldn't like it, but then a morning gift didn't belong to the bride-to-be but to her parents. Winfrith smiled to herself. At least someone else would eventually have to tell Ourdilic the jewel was not hers by right.

Whatever Winfrith's concerns were about the aestel, Alfred was too busy elsewhere to act on them, despite Milred's promise to raise the matter. As the days passed she grew used to seeing it on the small table and Ourdilic rarely left it out of her sight. When they had first arrived in Cheddar she had felt uneasy. The looming cliffs cast long shadows over the house and a constant wind hurried along the gorge, shaking twigs and dead leaves from the surrounding trees. The feeling had gradually lessened, helped by the knowledge that the cliffs prevented Guthrum approaching from the north and the narrow gorge made it easy to spot early any unwelcome visitors.

On the third morning after Eanflaed's visit Winfrith woke early. Leaving Olwen and Ourdilic sleeping, she walked towards the king's hall, hoping she might catch Cuthbert before he set off on one of his frequent forays towards Wells and Glastonbury. Across the road from the main door were the two ramshackle houses where Aethelnoth's Somerset men were lodged. Two long benches stood against the front wall, usually occupied by several unkempt ceorls. She rarely passed them without overhearing some remark about her looks or half-hearted invitation to join them, so it was surprising this time to see both benches empty.

Even more unusual was the absence of guards at the hall door. A sudden fear seized her. Had she and the two girls been abandoned in the night? Had Alfred got wind of Guthrum's army closing in on Cheddar? She put her shoulder to the door, feeling it creak slowly open. It took a moment for eyes to adjust to the gloom but it was soon evident that she had been right to be concerned. Instead of the usual ranks of sleepers lining the walls she could make out only untidy heaps of bedding, thrown aside as if everyone had left in a hurry. A movement at the far end of the hall caught her attention, gradually taking the shape of a tall, gangly figure slowly pushing a broom around the raised stone hearth.

"Hello! Where is everyone?" Winfrith called out.

The figure looked up sharply and she heard the clatter of the broom falling to the floor. He advanced cautiously towards her, head bent forward as he tried to make out who was there. Once he was near enough to see, he sighed with relief.

"Thought you were Alcuin," he said, giving Winfrith a gap-toothed grin. "Handy with his boot if he thinks I'm not going fast enough. None of Alfred's lot are here, if that's who you were looking for."

"Where are they? They can't all have gone?"

"Off after Aethelnoth's lot…that's where. Woke up this morning to find 'em gone. I said they looked a shifty lot as soon as they got here. Now it looks like they've all legged it back home."

"Why would Alfred's men have gone to look for them? Aethelnoth is ealdorman of Somerset though. He's surely the one who ought to know where they are?"

The tall man chuckled to himself. "He ought to for sure. He's gone with them."

Winfrith was briefly lost for words. Had Aethelnoth really just upped and left? It would be yet another huge blow to Alfred, losing one of his three remaining ealdormen. She'd be glad to see the back of him herself but she knew enough about their present plight to know others would see it differently. Cheddar might feel safe for the moment but Alfred's final destination was still ahead of them and no-one knew the moors and marshes of Somerset better than Aethelnoth.

"When did they set out?" she asked.

"At first light," the tall man answered. "In a mighty hurry they were too."

So they had not been gone long. Winfrith turned away, heading swiftly out of the door. Olwen and Ourdilic would soon be awake, wanting to know why everything was so quiet. It might be best to make sure they stayed inside the house until Alfred's men returned.

8

"Like looking for spit in a river," Cuthbert grumbled on his return. "A full day wasted and a night in a room not fit for sheep."

He stood with Winfrith outside the house she shared with Olwen and Ourdilic, watching the last of Alfred's men drop down the bank and cross the ditch separating woodland from the houses of Cheddar.

"Surely he won't have gone far?" she asked. "This is his own shire."

"You don't have to go far round here to find yourself up to your waist in marsh. Anyone who knows the land as well as Aethelnoth won't find it hard to stay hidden."

"Why do you think he left in such a hurry?"

Cuthbert shrugged, scraping a muddy shoe against the corner post of the house. "Who knows? Perhaps he decided there were too few of us to resist Guthrum any longer. Or he could be following Wulfhere's example. If Dorset's ealdorman thinks he can profit sharing a table with Danes, perhaps he thinks Somerset's would be better off doing the same."

Once the last thegn had dragged himself wearily over the ditch and passed down the narrow lane towards the king's hall, Cuthbert gathered up his spear and shield and prepared to follow. He nodded towards the door of Winfrith's house.

"How are the two girls in there? Still at war?"

"Slightly better," Winfrith replied. "They're both quieter than usual, though Ourdilic still expects to be waited on. She spends most of her time rearranging her clothes and sorting through the beads she brought with her from Cornwall. If anything she's too quiet. I know her head's full of her betrothal to Aethelwold but I've got used her making herself heard. I wonder if there's something else troubling her. She didn't even grumble when I swept a pile of dust over her feet this morning."

"Probably nothing," Cuthbert said. "Still, enjoy it while you can." No sooner were the words out of his mouth than the sound of raised voices carried through the half-open door. He was about to say something but Winfrith put a finger to her lips and indicated they should move closer. The first voice they heard was Olwen's.

"Calm down. Someone will hear. There must be something we can do."

"Like what? It will ruin everything. Even you can see that." Ourdilic sounded upset enough to persuade Winfrith she ought to show her face, but she hesitated a moment longer, hoping she would say what was the matter. Instead it was Olwen who spoke, clearly growing more irritated now.

"Well Winfrith will be back soon. She won't take long to work out there's something wrong, that's if she hasn't already. If you keep acting like this, she'll go on and on at you until you tell her. You know what she's like...never lets anything go once she's started."

Winfrith's was about to burst in on them and point out that someone needed to keep an eye on what they were doing but before she could move Cuthbert gave their presence away by giving way to laughter. Straight away Olwen appeared in the doorway, managing to look both alarmed and indignant at the same time.

"How long have you been standing there?" she demanded. "Have you been spying on us?"

"We've just got here," Winfrith said, "but if you don't want anyone to know what you're up to it would be a good idea to keep your voices down."

"What was he laughing at?"

"If you mean me," Cuthbert said, clearly still amused, "it was hearing someone other than me suggest Winfrith never lets anything rest until she has an answer. And that's the last answer I have time for, so I'll leave the three of you to sort this out."

Winfrith waited until Cuthbert had disappeared into the narrow alley opposite before attempting to discover what was wrong. Olwen had stepped outside the door, clearly determined to have further words before they went back in to face Ourdilic.

"You shouldn't eavesdrop," she said, staring hard at Winfrith. "You're always telling us that."

"We weren't, Olwen. I just came back to the house I live in and met Cuthbert as I got to the door. What's so important that I shouldn't have heard it anyway?"

Olwen hesitated, taking a deep breath before answering. "Nothing dreadful...I suppose.
Ourdilic was just a bit upset. She'll be fine in a minute. You know what it's like. She misses her family and everyone here hates her."

"Then why don't we go in and at least make sure she has some company? She doesn't usually sulk for long."

"Don't say I told you she was upset. We've only just got back on speaking terms. I'd rather not be on the wrong end of her temper again."

Winfrith followed Olwen back inside, unconvinced that the complaints she'd heard from Ourdilic were much to do with missing her family or being disliked. Neither had bothered her before and her betrothal to Aethelnoth had seemed to be exactly the reward she had been looking for since arriving from Cornwall. No, there was definitely something else amiss for Ourdilic to shout that everything would be ruined.

Cheddar was at last beginning to feel a little like home. There was no sign of Danish raiding parties coming this far west and Alfred decided they would wait until the roads became less boggy before resuming their journey. It was hard to believe how quickly the weeks were slipping by, but each day the mornings grew a little lighter and it was easier to imagine spring soon making its presence felt. Winfrith was growing used to the new Ourdilic too, though strangely there were times when she missed the girl's old fighting spirit. She had definitely become easier to live with, less inclined to answer back and offering only rare reminders that she was Aethelwold's betrothed. She and Olwen had become firm friends again, conducting long whispered conversations which ceased as soon as Winfrith came near.

Eanflaed's visits became more regular, though she rarely stayed for long. For the most part Ourdilic listened to what she had to say, perhaps because it was clear it was Alfred who was insisting on Eanflaed's guidance. He took little part himself in preparing Ourdilic for the life ahead and Aethelwold seemed to be avoiding her altogether. Winfrith had grown so used to this, not to mention relieved that her own responsibility was lighter, that she was surprised to find Alfred at the door one day, suggesting it was time Ourdilic's learning was put to the test.

"Let's see if she knows how to receive guests well. I'd like a small feast to be prepared tomorrow evening," he said, clearly not anticipating Winfrith raising any objections to the idea. "Milred, Cuthbert, myself, Aethelwold of course, you and Eanflaed…all people she knows. It will be my chance to see if she's taking in everything Eanflaed has told her and whether she can be a good host when all eyes are on her. My own kitchen will supply food and perhaps some wine."

"She can pour without spilling," Winfrith said, "though I'm not sure she can manage a smile at the same time."

"Then you and Eanflaed need to remind her that every thegn's wife must welcome her husband's guests. Don't tell her who will be sitting down at the table…just that, as Aethelwold's betrothed, she will be the one to see that they all enjoy being here."

Alfred departed as suddenly as he had appeared, leaving Winfrith to begin the task of sweeping the spiders' webs from the rafters and from under the sleeping platforms. The girls had not yet roused themselves from their beds, though both had shown signs of having been awake for some time.

"What are you doing?" Olwen complained. "Couldn't that wait? You're spraying muck all over my blankets."

"Then perhaps it's time you got up," Winfrith answered, giving her a gentle prod with the broom. "The house needs cleaning from top to bottom. We're about to get some visitors."

Ourdilic stirred, propping herself up on an elbow. "What visitors? No-one ever comes here…apart from Eanflaed."

"Well they are now, so the pair of you had better stir yourselves and give me a hand."

"Who? Who's coming?" Ourdilic demanded, showing no sign she intended to leave her bed. "And why would they want to come here? There's hardly room for the three of us."

Winfrith leaned the broom against the wall. Alfred had said not to name the guests but Ourdilic would have to know his plan for her to host a feast in the house sooner rather than later.

"We're having five guests to eat with us tomorrow evening. It'll be a bit cramped, but we'll manage. We'll move these chairs outside and place benches along the walls."

"We can't feed five extra mouths. We've barely got enough for us," Olwen said, not hesitating to take Ourdilic's side.

"Alfred has promised us food from his own kitchen." As soon as the words were out, Winfrith regretted them. The look on the faces of both girls told her they knew Alfred's involvement meant something important was going on. They were bound to insist on knowing who the guests were. "But he said I wasn't to tell you…" she added quickly, "I was to say nothing more except that you, Ourdilic, are to act as host. Good practice for when you become Aethelwold's wife."

Ourdilic threw off her blanket, swinging her legs over the side of the sleeping platform. "That must mean Alfred himself will be here…and Aethelwold of course." She gave a hurried glance around the gloomy room. "Does it really have to be here?"

"Alfred insisted," Winfrith replied.

"Then we'd better make it look more cheerful. I'm not going to welcome King of Wessex to a fox hole."

So it was that Winfrith found both girls lending a hand to make the room more comfortable and, even if Ourdilic was far more enthusiastic about what needed to be done than Olwen, the satisfaction of having two uncomplaining helpers was enough for her to overlook it. It even seemed that whatever had upset Ourdilic earlier had been swept aside by the prospect of the feast.

By the time the guests arrived and Alfred ushered Milred ahead of him through the narrow doorway a good fire blazed on the hearth and a long table had been set down the centre of the room. A suckling pig, supplied by Cuthbert, was roasting on a spit and Milred had instructed his servant to carry over a barrel of good ale, sharper in taste and without the greyish sludge which marked most of what was drunk in Cheddar. Ourdilic invited them in. Winfrith was pleased to see her smile but there was just a hint of unease in her voice as she came face to face with Alfred.

"Welcome to our house. There are seats for you all, along the benches…and you, my lord at the top of the table."

Yet once everyone was seated, Ourdilic filled Alfred's cup with a steady hand and, despite all eyes being on her, took her place alongside him as if that was where she belonged. As soon as all their cups had been filled, Alfred raised his towards Ourdilic.

"The greeting was well done, Ourdilic. Thank you. A new life beckons for you and I hope there will be many such gatherings along the way. You have lost a father and a homeland but in the years ahead you will gain a husband and come to think of Wessex as the place you belong." He turned to look down the table. "Lift your cups and join me in drinking to the health and prosperity of Ourdilic and my nephew Aethelwold."

Winfrith glanced at Aethelwold, sitting at Alfred's opposite elbow. He raised his cup as he was bid but even though his face was half in shadow he could not hide his scowl of displeasure. If there was any reluctance to wish Ourdilic well, the taste of good ale meant no-one would dare show it. Milred's servant began to slice the suckling pig and the sounds of eating and drinking replaced talk for a while. It was Cuthbert, catching sight of Ourdilic taking a cautious sip of ale, who made the first attempt to lighten the sombre mood which had descended on them all.

"Drink up, Ourdilic. If you're to be a thegn's wife in a year or two, you'll need a taste for good ale. Aethelwold won't want to come home to ditch water."

Ourdilic clutched her cup more tightly, glancing down the table as if she expected someone to rescue her from this challenge. Seeing no help coming, she threw back her head and gulped down the contents of her cup. The laughter had barely died down before she dashed outside and her harsh retching sounded clearly from beyond the doorway.

The eating and talking resumed but when Ourdilic had not returned after five minutes Winfrith excused herself and slipped outside to make sure she was alright. A full moon had just climbed above the dark edge of the cliffs, casting a pale eerie light across the yard. She could see no sign of Ourdilic, just a shadowy group of perhaps three or four man gathered round a fire at the head of the alley leading down to the king's hall. She called out the girl's name but there was no reply. She shouted again, this time answered by a call from one of figures huddled round the fire.

"Lost your Cornish princess, have you? Them spriggans have probably took her back where she came from." Winfrith stared across at the fire but it was impossible to tell which of the men had called out. She wondered if the obvious dislike of Ourdilic in the voice and the mention of Cornish evil spirits meant it was Beorhtric but the men's faces were not well lit and in any case they all wore low hoods. The shouts were enough to bring Cuthbert outside, wanting to know why Winfrith and Ourdilic had not returned to the table.

"She's disappeared," Winfrith said. "Not used to the strong ale by the sound of it. I'm sure she won't be far away."

"Did they say which way she went?" Cuthbert asked, nodding towards the men round the fire.

"They don't seem to have noticed her…though you might get a more sensible answer from them than I did."

Cuthbert opened his mouth to shout but thought better of it, instead striding briskly down the slope towards the crackling fire. Winfrith followed.

"You must have seen a girl leaving the house up there," Cuthbert called as he approached the three men. "Where did she go?"

The nearest of the three turned to look at Cuthbert, the flame of the fire casting just enough light on the face beneath the hood for Winfrith to see that she'd been right in thinking one of the men might be Beorhtric. He waved vaguely in the direction of the cliffs beyond the house.

"Somewhere up that way…over the ditch. Following the devil back to Cornwall probably."

Winfrith shivered as a sudden icy gust flattened the flames and sent smoke whirling into the night. She told herself to be sensible. Nothing dreadful had happened to Ourdilic. Despite her show of confidence, the occasion had simply proved too much for her. She had gone somewhere quiet to get a bit of fresh air. She would be back as soon as she had calmed down a little. Yet as she and Cuthbert began their return to the interrupted feast she found it impossible to hide her concern.

"She ought not to be out alone. Even if she only meant to get away from us all for a moment, it would be easy to get lost. She doesn't know her way around Cheddar even in daylight."

"It's not the first time she's disappeared," Cuthbert said. "She turned up quite happy the last time. Give her a bit longer. If she's not appeared by the time the plates have been emptied, we'll make a proper search for her…but I'm sure she'll be back long before then, expecting everyone to make a fuss of her."

The slices of suckling pig were soon gone and Winfrith spooned a stew of barley, carrot and parsnip, flavoured with thyme, onto the empty plates. In Ourdilic's absence Olwen quietly set about refilling cups with ale and Winfrith was sure she caught the hint of satisfaction on her face as she did so. Aethelwold, who had said little all evening, was the first to suggest that it was time they looked for Ourdilic, though whether it was concern for his future wife or a desire to be out of the present company was not obvious.

"She won't have gone far," he said, nudging the table as he got to his feet. "She did the same thing yesterday. Went off in a temper and turned up again in no time as if nothing had happened."

"Wait," Alfred said, catching his nephew's sleeve as he headed for the door. "Beorhtric thought she headed over the ditch towards the cliffs. Is that right?"

"It's the impression he had," Cuthbert said. "He didn't sound too sure."

"But if she did, she could have gone any one of four ways on the other side of the bank. It makes no sense for all of us to follow the same path and we'll need torches out there. The track leading down into the gorge is the toughest. Since you've got the youngest legs, Aethelwold, you take that one. Cuthbert and I will each take one of the paths going east and west. That leaves you, Winfrith, unless we fetch Beorhtric …"

"No, I want to help. Beorhtric looks as though he's had too much ale to be much use."

Alfred nodded. "In that case you could search the path up to the bottom of the cliff face. You won't have to go far before you reach a dead end. It's a bit of a scramble but easy enough if you watch where you're putting your feet. I think it's best if Milred stays here with Olwen in case Ourdilic returns while we're gone."

They waited, all a little uneasy now, while Milred's servant fetched torches and Winfrith could see from their faces that she wasn't the only one eager to begin the search. The servant was soon back and the torches lit and carried outside. As she followed the others uphill towards the ditch, glad of the comforting circle of flickering light cast by the torch, Winfrith whispered reassuring words to herself. Ourdilic is just lost. No harm has come to her. She'll soon be back at the fireside.

Once they had crossed the ditch, Alfred spoke a few words of encouragement before they went their separate ways. Winfrith made slow progress to begin with. It would have been impossible without the torch, although in places she could have wished for two free hands, especially where the track began to rise through a series of sharp turns, turning back on itself as it twisted through stunted trees and trailing brambles. Several times her skirt caught on thorns and each time there was a brief moment when she imagined someone or something clutching at her ankles, trying to drag her down. Once the path emerged into the open it levelled out for a stretch before starting to rise again. She raised the torch high enough to see the track ahead of her beginning to narrow as it gained height. As she started to climb she stumbled, catching her foot on a bare tree root and sending a flurry of loose stones rattling down the hillside.

Occasionally the clouds parted long enough to allow pale, shadowy moonlight to show through, enough at least to suggest where the charcoal sky ended and the black cliff began. All too often the dark night sky closed in again, leaving her with only the flickering light of the torch. Winfrith stopped to listen, hoping to hear Ourdilic's feet disturbing the stones somewhere ahead of her, but the path was eerily silent. She called Ourdilic's name, straight away wishing she hadn't as the sound of her own voice echoed around the cliffs like a forest spirit in pain.

The last few feet up to the cliff face were steeper and Winfrith had to lean forward, steadying herself with her free hand, to ease her way up. The ground flattened out beneath the rock and, as she held the torch above her head, it was easy to see why people had taken the trouble to follow this awkward path. The flickering light from the flames was just strong enough to enable her to pick out the mossy edges of a cave entrance. Much of it had been filled in by layers of flat stones and footprints at the base of the gap that remained suggested others must have come this way recently. Winfrith paused before stepping inside. Ourdilic had left the house without a torch. She would surely not have chosen such a dark, damp place as a refuge. She called the girl's name…softly, though she wasn't sure why, and breathed a little more easily when there was no reply.

Winfrith was about to turn back but at the last minute peered into the cave entrance again. She ought to check inside, just in case Ourdilic had braved the dark and then either fallen asleep or tripped and hurt herself. She edged through the gap, holding the torch high enough for the flames to lick at the uneven rock above her head. The space in front of her opened out and she advanced cautiously until she judged she had reached the centre of the cave. She turned slowly round, casting orange light around the walls. Trails of green slime ran down them, as water seeped slowly from above and occasional splashes marked the spots where puddles had formed on the cave floor. Yet despite the damp and the chill air, there were signs someone had been here. A grimy wooden bowl stood on a ledge cut into the wall and a blackened circle of stones on the floor showed someone had recently lit a fire here. There was no sign of Ourdilic however, though just to be sure she was not crouching in one of the clefts or hollows towards the back of the cave, Winfrith advanced a little further inside, holding the torch nearer to the ground. She had just satisfied herself that the cave was empty when a sharp, high-pitched scream pierced the air outside, echoing along the rock face before dying away.

Gripped by fear, Winfrith narrowly avoided dropping the torch. She hurried outside, her heart racing. It might be nothing of course…some wild creature, caught unexpectedly by a predator, crying out in pain. Or perhaps it was just the cry of an owl, distorted by the echoes of the cliff face. It could even have been a lone wolf howling at the moon. Yet she couldn't put the thought aside that it had sounded like a human scream, and not just one of pain either. There had been more than that in it, much more. It was the sound of someone coming face to face with something terrifying, something which had frightened the life out of them.

Every muscle in her body seemed to be telling her to hurry back to the safety of Cheddar, yet she couldn't go without making some effort to discover if the cry of terror, which had seemed to come from further along the cliff, was anything to do with Ourdilic. She began to work her way along the bottom of the cliff face, hoping that it was only travelling alone at night in such a strange place which was making her more afraid than she should be. Almost immediately she found herself on a clear path, made up of loose stones at first but soon giving way to a ledge of soft, springy grass. It made for swifter progress and she was almost running when she felt her foot catch in a tangle of trailing roots. As she bent down to free it, the torchlight illuminated a pale strip of cloth…good linen by the look of it…hanging loosely from a thorny branch beside her. Even before she saw what lay beyond, she knew at once the awful truth of that long-drawn-out scream. She glanced upwards. Somewhere up there was the cliff edge. There was no hope of seeing it but staring into the dark delayed having to look at what she now feared she was about to find not far from where she stood.

 Slowly Winfrith turned her back on the cliff face and began to move the torch this way and that, scanning the ground below her. For a moment she thought there might be nothing there and that the cloth had come there by chance but something white, lying just below a stunted bush to her left, stood out briefly as the torchlight swung past it. She forced herself to go closer but it was obvious already what she was looking at. A small
bundle, twisted into a quite unnatural shape but with pale hands protruding beyond rumpled linen sleeves, lay motionless on the slope below her. The dress was torn and streaked with dirt but the fingers were spread delicately, as if their owner had been in the process of admiring them. The face was hidden from view but there could be no doubt as to who was lying there. For the second time in minutes the cliff face echoed to an anguished scream, except that this time there was no rocky ground to break the fall and put an end to it.

9

"You were making no sense at all when we found you." Winfrith still felt very drowsy but she could make out Cuthbert and Milred sitting together on the wall bench opposite where she lay. Cuthbert leaned forward, sensing he had her attention at last. "We had to give you valerian root…just to calm you down."

"What about Ourdilic?" The name almost stuck in her throat but she forced herself to continue. "Did you find her? Find the body, I mean."

"Don't worry about that now," Milred urged. It was kindly meant but Winfrith could no more forget about it than she could stop breathing.

"Where is she? I want to know." A rush of thoughts flooded back into her head… climbing the path to the cave, hearing a scream, seeing the white-clad figure lying at the foot of the cliff. Before that Ourdilic had left the house feeling unwell and no-one had thought to follow her…not until it was much too late. And only a week ago Winfrith had got so cross with her that in an unthinking moment she'd hinted they'd all be better off without her. Could it really be true that she was dead? Surely she had been dreaming? Any moment now Ourdilic would appear at the door, demanding to know where her tunic was.

"We brought her back last night," Cuthbert said, getting to his feet and crossing to her side. He laid a hand gently on her shoulder. "There's nothing more you can do for her just now. She'll be buried tomorrow. Alfred is arranging it. The manner of it will be the same as if she was already the wife of the king's nephew."

Winfrith studied his face, hoping to some sign that he had some reason for pretending Ourdilic was dead, but his eyes showed only concern and perhaps regret.

"How could it have happened, Cuthbert? What was she doing up on the cliff top? And in the dark?"

"I don't know. You can only get up there by a path out of the gorge. I wouldn't have thought she even knew it was there. Perhaps she didn't care where she was heading. Finally had enough of all the hostility she met with here…"

"No, she wouldn't do that…risk her own life." Winfrith realised straight away from Milred's startled face that she must have shouted. "I'm sorry, but she just wouldn't. She was happy. Glad to be betrothed. Looking forward to lording it over the rest of us. Someone must have persuaded her to go up there, or more likely forced her. She was feeling a bit unwell…unused to the wine. She wouldn't have chosen to go to the top of the cliff in that state. Someone must have made her…someone who hated her enough to want her dead."

"But she was just a girl," Milred said. "She wasn't much liked but no-one would go to those lengths. Seeing her dead like that has upset you…would upset anyone. You're bound to look for someone to blame, but it's far more likely to have been misfortune."

"Someone pushed her. I know it," Winfrith insisted. "She'd got too much to live for to jump…and anyway, she'd more sense than to head for a cliff edge in the dark. Someone threw her from the top. We have to find them."

Winfrith searched the faces of Cuthbert and Milred, looking for signs they would help. Surely they must see that Ourdilic would never have ended up at the foot of the cliff without someone attacking her in the dark. Perhaps it had happened close to the house and her senseless body had been carried to the top. It would have been hard work, but then thegns like Beorhtric were always boasting of their strength. Milred seemed thoughtful but Cuthbert still looked unconvinced.

"How would she have got up there?" Winfrith demanded, lifting herself onto her elbows. "The path where I found her ends at the cliff face."

"Another, further along the gorge, leads up to the top," Cuthbert said. "Otherwise it's a ten mile walk to reach it from the west."

"So she must have been taken along the gorge." Winfrith thought for a moment. Alfred had divided the searchers when they set out to look for Ourdilic and it was Aethelwold who had been sent along the gorge. Could she have gone that way and might he have caught up with her? But if he had, would he have attacked her? He'd been ill at ease during the evening certainly. Perhaps the feast had made him realise the betrothal was a mistake. Winfrith shook her head. There were easier ways out of the arrangement than murder. Besides, Aethelwold surely wasn't ruthless enough to go through with the cold-blooded killing of a young girl. Beorhtric or Raedberht perhaps, but not Aethelwold. Even so, the sooner she could put a few questions to the king's nephew, the better she would feel. If Cuthbert and Milred weren't going to help, she'd find out what happened by herself.

"Why would anyone have taken her so far?" Milred asked. "Even if someone did mean to harm her…and despite your fears, I really think it's unlikely… why not do it along the gorge? There would be no-one to see it at that time of night. It's more likely she simply lost her way. In the dark she wouldn't have known she was near the edge."

Winfrith let her head fall back on the pillow. Neither Cuthbert nor Milred were going to be persuaded and she felt too tired to argue. She closed her eyes, pretending to sleep. If she kept insisting, it wouldn't be long before they started saying she was imagining things…that seeing Ourdilic's body had been too much of a shock. She yawned, drawing it out as long as she could, and pulled the blankets more tightly around her. After a few moments she heard whispers and some shuffling sounds and when she slowly opened her eyes again both men had gone.

Being alone did not bring Winfrith much peace of mind. Ourdilic had been placed in her care. Why hadn't she been more watchful? She ought never have allowed the girl to leave the feast on her own. She'd seen there was something wrong. It wouldn't have taken much to save her from what must have been a terrifying journey to her death. Yet Ourdilic had only been outside for minutes before Winfrith went to look. No-one expected her to have gone far. No-one else thought there was any danger. Would she have kept a better eye on Ourdilic if she had been more likeable? More like Olwen? However difficult Ourdilic had been, she deserved better than to be pushed over a cliff in the dark.

Winfrith might have gone on finding fault with herself for longer if the slim figure of Eanflaed hadn't slipped quietly through the door and advanced hesitantly towards the side of the bed.

"Are you alright?" she asked. "Milred said you might like someone to sit with you."

"She's gone, isn't she? I didn't imagine seeing her lying there."

Eanflaed nodded. "She's gone. She won't ever sit in here again, suggesting she knows better than all of us."

Winfrith propped herself up on one elbow and looked round the familiar room. Ourdilic, as much as anyone, had made it her own. Her glance settled on the small table Ourdilic kept by her bedside. The coloured beads were still displayed on the strip of red cloth but, even from across the room, Winfrith could see that they had been moved. Pride of place in the centre of the cloth had been reserved for Ourdilic's morning gift but now the beads took up the whole space. There was no sign of Alfred's beautiful jewelled aestel. Had she finally heeded advice and put it somewhere safer? Or had someone taken advantage of the confusion and upset of Ourdilic's death and taken it? Winfrith blinked away a tear. For a young girl to die like that was hard to accept. To think that someone might have chosen that moment to steal her morning gift as well was almost unbearable.

Eanflaed was watching her, waiting for her to say something. She could ask her to look for the aestel...check it had not fallen on the floor perhaps. Yet Winfrith hesitated. She wasn't sure why, except for a vague feeling that it would be wrong to allow anyone else to go searching through Ourdilic's few possessions. Even so, the more she thought about it, the less Winfrith thought it likely a thief had taken it. Who would have dared to take such a thing? She was sure it had not been found with the body. She tried to picture Ourdilic leaving the house. Was there any possibility that, even feeling unwell, she had thought of taking it with her? That would mean either she had lost it on the way up the cliff, or else the same hand that had forced the girl over the edge had kept it. If, on the other hand, the aestel had remained in the house, who else might have been tempted by its fine colours and skilled craftsmanship? Knowing it was the king's gift would surely have deterred most people?

Even as Winfrith asked herself the question, one possible answer came to her. Eanflaed had made no attempt to hide her admiration of the aestel. It had reminded her how unexciting her own morning gift from Beorhtric had been. Her envy had been plain to see and yet she was a thegn's wife, trusted by Alfred himself to teach Ourdilic the right way to behave. She more than anyone would feel how wrong such a theft would be. Winfrith pushed herself up into a sitting position, easing her legs over the side of the platform.

"I'm feeling more rested now. If I get up and do something, it might help to get Ourdilic out of my mind, at least for a bit. It's kind of you come, but I think I'd like to be on my own for a short while."

Eanflaed looked reluctant to leave, but by the time Winfrith had lowered her feet to the floor and searched under the sleeping platform for her shoes, she had crossed to the door and, with the slightest bow of her head, passed outside.

As soon as she was sure her legs would support her Winfrith knew what she intended to do. If neither Cuthbert nor Milred believed Ourdilic had died as the result of an attack not an accident, no-one else was likely to either. The only way to convince them otherwise was to climb the path to the cliff edge and look for signs of what had happened there. She saw no-one as she left the house and crossed the rainwater ditch, taking the route along the bottom of the gorge which Aethelwold had followed the night before. Despite the attempts of a pale morning sun to pierce the high cloud the air felt heavy and dark shadows fell across the path. It twisted its way between high banks, offering little chance to see what lay ahead. It was easy to imagine that anyone – a thief, a murderer, a forest spirit even – might be lying in wait around the next bend. Each sigh of wind or rustle of leaves raised the possibility of someone watching from the bushes above her. Every time a startled bird flapped out of the branches overhead she felt her heartbeat quicken. Yet she pressed on, telling herself over and over again that she must do more for Ourdilic in death than she had managed in life.

It didn't take Winfrith long to reach the fork leading off to the cliff top. A line of stones laid across the main path pointed the way to six steps cut into the hillside. From the top of these a narrow path twisted its way upwards until it disappeared behind a clump of wind-blown thorn bushes. Winfrith quickly found herself breathing more heavily as she began to climb. The path doubled back on itself several times so that it was not long before she could see below her the ground she had already covered. She stopped to look down for a moment, relieved that no-one appeared to be following her.

Several more sharp turns brought the cliff edge into view but, despite her eagerness to reach the top, she began to move more cautiously. The path was even narrower here, with the cliff face on one side and a steep drop into the distant trees below on the other. Perhaps thirty paces ahead of her the path turned out of sight behind a towering boulder. Once there, she edged her way along it, feeling for handholds in its rutted surface. She had almost turned the corner when a sudden clatter of stones stopped her in her tracks. Before she could move a small goat came clattering around the boulder, sending loose stones rattling over the edge and racing down towards the trees. Seeing Winfrith, the terrified creature tried desperately to turn back, its tiny hooves scrabbling madly on the stony path. For a brief moment it looked as though it would gain a secure foothold until with a sharp crack a heavy stone broke away from the path, carrying the flailing animal over the edge. She looked away, pressing her face against the rock, as the goat's desperate bleats rent the air before dying away into eerie silence.

In the moments that followed Winfrith remained rooted to the spot, feeling as though her heart was hammering against the cliff face. She took several deep breaths, telling herself she had been fortunate. A few paces further on and it might have been her, not the goat, tumbling to her death. It briefly crossed her mind that someone must have frightened the goat, driving it towards her in panic, but she quickly dismissed the idea. No-one could have known she'd decided to come this way, nor could they easily have seen her approaching. Even so, she rounded the boulder an inch at a time, clinging tightly to the small cracks and crevices in its surface, trying not to show herself until she was sure there was no-one lying in wait.

On the other side of the boulder the path rose more gently towards the cliff top and a line of rowan trees protected it from the drop below. As far as Winfrith could tell there was no-one ahead of her, though the trees might provide cover for anyone determined to stay hidden. She pressed on, more swiftly now, and emerged ten minutes later onto a grassy track which stretched away along the cliff edge. She followed it back towards Cheddar, all the time scanning the ground around her for signs of a struggle. The turf was soft and springy and, checking behind her, she could see that her own footfalls left no trace. She walked for twenty minutes, until she was sure she must have gone well past the point where Ourdilic had fallen, but she saw nothing to explain what had brought it about. Reluctantly she turned back, walking more slowly now in the slim hope she might spot something she had missed the first time.

But for a sudden gust of wind she might have missed the place a second time. She walked with her eyes fixed on the ground, looking for signs of a struggle. It was only the noise of a breeze rattling the dry branches of a thorn bush right at the cliff edge which made her look up. Caught up in the branches was a pale strip of linen, fluttering in the breeze. It was just what she had been seeking, yet the sight of it still came as a shock. The colour was unmistakeable, surely the same material Ourdilic had been wearing the night before?

Now that she had found the place, Winfrith hung back, unsure what she might find and unable to keep images of Ourdilic's last moments out of her mind. She forced herself to go nearer, taking in as she went the flattened grass and the dark scar of freshly disturbed earth leading right to the cliff edge. Carefully she loosened the strip of linen from the bush, sure on closer inspection that it had been torn from Ourdilic's dress. As the dark lines on the ground neared the cliff edge they grew more uneven and several deeper ruts appeared which to Winfrith's eyes straight away suggested heels being dug desperately into the soil.

She turned away, suddenly eager to be gone. She didn't need to see any more. A girl wandering up here by chance and falling in the dark did not leave marks like that. Now they would have to believe her. She hurried back to the path into the gorge, her mind full of what she would say to Cuthbert and Milred. She was perhaps half way down the descent and so preoccupied with how to find who had attacked Ourdilic that the sudden appearance of a shadowy figure, dropping onto the track perhaps fifty paces ahead of her, did not sink in for a moment or two and by the time she had started to think she might be in some danger, the figure was already disappearing around a bend.

10

    Winfrith advanced cautiously to the bend round which the figure had vanished. They had looked in a hurry to be gone but she couldn't rid herself of the thought they might be lying in wait for her. She ought to have been afraid but seeing the signs of that desperate scuffle on the cliff top had strengthened her resolve. She was not an unsuspecting child. If anyone thought they could dispose of her the same way they would get a surprise. She scanned the sparse hawthorn and juniper bushes which sprouted at the path's edge but none seemed to offer a branch stout enough to serve as a weapon. After several unsuccessful attempts she finally managed to unearth a lump of sharp-edged rock from under the roots. It was not as big as she would have liked but it was heavy enough to give someone a headache if they got in its way.

    She descended into the gorge with few alarms. A pair of rooks startled her, screeching at each other over some scrap of food on the hillside below, but otherwise she passed few places where anyone could easily stay out of sight. Once she had turned onto the grassy path into Cheddar she began to move more warily. Rows of coppiced ash and hazel and thickets of bramble offered more cover to anyone watching out for her. She gripped the sharp stone more tightly, trying to make as little noise as possible. Soon the path started to look more familiar and she began to breathe more easily once she had glimpsed a thatched rooftop through the trees.

    She was about to cross the rainwater ditch when her nostrils caught a powerful scent of thyme. She halted, overcome by a sudden memory of the first food she had cooked on arriving in Cheddar. She had mixed scraps of meat scavenged from the king's hall with barley and was lowering the pudding into boiling water when she had smelled the thyme on her hands. She had forgotten to add the herbs and Ourdilic had said it didn't matter. She preferred it without. Winfrith felt her throat go dry. It had only been a matter of days ago. Ourdilic wouldn't be eating meat pudding ever again…with or without herbs.

    Ourdilic's face as she dismissed the idea of adding herbs afterwards appeared so real that Winfrith failed to notice a stout, unkempt figure trudging towards her. It was only the sound of the woman's voice that made her realise she was no longer alone.

"If you're out to rob us, we've nothing worth having," the woman growled. She wore a mud-streaked cloak, long enough to trail on the ground behind her, and two pale-faced children, neither more than six or seven years old, huddled close behind her.

"I wouldn't take it if you had," Winfrith replied, giving the wide-eyed children a reassuring smile. "The children look as though they're ready for a rest. Where are you heading?"

The woman looked suspiciously at Winfrith. "Not far. The children will have to cope. They're used to it by now, thanks to their worthless father."

Winfrith looked along the path. "The way you're heading it'll be many hours before you see another house."

"Don't need you to tell me that. It's not the first time we've had to drag ourselves all this way."

"You could stop here a while…get the little ones something to eat. Cheddar is just through the trees, beyond the thatched roof you can see."

The woman glanced in the direction indicated, spitting on the ground as she did so.

"I know where it is well enough. It's where Aethelnoth was supposed to have been… except he's gone off chasing some dim-witted girl. Not the first time we've had to come looking for him."

Winfrith studied the woman more closely, recalling Ceolstan's warning that Aethelnoth thought all women fair game, despite having a wife and children in Frome. Could this angry red-faced barrel of a woman be the wife he had referred to? She was not as old as she'd first appeared, perhaps just worn out chasing an errant husband, and there was enough in the dark hair and eyes to suggest she might once have been handsome. Wife or not, Winfrith was curious to know why the woman had come looking for the absent Somerset ealdorman.

"You know Aethelnoth then?" she asked.

"Better than anyone…and if I catch him with anything in a skirt they'll feel the back of my hand." She returned Winfrith's stare. "Even you, if you've been anywhere near him."

"I steer clear of other women's husbands," Winfrith said. "Too much trouble."

"Looking at you, I can see Aethelnoth might keep out of your way too. Even if he wasn't put off by that scar, he'd likely prefer something younger."

Winfrith resisted the temptation to describe Aethelnoth's attempt to lay hands on her as she collected firewood. "You speak as if he's your husband."

"Why else would we be here?" the woman said, pointing to the children. "Look at these two…fathered by Aethelnoth. Does he think food to keep them alive is just going to drop out of the sky? If you know where he's run off to, ask him if he's willing to let Beornhelm and his children starve."

"I don't know where he is," Winfrith said. "He left some days ago with the rest of the Somerset fyrd. I can find the children something to eat though. It won't be much…bread and soup perhaps…but enough to keep them going."

Beornhelm shrugged. If she was grateful she wasn't going to say so, but the look in the children's eyes at the mention of food would have swayed even the hardest heart.

"We can't stay long. Aethelnoth will have boasted to someone about who he was chasing. He's not known for keeping his mouth shut. As soon as we find out, we'll be off. He's not going to leave us in the lurch that easily."

Winfrith turned towards the thatched house, beckoning to the children to follow. If their mother didn't appreciate her kindness, at least she could help the children. Knowing that she had failed Ourdilic still preyed on her mind. Giving these two food couldn't make up for that, but it might make her feel a little better.

They crossed the rainwater ditch in silence, the smaller child, a girl, refusing Winfrith's offer of a helping hand. She stopped outside the house, signalling to them to wait, and pushed open the door. She was slightly surprised to see Olwen sitting on the floor… unlike her not to find somewhere more comfortable…and surrounded by Ourdilic's collection of coloured beads. She looked up as Winfrith entered, her eyes glassy with tears.

"They didn't take her beads, just the aestel." She shook her head sadly, stroking the beads gently with her fingertips. Beornhelm and the two children hovered in the doorway, uncertain whether or not to follow Winfrith inside. The children stared at Olwen and the beads, their curiosity clearly beginning to overcome their shyness, though even as they began to edge their way into the room Olwen appeared not to see them.

"Who took the aestel?" Winfrith demanded, crossing the room and crouching down beside Olwen. "What do you mean?"

"It's gone. Someone took it in the night. Beorhtric said it was spriggans. They were angry with Ourdilic because she'd left Cornwall."

"But that's nonsense, Olwen. You know it. It's just a tale told by mothers to scare their children. There's no such thing as a spriggan."

"Then why was Ourdilic lured off the cliff? Spriggans lead lonely travellers into danger. It's what they do. Ourdilic herself told me that."

"Then she was just trying to frighten you. You've never seen one have you? You couldn't say what a spriggan looked like."

Olwen wiped her eyes with her sleeve. "Yes I could. They're skinny and crooked, with wizened faces, as if they've been stewed in ale."

Throughout this conversation Beornhelm's little girl had kept her eyes fixed on the beads and now she stepped forward to take a closer look, catching Olwen's attention for the first time.

"Who's that? What's she doing here?"

"This is Beornhelm and these are her children. They're exhausted, walking all the way here from Frome. I said I'd find them a bite to eat. Why don't you show them Ourdilic's beads while I get the food ready? It looks as though you've got all her things laid out there. Are you sure the aestel's not with them?"

"I told you. Spriggans took it. They'll take these two as well if you don't watch out, just like they took Ourdilic. She told me how they steal children and turn them into their own."

"It's just a story, Olwen and even if there were such things as spriggans, why would they take Ourdilic? She was hardly a child?"

Olwen looked confused and Winfrith didn't press her to answer. She was clearly shocked by her friend's death and Beorhtric filling her head with foolishness hadn't helped. Perhaps it was better to accept her explanation until Winfrith herself could find out what had happened to the aestel. She might have left it at that too if Olwen hadn't offered a belated reply.

"They had their reasons."

Winfrith stood up and would have started getting together what food she could find but Olwen's odd remark made her pause. She had turned her attention back to the beads and was clearly not intending to offer any kind of explanation. Without being quite sure why the idea should come to her now and not earlier Winfrith had a sudden thought...a thought she would not have wanted to accept but which might explain several things which had been puzzling her. Ourdilic's sudden sickness, her whispered conversation with Olwen, her claim that in Cornwall girls of her age were often married and already with child...had she managed to get herself into the same state herself? Winfrith considered the possibility and immediately the memory of Ourdilic disappearing and returning with such a triumphant look astride Aethelnoth's horse came to mind.

The only person who could confirm it was Olwen. Winfrith and Cuthbert had overheard them talking about something wrong which would ruin everything. Being with child would certainly have put an end to the betrothal, unless of course Aethelwold had been responsible. Beornhelm's girl had tired of looking at the beads and was casting an eye around the room, reminding Winfrith that until she'd fulfilled her promise and sent Beornhelm on her way she couldn't set about extracting secrets from Olwen.

The three visitors wolfed down the hunks of gritty bread and hard cheese Winfrith managed to find for them. The two children sat on the floor, their heads resting against the wall, and looked as though they might fall asleep at any moment. Beornhelm on the other hand was noticeably less hostile and now seemed in no hurry to be gone. Much as she wanted to talk to Olwen alone, Winfrith could hear the sound of the wind rising outside and the slap of rain against the walls. It would be cruel to turn the children out before they'd rested for a while.

"You shouldn't listen to the likes of Beorhtric," Beornhelm said, crossing the room and sitting down beside Olwen. "You didn't see spriggans take your friend away, did you?"

"Of course not. They come in the night...that's what Beorhtric said."

"He talks as much nonsense as any other thegn...probably more."

Olwen began scooping up the beads and piling them in the middle of the red cloth. "How would you know what he's like? You don't even know him," she said, edging away from Beornhelm.

"I know him as well as any of the other thegns who follow King Alfred. My husband Aethelnoth has made sure of that."

Olwen glanced up, her eyes wide with disbelief. "Aethelnoth? Alfred's ealdorman in Somerset? He doesn't have a wife. He would have told us."

Beornhelm leaned back, looking Olwen up and down. "Well, you're easy enough on the eye," she said, "not that he cares. So he came sniffing round you and this girl you say has gone off the cliff, did he?"

Olwen said nothing but Winfrith could see she was close to tears.

"Whatever he told you, it was lies," Beornhelm said. "Look. I'm his wife. Those are his children. Can't you see it in their faces? So if you're thinking you might win him for yourself, forget it. I'll make sure you don't…"

"Leave her," Winfrith said, taking Olwen's hand and helping her to her feet. "You can see she'd upset at losing her friend. I'm sure she had no more idea of encouraging your husband than I did. It's not her fault he thought anyone in a skirt fair game."

"Well I'm warning you…"

"And I'm warning you," Winfrith said, leaning over Beornhelm so that their faces almost touched. "Your husband is an animal. He tried to lay hands on me but I fought him off. So now I'm beginning to wonder if he tried the same with Ourdilic, the girl who died. Or perhaps you caught him the act and were angry enough to push her off the cliff yourself. You weren't far from the cliff path when we met, were you?"

Beornhelm pushed Winfrith away and scrambled to her feet. "If I'd caught the pair of them together, they'd have regretted it. Maybe the girl would have felt the back of my hand, but there'd be more chance of Aethelnoth going over the cliff than her." She grabbed the two children by their sleeves, pulling them up. "You think anyone goes wandering about cliff tops with two of these in tow? As for you, girl, if your friend was taken in by my husband, it doesn't seem to have done her much good, does it? Let it be a warning to you."

She ushered the reluctant children towards the door and they stepped out into the rain without a word of thanks for either the food or the shelter.

Winfrith stood in the doorway, watching as Beornhelm crossed the storm-water ditch,
the children already trailing several yards behind her. Did she know more about Ourdilic's death than she'd admitted? The woman had a quick temper and the difficult cliff path wouldn't have been beyond the strength of someone who had shepherded two small children all the way from Frome. She had threatened to harm any woman she found with her husband. Winfrith tried to picture again the figure she had seen ahead of her as she descended the path. Had that been Beornhelm? Probably not. Someone slimmer and more agile, she thought. And in any case she could hardly have taken the children up there, and certainly not at night. Besides, Winfrith had met them heading towards the cliff path not away from it. If Beornhelm had sent Ourdilic to her death, she'd surely want to make herself scarce.

Winfrith turned back inside, glad to get out of the freshening wind and steady rain. She stirred the embers of the fire, adding more logs and warming her hands as the flames took hold. Olwen had moved to the edge of the sleeping platform. She sat with her arms folded tightly across her chest, as if she were trying to comfort herself. She did not look up, even when Winfrith came and sat beside her.

"Did Aethelnoth bother you? You were clearly upset when Beornhelm said she was his wife."

Olwen shook her head but said nothing.

"Men like him tell girls they're not married. They think you'll lie with them. You didn't, did you?"

"Never...I wouldn't. I'm not stupid." Olwen was plainly shocked. "He was too old for us."

"And Ourdilic? What about her? Did she encourage him?"

"Not at first. It was just a game. We were bored. All that walking when we had to leave Chippenham. We decided to see which one of us could get a smile or a kind word from any of Alfred's thegns. That's all it was."

"But then it went wrong?"

Olwen nodded. "Ourdilic already had Aethelwold eating out of her hand. I wanted to show her I could be just as clever."

"And Aethelnoth looked most likely to oblige?"

"He was always watching us from a distance. I didn't think it would be hard to get a smile out of him."

"But if that was all it was, why were you so upset to learn he had a wife?"

"I wasn't upset because of anything he said to me. It's what I told Ourdilic…and what she might have done because of it." Olwen paused, swallowing hard. "I wish I hadn't. I never meant anything bad to happen to her."

Winfrith put her arm around Olwen's shoulder. "Whatever happened to her wasn't your fault, Olwen. She always knew her own mind."

"I lied to her. She kept going on about Aethelwold…how he would do anything for her. She kept saying a thegn would never look at me that way. Finally I couldn't stand it any longer. I told her Aethelnoth, a much better-looking thegn, had not only smiled at me but had promised me a gold ring in return for a kiss. I didn't think she'd believe me, but obviously she must have."

"Why? What did she do?"

"You know. You saw her. Pretended to get herself lost and then showed up on Aethelnoth's horse..all just to prove she was cleverer than me. I was so angry. Why would she do that when I was the only friend she had?"

"I don't know, Olwen. Probably because she was afraid. Ever since she came here she'd been fighting to be noticed. She lost her home and her father and mother, remember. Did she say anything about it afterwards?"

Olwen shook her head. "Nothing. We hardly spoke. She looked pleased with herself at first, but maybe a bit frightened too. I thought she might be worried Aethelwold would ignore her because of it."

Winfrith hesitated before continuing. "She and Aethelnoth were missing for quite a while, weren't they? You've heard what his wife says about him chasing anyone in a skirt. Do you think anything happened between them? Something was obviously troubling her the night she died."

"She didn't talk about it, and anyway I was too cross to ask."

"But you must have forgiven her. Two days later the pair of you were as inseparable as a rock and a limpet. And don't forget Cuthbert and I chanced to hear you discussing something that had gone badly wrong for Ourdilic. Was that to do with Aethelnoth?"

Olwen stared at her hands, clearly in no hurry to answer. "I promised I wouldn't tell anyone. She swore me to secrecy."

"It can't do any harm now to say. You want to know who killed her, don't you?"

"It can't bring her back."

"But they ought to pay for what they did. Her life must have been worth something. I'll tell you what. Why don't I describe what I think might have happened and you just nod if you agree? That way you won't have broken your promise to keep silent, will you?"

Olwen thought about this for a moment. Winfrith felt the girl's shoulders relax and took it as a sign of agreement.

"This is what I think you and Ourdilic were discussing. She had been troubled by sickness in the mornings and it didn't take long to work out the cause. She was pregnant, wasn't she?"

Olwen nodded.

"And that would ruin everything because she was betrothed to Aethelwold and, knowing how timid he was with her, it's unlikely he was the one to have got her with child. Am I right so far?"

Olwen nodded again and Winfrith was sure there was relief in her eyes now.

"So that leaves Aethelnoth as far as I can see. She spent an hour alone with him, perhaps having lured him away. His wife admits he's not to be trusted with girls…and now he's disappeared. Is that what she told you…that Aethelnoth was the father?"

Olwen shook her head, unable to resist the urge to speak any longer. "She didn't say it was him. She refused to talk about it, apart from admitting why she felt sick. All we discussed was what to do about it. She was going to tell you. I persuaded her you would help. You would have done, wouldn't you?"

"Of course I would," Winfrith said, drawing Olwen closer.

"She would have kept the child…no matter what anyone said…even if it ended her betrothal. She'd never have jumped…never."

Winfrith felt the girl's body begin to shake as she folded her arms around her. "I know. I know. Someone forced her over…and it's left to us to make sure whoever was responsible pays for it. It'll be our parting gift to Ourdilic…our way of saying sorry."

Slowly Olwen became still again and just when Winfrith thought she might be falling asleep she heard her whisper, "Who though? Who could have done such a thing?"

11

Ourdilic was buried at the summit of a slight rise just above the king's hall. The grave commanded a view over the roofs of Cheddar and out across the marshes, while behind it the sides of the gorge rose steeply towards a murky sky. Winfrith counted twenty faces gathered at the graveside. Some, like Alfred, Aethelwold, Eanflaed and Milred, she had expected to be there but the presence of Beorhtric and Raedberht, neither of whom had hidden their dislike of Ourdilic, was unexpected. She wondered what they were doing there, imagining how amused Ourdilic would have been if she'd been able to see their untroubled expressions and the pretence of grief on some of the other faces as they waited for Alfred to start the proceedings. Winfrith was surprised to see that Eanflaed looked more distressed than most. Perhaps she'd seen too late that she and Ourdilic had more in common than she'd realised…a long way from home, unloved and having to fend for themselves in a place where food and safety were far from certain.

Winfrith took hold of Olwen's hand as Alfred beckoned the priest forward, indicating that he should offer some consoling words. He had sent to Wells for the man but the severe look he gave him as the wheezing, bleary-eyed priest shambled forward suggested he was far from pleased with the result. He looked as though he had been roused from a drinking house rather than a church and he needed several prompts from Alfred to get him through a description of the afterlife. He was still trying to say what must be done to be sure of Heaven when Alfred cut him short.

"We should all be aware of what it takes to enter Heaven…all of us from the poorest servant to the king himself. Ourdilic was just a child. When I was a child there were two teachings I was instructed never to forget. The first was that the only reward from life is Heaven. The second was that it's the ploughman who feeds our bodies, but God who feeds our spirits. Ourdilic may have come from Cornwall. She may have done little to win herself friends among you, but she was as much God's child as any of you."

Winfrith glanced across at Beorhtric, sure that she saw the ghost of a smile flicker across his face.

"She wasn't with us long," Alfred continued. "Had she lived she would have married my nephew, Aethelwold, perhaps had children…" Winfrith was not alone in turning to look at Aethelwold. His face gave little away. He stared up at the cliff face, unwilling to return anyone's gaze. He did not look into the grave either and it seemed obvious that he would be glad when the whole business was over and done with. Whether or not he felt any grief at losing Ourdilic was less clear.

Alfred raised both his arms skywards. "In the end it matters little what any of us thought of her. Let God be the judge. Laying this frail body in the earth is our final duty to her. May God receive Ourdilic as she left us… a child with much to learn but with much to offer too. What she might have been here is no longer of any account. Therefore we commend her to God, in the belief that He will extend his goodness and mercy towards her. Let us pray for her."

Alfred nudged the priest who cleared his throat before mumbling his way through a short prayer. As he finished there were one or two muted amens and, at a signal from Alfred, two men stepped forward ready to begin filling the grave.

Winfrith felt Olwen grip her hand more tightly and as the first shovelful of earth struck Ourdilic's heavily bound body she could no longer contain her anger.

"So that's it? No word about how she came to die?" She didn't expect anyone to answer. She wasn't even sure she'd spoken loud enough for anyone to hear, so she was surprised when Raedberht, standing opposite her across the rapidly filling grave, replied.

"What difference does it make? She fell. Who cares what she was doing up there?"

"I do," Winfrith said, aware she was shouting now but not caring. "She was just a child, and she didn't fall…she was pushed. Some cowardly bastard pushed her and they won't get away with it."

Raedberht laughed, turning to Beorhtric for support. "See the company your wife's been keeping? Mad, the three of them…except there are only two now."

The exchange drew a reproving look from Alfred but before he could intervene Winfrith felt a firm hand grip her arm and Cuthbert began to drag her away from the graveside.

"It's not finished yet," she shouted, pushing those behind her aside. "You all hated her, but that didn't give anyone the right murder her. Someone did that and I'll find you... whoever you are."

"Let it rest," Cuthbert urged, shepherding her towards the path across the stormwater ditch. "You'll make yourself as disliked as Ourdilic was."

"I don't care. It might even bring the worm out of the woodwork. If I shout loud enough perhaps whoever pushed Ourdilic off the cliff will try and shut me up. Only this time I'll be expecting them."

"Don't. I don't want you to. Please." Winfrith looked over her shoulder. In her fury at Raedberht and Beorhtric she had forgotten all about Olwen.

"Don't worry, Olwen, I'll be careful."

"But you've already told everyone Ourdilic was murdered and that you mean to find out who did it."

It was true. It hadn't been wise to announce her intention but then who would take her accusation seriously? Before she could think of trying to persuade anyone she'd have to find a good reason why someone wanted Ourdilic dead. Hating her because she was Cornish didn't seem enough. Wanting to stop the betrothal to Aethelwold was the only reason she could think of, but that left the king's nephew as the only man who might care one way or another.

"Just keep quiet for a few days," Cuthbert said, as they approached the small thatched house that had been set aside for Winfrith and the two girls...not that Ourdilic would ever see it again now. "They'll put your outburst at the graveside down to grief. It'll be quickly forgotten."

"Just like Ourdilic," Winfrith said, unable to keep the bitterness from her voice. She stood in silence outside the house for a few moments, reluctant to enter, afraid of the reminders it would bring of the last time she'd seen Ourdilic. One or two others began to appear at the top of the ditch, making their way slowly back from the burial. Beorhtric and Eanflaed were among the first, unusually walking arm in arm. Raedberht followed a little way behind and made a point of staring hard across at Winfrith right up until the moment he turned into the king's hall. Aethelwold was not far behind him, walking alone, staring down at his feet and Alfred came in the final group of thegns, deep in conversation with Milred. Winfrith was about to face going inside when a last lone figure started a cautious descent into the ditch. It was the priest, shambling along as if he'd been forgotten. She watched him approach the king's hall and wander several paces past the entrance before stopping to turn back. He hesitated at the door, spending several moments peering inside before evidently deciding it was safe to go in.

Whatever her own feelings about returning to the house, Winfrith could see that Olwen did not share them. She seemed relieved to have got away from the graveside and sat quietly in a corner, sewing together a tear in the hem of her skirt. Cuthbert had promised to set someone he trusted to watch their door, at least for the rest of the day, and that seemed to have calmed Olwen's fears. They would still have to talk about what Winfrith had seen up on the cliff top and who might have been up there with Ourdilic but for now Winfrith decided it could wait. In the meantime she would do what little she could to try and establish who it had been.

The place to start was surely Beorhtric. He'd made no secret of his dislike of Ourdilic. He had a short temper and, if his treatment of Eanflaed was anything to go by, was capable striking a woman. Telling Olwen that spriggans had been to blame for Ourdilic's death was strange too. Everyone else assumed it was an accident, so why raise the possibility that there had been something odd about it? Yet Winfrith was by no means certain that Beorhtric was a murderer. He wasn't alone in being deeply suspicious of the Cornish and where their loyalties lay and she couldn't see that he had any personal reason for wanting the betrothal stopped. Either way she could be sure of one thing. He wouldn't welcome questions and she'd need to approach him in full view of others.

It was late afternoon before Winfrith thought it safe to leave Olwen. A young retainer from Cuthbert's estate at Easton guarded the door and Olwen had drifted off to sleep. She made her way briskly to the cheesemaker's house, the back room of which had been set aside for Beorhtric and Eanflaed. Confirming with him that she wouldn't find Beorhtric alone, she knocked and pushed open the creaking door.

"Anyone here?" she called.

Eanflaed got hurriedly out of a chair and crossed the room to meet her. A quick glance around the room showed Winfrith she was alone.

"It was your husband I wanted to speak to," Winfrith said. "He's been saying things to Olwen, upsetting her, and I want to know why."

"He's not here," Eanflaed replied. "Always got something more important to do than spend time with his wife."

"Do you know where I can find him?"

Eanflaed shook her head. "With his cronies probably…discussing horses or spears. He won't care who he's upset anyway. You'd be wasting your time asking him. And if he hears you've been here, it'll be me on the wrong end of his temper."

"Perhaps you know why he tried to frighten Olwen then. He obviously didn't like Ourdilic, but why turn on Olwen? She wasn't from Cornwall and anyone could see Ourdilic's death had hurt her badly."

"I don't know." Eanflaed sounded weary, but she had clearly not quite given up hope of presenting her husband in a good light. "I didn't know he'd said anything to her. Perhaps he thought it amusing. He doesn't always think what effect his words have. He means no harm by them. What was it he said?"

"Some tale about her being taken by spriggans, Cornish night spirits of some sort. Why would he suggest her death was anything other than an accident?"

"I don't know anything about that. He never said anything to me about it. I told you, he's hardly ever here these days."

"What is there to keep me?" Winfrith turned to see Beorhtric standing in the doorway. It was impossible to say how long he'd been standing there, but he seemed less surprised and less annoyed too at finding Winfrith with his wife than she would have expected.

"You didn't marry me just to have someone to gossip to," He said, crossing the room and taking the seat nearest the smouldering fire. "Getting away from Cornwall...that's what you wanted and that's what you got. What's she doing here, anyway?" He nodded towards Winfrith. "She doesn't need your advice now your Cornish bride-to-be isn't with us anymore."

"It's her I came about...in a way," Winfrith said. "Your wife tried to help her...more than most folk here did. So I wondered why you hated her enough to upset her friend Olwen yesterday. Wasn't it enough that Ourdilic had died?"

"The king ordered my wife to help. She didn't choose to. The girl's father, Drumgarth, betrayed good Wessex men. Why should anyone here befriend her?"

"Olwen did," Winfrith said, straining to keep the anger out of her voice. "She'd lost any family she'd ever had too. What made someone like you go to the trouble of frightening a girl like that? Were you worried she wouldn't believe Ourdilic fell without someone pushing her? You thought she might believe spriggans before she'd accuse a Wessex thegn?"

Winfrith glanced at the door, ready to run if Beorhtric threatened to turn violent. Instead his angry stare relaxed slowly into a sneering grin.

"So all that shouting at the graveside wasn't just guilt that you hadn't taken better care of her? Everyone knows about that by now, if they weren't there to hear it themselves. Keep repeating all that nonsense and they'll mark you down as a madwoman. No thegn would have ventured up there at night. They'd laugh at anyone who suggested it."

"So why bother Olwen with scary tales afterwards?"

He shrugged. "You wouldn't understand...any more than she did. Taken in by a mere girl who thought she could lord it over all of us. It was Ourdilic's kin who got Wessex hostages killed at Wareham, my brother among them. Yet you and Olwen think she deserved sympathy? She needed a lesson, that's all."

"So you picked on a young girl? Why not me? Or Eanflaed? Scared we'd fight back?" Winfrith could see straight away that for once Beorhtric was in no mood to be riled, though no doubt Eanflaed would be on the receiving end of his temper once she'd gone. He looked unconcerned, just as he had the night she and Cuthbert had come out of the house looking for Ourdilic. Could he have followed Ourdilic before they had organized a search? She supposed it was possible, but there was nothing in his manner now to suggest he was about to admit it.

"Hardly scared…just tired of listening to you," Beorhtric said. "The girl fell off a cliff. She's dead and buried. Her friend was persuaded spirits took her back to Cornwall where she belongs. I'm sure someone with as much to say for themselves as you will be able to convince her spriggans don't exist. Why don't you go and make a start? Perhaps my wife can find the time to get me something to drink then."

Winfrith glanced at Eanflaed who nodded back at her as if to suggest she would prefer to be left alone with him. She took a step towards Beorhtric, staring hard at him.

"I'm going…but next time your grudge against the Cornish gets the better of you, try picking on someone your own size." Without waiting for an answer she turned away and walked briskly out of the room, stopping only when she had passed the cheesemaker's row of empty buckets outside. She listened for any sound of raised voices but, despite waiting several minutes no sound reached her from inside.

Olwen was still asleep when Winfrith returned. She poured herself a cup of ale and set it down on the small table where Ourdilic had displayed her beads. Olwen must have wrapped them in the red cloth and put them somewhere safe and that reminded Winfrith she had forgotten all about the missing aestel. No mention had been made of it during the burial and it was well known that Alfred disapproved of the old custom of burying possessions alongside the body. She'd heard him ask what purpose gold and garnets would serve at the gates of Heaven. Yet the aestel was worth many shillings, enough to buy much needed food and weapons. He'd surely want to know what had happened to it before long.

Winfrith tried hard to recall the last time she'd seen it. She was sure it had been in full view on the table before the guests arrived to eat. Had she seen it after that? The trouble was she had been in such a state of turmoil after finding Ourdilic dead that it was difficult to recollect anything with certainty. She remembered standing above the rainwater ditch, yelling over and over again that Ourdilic was dead, but she couldn't recall entering the house again or anything else until she woke the following morning. Cuthbert and Milred were sitting watching her but she'd sent them away in her haste to go and search the cliff top in daylight. Olwen thought spriggans had taken the aestel in the night. That was nonsense of course, so who else had been inside the house? Eanflaed had come, supposedly to see if she was alright, and Beornhelm and her two children had returned with her to get something to eat. Eanflaed had openly admired the aestel, but would a thegn's wife risk stealing the king's gift? Beornhelm might have had greater need of money but the aestel had disappeared from the table at least before she and her children had entered the house. The only other possibility was that Olwen, perhaps envious of all the attention Ourdilic had received, had hidden it away somewhere, hoping to keep it for herself. Winfrith sighed. None of the names she'd come up with seemed likely thieves.

She took a mouthful of ale, pulling a face as she swallowed and wishing there was honey in the house to disguise the sour taste. She then began a quick search of the room, taking care not to wake Olwen. She looked under all the sleeping platforms and sorted through a heap of discarded clothes without finding the aestel. She had no more success feeling along tops of the rafters or rummaging through the bags they had travelled with to Cheddar. If Olwen had hidden it, and she didn't really believe she had, it must be somewhere outside.

Wherever the aestel had got to, Winfrith decided Alfred would have to be told it was missing and with that in mind she set off for the king's hall, first checking that the young thegn would continue to watch the door until her return. She found the king sitting with Milred at a small table, poring over a well-used sheet of parchment. Aethelwold stood behind them, looking over his uncle's shoulder. Alfred looked up as she approached and pointed to a bench against the wall.

"If it's Milred you want, he won't be long," he said.

"It's you I have news for," Winfrith answered, "something you should know."

Alfred looked momentarily intrigued but quickly turned back to the parchment. "Right, let's sum up our position before I hear what Winfrith's got to say. No-one has seen any Danes on any of these roads north of here. Villages haven't suffered heathen raids either.

That means Guthrum doesn't know food here is in short supply. If we cross the River Axe here and head for the Mendip Hills the marshes will make it very difficult for Guthrum's men to follow."

"It would be hard going for us," Aethelnoth said. "We can still hunt food here."

"But the rider from Wedmore who brought two sacks of flour this morning said they were the last," Milred said. "If we want Somerset men to fight with us we can't bleed their villages dry."

"There'd be more chance of that if Aethelnoth hadn't run away," Aethelwold said, loudly enough for several heads to turn his way. "We can't even trust our own ealdormen now...first Wulfhere and now Aethelnoth going over to the enemy."

"We don't know Aethelnoth has joined Guthrum," Alfred said. "There could be many reasons why he left Cheddar."

"Cowardice," Aethelwold said with enough force to dot his tunic with flecks of spit. "I wouldn't trust him to tie my shoe straps." Alfred looked up at him, clearly surprised at how angry he was and Winfrith found herself wondering if it was anything to do with Ourdilic. As far as she knew Aethelwold hadn't known she was pregnant, but what if he'd found out and suspected that Aethelnoth was responsible? That might rouse even a timid man to ire.

"We've little choice but to trust him," Alfred said. "Once we leave here there's no-one else to organize resistance against Guthrum in Somerset. We'll need his help if we're to strengthen our own forces before the days begin to grow longer again. Now, Winfrith has been waiting long enough. Perhaps, nephew, you would go and start spreading the news that we leave here at first light tomorrow."

Aethelwold didn't move. It looked for a moment as though he might refuse to do Alfred's bidding but he thought better of it and turned away, heading for the thegns gathered at the far end of the hall.

"Now then, Winfrith," Alfred said, "you have something urgent to tell me?"

"It's the aestel...Ourdilic's morning gift. It's gone missing."

A flicker of surprise passed across Alfred's face but otherwise he seemed to take the news calmly.

"You're sure? She didn't hide it away somewhere for safe keeping?"

Winfrith shook her head. "It's not in the house. I haven't seen it since the night you and Aethelwold came to dine with us."

"Then we must organize a search for it. It can't have gone far. I sent Eanflaed to advise Ourdilic about her betrothal. Perhaps she knows what she did with it."

"Unless someone stole it," Cuthbert said. "It must have been worth a lot."

"It was," Alfred said, "but let's see what Eanflaed has to say before we start accusing anyone. Stealing my gift would bring down a heavy punishment on the thief."

He summoned a thegn from a group in the doorway and sent him to fetch Eanflaed. She appeared looking pale and worried, nervously twisting her hands together when Alfred asked about the aestel.

"I don't know what happened to it. When Winfrith was brought down from the cliff and I went to sit with her, I think it was still sitting on a red cloth covering a small table. I never saw it after that."

Winfrith thought back to the moment she had woken to find Eanflaed watching her. Her mind had been in a whirl, full of images of the cliff path and Ourdilic's body. Yet even in her confusion the fact that the aestel was not in its usual place had struck her. Why would Eanflaed say that it had still been there on the red cloth, unless she herself had taken it?

"And she didn't confide the place she'd hidden it to you?" Alfred asked. Eanflaed shook her head.

"Then we'll search any likely places, starting with the other houses here. Go with Winfrith…you two know best what the aestel looks like…and search each house, starting with the ones that are empty. Cuthbert can go with you to make sure there's no trouble.

It soon became clear that few of the houses in Cheddar contained anything of much value. Chairs, tables and benches, most of them showing signs of wear, were common but otherwise possessions consisted of little more than clothes, shoes, buckets, knives, spades and assortments of bowls and cups. Few householders protested about the search once they knew the reason, the only exceptions being two rickety buildings sheltering under trees at the entrance to the gorge. A search of even the darkest nooks and crannies inside revealed that the reluctance to admit the searchers had nothing to do with the aestel but rather because the houses concealed secret stores of food and ale. Cuthbert was quick to order their removal to the king's hall and to send the culprits to wait for the king to decide what their punishment should be.

They had not discussed leaving the search of the cheesemaker's house until last. Even so it was clearly going to be more awkward for Eanflaed to lead them through to the back room she shared with Beorhtric if her husband was there and so perhaps they had all been happy to put it off. Cuthbert suggested she wait outside while he and Winfrith went in. They passed between the empty vats and buckets, reminded by the cheese-maker that without milk there was no work for him to do. They were still ten paces away when the door of the back room was flung open and the disheveled figure of Beorhtric stood in the doorway, barring their way.

"What do you want?" he demanded. "Can't I ever be left in peace?"

"We're looking for the jeweled aestel Alfred gave Ourdilic. It's disappeared," Cuthbert said, advancing towards him.

"What would it be doing here? Hasn't that girl caused us enough trouble, having my wife run around after her? She was from Cornwall. She probably sold it to a passing pedlar."

"Alfred ordered every house searched, including yours, so step aside." Beorhtric returned Cuthbert's stare, making him wait several moments before moving out of the way.

"You won't find anything," Beorhtric said. "Just because Eanflaed was told to waste time with the girl, it doesn't make her a thief. She's a thegn's wife. If you had one of your own, you'd know they're incapable of stealing." Cuthbert ignored him, circling the room, turning over piles of clothes and searching through the only obvious hiding place, a heavy wooden chest in the far corner. He reached down and drew out a box. Its surface was covered with inlaid beads, suggesting to Winfrith's eyes something a thegn's wife might use to keep brooches and necklaces in. Cuthbert carefully lifted the lid, holding out the box so that Winfrith could see the contents. There were brooches and necklaces, several rings too, enough to suggest the owner's fondness for silver and precious stones but of Ourdilic's morning gift there was no sign at all.

"Told you you wouldn't find anything," Beorhtric said, waving them towards the door. In his haste to get rid of them, he caught his foot on a small table knocking over a bowl so that broken pieces of pot scattered across the floor. "Tell Alfred he should trust his thegns better, not treat them like common thieves."

Cuthbert and Winfrith left Eanflaed outside the cheesemaker's and set off towards the king's hall to report back to Alfred. The afternoon light was fading fast but the torches marking the entrance to the hall had already been lit and from somewhere further along the wall, out of the circle of light cast by the flames, they could hear the sound of shouting. There seemed to be two voices and, as they stopped to listen, Winfrith was sure one of them belonged to Aethelwold. Cuthbert put his finger to his lips and motioned to Winfrith to follow him along a broad ditch which skirted the hall and which would bring them close to the argument without being seen. She trod as softly as the rough ground would allow but as they drew closer it became clear that the argument was fierce enough to mask all but the loudest noise. She also realized that the other voice was familiar too and that the last time she'd heard it, at Ourdilic's betrothal feast, it had been confronting Aethelwold. Raedberht, Wulhere's nephew, had been threatening Aethelwold then as well. It seemed he hadn't finished yet.

"Why deny it? You're glad she's dead. What kind of a wife would she have made? She'd have lost you the few friends you've got."

"You'd know about that. You've none here. Off to join Guthrum soon, are you?" The faintest of hesitations in Aethelwold's voice suggested he was getting the worst of the argument and Raedwald sneering reply suggested he knew it.

"Or did you have your reasons for not wanting her? Did she think you weren't man enough? Limp as old rope? And then you heard she'd been got with child by someone else? Even a sheep like you might have killed her for that."

Much as she wanted to shout accusations of her own, Winfrith forced herself to stand and listen. Was Aethelwold going to admit killing Ourdilic? Much to her frustration, instead of an answer there was a growl of rage from somewhere just above them, followed by a thud and the rattle of stones tumbling into the ditch.

She heard Cuthbert scrambling up the bank, shouting for them to stop as he went.

"Leave it," he shouted. "Save the fighting for Guthrum." It was too dark to see clearly but Winfrith heard what sounded like a scuffle ending in a sharp cry of pain and the sound of retreating footsteps. Cautiously she felt her way up the bank, almost colliding with Cuthbert at the top.

"King's nephew or not…he'll pay for that." She could see now that Cuthbert was kneeling over Raedwald, holding a cloth to his forehead.

"If Alfred gets to hear of it, you'll both pay. He hasn't done you much harm from what I can see."

"Let him try in daylight, without a rock in his hand. He'd know about harm then."

Winfrith would have liked to ask Raedberht where he'd got the story about Ourdilic being with child and whether he had any idea who the father was if it wasn't Aethelwold but Cuthbert was already heaving him to his feet and guiding him back towards the torches at the entrance to the king's hall.

12

 Winfrith took a last look around what had been her Cheddar home for almost a month now. She wasn't quite sure what she expected to see…some last sign of Ourdilic's presence perhaps? Or maybe the miraculous reappearance of the aestel? If either hope had truly been lingering at the back of her mind, neither was realized and she extinguished the last of the tallow candles and went to join Olwen outside.

 Daylight was slow in coming with a strong westerly wind sending thick grey clouds scudding across the sky. On the far side of the yard Alfred was pacing impatiently among his thegns as they argued about who would carry which loads and what could be strapped to the few horses they had left. Even to Winfrith's eyes the numbers gathered there brought home how low Alfred's fortunes had sunk. Two ealdorman remained among them, Aelfstan and Cuthred, but both were far from their own shires…too far to raise a fighting force easily. The longest-serving members of the witan, Milred and Eadwulf, would follow Alfred to the ends of the earth but they were too old to take up arms and even the journey ahead might prove beyond them. Not that Winfrith herself was relishing the prospect of several days crossing hills and marshes. She, Olwen and Eanflaed would be the only women among the thirty or so setting out. The rest were Alfred's thegns but they would not amount to much of a force when put against the thousand Saxons who had fought off the Danes at Ashdown.

 Winfrith took a last look back at the house. Just beyond the door the branches of an alder with its dull red catkins waved in the breeze. She reached up and broke off a small branch, tucking it into her bag, unsure why until she remembered seeing Ourdilic do the same thing just a few days earlier. She and Olwen crossed towards where the final bundles of blankets, pots, weapons and tools were being loaded onto two battered carts. Milred was being helped up onto the back of one of them but it looked as if there would be no room for anyone else. Finally Alfred raised his arms and pointed ahead. They were ready to go. Slowly an untidy line of marchers began to drift down the slope to the south and onto the track towards Wedmore.

Once they were below Cheddar and out onto the flat, marshy land which lay between them and the River Axe the wind grew stronger, bending the uncut willow canes alongside low to the ground. The track itself, already hollowed out and churned up by heavy use, quickly became waterlogged and they were frequently forced to leave it altogether to bypass stretches of water. Alfred seemed slightly surprised at the amount of flooding, given that they were still a considerable way from the river and looking back the way they had come did nothing to soothe their disquiet. Some fifty paces behind them a surge of water pressed its way into the path and sent a ripple of waves towards them. A rapid discussion between Alfred and Milred, the only men who had followed this route before, led to urgent orders being passed down the line.

Cuthbert, urging everyone to get moving again, fell into step alongside Winfrith.

"See the hill just to the left of those trees?" he said. "That's Clower Hill, where this track meets the river. The water's still rising but we're going to try and cross using a rope. You'll get wet, but someone will make sure you reach the other side safely."

As soon as they got within sight of the river it became clear that reaching Wedmore would not be easy. A broad lake lay between them and where the river's edge ought to be. The wind whipped up white-topped waves across its surface and one of the horses wading across it suddenly reared up in alarm as a burst of spray lashed against its flank. The party threaded its way carefully across the flooded meadow, gathering in a tight cluster on a small raised section of river bank. In the lee of the hill opposite it was at least possible to be heard without yelling.

"It's still not too late to go back," Aethelwold said, looking nervously at the swirling current ahead.

"Half an hour ago you might have been right," Alfred replied, looking back the way they had come. The flow of water along the path was growing stronger by the minute, the banks alongside glistening where fresh currents were beginning to slide through the willows which flanked it. "Now it would be a greater risk than going on. It's not river water behind us…that's the sea."

"It can't be," Aethelwold protested. "We've hunted this way before. We must be ten miles from the sea."

"Go back and taste the water back there. You'll soon see it's salty. I was here as a boy and I remember then strong winds could drive the sea miles across these marshes. It's easy to drown when that happens. We have to go on. The river's not so deep and if we attach a rope we should be able to pull ourselves across."

Perhaps aware he might have appeared afraid of the river, Aethelwold busied himself attaching a length of rope to the only tree near enough to the river to allow the rope to stretch to the far bank. Beorhtric offered to carry it across, once one of the horses had been unhitched from its cart. Urging the nervous animal forward, he plunged into the water, disappearing from view in plumes of spray. The horse floundered for a moment before securing its footing and, despite the swell of water rising half way up its flanks, inched its way across. Several times the current turned the horse sideways but with Beorhtric slapping its neck and shouting encouragement it eventually battled its way into shallower water and from there onto the far bank. Several shouts of approval went up as Beorhtric secured the rope to a solid-looking oak trunk close to where he had emerged. Immediately Alfred and Cuthbert set about distributing the heaviest loads among the strongest men. It would be difficult to keep everything dry but at least they hoped to avoid losing much.

"No more than three at a time on the rope," Alfred called, struggling to make himself heard against the howling wind. "Get on with it. Move!" Looking back across the flooded meadows Winfrith could see the reason for the urgency. Fresh waves were sweeping across the surface, lapping greedily at the bank they stood on. It would not be long before it was under water. The first three thegns entered the water, one arm clenching the rope, the other balancing bags on their shoulders. By the time they had reached midstream the slender tree Aethelwold had attached the rope to had almost bent double and Winfrith could see she was not alone in breathing a sigh of relief when the three men finally clambered onto the far bank. Aethelwold held up a hand before three more thegns set off, making a great show of tightening the knots around the tree before waving them on.

Alfred's plan was for the strongest to go first, both to test the rope and to ensure that as much as possible in the way of goods and provisions were carried without a soaking. The numbers on the far bank had swelled to twenty or so by the time Eanflaed and Olwen stepped forward to grip the rope. Winfrith made as if to follow them but felt a firm hand grip her shoulder, holding her back. She tried to shrug it off but Eanflaed and Olwen were already almost up to their waists in the water. She turned angrily to face Aethelwold.

"What are you doing? Three at a time was the plan. I should be out there helping the girl."

Aethelwold relaxed his grip. ""Look at the rope. It's getting more and more stretched and this tree won't take much more weight. Better the two of them get across first. You can follow as soon as they're across."

Winfrith had little choice but to watch as Eanflaed and Olwen battled against the current. They seemed at times to be hardly moving and at one heart-stopping moment Olwen appeared to lose her footing and Winfrith thought she was about to be swept away. Somehow she managed to keep hold of the rope and pull herself upright again and she and Eanflaed emerged on the far side. Olwen sent her a reassuring wave and Winfrith took hold of the sodden rope and stepped down into the water without waiting to see if anyone meant to cross with her.

As soon as she moved away from the bank she felt the current dragging her skirt downstream. Each time she lifted a foot it seemed harder to force it back to the river bottom. The water numbed her fingers making each grab for the next section of rope harder. She glanced back to see if anyone was following but for some reason the few thegns still waiting to cross were holding back. Before she had time to wonder why she heard a loud crack and the rope suddenly gave way. The force of the water swept her feet from under her. She flapped her arms wildly, struggling to stay afloat. She felt her head dragged under, water blinding her eyes, forcing its way into her ears and nose. She clamped her mouth shut, flinging her arms upwards and kicking against the clinging weight of her skirt. She felt one hand break the surface but before she could lift her head out of the water her back and elbow crashed into something hard, twisting her body onto its side. Instinctively she grabbed at it, closing her fists tightly round it and heaving herself upwards.

Winfrith found herself beneath the black, tangled branches of a thorn bush. She had been swept across to the far bank of the river and had managed to grab hold of a submerged tree root. She dragged herself into a sitting position, sucking in huge gulps of air, trying to take in what had happened as she watched the turbulent current racing past her feet. She sat for a moment, still waist deep in water, before realizing how cold she was. She needed to get onto dry land quickly but before she could move a coughing fit seized her, muddy-tasting river water filling her mouth. The effort seemed to drain her of what little strength she had left. She lifted an arm from the water to try and push the thorn branches aside but they were thick and tangled and barely moved. Surely she hadn't survived drowning only to freeze to death? She had to get up somehow. She had just started to arch her back in the hope of reaching a thicker branch overhead and pulling herself up when she heard a shout from somewhere behind her.

Turning her head in the direction from which the shout came, she thought for a moment she must be dreaming. A small gap between the thorn branches offered a view along the riverbank and, though she was sure Aethelwold had still been waiting to cross when the rope broke and she was swept across the river, he was now on this side running towards where she had come ashore.

His lank hair was plastered flat against his head and as he came closer Winfrith could see every inch of his clothing was dripping wet.

"She's safe," he called out, pushing at the outer thorn branches with his foot and stretching out a helping hand towards her. She hesitated, a fleeting thought that he might help her back into the rushing current crossing her mind. Before she could decide another voice spoke from somewhere behind Aethelwold and she felt a surge of relief hearing Cuthbert join him.

"No thanks to you. What were you doing trying to retie the knot while she was still clinging to the rope?"

"I had to. It was slipping. And anyway it wasn't the knot. It was the tree snapping that set her adrift. I couldn't have done anything about that."

"Chosen a stronger tree," Cuthbert said, crouching down to get a better look at where Winfrith was.

"There weren't any. You could see…" Cuthbert ignored his protests, kicking away thorn branches and sliding down the bank and into the water. He leaned down, resting Winfrith's arm across his shoulder and slowly raised her onto her feet. Her clothes felt almost too heavy to carry and so wet and cold that she couldn't stop shivering. As Cuthbert tried to get her moving up the bank every joint ached, as if she had been bounced on every stone on the river bottom. She was vaguely aware of Aethelwold's hand helping to pull her upwards and wondering whether he had meant her to drown by loosening the rope. Why would he do that? Because he'd killed Ourdilic and guessed she was on to him? But had he? Did he even know she was pregnant? What had he said when Raedberht goaded him about it? She felt herself laid down on the grass and warm blankets laid over her. She shut her eyes trying to picture the argument between Aethelwold and Raedberht, but the words they'd used just wouldn't come.

The rest of the journey on to Wedmore passed in something of a blur. All Winfrith remembered was Olwen throwing her arms around her, sending a sharp pain up her spine, and Cuthbert pestering her with questions about the rope. Someone must have carried her away from the river because the next thing she was aware of was waking up with the unfamiliar feel against her skin of a scratchy woollen tunic which was clearly not her own. She was lying on a thick straw mattress, facing a gently glowing fire and two faces watched her from the shadows beyond. One was Eanflaed but the other, a fair-haired girl not much older than Olwen, she didn't recognize.

"She's waking," Eanflaed said.

"She looks better than when you got here," the girl said.

Winfrith shook the front of the tunic, trying to cool her skin. "Where are my clothes?"

"Drying off," Eanflaed said. "They were drenched. Hendraeth had to lend you some of hers." Eanflaed nodded at the girl who smiled shyly. "Olwen's gone to see if they're ready yet."

A small movement in Hendraeth's lap caught Winfrith's eye, a tiny pale arm lifting and a small hand catching at the girl's dress.

She had a sudden picture of Ourdilic with a child in her lap, smiling down at it. She forced herself to put the thought aside. There was no use dwelling on what might have been.

"Thank you, Hendraeth. It was kind of you."

Hendraeth smiled, looking more assured now. "It's dangerous when the sea floods here. People have been swept away before. You have to be watchful."

As she spoke the door was being nudged open and Olwen edged her way inside, her arms laden with fresh logs and a cloth bag slung over her shoulder.

"She was watched by at least thirty people," Olwen said. "A rope strong enough to support three fully grown men at a time gave way when only Winfrith was holding it. That shouldn't happen, should it?"

"The rest of us crossed without mishap. It was just bad luck," Eanflaed said.

"Or someone didn't want her to get to the other side," Olwen said, dropping the pile of logs next the hearth and holding the bag open to show Winfrith her dry clothes. She set the bag down within Winfrith's reach and sat down on the edge of the mattress.

"Why? What possible reason could anyone have?" Eanflaed asked.

"It's obvious," Olwen said, "Aethelwold had charge of the rope. He must have loosened it."

"But why? What has he got against Winfrith?"

Winfrith eased herself up onto her elbows. "Probably nothing. He did attach the rope and I must admit it crossed my mind that it was odd for it to give way when only I was on it. But I'm not sure he'd go that far…not with so many folk watching."

"But what about Ourdilic?" Olwen insisted. "If he changed his mind about the betrothal? Maybe he found out she was pregnant and killed her. He'd want to silence anyone who'd made it clear they were hunting Ourdilic's murderer, wouldn't he?"

Winfrith wasn't sure what to say. With everything going on around her she had given little thought to Olwen. The girl was no fool and she had more reason than most to want to know why Ourdilic had fallen from the cliff. They should have talked about it sooner and now it felt awkward with Eanflaed and Hendraeth listening in.

"Ifs and maybes don't make him guilty," she said at length. "It was probably just a mishap, but we'll keep an eye on Aethelwold from now on."

They fell silent for a moment and Hendraeth gently lifted the half-awake baby from her lap to her shoulder. "You're not the first to be dragged into the river," she said. "Old Alaric who lives across the street was pulled from the riverbank. He felt something clutch his ankles and drag him under the water. He struggled to free himself but the more he fought the more water he swallowed. Finally he managed to grab a branch but each time he tried to haul himself out of the water something pulled him back. He felt his arms and legs go numb and the branch slipped from his grasp." She paused, gently rocking the baby.

"Was he found?" Olwen asked.

"He came staggering back at noon the next day. Said he'd woken at dawn, lying in a muddy reed bed. His feet were covered with a tangle of trailing weeds so thick that at first he couldn't move his legs at all. He cast his mind back to the night before. He'd been sure some monster or spirit had been trying to drag him into the river. Now the daylight had come he wasn't so sure. So you see you wouldn't be the first to imagine the worst because you've had a fright."

"You're probably right," Winfrith said. "After all it was Aethelwold who was the first to come to my aid."

Olwen was clearly still not satisfied. "But that could have been him trying to cover up what he'd done when he saw you'd survived. He wouldn't be blamed if he looked as though he was trying to save you."

"You can't think that," Eanflaed said. "He went into the river after you…without the rope to cling to. He could have been swept away himself."

It did seem a big risk to take and to show more courage than Winfrith would have expected from Aethelwold, though why Eanflaed should be so eager to defend him was harder to understand.

"But he wasn't, was he?" Olwen insisted.

"Well even if he did cut the rope," Winfrith said, taking Olwen's hand, "I'm still here and there's nothing I can do unless someone's willing to say they saw him. Besides, if he did his face will give him away sooner or later. He's no good at hiding his feelings. There's no point in dwelling on it now. Come and walk with me by the river. A bit of fresh air will do us both good."

Olwen looked keen to continue the argument with Eanflaed but as Winfrith struggled to her feet she seemed to think better of it, taking Winfrith's elbow and guiding her towards the door. As they made their way outside Hendraeth called after them.

"Watch one of those river spirits doesn't make a grab for your ankles."

13

It soon became clear the following morning that there was little or no hope of an early departure from Wedmore. With Olwen's help Winfrith managed to walk as far as a ridge which overlooked the flooded marshes. Each step reminded her of the battering she had taken in the river and staring down at the wide expanse of water it was easy to see how fortunate she'd been not to drown. The wind had dropped, at least for the time being, and they sat together on a flat rock, watching the reflections of lumpy clouds drifting slowly across the glassy surface of the floodwater. Occasional lines of willow, sprouting up from the water, were the only indication of the network of paths they had crossed only a day ago.

Winfrith yawned. She had not slept well, but then she doubted if anyone had managed a peaceful night. With five or six extra bodies in every house it was difficult to lie down without nudging into someone else's stray arm or leg. She was probably not alone in being hungry either. The strips of dried salted eel that Hendraeth had offered had been difficult to swallow and Olwen had refused to touch them altogether. She had barely said a word since waking, or indeed the previous evening, but Winfrith was sure there was stil much on her mind.

"At least we know Cuthbert will keep an eye on Aethelwold," Winfrith said. "They both slept in the half-timbered house at the top of the hill. Trust them to find the sturdiest building in Wedmore. No draughts there…"

Olwen glanced towards the house. "He'll never admit it," she said.

"Maybe the branch just snapped. It was blowing a gale."

Olwen sighed. "Everyone else crossed safely. It just happened to give way at the moment you were in midstream? He wanted to shut you up and that can only be because he killed Ourdilic."

"Cuthbert was there. He thought it was an accident."

"He's a thegn. He's not going to accuse the king's nephew."

"We'll talk to him again. He's spent the night in the same house as Aethelwold. He might have seen or heard something to make him change his mind."

"Aethelwold could say he cut the rope and Cuthbert would find himself suddenly deaf. Thegns always stick together."

Winfrith slipped an arm round Olwen's shoulder. "We'll find out what happened to Ourdilic, whatever Aethelwold or anyone else thinks. I promise you that. My husband Leofranc served Cuthbert loyally and I've lived among his household for a number of years now. He's not so fond of Aethelwold as you might think. But we need to tread carefully. Shouting to the rooftops that Aethelwold killed Ourdilic will land us both in trouble. Promise me you won't do that until we know more."

Olwen took her time answering, and it wasn't until Winfrith had asked again that she offered a grudging reply.

"I suppose so." It hardly sounded as if she was convinced, but a hesitant promise was better than no promise at all. Winfrith smiled to herself. She wouldn't have been sure she could contain her own urge to accuse Aethelwold had she still been Olwen's age. It was hard enough now! One thing was clear though. Difficult as it might be, she must not let Olwen out of her sight. She had to be absolutely sure there was no chance of her wandering off alone as Ourdilic had done. If that meant following her everywhere or setting someone to stand guard over her then that was how it would have to be.

Olwen seemed happy enough to keep Winfrith company, even when she suggested paying an afternoon visit to Cuthbert. No-one stood guard outside the timbered house and Winfrith eased open the heavy door without knocking. A broad hearth, on which a fire burned fiercely, took up the middle of the room while the occupants filled the spaces on either side. To the left flickering yellow light from the fire lit up the faces of several of Alfred's thegns, Aethelwold among them. The right hand side appeared more crowded, mostly Wedmore folk, though Winfrith did pick out Cuthbert sitting among them. Most of the noise in the room came from group of thegns round the fire. They were passing a large jug between them and the loud voices and clumsy movements suggested it was not the first ale they had tasted that day.

Taking Olwen's hand, Winfrith led her inside and began picking her way through the Wedmore crowd towards the wall bench where she'd glimpsed Cuthbert. He looked surprised to see them but edged into a corner, making room for them to sit.

"I thought you'd be resting...saving your strength for when we set off again," he said.

"It doesn't look as though your fellow thegns are preparing for a long march," Winfrith replied, nodding in Aethelwold's direction.

"They'll tire of drinking soon enough...that's if the ale doesn't run out first. We might all get a bit of peace then." He was about to add something, when a chorus of shouting from round the fire made all heads turn. A young thegn was being pressed to drink but was holding up his hands, attempting to push the jug away. His efforts were greeted with much laughter, quickly followed by jeers and curses.

"Fools," Cuthbert said, loudly enough to draw some startled looks from the Wedmore folk around them. "The lad will be sick and the rest will be good for nothing tomorrow."

"You could stop them," Winfrith said. "He's only a boy."

"You don't know who he is then? That's Aethelhelm, Aethelwold's younger brother. Just arrived here yesterday. Seems like his first lesson is to be how to get drunk."

"Then why not stop it?" Olwen said. "There must be better things he could be learning."

"There certainly are," Cuthbert replied, "and he'll be taught them in time. But for now his companions, including his big brother, are in no state to pick an argument with. Aethelwold would say the lad is his kin and what he does with him is none of my business. If nothing else it might teach the boy that moderation is a better way."

Winfrith looked across the room in time to see Aethelhelm give in and reluctantly raise the jug to his lips. As he was about to drink Aethelwold leaned across and placed his palm underneath the jug, tipping it so that the ale spilled down the boy's cheeks and spattered the front of his tunic. He jerked his head back, coughing and spluttering to clear his throat, and Aethelwold just managed to grip hold of the jug before it fell to the floor. With hoots of laughter ringing in his ears, Aethelhelm got unsteadily to his feet and, clutching his stomach, made a desperate rush for the door.

Olwen stood up, perhaps intending to follow him, but Winfrith caught hold of her sleeve, worried she might be thinking of telling Aethelwold what she thought of his treatment of his brother.
"Wait. Wait until they've forgotten him. If that's Aethelwold's younger brother he might be able to tell us something useful, but we don't want Aethelwold to see us follow him outside."
Olwen sat down again and they watched the drinkers resume their emptying of the jug. Once they seemed settled, Winfrith turned to Cuthbert.
"We'll go and see if he's all right. Will you watch and see no-one follows us?"
"Of course, but be careful what you say," Cuthbert said. "It will all get back to Aethelwold in the end…that's if the lad is sober enough to make any sense."
"Don't worry about that. Olwen's coming with me. Young men will always talk to beautiful girls…or is it so long ago you've forgotten?"

Aethelhelm had not gone far. Olwen spotted him straight away, slumped against a tree. He must have heard them approaching because he looked up, hurriedly wiping his sleeve across his face and trying without much success to push himself upright.
"Can we help?" Winfrith asked. "You look ill."
"Be fine in a minute. Just a turn." Something in his look reminded Winfrith of his father, old king Aethelwulf. He had the same red hair as his brother but his broader face and darker eyes suggested he had inherited at least some of his mother's looks. He took a deep breath and tried to step away from the tree but straight away had to reach out for support. Winfrith just managed to catch his arm before he fell and Olwen was just as quick to take hold of his other arm.
"It'll take more than a minute by the look of you. Come with Olwen and me. It's nothing a potion of herbs and a good sleep

won't cure. Best to avoid your brother and his friends for a bit. We promise not to mock you, don't we, Olwen?"

Olwen nodded, already beginning to guide him away from the tree. Aethelhelm allowed himself to be led, though several times he stumbled and insisted he should be left alone. Just before they reached Hendraeth's house, a grassy path branched off to the right and followed the ridge overlooking the flooded marshes.

"We'd better get him a bit of fresh air first," Winfrith said, nodding towards the path, "just in case there's any more ale he still needs to bring up."

It proved a wise precaution but, after retching violently into the bushes, Aethelhelm's cheeks at least began to regain a little colour. He sat down, taking deep breaths and gently rubbing his stomach. Winfrith watched him, trying to decide how freely he might talk about his brother. It was strange to think that, had their father lived a few more years, they would have been old enough for one of them to become king instead of Alfred. She wondered if they resented it and whether it had drawn them closer. She'd seen no sign of it. Only half an hour ago Aethelwold had taken great delight in making a laughing stock of his younger brother and had shown no concern at his obvious distress.

"You're looking a little better," she said. "I'm sure Aethelwold will be pleased."

Aethelhelm stared vaguely at Winfrith, as if he'd heard the words but could make no sense of them at all.

"You're fortunate to have someone to look out for you. It's what older brothers are for, I suppose…not that I had one myself."

Aethelhelm frowned, still struggling to make sense of what Winfrith had said. He opened his mouth to reply but the words were lost in a fit of choking laughter. He shook himself free of Winfrith and Olwen's supporting arms, staggering to the side of the path and sitting down heavily. He took another deep breath, clearly struggling to control his anger.

"Fortunate? With a brother like Aethelwold? Be better off without him…and his dim friends. Looking out for me? The only thing he looks out for is the ale pot."

He waved a fist in the direction of the timbered house but the effort of speaking seemed too much for him and his head slumped against his chest. Winfrith motioned to Olwen to assist her in helping him up but he pushed them away.

"Don't need any help," he insisted, more quietly now, almost as if he was talking to himself. "Hated us when we were small... me and Aethelwulf. Father's name and father's favourite, see? Aethelwold couldn't stand it. Laughed when they found him. Laughed himself stupid."

Not for the first time Winfrith cursed Wessex kings and their fondness for giving their sons their own names. It was confusing enough trying to make sense of this youth's drunken ramblings without so many Aethelthises and Aethelthats. What was wrong with the occasional Godstan or Burgred? The talk of brothers had clearly sparked some strong childhood memory, one that he still found upsetting. She knelt down beside him, doing her best not to sound too eager.

"Found who, Aethelhelm? Who did they find?"

Aethelhelm stared at her, as if astonished that anyone would need to ask. "Aethelwulf. They found Aethelwulf...dead. Everyone knows." Even allowing for the effects of the ale it was obvious he was not simply confused and that this Aethelwulf was not his father but someone sharing the same name. A brother perhaps? Winfrith was sure he'd said Aethelwold hated us, not me. Did that mean there had been another brother...one who'd died young? Yet she'd never heard it said the old king had more than two sons, apart from the bastard Oswald, and he was reported to be alive enough to be making fresh enemies in his exile in Devon. She was about to ask when Olwen, who had remained remarkably patient and quiet so far, sat down next to him, putting an arm around his shoulder and asking gently,

"Did you lose a brother? I know how hard that is. I had an older brother, Rhodri. We ran away together from a cruel father. We became slaves before Winfrith rescued me. Rhodri went away into Wales and I miss him terribly. It's very hard being separated from someone you were once very close to."

Aethelhelm stared at her. At first he looked bewildered, but when he spoke again he had clearly taken in what she'd said.

"I do miss Aethelwulf. Just kids...that's all we were. Aethelwold should have been looking out for him. If he'd been my twin, I'd never have left his side."

"So Aethelwulf was Aethelwold's twin?" Winfrith asked, no longer able to keep the excitement from her voice. "I've never heard anyone mention that before."

Aethelhelm groaned, shaking his head. "I feel sick. I don't want to talk about it anymore. I told you already. He's dead. Shouldn't have been up there on his own."

"Up where, Aethelhelm? What happened? Did he fall? Just tell us this one thing and we'll leave you in peace. No more questions, I promise." Despite using her softest pleading voice Winfrith could see that they were not going to get much more from him, however hard they pressed him. He closed his eyes and she thought for a moment he had actually fallen asleep when she saw his lips move. The sounds he made were barely audible, little more than a whisper, but what Winfrith thought she heard immediately set her mind racing. He seemed to be saying,

"Over the cliff…over the cliff…over the cliff he went."

Winfrith leaned closer, hoping to hear more, but already Aethelhelm's head had slipped sideways so that it rested on Olwen's shoulder.

"He's worn out," Olwen said. "We should let him sleep for a while." He certainly looked comfortable but, much as Olwen might be enjoying the moment, it was growing chilly and dusk would soon be on them. Winfrith stood up.

"He'll sleep just as well inside. The pair of you will get frozen to the ground if you stay here. Come on, let's get him on his feet."

Olwen made no effort to hide her disappointment. "It seems a shame to move him. He looks so peaceful. And he's got a lot of questions to answer, hasn't he? What did he mean about the cliff? Was he saying Aethelwold's twin died falling from a cliff? That's what it sounded like. It's just the same as what happened to Ourdilic. Maybe Aethelwold killed them both."

"We don't know that," Winfrith said. "It's unwise to believe everything a man who's drunk a lot of ale tells you. Once he's safely in Hendraeth's house I'll go and look for Milred."

"Milred? What's he got to do with it?"

"He's been at Alfred's side since he was a babe in arms. If Aethelwold did have a twin he's the most likely person to remember it. He's a lot easier to get a story out of than that young man too."

Aethelhelm protested mildly as Winfrith and Olwen prepared to lift him but, once he was on his feet, he seemed not to mind their arms around his waist or his own resting on their shoulders. He allowed himself to be led inside Hendraeth's house and a space was cleared at the far end for him to lie down. A blanket thrown over the rafters kept him from the curious eyes of the children and Olwen sat down just inside it, determined to see that he was not disturbed.

"I'll try not to be too long," Winfrith said softly, though Olwen looked as though she was very happy with the company she had. "If he wakes up don't forget he's Aethelwold's brother. When the ale's worn off he'll be a lot more wary of talking about his brother. He may be young, but he's still a thegn."

"I know," Olwen said, smiling.

"I'll keep an eye on her," Hendraeth said as Winfrith prepared to leave. "Mind you, from what I can see there's no danger of her going anywhere but the foot of that mattress."

Milred was delighted to see Winfrith, insisting on finding her a chair, a thick cushion and a cup of ale before he would listen to the reason for her visit.

"It's a bit out of the way, this little room of mine," he said, smiling and taking a seat opposite her, "but it does mean I don't often get disturbed. Now, you have an impatient look about you, which usually means you've something to ask me. What can it be that you'd like to know this time?"

"It's about Aethelwold. You probably know his younger brother has just arrived in Wedmore. He said something strange to Olwen and me this afternoon. He said that Aethelwold had a twin…called Aethelwulf. It seems he died young. Can that really be true? It would surely be widely known if it was, but it's the first time I've ever heard it spoken of."

"That's probably because there was much doubt about the story, even at the time. I'd quite forgotten it. It must be twelve years or more since I last heard it mentioned. They were very difficult times. Aethelred, Alfred's older brother, was not yet king and but like all his brothers was heavily involved in defending Wessex from outside threats. His wife rarely saw him. It's a miracle that kings, or thegns for that matter, ever had time to produce offspring."

"But Aethelred's wife did give birth to twins?"

Milred pulled a blanket more closely over his lap, enjoying the chance to recall a story from the past and clearly unwilling to be rushed.

"There was gossip…a rumour, that's all."

"But there might have been some truth in it?"

"It was a long time ago and my memory's not what it was but I'll do my best to tell you how it was. Aethelred wasn't yet king when Aethelwold was born. He was often away fighting the Danes and so saw little of his wife and son. As a child Aethelwold was sickly and rarely left his mother's house in Wallingford. Aethelhelm, who I hear is newly arrived in Wedmore, was born a few years later and shortly afterwards Aethelberht died and Aethelred became king. Ah, that was a day to remember. Perhaps the best feast ever seen in Wessex. There were roasting pigs, wildfowl, fish, fresh baked bread, even wine from across the sea. It was the first time many of us had seen Wulfthryth, Aethelred's wife, and, as it turned out, the last time as well. She performed her duties as the king's wife, serving him the first cup and making sure none of our plates stayed empty for long. And then there was music and stories. Scops came from all corners of the kingdom. Rarely can a new king have had a better welcome…"

"But what about the twin, Milred? Did anyone see the boy?"

Milred smiled, raising his hands and gesturing for patience. "I shall get to that in good time but it's no use hurrying me. I shall lose my thread. Now, where was I? Ah yes, the evening was almost at an end. We had eaten and drunk well and most were ready for sleep. There was a sudden commotion outside and we all turned to see a disheveled serving woman at the door, demanding that she be allowed in to speak to Wulfthryth. Guards tried to drag her away but she struggled desperately, shouting that Wulfthryth must go at once because something dreadful had happened to one of her children."

"And that was the twin," Winfrith said, recalling Aethelhelm's words about going over the cliff.

"No-one thought any such person existed. We assumed something had happened to Aethelwold or Aethelhelm, but when we went to look they were both found playing safely where they'd been left. The only odd thing was that the woman who had tended them since birth and who should have been watching over them was nowhere to be seen."

"So how did the woman explain why she believed something dreadful had happened to one of Wulfthryth's children?"

Milred scratched his chin. "Well, that's when the story began to seem like something the woman had dreamt. She led us beneath a high rock and swore that a child had fallen from it and broken its neck. She even pointed to the spot on the ground where she'd seen the body lying. The earth was scuffed and there was a dark patch which might just have been blood but there was no sign anywhere of a dead child. The poor woman must have imagined the whole thing."

"Then where did the rumour about a twin come from?" Winfrith asked.

Milred considered this for a moment. "There were plenty who dismissed the whole thing and said the woman was plainly mad. Yet a few were so convinced by the woman's obvious distress that it set their tongues wagging. One of these had been a woman who had attended both of Wulfthryth's confinements. She apparently made much of the secrecy which had surrounded both of them. Hardly anyone saw the actual births and soon the gossips were busy asking what Queen Wulfthryth had to hide. One of the answers someone came up with was that perhaps there had been a twin, though most agreed that if that was so the child couldn't have survived the birth, otherwise someone would have seen it."

"But if it had, that could have been the dead child the woman saw?"

"I don't think anyone took the idea seriously. Why would Aethelred and Wulfthryth have concealed the fact that they had another child for ten years or so?"

"What did Wulfthryth make of it then? She must have been terrified until she saw Aethelwold and Aethelhelm were safe. Did she behave as if there might have been another child?"

"Well that is a little strange. No-one really had a chance to tell. Wulfthryth left Wallingford early the next morning and she and her sons entered the monastery at Abingdon. Aethelred laughed it off as the rantings of a madwoman and little more was heard about it."

"And no child's body was ever found?"

Milred rested his head in his hands for a moment. "It's hard to separate truth from gossip when I think of what happened afterwards. Nothing was found anywhere near where the woman claimed to have seen the child. A body was found weeks later a few miles away, half hidden in a ditch. Foxes and crows had left nothing of the face for anyone to recognize. A woman from a nearby village said it was hers and had wandered off perhaps a month ago. That seemed to be the end of it, though I did hear later that the woman hadn't all her wits about her and it was rumoured she'd had no children of her own. And that, I think, is all I can tell you, Winfrith, unless there's any other old tale you'd like to hear."

"Later perhaps," Winfrith said with a smile. "Just one more question. If Wulfthryth had given birth to twins why would she and Aethelred go the trouble of concealing one of them and then show little concern when one of them was reported dead? They surely wouldn't leave the body in a ditch either. And what about the serving woman? Why did she think the dead child was Wulfthryth's?"

Milred laughed. "You don't change, Winfrith. That sounds like at least three questions to me."

"Well, it's not surprising I'm curious. Ourdilic is killed in a cliff fall shortly after she's betrothed to Aethelwold and now I find out Aethelwold may have had a twin brother who may also have died young as a result of a similar fall. You've got to admit it looks very suspicious."

"If any of it's true," Milred answered. "No-one ever admitted seeing a twin. Aethelhelm would have been very young, so perhaps he was confused by hearing adults gossip. Aethelred didn't take the story seriously and Wulfthryth was dead within the year. I don't know what happened to the serving woman. Perhaps she went with Wulfthryth to Abingdon."

Winfrith got to her feet. It seemed there was nothing more Milred could tell her. She was about to take her leave when another thought struck her. "When I lived with my father in Twyford, there was a woman in the village gave birth to a boy. Her husband disappeared soon afterwards and she kept the boy close by her and rarely ventured far from the house. Neighbours began talking of strange noises at night, as if she kept a pig or a goat inside. Not long afterwards, someone spotted a child in the doorway, not the boy but a girl of similar age. The girl's arms were withered and twisted and her eyes blank. She had begun to feel her way outside when her mother reached out and dragged her back inside. Wulfthryth wouldn't be the first to keep a child like that hidden."

Milred nodded. "It's not unheard of in villages, I know, but a queen would find it much harder to keep something like that secret. You say it was Aethelhelm who gave you the idea there was a twin?"

"He was suffering from too much ale, thanks to Aethelwold and his friends, but he definitely talked of a twin, Aethelwulf, who died falling over a cliff."

"You're sure he wasn't just confused? Strong ale has strange effects on those not used to it."

"He wasn't feeling well, but Olwen heard him and she thought he must mean the same as I did."

"In that case you'd both better be careful who you repeat it to, especially if you bring Ourdilic into it. The last thing you want is Aethelhelm or anyone else telling Aethelwold that you've decided he killed both Ourdilic and his twin brother."

"I won't say a word." Winfrith crossed to the door and eased it open an inch or two before glancing back at Milred. "Unless I see or hear anything that shows Aethelwold was guilty." She swiftly stepped outside, banging the door behind her without giving Milred the chance to reply.

14

Winfrith took her time returning to Hendraeth's house. Milred's advice was no doubt wise but Aethelhelm was likely to remain in their care for a few hours yet. If he had slept his head ought to be clearer by now and it might be possible to get a little more out of him without arousing his suspicions. From what she had seen he was not over fond of his older brother, even if he did owe him some family loyalty. Yet by the time she reached Hendraeth's door she had still not decided how she might tease more out of him without alerting Aethelwold.

As soon as she stepped inside she saw Hendraeth coming towards her, a finger pressed to her lips in a gesture of silence. She motioned to Winfrith to follow her past the children, asleep on the floor, and over to the corner where they had earlier hung the blanket from the rafters. There was no sign of Olwen standing guard in front of it and the reason soon became clear. Two distinct voices could be heard from behind the blanket, talking in soft but animated tones. Hendraeth nodded in the direction of a gap several inches wide between the edge of the blanket and the wall and, taking Winfrith's arm, guided her towards it. She hesitated, reluctant to eavesdrop, but curiosity swiftly got the better of her. Who would be most likely to get Aethelhelm talking – Winfrith herself or a good-looking young girl like Olwen?

Straw rustled under her feet as she leaned forward to peep through the gap. She froze, sure that she would be discovered, but the voices continued with no sign of alarm. She felt her hair brush the wall as she searched for the position that would give her the best view. She could see the back of Olwen's head and beyond that enough of Aethelhelm's arm and hair to suggest he was sitting up with his head against the far wall. It sounded as though Olwen had already won his trust enough for him to be talking quite openly about his brother Aethelwold.

"I can't believe it," he said. "I haven't seen him for a year but he can't have changed that much. He can't have got himself betrothed. If a girl so much as speaks to him he wants to run away."

"Not like his younger brother then." Aethelhelm didn't answer but Winfrith imagined he and Olwen exchanging a smile. "It's true anyway, even if he did have to be encouraged. I'm surprised you didn't know."

"I was in Abingdon until three days ago. We rarely heard news from outside and the monks kept me at my studies much of the day. So who was this girl my brother was set to marry?"

"Her name was Ourdilic and she was the daughter of the late king of Cornwall. She was very beautiful, but very proud too. We were friends but we argued as much as we laughed. She was excited that she would one day be the wife of the Wessex king's nephew. She liked people to think she was important."

"You said she was excited. What happened? Did my brother change his mind about the betrothal?"

"He didn't look very happy about it, but he never got chance to change his mind. She died."

There was a brief silence and Winfrith saw Aethelhelm's arm reach out far enough to take hold of Olwen's hand. Someone, perhaps one of the children, sneezed and Olwen's head shot round. Winfrith jerked her head back out of sight and held her breath, certain she was about to be discovered, but it seemed Olwen hadn't seen her because Aethelhelm quickly resumed the discussion of his brother's betrothal.

"I'm sorry. You lost a friend as well. What happened?"

"I'm not sure I ought to tell you. Some of it was secret. I promised Ourdilic I'd tell no-one. Not even Aethelwold."

"But Ourdilic's not here now and if it concerns my brother surely I should know about it? At least it might explain why he's in such a foul mood."

"He might not know all of it, but if he does he won't want anyone else to know."

"You're talking in riddles now, Olwen. Just tell me what happened. Aethelwold and I are hardly on speaking terms. I promise I won't repeat anything to him that you don't want him to know."

"You promise? You wouldn't lie to me?"

"I promise. I won't say a word. Tell me what happened."

Olwen took her time replying and Winfrith briefly considered stopping her saying more but the opportunity passed before she could make her mind up to do it.

"Then what few people knew was that Ourdilic was pregnant when she died."

Aethelhelm made a choking sound and when he spoke his disbelief was unmistakable. "You mean…she and my brother? They…they actually…"

"They what? Lay together, do you mean?" Olwen began to sound as though she was enjoying herself. "Isn't that what man and wife do? They were betrothed…"

"Yes, but…Aethelwold…I just can't see him…you know…"

"It's what all men want, isn't it?" Aethelhelm didn't answer and Winfrith leaned forward again, thinking she might have to intervene this time if Olwen pressed him any harder with such a question. Much to her relief it seemed Olwen was intent on nothing more than teasing Aethelhelm. "Perhaps not everyone then. Maybe Aethelwold showed less interest than some."

"But if he didn't father the child, someone else must have, despite the fact that Ourdilic was betrothed to my brother."

"And if that was so, and your brother did learn of it…"

"He might have been very angry. You can't believe he would have harmed Ourdilic though?"

A shout from somewhere outside delayed Olwen's answer. Another voice answered, coming nearer and the sound of passing footsteps grew louder before fading away again. The house fell silent and Olwen decided it was safe to speak again.

"All I know is that it wasn't an accident. She disappeared late one evening and was found a long way from the house. She would never have wandered up there in the dark…she was much too careful. She fell off a cliff, you see…just the same way Aethelwold's twin died."

Though she couldn't see his face there was no doubt in Winfrith's mind that Aethelhelm had received his second shock of the morning. He withdrew his hand from Olwen's and forgot himself enough to raise his voice.

"How did you know about that? No-one's supposed to know. It's never spoken of."

"Shush…Hendraeth will hear you. It's your fault I know anyway. You had so much ale you talked all sorts of nonsense, but that story sounded as though you remembered it clearly…from when you were a child. Aethelwold did have a twin who died, didn't he? Why does no-one ever talk about it?"

There was another long pause. It was clearly not an easy question to answer and Winfrith found it hard to keep still in her eagerness to hear how Aethelhelm would respond. Finally she heard him clear his throat and begin his attempt to explain.

"It was such a long time ago. I was only a child, four or five years old, so I don't remember it very clearly. Aethelwold's twin was called Aethelwulf, after his grandfather. I remember him always smiling and singing to himself. The trouble was he never learned to speak. He'd chatter away like a magpie but none of it made any sense. Our father must have been disappointed and perhaps he took out some of his feeling on Aethelwold too. There was never much love between them."

"So what happened to him… to Aethelwulf? How did he die?"

"We'd been left in the care of the wife of one of our father's thegns. She must have left us alone for some reason because Aethelwold and Aethelwulf went off together, telling me I should wait until she came back and say they wouldn't be gone long. All I remember is that Aethelwold came back on his own saying they had got separated. After that it's all a bit confused. I remember my mother screaming and crying, and Aethelwold and I being taken away on a cart to the monastery at Abingdon. The nuns said Aethelwulf was dead and that our mother was too ill to look after us. No-one was to speak of Aethelwulf for fear it might kill her. I suppose over the years I got used to not talking about him. I asked Aethelwold once or twice what could have happened to him but he just got angry. He said we should forget Aethelwulf. He'd never have had a good life and would only have brought shame on the family."

"And you've no idea how he died? It's just that when the ale still had its grip on you, you seemed to be saying he'd fallen from a high rock."

"Did I? I don't remember. There was a story I heard many years later that a child had died in a fall not far from Wallingford. I don't know if it was true or not. I suppose I'd often wondered how

Aethelwulf had met his end...drowned, attacked by thieves or wild animals, or just beaten by cold and hunger. I might have imagined Aethelwulf could have been the child in the story."

"It's just how Ourdilic died...in a fall from a cliff."

"But that was years later. It can't mean anything." He sounded unworried, a little slow to grasp what Olwen was hinting at but suddenly seeing it. "You think my brother...that he was there both times. You can't think he..."

"He did what? Pushed them?" Winfrith braced herself. How would Aethelhelm react to the accusation? To her surprise he said nothing and it was Olwen who calmly continued. "I'm not saying he did...just that it's strange they both died the same way and Aethelwold had reason to be displeased with them both. And he was in the same place each time of course."

Aethelhelm took his time replying. To Winfrith's relief when he did finally speak he sounded more bewildered than angry. "I don't know. It doesn't seem possible. Aethelwulf was harmless. Who'd have wanted to harm him? From what I know of my brother, he does have a temper but I've never seen him so much as strike anyone. I just can't see him doing something as evil as that."

"Well I don't suppose he'd tell you if he had," Olwen said, "unless you think you can see if he's as talkative as you after too many cups of ale. If you haven't seen each other for years it would be natural to talk over old times."

Aethelhelm groaned. "I won't be sitting down with a barrel of ale for a long time. But since you've been so good to me, I'll keep an ear open for any mention my brother makes of Aethelwulf or Ourdilic. If I hear something interesting at least it will give me an excuse to talk to you again."

"Then be careful. We don't want anyone else having an unexpected fall."

"I can look after myself." Aethelhelm paused, clearing his throat. "So you'd miss me if my brother finishd me off then?"

Winfrith leaned her head against the wall, so that she could see a little more of Aethelhelm. He appeared to be leaning forward and sliding his arm around Olwen's shoulder. Winfrith stepped quickly back and called out a greeting to Hendraeth, hoping it sounded as though she was just returning to the house. Allowing herself time to have removed her cloak and crossed the room, she pulled the blanket aside and stepped through. It was difficult to say which emotion was stronger on the faces of Aethelhelm and Olwen – annoyance or embarrassment.

"You're looking better," she said to Aethelhelm. "Olwen has obviously been taking good care of you. Perhaps it's time you rejoined your fellow thegns. They'll be wondering where you've got to."

Once Aethelhelm had gone, albeit with obvious reluctance, Olwen seemed restless and Winfrith suggested they repay some of Hendraeth's hospitality by fetching some clean water from the river. The only well in Wedmore was beginning to show the effects of so many extra thirsts to satisfy and clothes to wash, offering up half buckets of increasingly muddy water. Winfrith felt a moment of panic as she stood by the swollen river again but she steadied herself, making sure her feet were firmly planted on the bank. At least the conditions underfoot were starting to improve, suggesting it might not be too long before they could be on their way again. The floodwater had retreated far enough to leave banks, ridges and clumps of trees exposed and those paths built on causeways looked passable again. It was certainly timely. Alfred's followers had surely outstayed their welcome in Wedmore by now. There was little for them to do and the increasing shortage of food meant tempers were beginning to fray. Sleep was hard to come by on the overcrowded floors too. Even in Hendraeth's house, Winfrith's nights had been frequently disturbed by complaints of stray feet and elbows waking yet another sleeper.

While they were out of the house Winfrith had meant to talk to Olwen about Aethelhelm, and perhaps Aethelwold and Ourdilic too, without Hendraeth listening in but now the chance had come she was unsure how to begin. So much of what she might say would give away the fact that she had eavesdropped on the two of them. They were on their way back, moving slowly for fear of spilling water from the awkward, broad buckets favoured in Wedmore, before she broached the subject.

"Let's rest a minute. These are heavy. We could do with young Aethelhelm to give us a hand. He seems to have taken a liking to you."

Olwen put down her bucket firmly enough for water to splash over the top and looked enquiringly at Winfrith. "I don't think so. He's a thegn and I'm little better than a servant."

"But a fine-looking one…and he has noticed."

"Well even if he has, what difference does it make?"

"Only that you should be careful. Remember what happened to Ourdilic and she was a king's daughter. We don't want that happening again."

"What are you saying? That Aethelhelm would harm me? You can't think that."

"We didn't believe Ourdilic could be pregnant either."

"He wouldn't try that. I'm sure he wouldn't. I wouldn't allow it."

"Given the slightest encouragement he would. I saw how he looked at you."

"Well he won't get the chance. Besides, you've hardly let me out of your sight since we got here."

Winfrith smiled. "Well you know why that is. You were Ourdilic's friend and I think someone killed her. I mean to make sure you won't go the same way."

Winfrith hesitated, trying to think of the safest way to introduce the subject of Aethelwold's twin when she saw that Olwen had turned away and was staring uphill to a point where the track turned out of sight behind a thick clump of bushes. A woman had stepped out of them and was now brushing her clothes, as if leaves or twigs had caught in them. As they watched she appeared to tuck something into the folds of her cloak before turning and heading back up the hill. The woman had been tall and she held her back straight as she walked. Even at a distance her clothes had looked well made, thicker and warmer than most Wedmore women could afford. Winfrith and Olwen exchanged glances. It was clear they had both recognized Eanflaed.

"What do you think she was up to?" Olwen said. "Not like a thegn's wife to be rooting about in the bushes."

"Even thegn's wives are caught short sometimes," Winfrith replied, "though why Eanflaed would leave the fireside I'm not sure. Let's get these buckets moving again. We can take a look at the spot we saw her as we pass. You never know…she might have been meeting a man. No-one would blame her with a husband like Beorhtric."

When they reached the bend in the track at first sight the bushes looked too dense to find a way through. They put down the water buckets again and began to pull branches aside looking for a gap.

"Here," Olwen said suddenly, disappearing from sight as branches sprang back behind her. Winfrith followed, holding one arm up to protect her face and using the other to free her clothes. She emerged behind Olwen into a small hollow flanked by thorn trees. Glistening grey rock showed through in various places around the sides of the hollow and ancient rainwater had worn a series of channels into the surface. The largest of these opened out near the ground into a dark hole the size of a man's head. Winfrith walked slowly around the edge of the hollow, searching for anything which would explain Eanflaed's presence there. There was nothing obvious and she was about to return to the path when Olwen knelt down and reached inside the hole in the rock. For a moment it seemed as if she had found something, for she quickly withdrew her hand and held it up towards Winfrith. It was a lot less interesting than they might have hoped…a strip of brown cloth, neatly stitched along one edge but roughly torn along the other as if it had caught on the sharp edges of the rock.

"Is that all?" Winfrith said, surprised at how disappointed she felt. Olwen reached inside again but, aside from a handful of twigs and dead grass, came across nothing else.

"What a shame," she said. "Eanflaed thinks she's better than us. It would have been good to find she had a guilty secret."

"Perhaps she has," Winfrith said, laughing, "but if she has it's not here. We'd better get back before Hendraeth starts thinking we're lost."

They began to push their way back onto the path. As they went, Winfrith couldn't get the idea of a guilty secret out of her head. Eanflaed had been acting strangely. Had she been hiding something? There was one explanation which would account for her behaviour, a suspicion that Winfrith had considered before. If Eanflaed had stolen Ourdilic's morning gift she would go to some lengths to ensure no-one knew she had it. Was that what she had hidden under her clothes…retrieving it because she knew they would shortly be leaving Wedmore? There might be nothing in it but Winfrith determined she would keep a close eye on Eanflaed once they were ready to depart.

As it turned out the departure from Wedmore took longer than expected. Though the floodwater was retreating it was a slow process and Alfred and his closest advisers retired inside to consider their next move. Guards were posted on the door, leaving those outside curious to know what was going on. On the rare occasions when anyone stepped outside they remained tight-lipped whenever a question was put to them. Winfrith had hoped either Cuthbert or Milred might drop her a hint but even they were disinclined to talk. In the end it was Hendraeth, pausing in an effort to feed her youngest child a mash of medlars, who suggested a possible answer.

"There's a story going round that Alfred's planning a raid on Chippenham," she said, putting down the bowl and wiping the protesting child's face. "They're hoping to go by night and surprise Guthrum."

"I don't know where you heard that," Winfrith replied, "but it doesn't sound very likely. All that way across flooded land with so few men…and most of those half-fed? They'd have little hope of success."

"That's what I told them," Hendraeth said with obvious satisfaction. "Someone would warn the Danes anyway. There are folk out on the marshes would sell their mothers for a shilling. I think Alfred's cooped up in there for some other reason…something he doesn't want too many people to know about."

"And what would that be, Hendraeth?"

Hendraeth lifted the child onto her lap, settling into a more comfortable position. "It's obviously something very serious. Otherwise they wouldn't have been so long about it. I think it's to do with the king himself. What if he'd been taken ill? Maybe it's serious. None of his brothers lived to old age. They'd all be worried if they thought he might die. Who'd succeed him? His sons are too young. No-one likes his nephew Aethelwold. And if Guthrum got to hear of it he'd think the end of Wessex as very near."

"It's an interesting idea, Hendraeth, but Alfred looked well enough the last time I saw him. I'd have thought it's more likely he means to take us somewhere out of Guthrum's reach, at least until he's raised more men. They're probably talking about how they can feed themselves through the winter if we go further west."

Hendraeth nodded, though she did look entirely satisfied with this explanation. "It's wild country that way. Travellers have gone and never returned. He might be better off sending men to Chippenham to make peace with Guthrum. That's what his Dorset ealdorman, Wulfhere, did."

"And made himself the most unpopular man in Wessex," Winfrith said. "Most of Alfred's thegns who've followed him this far see Wulfhere as a traitor. I think they'd sooner die than kneel before Guthrum."

"Well dying is what they might finish up doing if they go on. It's probably why they're taking so long. Some will need a lot of persuading."

"Whatever the reason, I don't think we'll be staying here once the floodwater has gone down. You've been very kind to Olwen and me. I'm only sorry we've nothing to repay you with."

"Glad of the company," Hendraeth said. "Besides, it's not every day a king comes to Wedmore."

15

Despite her best intentions, when the moment did finally arrive for leaving Wedmore Winfrith had little opportunity to watch out for either Eanflaed or Aethelwold. What with taking leave of Hendraeth and her children and hurrying Olwen along she saw neither of them until they were already some way out of the village. Alfred had hired a local drover to guide them the first part of the way. He directed them along a well-worn track which he named Black Way. It would lead them across high ground before dropping onto Till Moor. From there the route lay across treacherous marshland and, as the drover frequently reminded them, without knowing how to find the few well hidden wooden causeways strangers would quickly become lost.

Winfrith and Olwen joined the line heading out of Wedmore in something of a rush. Some of Alfred's thegns were already too far ahead to recognize but there were enough sounds of others coming along behind to feel confident they would not be allowed to lose touch with the leading group. They had walked a mile or so before Winfrith, hearing footsteps approaching rapidly, glanced over her shoulder to see Aethelwold bearing down on them. She caught Olwen's arm, guiding her closer to the edge of the path to give him room to pass. He looked to be in a hurry though Winfrith was sure no-one would threaten any harm to them while other thegns were not far behind.

"Get a move on," he said as he passed. "Don't know why my uncle thinks women and girls are going to be much use." His pace didn't slacken and he was soon far enough ahead to be out of earshot.

"As much use as he'll ever be," Olwen said as they set off after him.

"We could speed up a bit," Winfrith said. "We don't want to get left."

Aethelwold's scorn seemed to have provoked Olwen enough to make her walk faster and so it was something of a surprise when a few hundred paces further on Cuthbert caught up with them.

"Putting the stragglers to shame," he said, waving back down the path. "I saw Aethelwold pass. Not causing you any trouble I hope?"

"He wasn't pleased to see us," Winfrith replied, "but no trouble. If there are any more rivers to cross I'll choose a different helper next time."

Cuthbert watched the distant figure of Aethelwold for a moment. "He's probably not the only one who thinks you shouldn't be here…but he's making no secret of it. Why's that do you think? Did you accuse him of trying to drown you?"

"Well he did," Olwen said. Winfrith put a restraining hand on her arm before she could go on.

"I didn't say anything to him. Perhaps he has other things to feel guilty about."

Cuthbert smiled. "Well none of us are saints. Did you have some particular matter in mind?"

"Apart from having a hand in Ourdilic's death, you mean? As if that's not bad enough. I have heard another story about him which, if it's true, might explain a lot."

"He's the king's nephew. There's bound to be gossip. What's this tale about?"

"About when he was a boy. He had a twin brother, Aethelwulf."

Cuthbert looked up to the sky. "That's utter nonsense. So where is this twin? No-one's ever seen one, have they?"

"Because he died…falling off a cliff…just like Ourdilic. No-one ever spoke of him because he was born without speech…not fit to be a king's son. That's why it was easy to hide the whole story, but Aethelwold was the only person with him when he fell."

Cuthbert turned to look behind them, checking no-one was following closely. "Someone's got a good imagination. Where on earth did y ou hear that one?"

"It's true," Olwen said. "I heard it too…from Aethelhelm."

"Ah, Aethelhelm…I see. That explains it. He's still just a boy…and not very fond of his brother either. He probably dreamed it."

"I could hardly believe it myself," Winfrith said, "until I spoke to Milred. He'd heard the story too…long ago. No-one could be certain it happened but there was a woman claimed to have seen the dead boy and Aethelwold's mother, Wulfthryth, was very distressed. She disappeared into the nunnery at Abingdon straight after."

Cuthbert sighed. "Milred knows more about the kings of Wessex than most, I suppose, but even his memory's not what it was. It sounds as though it's something that started from some child's death and got built up into quite another story over time."

"But when you put it together with the way Ourdilic died and remember Aethelwold was there both times, it seems more likely. He was reluctant to get betrothed to Ourdilic and Aethelhelm says he was pleased his twin was out of the way. Then when I say I mean to find out what happened to Ourdilic, I'm nearly drowned."

"And so he killed them both by pushing them over cliffs and then cut you loose in the river?" Winfrith nodded. "He's not much liked. That's clear enough. He was brought up expecting to be king and he's angry that he was too young to succeed his late father. But the cold-blooded murder of a child and then a young girl? This is Aethelwold we're talking about…not a Danish jarl."

"But surely there's enough in it to be very wary of him at least?"

"I'll see that he's watched, especially when there are rivers to be crossed. In the meantime I'll drop back and have a word with Milred. I'd like to hear what he has to say about this mysterious twin."

Once Cuthbert had left them, Winfrith and Olwen fell silent, walking on at a steady enough pace to begin closing the gap between themselves and a small group ahead. As they drew nearer two figures appeared to slow down, separating them from the group, and from the gestures and occasional sounds of raised voices it seemed they were arguing. Ordinarily Winfrith would have hung back and let them get on with it but she had recognized the pair as Beorhtric and Eanflaed and that made her suddenly eager to hear what the disagreement was about. She pointed towards them, putting a finger to her lips for silence, and she and Olwen approached as quietly as the ground under their feet would allow. Taking care to avoid loose stones and tussocks of grass they gradually got within hearing distance. It was Eanflaed who was protesting the loudest.

"Why not? Why shouldn't we go? It would be better than this. We'd have a home."

"How can we?" Beorhtric shouted back. "What about all those who died fighting the Danes? What about my brother? Doesn't he deserve vengeance?"

"Haven't you done enough killing? It'll be your turn one day unless you choose a different life."

"We'll all be dead if we hand over everything to Guthrum. What you need to remember is…" He stopped, alerted by the scrape of a foot on gravel to the closeness of Winfrith and Olwen behind him. Winfrith smiled and made as if to overtake them but Beorhtric stepped in her way. "Were you listening? Whatever you heard wasn't meant for your ears. Best to forget it…the pair of you. My wife occasionally gets these strange ideas about returning home, wherever that might be. She always changes her mind. Don't you, Eanflaed?"

Eanflaed nodded, but said nothing.

"You see? Just like a woman to want something and straight away to be dissatisfied with it. Always dreaming, that's all it was." He stared hard at Winfrith before stepping aside, leaving her certain that there had been more to the argument than simply the possibility of deserting Alfred. Even if Eanflaed was serious, why choose such a wild place where they would surely struggle to survive on their own? Yet even at Wedmore she and Olwen had seen Eanflaed behaving very oddly. The real question was whether the reason for it was that had she had some knowledge of how Ourdilic had died and if, as Winfrith suspected, she had stolen the morning gift too, then she would be afraid that would point to her guilt. The thought led her to look back over her shoulder to where Beorhtric and Eanflaed looked to have resumed their argument.

"She'd be better off without him," Olwen said, following Winfrith's glance.

"Not out here, she wouldn't," Winfrith replied, "thought I doubt if we've heard the last of that argument yet."

They walked on in silence for a while, until the track began a slow descent towards flatter, marshy land. Ahead of them it disappeared into woodland and a dark grey line of hills rose beyond the trees.

"Westhay," Cuthbert said, catching them up once again and pointing to the nearest of the hills. "That's where we cross the

River Brue. On the other side there's a wooden trackway across the marshes to Shapwick, in the middle of that black line of hills. Alfred thinks we'll be there by mid afternoon at the latest."

"Let's hope they're expecting us then…a lot of mouths to feed."

"There are half a dozen villages up in those hills. Alfred's expecting them to provide fighters as well as food. This is still Wessex remember."

"But its ealdorman looks to have deserted the cause. Who's to say other Somerset men will be any more loyal?"

"Aethelnoth will be back. It's not the first time he's argued with Aethelwold or offended the king. The truth is he hates Guthrum far more and Alfred knows his word carries more weight here in Somerset than anyone he could replace him with. They'll settle their differences I'm sure."

"And what about Milred? What have you done with him?" Winfrith asked. "I thought you went back to help him."

"And I did. Unloaded a pack horse and put him on instead. He protested of course but he wouldn't keep up otherwise. He won't be far behind us now. And now, if you get a move on, the river lies just behind those trees and you might like someone a bit more trustworthy than Aethelwold to help you across this time."

They reached the gently sloping river bank in time to see Raedberht adjusting a heavy bundle of spears, strapped across his shoulders, before stepping into the water. Winfrith watched as the water rose above his knees, slapping and bubbling around his thighs as he reached midstream. To her relief it appeared to get no deeper and he made steady progress to the far bank, despite his awkward load. Once there he dropped the bundle of spears to the ground and sat down, watching as Winfrith, Cuthbert and Olwen followed, linking arms as they went. Despite the drag of the current against her dress and the icy chill which swiftly gripped her feet and legs, Winfrith stared straight ahead, determined to shut memories of being dragged helplessly along in the current from her mind. Even so, she felt a surge of relief as she emerged on the far side without alarm. From there they skirted the hill on which Westhay stood, making straight for the wooden causeway to Shapwick.

"It's called the Sweet Way for some reason," Cuthbert said, "though, looking at it, it's hard to see why. Looks more like a trap for the unwary to me. Watch where you put your feet. I don't want to be fishing you out of the water again."

Cuthbert stepped cautiously onto the first of the oak planks. Ahead of him, a double line of posts snaked across the marsh towards the dark line of the Polden Hills. The drover leaned against a stunted tree, watching them, no doubt pleased he would soon be heading back to Wedmore.

"You can't get lost now," he called as they passed. "Follow the posts and you'll be in Shapwick well before dusk."

Winfrith motioned Olwen to go ahead of her and together they followed Cuthbert, keeping an eye out for broken or slippery planks. Now and again they came to a halt where awkward gaps had to be crossed. Either side of them lay an uninviting landscape. Stagnant pools, their dark brown surfaces making it impossible to tell if they were inches or miles deep, were dotted everywhere. Clumps of reed surrounded them and the surfaces of any humps and islands which rose above the water were masked by marsh grass, bedstraw and spiny teasel heads. A strong smell of rotting leaves filled the air. It was easy to imagine lost travelers sinking out of sight in this morass or worse, some misshapen creature rising steaming and mud-splattered from the depths of one of the dark pools.

Winfrith shuddered and hurried after Cuthbert and Olwen.

The unreliable surface of the causeway meant they made slow progress. Once Olwen lost her footing and only Winfrith grabbing her arm stopped her from sliding onto the marsh. Yet gradually the line of hills ahead of them grew more distinct and the drifts of smoke from Shapwick fires suggested it was not too far off. They were not the only ones encouraged by the sight. The sound of rapid, heavy footsteps sounded on the boards behind them and made them both turn. They had barely time to move aside before Raedberht, the bundle of spears across his shoulders, strode past without a word.

"He's in a hurry," Winfrith said, watching Raedberht's rapidly retreating back.

"A man with a thirst," Cuthbert said, "unless Alfred's sent him ahead with a message for the good folk of Shapwick."

Winfrith looked back the way Raedberht had come. Seven or eight of Alfred's men, most likely bringing up the rear of the party, were making their way steadily towards them. There ought to have been nothing strange in that but Winfrith found herself stopping to look more carefully. Milred was clearly one of them. The horse had been abandoned now they were on the walkway but two young thegns, one on each side, were supporting him. They were close enough to pick out other individuals now and she realized what had struck her was not who they were but who was missing. Despite having passed them earlier, there was no sign of either Beorhtric or Eanflaed.

"Why don't you two go on?" she said. "It can't be far now. I'll just wait for that group behind us. I just want to check Eanflaed is all right."

Olwen shot her a questioning look, and Winfrith gave her a reassuring pat on the arm. "I won't be long. I'll catch you up before you reach Shapwick."

It was easy to see why Alfred's group were lagging behind. Most carried heavy bundles or sacks lifted from the pack horses at the start of the causeway. It looked likely that Milred too, despite the help he was getting, was slowing them down. Winfrith flattened herself against one of the stouter looking posts as they edged their way past. She was relieved to see that further back, perhaps two hundred paces away, two more figures were following. One was certainly Beorhtric and the other tall and slim enough to be Eanflead. Yet as she waited for them to draw nearer, Eanflaed appeared to be moving awkwardly. At first she thought it was because she was taking a turn carrying Beorhtric's pack but she soon saw that the figure was not Eanflaed at all but Beorhtric's servant, Wicstan.

Beorhtric slowed slightly when he saw Winfrith, so that Wicstan stumbled into him and grabbed hold of a post as the weight of his pack threatened to swing him off the boards. The pole bent outwards, sending up ominous gurgling sounds from somewhere below it. Wicstan made a last effort to push himself backwards, just managing to let go of the pole and regain his balance before it slid slowly over into the mud.

"Look where you're going, oaf!" Beorhtric said, gesturing towards the murky pool below. "I'm not pulling you out if you end up in there." He made as if to pass Winfrith but she held her ground in the middle of the boardwalk.

"Where's Eanflaed got to?" she said. "I thought she was with you."

Beorhtric shrugged. "How would I know? You heard her. She made it pretty clear she didn't want to be here with me."

"So you left her to walk on her own? In a place like this?"

"Better than listening to her complaints for another hour. Anyway, what's it got to do with you? Spending time with you and that Ourdilic child didn't improve her temper."

"Nor yours by the sound of it."

Beorhtric glared at her, taking a step closer. "Why don't you get out of our way? I wouldn't like to see you slip over like my clumsy servant here…especially if there was no-one waiting to help you out. So step aside. There must be a fire and a cup of ale waiting for us and I'm more than ready for it."

Winfrith did as she was bid, watching the two men until they were out of sight. There was still no sign of Eanflaed ahead of her. Should she go back and look? The light was still good and the posts were visible for perhaps five hundred paces, before they disappeared behind a tall bank of reeds. There was something about the place which made her uneasy and reluctant to go too far alone but it could do no harm to return as far as the reed bed. Eanflaed would surely not be any further behind than that.

She was tempted to hurry and get the search over with but the occasional loose boards and patches of damp, slippery timber had to be crossed with care. She reached the reeds without mishap. Passing them the first time she hadn't noticed that the bend in the track had been made to pass round a dark pool, partly hidden by the reeds. She wouldn't have seen it now either, but for a gap, made where something had flattened down the reeds. She was not sure whether she imagined it, but the breaks in the reed stems looked pale, as if they had been recently made. She found herself wondering if someone had stepped off the causeway and for some reason risked pushing their way through the reed bed.

She walked on a few paces, rounding a corner so that the track twisting its way back towards Westhay came into view. Though it stretched into the distance there was no sign of anyone moving along the boards. She was suddenly afraid that some harm had come to Eanflaed and hurried back to the gap she had seen in the reeds. Telling herself that something or someone had already safely taken the same route, she began to lower herself off the walkway. Clinging to one of the posts, she felt the muddy water creep up her calves and her feet sink into soft mud before settling on what she supposed were tough, springy roots. She began to wade forward. Each step was an effort as the cloying mud clung to her feet and the murky water pulled at the hem of her skirt. She brushed the reeds ahead of her aside, casting her eyes around the dark surface of the pool. It lay flat and unmoving, a peaty brown colour that hid from sight anything beneath the surface. She breathed out slowly. Perhaps after all there was nothing to see. Maybe Eanflaed had somehow passed without her noticing and this gap in the reeds was simply the result of some animal coming to drink.

It had been rash, stepping off the walkway, letting her imagination get the better of her again. That's what Cuthbert would say. She turned to go back and, as she did so, her foot caught on something too thick to be roots, nudging it to the surface. It took her a moment to regain her balance, time enough to dismiss it as some long ago discarded pole from the walkway. And then she looked down again. She froze. She turned away, feeling her heart race. Not again. Please not again. Finding Ourdilic was bad enough. She forced herself to look down again. No piece of wood was ever clothed in leggings or wore a finely-stitched shoe. Even coated in muddy water it was clearly not footwear belonging to poor folk. Perhaps she was dreaming. She screwed her eyes shut, trying to rid herself of the image. Perhaps she would never open them again. The longer they stayed closed, the longer she could still believe this wasn't Eanflaed lying dead under the water.

16

Cuthbert insisted on returning with Winfrith as soon as sense could be made of her breathless account of what she had seen under the surface of the pool. Beorhtric followed with two other thegns and, after taking a swift look at his wife's corpse, moved away and the three of them stood in a close circle. Every now and again Winfrith caught a terse angry whisper from Beorhtric, while his companions glanced frequently back towards Shapwick.

"I should have gone to look for her sooner," Winfrith said. "I knew she was lagging behind."

"You're not to blame," Cuthbert said. "She wasn't your responsibility. She was a grown woman with an able-bodied husband… quite capable of looking after herself."

"Except she wasn't, was she?" Winfrith shook his consoling arm from her shoulder, stepping closer to where Eanflaed's dripping body had been lifted out of the water and onto the boards of the Sweet Way. Her mouth was twisted into the faintest of smiles and, but for the livid bruise on her cheek, it would have been easy to believe she had died peacefully.

"Beorhtric doesn't look overwhelmed with grief, does he? Maybe he gave her that bruise…or worse, forced her under the water."

Cuthbert glanced towards Beorhtric but the thegn was staring morosely along the boardwalk, paying little attention to anyone. Cuthbert leaned closer, speaking barely above a whisper,

"Not so loud. If he knows anything about this he can explain when we've moved the body to Shapwick. Start accusing him now and we might have a third dead woman on our hands."

"So you agree this wasn't an accident?" Winfrith whispered back.

"I didn't say that…"

"But you can see it's possible? She didn't have that bruise this morning and I heard the two of them arguing earlier. Beorhtric's got a violent temper and he was with her at the back of the line."

Cuthbert put his finger to her lips. "Let's do this later," he hissed. "The last thing we need is another fit of his temper just now. Arguing with his wife doesn't mean he killed her and he had no reason to attack Ourdilic. You thought that was Aethelwold a day or two ago."

Winfrith opened her mouth, unwilling to give up trying to get a reaction from Cuthbert, but hesitated as she caught sight of Beorhtric glancing again at his wife's body and stepping towards Cuthbert.

"How much longer do we have to wait? It'll be dark before long and we've no torches."

"We can't leave her here, can we?" Cuthbert answered, forcefully enough to make Winfrith think he'd forgotten his own advice about not provoking Beorhtric. "And I don't suppose you want your wife's dead body on your back all the way to Shapwick. The man I sent back for a stretcher won't be long."

Beorhtric muttered something under his breath before turning to Winfrith. "Looks like you've poked your nose into my wife's business for the last time. See where it got her."

Winfrith drew back an arm to strike him but Cuthbert was too quick for her, catching her sleeve and pulling her away.

"It wasn't me brought her to this," she shouted. "You argued with her. You've hit her before. Had you had enough? Held her under the water, did you? Just like you pushed Ourdilic."

Cuthbert dragged her further away as Beorhtric advanced angrily towards her, fists clenched. Yet even as Cuthbert turned and positioned himself between them, Winfrith thought she saw something else in Beorhtric's look. It was hard to say what…it had come and gone in an instant…something between bewilderment and amusement she thought. When he did speak again, he seemed already to have got over his rage.

"Bruises come easily…just like scars. She probably fell. As for me trying to drown my wife, why would you think that? Unless of course you were trying to hide your own part in it. You were the one who went back and found her. It's you has the explaining to do."

"And I will," Winfrith said, despite Cuthbert's warning look. "I'll explain how Eanflaed and Ourdilic both had marks suggesting they were attacked before they died and how you seemed to have taken a dislike to both of them."

"Enough," Cuthbert said before Beorhtric had chance to reply. He grasped her firmly around the waist, hurrying along the walkway until they were out of earshot. "You've said enough. Finding Eanflaed dead was a shock, especially after Ourdilic. Unless you saw Beorhtric knock her into the water, you'd be wise not to accuse him. He'll say you're mad and that will leave Alfred with a choice. Get rid of a fighting thegn or get rid of a madwoman. You know what he'd do."

Winfrith did of course, and she hadn't seen Beorhtric strike his wife. She could have got the bruise when she fell, though why she'd waded away from the walkway first was unclear.

"So no-one will even ask why she died like that?"

Cuthbert relaxed his grip on Winfrith's waist. "Usually it would be up to the local ealdorman to decide whether there were any questions to be answered."

"And Aethelnoth has made himself scarce, just when he's most needed."

"He'll be back," Cuthbert said. "He needs Alfred as much as Alfred need him."

"And in the meantime? You could offer to look into it. Alfred trusts you."

Cuthbert sighed. "We'll see. I'll mention it on one condition…that you promise to keep your mouth shut. We don't want another body on our hands."

"So you believe me? You think Beorhtric would attack me too?"

"I didn't say that. He has a temper, that's all, and any of us would be angry if someone accused us of killing our wives."

There seemed little point in further argument. Winfrith stopped and looked back, thinking it might not have been wise to leave Beorhtric and his friends in charge of Eanflaed's body. Yet they could do her no further harm and two figures had already appeared in the distance ahead of them. As they drew nearer she could see that they carried the poles of a makeshift stretcher between their shoulders. They looked far from happy, but then leaving a warm fire on a cold afternoon to carry a dead body the mile or so back to Shapwick was not a task anyone would welcome. Cuthbert pointed to where Beorhtric and his companions were waiting and, as soon as he saw them lift the body onto the stretcher, indicated to Winfrith that they should go on ahead.

Eanflaed was buried the following morning on a frosty hilltop just above Shapwick. There were no more than a dozen gathered around the graveside. Beorhtric was among them, though as far as Winfrith could see his face showed little sign of grief. More surprising was the presence of Aethelwold, standing silently alongside Alfred. Once the body, wrapped in white cloth, had been lowered into the grave, Alfred pressed his hands together as if at prayer.

"We hereby commit this body to the earth and the soul of Eanflaed to God. She was a good woman and a loyal wife. Her life was cut short and should serve as a reminder to us all of the dangers we face. We should always be ready to meet our Maker."

He signaled to the two Shapwick men who had dug the grave to begin filling it in and Winfrith felt her anger rising at the haste with which Eanflaed's death was to be put behind them. She would not lose control this time though. Shouting accusations at Ourdilic's funeral had achieved nothing. Even so, the unmoved faces of Aethelwold and Beorhtric made her seethe inside. If either of them was hiding a guilty secret she would do everything she could to uncover it.

Once the grave was filled and a roughly carved wooden cross pressed into the ground Alfred took Cuthred's arm and led him to one side. Winfrith moved a little closer to where they stood in the hope of overhearing what was being said. She couldn't hear every word but it looked as though Alfred had been asking for Cuthred's help. Eanflaed's name was mentioned and Cuthred nodded as if he had agreed to Alfred's request. In Aethelnoth's absence, Cuthred was the only ealdorman in Shapwick. Winfrith felt a surge of hope. Perhaps Alfred thought the death needed explaining too and was asking Cuthred to look into it. She looked quickly away as the two men rejoined the others and set off back towards Shapwick.

Winfrith followed, keeping close enough to Beorhtric to observe his reactions. She was not disappointed. Half way down the hill, Raedberht was waiting, leaning against a tree. The moment he saw Beorhtric he fell into step alongside him, clapping him lightly on the shoulder.

"An unlucky day for you, Beorhtric," he said, louder than really seemed necessary. "You wouldn't think your wife could step off a good track into a treacherous marsh, would you?"

Beorhtric pushed him away. "Go hang yourself, Raedberht. Find someone else to annoy."

"Why would you be annoyed? Even you must have thought it odd she was hanging back there on her own. What could she have been up to?"

"Who knows? Maybe she dropped something and went back for it. Maybe she was just weary. What does it matter now? So, if that's all, why don't you shift yourself? There's a funny Danish smell around here all of a sudden."

"Is that right? Then I wonder where it's coming from. If anyone was planning to send a message about Alfred's whereabouts back to the Danes in Chippenham, they'd need to hang back until everyone had passed. Those reeds would make a good hiding place."

The raised voices were beginning to attract attention with four or five thegns slowing down and looking round expectantly. Beorhtric stopped and turned to face Raedberht, slipping his hand inside his tunic as he did so.

"She wasn't the only one hanging back, was she? And there's only one way of dealing with traitors and that's to make sure they're dead."

Raedberht laughed. "Just like Eanflaed you mean?"

"She was no friend of Guthrum, unlike you. She never had an uncle who kisses Danish arses."

Raedberht's grin vanished. He looked about him, as if seeking support, but no-one spoke. "Wulfhere's got nothing to do with this. Your wife went back for something. I don't suppose she found it in the bottom of a lake."

Beorhtric let out a low growl and launched himself at Raedberht. There was just time to see the flash of a blade and Raedberht's arm raised to ward off the strike before arms were flung around Beorhtric and he was dragged off. Raedberht pulled up his torn sleeve, inspecting the scratch on his forearm.

"You all saw that," he said, holding up his arm. "All over a few words in jest. Let's hope his wife didn't say anything that displeased him."

Beorhtric struggled to free himself but the two thegns holding him pulled him back while a third wrestled the knife from his hand.

"Say that when there's no-one to protect you," he said, spitting out the words. "It'll be the last words you speak."

Raedberht laughed, beginning to walk away. "Save your threats for someone who fears them," he called over his shoulder. "Another woman perhaps."

Winfrith watched him go, trying to decide whether he might have seen Beorhtric strike his wife and whether Eanflaed could possibly have been intending to betray their position to Guthrum. If the first seemed possible, the latter seemed unlikely. Eanflaed might have wanted to escape this apparently endless flight but she'd shown no desire to put her trust in Guthrum's protection. If none of it was true, why had Raedberht gone to such lengths to provoke Beorhtric? If Alfred got to hear of it, neither of them would escape without punishment. Of one thing she was sure. It would not be easy to get either Raedberht or Beorhtric to talk freely about what they saw crossing the Sweet Way.

They returned to Shapwick without further incident. Eanflaed's burial had not been a promising start to their stay but it soon became clear that this was a more comfortable stop than Wedmore had been. The village was made up of two main streets with a succession of narrow alleys linking them. These alleys were lined with houses, wedged close together and providing shelter from the wind. Some were occupied but news of the king's arrival had led some families to depart to neighbouring villages, leaving enough space for the new arrivals to bed down without having their feet in someone else's ears. Others belonged to the monks of Glastonbury and were only occupied when the abbot gave his blessing to a leave of absence. Winfrith and Olwen had spent their first night in a draughty hall but now Cuthbert escorted them to one of the monks' houses, suggesting they would be safer there than on either of the main streets. Alfred had been assured it was both secluded and presently occupied by a woman and her daughter who would be better company for them than his own thegns.

The house was certainly well hidden. They reached it by following a grassy track downhill until it reached the edge of a hollow. Ahead of them a dense cluster of holly trees appeared to block the way, forcing them to turn aside. They followed the line of trees for perhaps fifty paces until they came to a narrow gap, just wide enough to pass through one at a time. Holly branches closed over their heads, allowing through very little daylight. A slit of flickering orange light guided them towards a solid oak door, slightly ajar as if they were expected. Cuthbert knocked and ushered Winfrith and Olwen inside. Two women sat close to the fire and the older one leapt up and came to meet them.

"Come in. Come in," she said, a little breathlessly. "Come and warm yourselves. I'm Heafa and this is my daughter, Flaedda." Fleadda glanced towards them and coughed nervously. "She's not used to strangers," Heafa said. "She'll liven up once you've been here a while. Fetch us a jug of ale and some cups, Flaedda. Our guests must be thirsty."

Cuthbert excused himself, leaving the four women to gather round the fire and get to know each other.

"He's a fine man," Haefa said, once Cuthbert had closed the door behind him. "Wealthy too by the look of him. Not looking for a wife is he?"

Winfrith smiled. "He's too busy I think and he likes his own way too much to consider getting wed."

"Shame. The only unmarried men in Shapwick are dolts without a shilling to their name." She nodded towards her daughter. "That girl has more chance of flying than finding a husband here."

Flaedda glared at her mother but remained silent.

"What does her father think? Olwen asked, offering Flaedda a sympathetic smile.

Heafa hesitated before answering. "Died ten years ago. Not that he'd have been any help to the girl. Never here…"

Flaedda looked on the point of challenging this until she was seized by a fresh bout of coughing and Heafa sighed impatiently, getting to her feet. "Where's the potion I got for you? I have to do everything for this girl."

"No you don't," Flaedda said, finding her voice at last. "You're always finding me work. The potion's on the table, where you left it."

"I'm sorry to hear about your husband," Winfrith said, hoping to put an end to the bickering. "I lost mine too…killed by Danes."

"And left you to provide for this growing girl? It's a great weight to bear…"

"Oh, Olwen's no trouble," Winfrith said swiftly without quite knowing why. Arguments between them were hardly unknown, especially once Ourdilic had joined them. "But she's not my daughter. She'd been mistreated and I took her in."

Winfrith realized they were all staring at her...Heafa disbelieving, Olwen a little embarrassed, and Flaedda more difficult to tell but Winfrith thought there might be a trace of envy in her look.

"However she came to me, I wouldn't be without her now."

"You might have to one day," Heafa said, brushing her fingertips against Olwen's cheek. "She's pretty enough to get a husband anywhere but Shapwick. Perhaps that's why that Cuthbert was so eager to find you a warm house."

"More likely because he wants to keep an eye on us," Winfrith said. "My husband was one of his retainers and I remained part of Cuthbert's household after he was killed."

Heafa's curiosity was clearly still far from satisfied but before she could ask any further questions Flaedda was gain seized by a bout of coughing and, sighing impatiently, her mother got up and went to fetch the potion. Patting her daughter's back she spooned some it into her mouth, sighing again as the girl struggled to swallow it. Winfrith watched, glad of the chance to satisfy her thirst. Flaedda did not take after her mother, lacking her long beak-like nose and jutting chin. Nor did she constantly nod her head like a hen searching for grain.

"There...that should keep you quiet for a bit, or else it's a waste of the cup of barley I gave the widow Fraeda for it." Heafa turned back to Winfrith. "Now then, you were about to tell me about the sort of household Cuthbert keeps I think."

Olwen yawned and Winfrith was quick to draw attention to it. "You've made us so welcome, Heafa, that you deserve an interesting tale about our lives and how we came here and I promise I'll do my best to oblige. But as you can see, we've just come from burying Eanflaed, a woman we knew well, and we're still exhausted from the hours of dragging ourselves up hill and down dale yesterday. Perhaps if we have an hour's rest, I'll be able to tell a better story."

Heafa looked disappointed and with obvious reluctance got up and led Winfrith and Olwen to the far end of the room where two straw mattresses lay side by side.

"There are blankets against the wall there. Flaedda can come outside with me and gather some fresh kindling. You'll have a bit of peace then."

"You didn't really want to sleep, did you?" Olwen whispered as soon as Heafa and her daughter had gone.

"No…just a chance to think. Who really wanted both Ourdilic and Eanflaed dead? I'm sure neither death was an accident. What links them?"

Olwen thought for a moment. "They were both women. They both came from Cornwall."

"Enough for most thegns to mistrust them…but did anyone apart from Beorhtric know Eanflaed was Cornish?"

"Maybe not. Some people accused Ourdilic's father of helping the Danes at Wareham, getting Saxon hostages killed."

"There was someone who suggested Eanflaed was capable of betraying us to the Danes as well."

"You mean Raedberht? I heard him. At the end of Eanflaed's burial. He was obviously trying to make Beorhtric angry."

"He succeeded…not that it's hard. Beorhtric would have taken a knife to him if someone hadn't stopped him."

"What I couldn't work out," Olwen said, raising her head and resting on her elbows, "is where Raedberht got the idea from in the first place. Beorhtric doesn't like letting her out of his sight. How would she have made contact with any Danes?"

Winfrith nodded. Did Raedberht have a particular reason for accusing Eanflaed? "It's a good question. At the time I thought he was just enjoying provoking someone known to have a short temper. But now…I'm thinking perhaps there was more to it. The only thing I know about Raedberht is that his Uncle Wulfhere, despite being Alfred's appointed ealdorman in Berkshire, switched his loyalty to Guthrum. That makes Raedberht himself more suspect than someone like Eanflaed."

"I probably shouldn't speak ill of her," Olwen said, hesitating before going on, "but I didn't really like her. She might have given Ourdilic advice about her betrothal, but only because she'd been told to. She was afraid of her husband too and she hardly ever spoke to me. But she never seemed like the sort of woman to take risks."

"You might be right, Olwen, but how well did we know her? You remember we saw her acting very strangely outside Wedmore...when we thought she'd hidden something?"

Olwen sat up, her voice rising with excitement. "We didn't find anything though. What if she wasn't hiding something but collecting it? We were due to leave the next day. And there's one thing she wouldn't want anyone to know she had. I don't know why I didn't think of it before. What if she'd stolen Ourdilic's morning gift? You could see how much she envied Ourdilic being given it."

Winfrith smiled. She'd been uncertain whether or not to share her suspicions about the aestel with Olwen. She still felt protective enough towards the girl to keep some things from her but this was a reminder, if one were needed, that Olwen was sharp enough and observant enough to work much out for herself.

"It'd crossed my mind too. She clearly admired it and made much of the meagreness of the morning gift she received from Beorhtric."

"Could she have been killed for it, do you think?"

Winfrith glanced behind her, thinking she'd heard Heafa returning but the door remained shut. "I don't know, Olwen. Who else desired it? And why not just steal it rather than risking murder?"

"Perhaps they tried and Eanflaed fought back."

Winfrith rolled back the blanket and sat up, her back against the wall. It was clear neither she nor Olwen were inclined to sleep. "Whatever happened to her took place on the causeway. If someone she knew did attack her they must have been behind us."

"Like Beorhtric, you mean?" Olwen said.

"Him and a few others. The trouble is, finding her body was a shock. I didn't really notice who came along after us. And I'm not sure it was anything to do with the aestel because that doesn't explain Ourdilic's death. No-one would have taken her all that way up to the cliff top just to take it...certainly not Eanflaed."

"Perhaps Beorhtric lured her up there to make stealing it easier."

Winfrith thought back to the night Ourdilic disappeared. Beorhtric had been outside, drinking with friends. He'd seen her pass but whether or not he might have followed Ourdilic was impossible to know.

"I didn't think he'd done it at the time. I suppose I couldn't see he had a good enough reason."

"You thought it was Aethelwold then, didn't you…because he found out she was pregnant?"

Winfrith nodded. "It gave him a reason, though whether he had the courage to do something like that…and anyway, the father of the child, Aethelnoth, might have wanted her silenced just as much."

"But if the same person was responsible for both deaths why would either of them have attacked Eanflaed? And anyway Aethelnoth wasn't with us on the causeway."

"As far as we know," Winfrith said. "Don't forget he's ealdorman of Somerset. He's supposed to know these moors and marshes like the back of his hand. But you're right. I can't see he'd have anything against Eanflaed."

"Perhaps he made her pregnant too."

Winfrith couldn't help smiling at the thought. "He does think he has a chance with any woman. I've seen that for myself. I doubt if Eanflaed would have encouraged him though. Too scared of Beorhtric for one thing...and she's never so much as hinted that she'd borne a child."

"So what are we going to do?" Olwen asked.

"Hope that Alfred takes the death seriously enough to look into it. I overheard him talking at the burial. I'm almost sure he was telling Cuthred, the new ealdorman of Berkshire, to find out what had happened to Eanflead. I might go and look at the grave again. See if anyone revisits it. It might at least show if anyone was upset by Eanflaed's death. I've seen no sign of it so far."

Any idea Winfrith had of carrying out her plan straight away was halted by the return of their hosts. Heafa came bustling into the room, groaning under the weight of an armful of firewood, and Flaedda followed, dropping a similarly large bundle of sticks and branches on the floor before retiring to a chair in the corner of the room.

"Awake already?" Heafa asked, laying down her own burden and nudging the two heaps together with her foot. "Eat first; sleep later. That's what I always say. Not that food's plentiful with all of you visitors here. I'm sure I can manage some soup though. Flaedda can help me get it ready."

The soup was a long time coming. Heafa was too full of questions about Alfred, about Cuthbert and about life in a lord's hall to work quickly and Flaedda seemed in no mood to hurry her mother along. The result was that it was well into the afternoon before Winfrith and Olwen set off up the hill towards where Eanflaed had been buried. Where they could they kept in the shadow of the trees lining the path, hoping not to be noticed if anyone else had the same destination in mind. Once they stopped to look back across the marsh, their attention caught by a flock of starlings, a dark flowing mass wheeling and circling across a pale sky.

They reached the ridge beyond which the ground flattened out without seeing anyone. The freshly turned earth of Eanflaed's grave stood out against the grass and had attracted a pair of crows, pecking impatiently at the soil. Winfrith ran towards them, flapping her arms, and they flew lazily up into a nearby tree, waiting patiently to resume whatever they had found to feast on.

"No-one here," Olwen said, joining Winfrith at the graveside.

"I didn't really expect it," Winfrith said. "I couldn't think when I was here yesterday. I thought coming back might help me decide who might have done this."

"And has it?"

Winfrith took a deep breath, slowly blowing it out again. "At first I was convinced it was Beorhtric, then I persuaded myself Aethelwold or Aethelnoth had better reason to silence both Eanflaed and Ourdilic, now I'm not even sure it wasn't someone else altogether."

She felt Olwen take her arm. "We won't give up though. We'll never know if Eanflaed was pregnant or not but the aestel might show up somewhere. Whoever had that would have some explaining to do."

Winfrith smiled. It was definitely time to stop thinking of Olwen as a child. "Of course we won't," she said. "Someone believes women are easily silenced. Well we'll teach them otherwise. Come on, back to Shapwick. From now on we keep our eyes and ears alert. Guilty secrets have a habit of escaping sooner or later."

17

Heafa was waiting expectantly by the door as Winfrith and Olwen emerged from the tunnel of holly trees.

"You've been gone a long time," she said, twisting her long face into a smile. "I was beginning to think we'd lost you."

"Just stretching our legs," Winfrith said. "We'd a lot to think about."

"Well come on. Get yourselves inside and you can tell me all about it. Flaedda's grinding flour and we shall have some flat cakes later on."

Heafa stood aside to let them pass. The harsh scraping of a quernstone coming from the far end of the room suggested Flaedda was indeed occupied as her mother had suggested, though it was difficult to make her out clearly with only the glowing fire and a single flickering oil lamp giving any light.

"I have some news as well," Heafa said, waving them towards a wall bench near the fire and setting down a stool for herself facing them. "My sister has been to visit her daughter in Chilton. You won't know it but it's a poor place…half a dozen windswept houses and as miserable a bunch of people as you'd meet anywhere."

"Sounds a place to steer clear of," Winfrith said, holding her hands out towards the fire.

"And so it is," Heafa continued, "and all because Aethelnoth has a house there. Chilton folk think they're too important to have anything to do with us."

"Except for your sister," Olwen said, yawning.

"Well that's what I was coming to," Heafa said. "Usually she…"

"Did you say Aethelnoth?" Winfrith said, realizing she too had not been giving Heafa her full attention. "The ealdorman of Somerset?"

"Who else? That's what I was telling you. My sister visits her daughter perhaps once a month. She rarely comes back with much to tell us. Her daughter is quiet and no-one else in Chilton talks to her…until yesterday that is. Not that anyone told her anything then. It's just who she saw there. You'll never guess."

"As long as it wasn't Guthrum," Olwen said, beginning to sound irritated.

"Don't be foolish. We wouldn't still be sitting here if it had been. It wasn't him, it was Beornhelm, Aehelnoth's wife."

Winfrith did her best to hide her surprise at the mention of Beornhelm. So Aethelnoth's wife was nearby. She'd arrived in Cheddar very shortly after Ourdilic's death too…not that she was going to tell Heafa, not until she'd had the chance to think it over.

"You told us Aethelnoth has a house there," Winfrith said. "I suppose she must visit from time to time."

"Not often. She prefers Frome. Mind you, she stirs up enough trouble on the few times she is there. There are enough soft-headed women in Chilton who'll listen to her."

"It can't be easy being married to Aethelnoth. He's always on the move and it's well-known he can't keep his eyes off other women."

Heafa gave Winfrith a searching look. "It's true enough. She ought to rope his ankles together. He's tried it on with you, has he?"

"He regretted it," Winfrith said, smiling at the memory. "He retreated from the skirmish in some discomfort."

"Now that's a story I'd like to hear more of. It must surely bear repeating."

"There's little more to tell," Winfrith said. "Olwen appeared and he went off as if nothing had happened…which it didn't really. Anyway, you were telling us about Beornhelm stirring up trouble."

Heafa rubbed her hands together, clearly enjoying herself. "The older she gets, the stranger she gets. It used to be just accusing different women of bedding her husband. She'd scream at them, sometimes scratching and kicking until someone stopped it. Often they hadn't even set eyes on Aethelnoth. Then she started calling on God to punish them, and when that didn't work she turned back to the old beliefs. My sister says she persuades women to join her and they chant strange words and sacrifice hens."

"She sounds mad," Olwen said, stretching her legs closer to the fire.

"But still the ealdorman's wife, which means some folk listen to her," Heafa said. "Now what I'm wondering is why she's here now, just when Alfred arrives unannounced in Shapwick. They say

Aethelnoth's been seen too and riders have been in and out of Shapwick like hornets round a nest. Something's going on, isn't it?"

"I don't know, Heafa," Winfrith said. "Just the king hunting for safe winter quarters I think."

"So far away from the long halls and fineries he's supposed to have? Times must be bad if he's planning to stop here. Mind you, Guthrum won't find it easy to follow. They say a blind man finds his way easily round his own house while a sighted stranger trips easily on a stool."

"You can see why Alfred had to put some distance between us and Guthrum. He's short of fighting men...especially since Aethelnoth's men left."

"You can't blame them for that," Heafa said. "Marching the country for a month with no pay. They've families to feed and roofs to mend."

"I suppose so. Guthrum's probably too comfortable in Chippenham to chase us into these bleak wastes in the middle of winter anyway."

"Let's hope so." Heafa stood up suddenly, perhaps deciding there was no more to be learnt without the encouragement of some food inside them. She moved swiftly to the far end of the room where Flaedda was now idly stirring water into whatever she had been grinding. Winfrith could just about make out her pale face as the girl looked up, startled by her mother's sudden approach. A burst of flame from the fire lit up the girl's face and it struck Winfrith that Flaedda was younger than she had first supposed... probably not much older than Olwen. To judge from the look she gave Heafa, it would not be long before she began to rebel against her mother's tyranny.

Once the flat cakes had been spooned onto the stones which ringed the fire, Heafa resumed her seat opposite Winfrith and Olwen and Flaedda joined them, casting occasional shy glances at the two visitors.

"You had a woman drowned, I hear," Heafa said, leaning forward to push one of the cakes closer to the heat. "A thegn's wife too. That must have upset a few folk."

Winfrith nodded. She would rather not have talked about Eanflaed but the smell of the slowly cooking cakes reminded her how hungry she was. Heafa was providing her and Olwen with comfortable beds and was sharing her supper with them. The least she deserved was some good company.

"Not so many," Winfrith said. "Her husband, Beorhtric, didn't like her befriending others. She was from Cornwall as well...never likely to make her popular with Saxons. I don't think she was very happy. She and Beorhtric were constantly arguing."

"Any wife should be used to that," Heafa said, flipping the paler side of the cakes towards the fire. "What man doesn't like the sound of his own voice? It's not a good enough reason to drown yourself though, is it? There'd be no wives left in Wessex if we all threw ourselves in a lake the moment a husband shouted at us."

Winfrith nodded, content for the moment to let Heafa draw her own conclusions. Of course she would assume Eanflaed had taken her own life. She'd not seen the bruised cheek or the shallowness of the water.

"I'm sure you're right, Heafa. It doesn't...it's...most wives just learn to put with it."

Heafa was quick to seize on Winfrith's momentary hesitation. "So you don't think she drowned herself? So that leaves only accident or murder and I never heard of anyone falling off the boardwalk in broad daylight unless they were drunk or blind. She wasn't either, was she?"

"Not as far as I know."

Heafa leaned forward, her eyes wide with excitement. "Then it was murder? Someone pushed her off the walkway and held her under the water perhaps? Who would do that?"

Winfrith did not answer straight away, despite the eager hand laid on her sleeve and Heafa's obvious curiosity. Olwen raised her eyes sympathetically to the rafters and even Flaedda looked up from the fire long enough to reveal an interest in the answer.

"I'm not saying it must have been murder," Winfrith said, turning to Heafa and choosing her words carefully. "Eanflaed...that was the woman's name...didn't seem the sort of person to drown herself, that's all." For once Heafa was slow to reply. The room was not well lit but just for a moment Winfrith thought she had seen a flicker of recognition in Heafa's face at the mention of Eanflaed's name.

It didn't take Heafa long to find her voice again. "So it must have been that husband of hers, the one with the violent temper. I'd have done the same for mine if he'd ever stuck his head near water. He didn't need my help in the end. Drank a month's ale at one sitting and never woke up."

"Leaving you and Flaedda to fend for yourselves."

"We were used to it even when he was alive. Never had time for anyone but himself. It's not surprising we had no children of our own."

"Flaedda's not yours then?"

Flaedda looked up at Winfrith, just long enough for her to see something other than shyness in her eyes...defiance perhaps.

"I was born for something better than this," she muttered. Heafa watched her for a moment, then turned again to Winfrith, speaking more gently now.

"It's true...in a way. We took her in as a babe and told everyone she was our daughter. Her father paid us to keep it quiet."

Heafa, perhaps reluctant to say more, reached forward to test whether the flat cakes were ready and motioned to Winfrith and Olwen to help themselves. They were hard and dry and chewing them made talk nigh impossible until the cakes were finished.

"A cup of ale to wash them down?" Heafa asked and without bidding Flaedda got up and went to pour drinks for them all.

"So does Flaedda's father never come to see her?" Winfrith asked, once they were settled again.

Heafa shook her head. "She's not the only bastard child he's fathered. He's wealthy enough to keep us in bread and a roof over our heads but he's no interest in seeing her."

"He's too busy," Flaedda said. "He doesn't have time."

"So you know who your father is?" Olwen asked. "I hardly remember mine."

Flaedda looked towards Heafa and it was clear neither was eager to answer the question. Eventually Heafa decided she ought to be the one to do so.

"She does...as does most of Shapwick by now. It's impossible to keep a secret in a place like this. We don't talk about it much though. We don't want to lose the food or the house."

"It can't hurt your father if people know," Olwen said, "especially if he's giving you a home and food."

"It's not as simple as that. I suppose I'll have to explain now you know most of it. The truth is there's someone else to think of. That's why I was telling you earlier about Beornhelm, the woman my sister saw in Chilton."

"Beornhelm? Aethelnoth's wife? What's she got to do with it?" Even as she asked the question Winfrith arrived at the answer herself.

"That's the one," Heafa said. "Not a woman to get mixed up with."

"And she would be very angry if she knew Flaedda was Aethelnoth's child?"

"And that her husband was paying to feed and house her," Heafa added.

"If everyone here knows, and she's not far off in Chilton, won't she find out sooner or later?"

Heafa shrugged. "Chilton and Shapwick folk rarely speak to each other and no-one's keen to speak out against Aethelnoth. An angry ealdorman could make their lives very difficult. I think the secret's safe, as long as neither of you two let it out."

"Of course we won't," Winfrith said. "It's a shame for Flaedda though, not seeing her father. Was her mother from Shapwick?"

"Aethelnoth wouldn't say who she was," Heafa said, looking thoughtful, "only that she came from distant parts and that the child's birth had been kept from her family. I did wonder why. Perhaps she was married. It wouldn't be the first time Aethelnoth had chased someone else's wife."

Winfrith turned to look at Flaedda, wondering why she had thought her face resembled Heafa's. She had assumed they were mother and daughter but, unless Heafa was hiding her own infidelity, there must be hints of someone else in the eyes or nose or mouth. Flaedda did not return her gaze and in any case the firelight was not strong enough to allow a thorough study. It occurred to her that another reason the birth might have been concealed from the family was that they were not villagers but people of rank. Perhaps the wife had been mistreated by her husband and had looked for comfort with someone else. Someone like Eanflaed in fact. There was nothing she knew of to link Eanflaed and Aethelnoth of course and she had more or less dismissed the idea when Heafa sent her daughter to refill the ale jug. Hearing Flaedda's name spoken aloud suggested something obvious. The names Flaedda and Eanflaed were similar enough to suggest kinship. And hadn't she thought Heafa had reacted when she'd named Eanflaed as the dead woman? When the girl returned Winfrith searched her face again, looking for a likeness, but if it was there she couldn't make it out.

"Anyway, that's enough about us," Heafa said, taking a long swig of ale. "You were telling us about the thegn's wife. Are you sure her husband didn't drown her? Who else could it have been?"

"I don't know, Heafa. Perhaps she fainted or fell ill. We've walked a long way in the last few days."

It was clear Heafa was not very satisfied with this answer, but Winfrith resisted the temptation to add to it. The less Heafa knew, the less there would be to gossip about. She might have said more if she'd seen any sign that Heafa's interest was because Eanflaed had been Flaedda's mother but neither she nor her daughter seemed very concerned about Eanflaed's death, merely curious.

"But you don't think it was an accident. I can see it in your face. And your girl, Olwen, is troubled by it too."

"I'm not worried," Olwen said sharply. "She's buried now and nothing can change what happened."

"She's right," Winfrith said. "We can imagine what we like, but we weren't there. So, unless anyone stands up and swears they saw what happened, that's the end of it."

She'd spoken more forcefully than she'd meant to but it had the desired effect. Heafa frowned but swiftly recovered her temper and began a long story about a feud between two of her longstanding neighbours.

Winfrith woke early and, slipping quietly from her bed, crossed the room and helped herself to some of the leftover flat bread. No-one else was stirring and it seemed the perfect chance to carry out a plan she had been mulling over since the mention of Beornhelm the previous evening. Was it mere chance that had brought Beornhelm to Chilton at the same moment Eanflaed died or were Winfrith's thoughts about Eanflaed, Flaedda and Aethelnoth more than just vague possibilities? The only way to find out was to make the short walk to Chilton and speak to her. Heafa would want to know why she was so interested of course…all the more reason for setting off before she woke.

She emerged from the tunnel of holly into the daylight. Immediately she felt her spirits lift. A few thin feathery clouds streaked a pale blue sky and a creamy sun was beginning to make its presence felt. Frost marked out the dips and hollows, sending up a satisfying crunch of grass as she crossed them. She walked briskly, easing the stiffness from her bones and enjoying the view towards Westhay, where wisps of morning mist drifted across the marshes toward the purple line of hills beyond.

Once she was well clear of Shapwick Winfrith began to think about how she could introduce the subject of Eanflaed to Beornhelm without betraying her own suspicions. Something she hadn't thought of before was Flaedda's age. If Eanflaed had been her mother, she must have been very young when she gave birth. Not that that would have troubled Aethelnoth from what she knew of him. It would though have been an added reason for Eanflaed's family to keep it quiet.

As Heafa had said, Chilton and Shapwick were not far apart. It was still early morning when Winfrith reached the top of a short rise and saw the rooftops of six low houses below her. They were ranged in a wide circle around what might once have been a pond but which was now a muddy hollow fringed by brittle straw-coloured reeds. A haze of blue smoke hung over the houses and from somewhere beyond them Winfrith could hear the dull rhythmic thud of an axe falling.

She was still some fifty paces off the first house when a black dog dragged itself onto the path and limped towards her. Its warning bark did not sound too threatening but it was enough to bring a grubby-faced girl to the doorway. She stared at Winfrith for a moment before a shout from inside sent her dashing off around the dried up pond and out of sight behind the house opposite. A stout, red-faced woman emerged after her, waving her fist in the direction the girl had gone. She was about to go back inside when she caught sight of Winfrith and stood watching as she edged past the now silent dog and approached.

"Who are you?" she said as Winfrith drew level with her. "We don't see strangers much up here. They're not welcome."

"I mean no harm. I was looking for Beornhelm. I was told she'd been seen here."

The woman regarded her suspiciously. "What would you want with that old battle-axe? There aren't many choose her company."

"She and her children came to my house when they passed through Cheddar. I thought since I was nearby they might return my hospitality."

The woman gave a contemptuous laugh. "Hospitality? Beornhelm? You'd get more out of a beggar in rags. The only folk here who'll sit with her are a pair of old crones who share her mad ideas. You'll find them there now, over in the long timbered house you can see. You're wasting your time though. You won't get any sense out of her."

Winfrith thanked her and hurried round the edge of the pond, the limping dog trailing in her wake. The door to the timbered house was not firmly closed and she could hear Beornhelm's voice, loud and measured, as if she was delivering a speech. She nudged the door open far enough to squeeze through. As soon as she was inside she recognised Beornhelm at the far end of the room…the red face, the wild hair and the broad hips just as they had been in Cheddar. The only difference was that she had exchanged the plain woollen clothes for a brightly-coloured gown. She was seated on a carved high-backed chair and facing her Winfrith could see the backs of two women and a child who looked very like the girl who had run off when she arrived in Chilton. None of them appeared to have noticed Winfrith's entry and it seemed a good idea not to disturb them. Listening to Beornhelm for a while might provide her with an idea of how to get her talking about her husband and perhaps about Eanflaed and Ordilic. She crept over to one of the gnarled posts supporting the rafters and sat down with her back against it.

"Nothing is like it was in the old times, is it?" Beornhelm demanded, spreading her arms wide. "Famine, disease, Danes killing our menfolk and carrying off our women. Unfaithful husbands, thieving children, greedy landlords…but we know the cause, don't we? Why has everything gone bad?"

"Because Erce is angry," one of the women replied.

Beornhelm nodded vigorously. "That's right. Erce is angry. The days are darker and the earth stays cold. And we know why. We have forgotten Hretha, mother of the Saxons. How is she to defeat winter if we don't feed her?"

Both her listeners murmured their approval.

"What use is this God of monks and priests? Does Guthrum pray to him? Of course he doesn't. And look how these Danish invaders thrive…living in our best houses, feeding on our bread, taking what treasures we've gathered. Our troubles began the moment we abandoned our old ways. Anyone with eyes can see that."

Beornhelm paused, taking a deep breath and gathering the coloured gown tightly around her shoulders. "Spring will be here soon. The plough waits, the oxen are stirring, the seed is ready. Remember the good harvests you used to have. Why was it? Why did Erce nourish the seed and Eostre warm it?"

Winfrith was suddenly back in Twyford, a small child listening to but not understanding the complaints of the old women. She smiled at the memory of these once familiar names.

"You stopped feeding them and famine came. Once bread was placed in the ground and blood on the hearth. Now you…"

Winfrith was knocked aside as the door flew open and the stout woman Winfrith had seen earlier barged into the room. She advanced quickly down the room, shouting as she went.

"Don't listen to her. She's only trying to cheat you out of your own bread and a fowl or two. Just like she gets that girl there to steal from honest folk. Just wait till I get my hands on her."

"You'll do no such thing," Beornhelm said, coming to meet her before she could get near the girl. "You should be careful who you accuse of thieving. Don't forget my husband is still ealdorman of this shire. There are punishments for folk who spread lies."

The woman laughed, continuing to advance until she stood face to face with Beornhelm. "Your husband? Punish anyone here? When was the last time he set foot in this place? And what did he do when he was here?"

Beornhelm's cheeks reddened and she clenched her fists. "I'm warning you…"

"Warn all you like," the stout woman said. "He won't come here again. The child he left needs feeding and clothing. He doesn't like parting with money."

Beornhelm turned to look at the two old women still seated in front of her. "Listen to her. Believes in an old lie just to try and get money. My husband hears it all the time. No wonder she's stout…takes everything she can and grumbles when a hungry child begs a crust."

"Steals a crust," the stout woman shouted. "At least I know where my husband is. You two should have more sense than to listen to this mad goat's nonsense. Try putting some bread in the ground. No old god eats it. Dig it up and see. It rots. Food's for eating not wasting, and certainly not for giving away to those who have plenty already. You're fools, all of you, and as for that girl, keep her out of my arm's reach or she'll regret it."

She turned and headed for the door. Winfrith waited for her to pass, before stepping from behind the post and heading towards Beornhelm. If she was going to speak to her and get back to Shapwick in reasonable time it might be a good idea to do it before Beornhelm resumed her lecturing of the two old women.

18

It was not a promising beginning. Beornhelm fixed Winfrith with a hostile stare, planting her hands on her hips and drawing herself up to her full height. The two old women looked nervously over their shoulders as Winfrith approached.

"Who are you? No-one asked you in, did they?"

"Don't you remember me? You and your children stopped at my house in Cheddar only a few weeks ago. I gave you food and ale."

Beornhelm took a step forward, screwing up her eyes. Suddenly recognition dawned. "Of course…the spriggans. It's all coming back to me now. The girl lured off the clifftop and her young friend unable to believe what had happened to her. That's it, isn't it?"

Winfrith smiled. "That's right. The friend, Olwen, is with me now in Shapwick. I heard you were here so I thought I'd come over and see how you and the children were."

Beornhelm frowned. "Nothing better to do than gossip, Shapwick folk. I wouldn't stay there any longer than you have to. Here we have as little to do with them as possible."

The two old women nodded furiously. "We keep to ourselves."

"I didn't mean to disturb you," Winfrith protested. "I just hoped you'd all got back safely and that you managed to find your husband after all the trouble you went to."

The mention of Aethelnoth did little to improve Beornhelm's mood. She glared at the two old women, as if daring them to challenge what she was about to say. "Ealdormen lead busy lives. Their wives have to travel to see much of them. It can't be helped. Anyway, you didn't come here to talk about my husband I'm sure. My children are as noisy and tiresome as when you last saw them, so if there's nothing else we have business of our own here."

"I'm glad they're well. As it happens I was slightly curious about Aethelnoth. I thought you might be able to answer a couple of questions for me. Nothing serious…just to satisfy my curiosity. We could have a few words after you've finished here if you like."

Beornhelm considered this for a moment, before taking Winfrith's arm and guiding her towards the door. "I don't know what business of yours my husband is but you better ask whatever it is you want to know away from flapping ears. Those old crones might look half dead but they'll repeat everything they hear."

To Winfrith's surprise Beornhelm did not wait once they were outside but set off towards a grassy track which disappeared into a small copse. Winfrith hurried after her, doing her best to put her misgivings about where they were heading aside. They quickly emerged from the trees onto a low ridge which sloped gently downwards in front of them. At the foot a wooden walkway twisted its way through a patchwork of reeds, sedges, silvery channels of water and scars of blackened peat towards the distant pale grey of the sea.

"See that?" Beornhelm said, stopping to survey the view. "My husband knows that like the back of his hand. No-one will find him there if he doesn't want to be found."

"I hope he comes back. Alfred's much in need of him now. Otherwise what's to stop the heathens coming this way? They'll take everything you've got."

"He'll be back, when he's ready. He gets tired of Alfred preaching at him. God has brought all these hard times on us because of our sins. You must do this and that to get to Heaven. Look at Guthrum. Danes don't believe any of it and they have food, ale, warmth and silver. Folk have forgotten the old ways. That's why there are famines and sickness, not because we don't spend hours on our knees in prayer."

Beornhelm gave Winfrith a fierce look, as if daring her to disagree.

"My father would have agreed with you ," Winfrith replied, smiling. "He had no time for monks and bishops. They live better than most and give nothing in return he'd say. But it doesn't really matter if your husband shares Alfred's faith does it? If he doesn't fight to save Wessex, Guthrum will overrun it and we'll all be killed or made slaves."

"He'd have to find his way here first. Not many do. It's easy to get lost and the tides and marshes often trap the unwary."

"That's true enough," Winfrith said, suddenly seeing a chance to introduce Eanflaed's name into the conversation. "We lost one of our own on the way here….fell from the walkway somehow and drowned."

"Look at it from up here," Beorhhelm said, waving an arm along the line of the horizon. "Plenty of traps for the unwary. You're not the first to arrive here without someone you set out with."

"You might know her. Her name was Eanflaed, wife of Beorhtric, one of Alfred's thegns. He'd have fought alongside Aethelnoth I expect."

Beornhelm nodded, though as far as Winfrith could see the mention of Eanflaed had not sparked any strong reaction. "I've seen her a time or two on the rare royal visits to Somerset. Not much liked, was she? Thought marrying a man with a big mouth and a few hides of land would get her noticed. Wasn't above lifting her skirts for tanners and ploughboys I heard."

Winfrith said nothing, taken aback by the accusation, even if it was probably no more than malicious gossip. She'd seen no sign of Eanflaed chasing other men. She had surely been too afraid of Beorhtric even to think of it.

"She wasn't always easy to get on with," Winfrith said at length, "but I never saw her even look at a man other than her husband in that way."

Beornhelm shrugged. "Well she won't be troubling any of them again, will she?"

"She won't," Winfrith said. "These are hard times for women. She's the second to have died before her time recently. You remember when we met in Cheddar the body of a girl, Ourdilic, had just been found."

"Fell over a cliff in the dark, didn't she? It seems neither of them had much respect for the dangers lurking around them."

"They didn't expect to die though. It's odd that it should happen twice among the same group of travelers."

"Folk have forgotten the spirits that still live in the forests and marshes. No-one with sense walks in them alone, especially at night. The cliffs at Cheddar and the Sweet Way aren't places to linger in."

"You know Eanflaed fell from the Sweet Way? I don't remember saying that."

"How else would she get here?" Beornhelm said, clearly irritated. "There's no other way to get here from Cheddar."

She could have fallen, or been pushed and held down, before they got to the Sweet Way, but one look at Beornhelm's face was enough to persuade Winfrith not to pursue the point.

"I suppose someone will miss her," Winfrith said, trying hard to sound as though she was merely thinking aloud and not leading up to anything in particular. "Beorhtric is without a wife now. Still, at least there's no child to grieve for her mother. I know what it's like to lose a mother when you're still young. All villages seem to have someone who's had to face it. In Shapwick, where we've halted our journey, a girl in the house we share never knew her mother."

"Half the women in Shapwick have bastards. There's hardly a child there knows its father."

"This girl seems to think her father was high born. Her mother gets money for food and shelter from somewhere. It could be the girl's father."

"More fool him," Beornhelm said, turning round as if she intended to return to the house. "There's no-one in that place worth supporting."

"Aethelnoth must look a bit more kindly on them though? He must collect rents and service from the men who own land there."

Beornhelm gave Winfrith a searching look. "He has as little to do with them as possible. You seem very curious about my husband. Why's that? If I hear the pair of you have been up to anything you'll have another scar or two to add to that one."

"You won't. There's nothing to hear. Not about me. But perhaps that's why you said what you did about Eanflaed? Did you suspect they'd been up to something?"

Beornhelm stepped towards Winfrith, angry now. "That's why you're so nosy about Aethelnoth is it? You think just because this Eanflaed had a wandering eye my husband must have been one of her conquests. What's he going to be accused of next? Befriending the queen? Siring Alfred's children maybe?"

Winfrith backed away. "I'm not accusing him of anything. I'm just trying to understand what happened to Eanflaed."

Beornhelm grabbed her sleeve, pulling her close enough for Winfrith to catch the sour reek of her breath. "What happened to her had nothing to do with my husband. Do you understand? Anyone who says otherwise had better watch out. I'd forget all about that woman if I were you. Everyone else will. She can't be helped now."

"You're probably right," Winfrith said, gently loosening her sleeve from Beornhelm's grip. "I just feel sorry for the girl, Flaedda. She may have had nothing to do with Eanflaed but she deserves more than slaving away for the woman who took her in."

Winfrith watched Beornhelm's face, hoping for a sign that the name Flaedda meant something to her, but she showed no surprise, turning away with the obvious intention of heading back towards Chilton.

"That's Shapwick for you," Beornhelm said, setting off downhill. "Treat children as slaves and slaves as beasts of the field. Stay long enough and they'll have the king digging vegetables."

Winfrith watched her go, unsure whether she had actually learned anything at all. Could Beornhelm be right about Eanflaed lying with other men? It would be a dangerous thing to do with a husband like Beorhtric but if he had found her out it would have given him a good reason be angry with her and perhaps in his rage he had gone too far. Asking him about his wife's faithfulness would probably yield as much information as asking Beornhelm about Aethelnoth had done and probably provoke just as much anger. Yet answers about how Ourdilic and Eanflaed had died wouldn't be got by sitting silently at Heafa's fireside. Winfrith looked out across the marshes before taking a deep breath and setting off after Beornhelm.

She passed swiftly through Chilton, seeing few signs of life despite it being almost midday. The walk back to Shapwick at least gave her time to reflect further on the four names she had at one time or another thought might have had reason to want both Ourdilic and Eanflaed dead. Beorhtric hated anything Cornish and might, if Beornhelm was to be believed, have found his wife to be unfaithful. Beornhelm herself might have got the idea that her husband could not be trusted with either Ourdilic or Eanflaed. Aethelnoth might have feared his wife was about to discover he had got both of them pregnant. That left Aethelwold. He might have regretted his betrothal to Ourdilic and even found out somehow about the child she was carrying. Might he have been tempted by Eanflaed and then afraid she might let it be known? Winfrith kicked impatiently at a drift of dead leaves. Aethelwold was not easy around women and, as for the others, it was all mights and could haves. She still had nothing that could push anyone nearer to a confession. There was only one thing for it. She would have to tackle Beorhtric again. Whether he had killed his wife or not, her death must have affected him. His quick temper could easily lead him to say more than was wise. He'd certainly not take the accusation that his wife had been free with her favours lightly. She smiled to herself, quickening her pace. She wasn't going to give up just because Beorhtric was easily angered.

Beyond Chilton the path entered a dense copse, winding its way up and down a series of shadowy hollows. Here and there small clearings had been cut and narrow shafts of winter sunlight slanted across the ground. The dull thudding of an axe sounded somewhere ahead of her and then ceased as quickly as it had begun. A brief breath of wind lifted a handful of dry leaves, scattering them across a patch of flattened grass. Winfrith quickened her step, eager to be clear of the gnarled tree trunks and twisted branches hugging the hillside. There ought at least to be birdsong among the trees but even the birds seemed to have deserted the place.

Ahead of her, jutting into the track, was an ancient moss-covered boulder. She remembered passing it on the way to Chilton and hurried towards it, sure that it meant she would soon be out in the open again. She squeezed past, looking up at a small patch of sky overhead. The next moment she caught her foot and felt herself falling into a tangle of branches. She flung out her arms, feeling her knees scrape over a log as she pitched forward. Small branches dug into her as her elbows hit the ground. She lay for a second, cursing her carelessness in not looking where she was going. Before she could move a fearsome crack sounded above her, followed immediately by the creak of splitting wood and the swish of pine needles sliding past neighbouring branches. She looked up in alarm. A dark tree trunk was falling rapidly towards her. There was no time to move. She turned her head aside, shutting her eyes, waiting for the impact. There was a deafening noise as something thudded into the back of her head and everything descended into blackness.

She wasn't dead…unless of course she was dreaming something was crawling up her neck. She tried to reach up and brush it off but her arm wouldn't move. She tried looking down to see why but it was too dark to make out anything. It must be night time then. She raised her head a few inches, relieved to find that at least was possible. Something brushed against her hair and she was suddenly aware of the strong scent of pine all around her. Gradually where she was and what she was doing here began to make sense. Walking to Chilton, Beornhelm, the falling tree…that was it. She shuddered at the memory of the falling trunk and the moment she thought was going to be her last. But she was still breathing and thinking. She tried wriggling her fingers and toes and was reassured when she felt them moving. She twisted her ankles from side to side and flexed her knees as far as they would go. She arched her back and attempted to bend her arms, convincing herself that, though she was trapped by the fallen tree, she had suffered nothing worse than scratches, bruises and a bang on the head sufficient to leave her with a headache.

It took her a minute or two to realize that while one arm was caught up in a tangle of branches she could lift the other. She reached up, feeling the pricking of pine needles on the back of her hand. Her eyes were blinded by a sudden shaft of light as the branches parted. So it wasn't night. That was a relief, as was the discovery that no part of her felt weighed down by the trunk itself. It had to be the lighter side branches which were pinning her down.

She lay still, considering the best way to try and free herself without further injury. She was still undecided when she heard someone shout. Her first thought was that someone had seen the tree fall and heard her cry out. She was about to call back but at the last moment checked herself. What if the voice belonged to whoever had cut down the tree? She'd stumbled on a tree trunk which had not been there on her outward journey. Had it been placed there deliberately, so that a second tree, already half cut, could be felled where she had tripped? She thought she'd heard the sounds of an axe as she approached the copse. Someone could have been lying in wait…Beornhelm perhaps. She'd set off back to Chilton ahead of her and might have been much more concerned about Winfrith's talk of Eanflaed and Aethelnoth than she'd shown.

"Anyone there?" The shout came again, high pitched...too much so be Beornhelm. It was swiftly followed by the noise of snapping branches and then the thuds of an axe blade biting into thicker wood. Winfrith tried to roll onto her side, allowing more space to free her trapped arm. If it wouldn't budge she'd have to answer the shouts or else risk being caught by a careless blow of the axe. She felt her sleeve rip as she tried to tug her arm free. Whoever was wielding the axe paused to listen. There was no choice for Winfrith now but to announce her presence.

"Be careful," she called back. "I'm trapped in the branches."

"Who are you? Show yourself," a voice answered, sounding more afraid than threatening. He might have been surprised by hearing a woman's voice or perhaps he was scared of what sort of creature he was about to face. Winfrith allowed herself a quick smile. He didn't sound as though he was coming to finish her off.

"There's nothing to be afraid of. I was caught when the tree fell. My arm's trapped. My name's Winfrith. I was just walking back to Shapwick."

There was no response for a few moments, then the thudding of the axe resumed. Winfrith waited until she felt the branches holding her arm shake before calling out again.

"Be careful. You're very close now." She could hear smaller branches being snapped off and then there was the sudden glare of daylight as the branches above her were held aside and a face stared down at her. Her rescuer was young, no more than fifteen years old she guessed. His cheeks, red with effort, were flanked by a tangle of black hair and his eyes regarded her with obvious disbelief.

Winfrith smiled up at him. "Thank God you came," she said. "I'd never have got out of this without help."

The boy didn't answer. Climbing onto the pine trunk, he scanned the trees behind him before calling out to someone Winfrith couldn't see.

"It's a woman. Come and see."

Winfrith wasn't sure who she expected to appear but it certainly wasn't the ealdorman of Somerset himself, Aethelnoth. He stepped out from behind a broad oak and cautiously approached. Perhaps it wasn't so surprising to find him here. This was his shire after all and no doubt he was keeping an eye both on his wife and on Alfred and his men. Winfrith was less sure what he'd make of her presence here. She'd left him in some pain the last time they parted and she was in no position to fight him off this time. He patted the boy briefly on the shoulder, stepping up alongside him and looking down at Winfrith. He slowly raised his eyebrows when he saw who it was, then ran his fingers through his hair and Winfrith had the fleeting thought that it was thick and black just like the boy's.

"You again," he said, a grin spreading slowly across his face. "You do seem fond of wandering remote paths alone."

19

Aethelnoth stood watching Winfrith for a few moments. He was clearly enjoying himself and she felt some relief that he had not sent the boy away.

"You'd be safer if you travelled with company," he said, making no move to free her.

"That depends on who the company was," Winfrith replied, tugging again at her trapped arm.

"Ours is not good enough for you then?" Aethelnoth turned and grinned at the boy. "Perhaps we should leave her in peace."

"It would be a shame to waste all your efforts. A few more small cuts and I can be on my way. I'm obviously not very welcome around here."

Aethelnoth scratched his chin, pretending to give the matter serious thought. Winfrith watched him, trying to decide whether he had been responsible for the fallen tree. If he had killed Ourdilic and Eanflaed, he'd want to silence anyone accusing him. Yet if he meant to finish her off, he'd surely not want the boy to witness it?

"A little gratitude wouldn't hurt," he said. "If this lad hadn't seen the tree falling towards you you'd have been stuck here for good."

"I'll thank one of you to get me out of here," Winfrith said, struggling to contain her impatience. "It's not my fault if you've got some careless tree fellers hereabouts."

Aethelnoth studied the fallen tree for a moment. "It's a very old tree and not the first one to come down this winter. A bit of breeze would be enough."

"Someone was cutting trees down as I entered the wood. I heard them. You two had an axe with you too."

"We didn't cut it," the boy said hurriedly. "We were over there." He pointed vaguely to the trees behind him.

"Well if you cut my arm free we can look, can't we? It's easy enough to tell if an axe brought the tree down."

The boy glanced at Aethelnoth who nodded his agreement and he set to work cutting through the remaining tangle of branches. It did not take long and Winfrith was soon able to sit up and begin the task of rubbing some feeling back into her numb arm.

"There, you survived," Aethelnoth said. "You might not be so fortunate next time."

"I'll just have to hope someone who is as concerned for my safety as you is watching again, won't I?"

Winfrith caught the barest hint of irritation on Aethelnoth's face before it broke into a smile. He turned towards the boy, spreading his arms wide. "See what we men have to put up with? Who but a woman could be so ungrateful? We rush up here, blister our hands hacking our way through this tangle, save the woman from a night tormented by woodland demons and what do we get in return? No thanks and a hint we tried to land the tree on her skull in the first place. Who'd be a man, eh?"

The boy looked uncomfortable, staring down at his feet and saying nothing.

"He's welcome to my thanks," Winfrith said, nodding towards the boy. "He's the one risked getting the blisters." She reached out towards the pine trunk and, grasping the base of one of the cut off branches, tried to pull herself to her feet. She had barely lifted her weight from the ground when her arm gave way and she slumped back onto the grass. The boy stepped swiftly forward, reaching for her elbow too late the break her fall.

Aethelnoth stood by while the boy helped Winfrith to her feet. The thegn held out his arm towards Chilton. "You won't get far in that state," he said. "Come back to Chilton and get some rest."

"I'll be fine," Winfrith said. "Shapwick's not far. May be your lad can come with me a bit of the way."

Aethelnoth shrugged. "As you wish. I can't see why anyone would choose to take a boy before a man, but then what man does understand how a woman thinks?" He shook his head and, giving a brief wave, set off back towards Chilton.

Once she was moving Winfrith began to find it easier to move her arm, though a quick look under her sleeve revealed a colourful array of scratches and bruises. The boy, Raedwyn, quickly relaxed once Athelnoth had gone and, prompted by Winfrith's gentle questioning, began to tell her something of his life in Chilton.

"I've always lived in the hamlet," he said, "with my mother and sister."

"But not your father?" Winfrith asked.

"I never knew him. My mother said he went away to fight the Danes and never came back. She doesn't like being asked about him and I don't like to upset her."

"That's a shame. Every boy wants a father to admire. What about Aethelnoth? How is it that you were out with him? You seemed to know each other well."

"He visits Chilton from time to time. All the young men listen to him. He tells stories of battle and teaches us the right way to use a spear and shield."

They were quiet for a moment as they picked their way down a rocky slope leading into a gully lined by thorn trees, bent sideways by long exposure to hilltop winds.

"My father sometimes took me in his cart down to the sea," Winfrith said, once they were on flat ground again. "It was exciting watching ships being unloaded and seeing strangely dressed sailors from other lands. It made life back in my village seem very dull."

"Chilton isn't always dull," Raedwyn said, his face brightening. "There's plenty to keep us busy…ploughing, harvesting, hunting, cutting wood. And then people passing through stop to tell stories of what they've seen on their travels. Like Aethelnoth and his wife Beornhelm…she's there now."

"Yes, I spoke to her…a strange woman."

"Some people are afraid of her, but the old ones like her. She reminds them of how things were before the monks came, before God got angry with us and brought famine and disease here."

"I'm sure even Beornhelm can't prevent those. Every village suffers them some years."

"She can. She says the earth must be fed before ploughing and harvest. Otherwise nothing will grow."

"I see. And does everyone in Chilton share her beliefs? I don't suppose her husband, being one of King Alfred's ealdormen, would admit to such a heathen idea?"

The boy looked puzzled. "Why not? Beornhelm's not heathen. She was born here. Anyway, ask them in Shapwick who has better harvests, us or them? And they have more babies die. We do what Beornhelm says and it brings us good fortune. We have another chance tonight, as long as I get back in time."

They were emerging from the tree-lined gully and Winfrith stopped to look back. "I'll find my own way well enough from here if you want to return now. I wouldn't want you to miss any excitement. What has Beornhelm got you doing tonight?"

"The old ox that ploughs our fields is sick and about to die. Beornhelm says we must take him to the grove and slaughter him there by torchlight. She'll collect the blood and spatter all those watching with it. The more spots you find on your clothes in daylight the better you will eat as the warmer days come near. It will keep the tree spirits from tormenting your dreams too."

Winfrith smiled. It wasn't so different from the tales her neighbours had told her as a child. Her father had scoffed at them and visiting monks had done their best to dismiss them but, left to themselves, villagers still clung on to old ideas. Even so, she was sure Aethelnoth praised God whenever Alfred was in earshot.

"You'll be back well before dark if you turn around now," she said, giving the boy a grateful pat on the arm. "Thank you for seeing me safely this far. I should be able to make out the rooftops of Shapwick fairly soon now."

Raedwyn nodded awkwardly, rubbing his hands together, then, after the briefest of waves, turned and broke into a run.

Winfrith's hopes of returning unnoticed to Shapwick were foiled at the last moment. She had almost reached the sanctuary of the tunnel of holly leading to Heafa's door when a figure stepped unsteadily out of a tumbledown shack bordering the track. Winfrith recognized the gaunt, stooping frame and red hair of Aethelwold straight away. He was joined by three of Alfred's thegns who linked arms, more to keep themselves upright than out of companionship. Indeed, as Winfrith drew nearer she could hear that they were arguing.

"It's no use at all," the tallest of the three said, swaying as he turned to look at Aethelwold. "Ask anyone. See this woman coming? Ask her if she'd like to see your tiny weapon."

His two friends found this highly amusing, laughing loudly enough to drown out Aethelwold's reply. He pulled something from underneath his tunic and for a moment Winfrith, seeing a glint of light on metal, thought he was about to attack the speaker.

Before she could shout a warning, he thought better of it, holding a small knife in the palm of his hand, inviting the others to inspect it.

"It might be small, but if I stick this between your ribs you'll die quicker than from the swing of an axe. This blade will cut through anything."

As she drew closer Winfrith slowed down. She hoped no-one would notice her disheveled state and turn their attention on her as she passed. She was also a little curious to know where this argument was leading.

"Sharp it might be," another of the thegns said, "but look at the handle. It's got flowers on it. It was meant for a woman. Unpicking stitches is all it's good for. Ask this woman. She'll tell you."

Winfrith had almost drawn level with Aethelwold and glanced across at the knife he was holding. The blade was certainly short and the handle, made of polished yellow wood, showed the black outline of what could be small flowers.

"I'm sure it's very useful," she said, trying to sound serious.

"More useful than his own weapon," the tall thegn said, leaning hard enough on the other two to make them stagger forward.

"At least I can stand," Aethelwold said, clearly furious.

"He can stand..." The three thegns collapsed again into fits of laughter until one fell to the ground, dragging the other two after him.

"Look at you," Aethelwold shouted. "Drunk. Can't hold your ale...and jealous because you haven't got a single well-made weapon between you."

"Someone took care making it," Winfrith said, hoping to calm Aethelwold. "Where did you get it?"

"Found it on the walkway across the marshes, didn't he?" the tall thegn said, struggling not very successfully to get to his feet. "So he said. More likely it came from some woman's purse, I'd say."

Aethelwold stepped angrily towards him, pushing him back to the ground. "Are you calling me a thief? Take it back or you'll feel the point of this." He closed his fingers around the knife handle and made a small striking movement towards his accuser. The thegn looked briefly surprised but then a grin spread slowly over his face.

"Just jesting, Aethelwold. Of course you're not a thief. You get angry so easily we can't resist setting you off."

"It's very well made…just like me," one of his companions said, eyeing Winfrith. "Perhaps the lady would like to see." He began fumbling with his belt and Winfrith decided it was time to move on.

"You're incapable even if she liked the look of you," she heard Aethelwold say as she walked away. The argument probably meant nothing…just thegns a long way from home, bored and with no battle to prepare for. The knife had looked like something a woman might carry though. For some reason Winfrith found herself thinking of Eanflaed and her unfinished journey across the Sweet Way. Could it have been hers? There was no way of knowing, but as Winfrith entered the tunnel of holly she couldn't rid herself of the idea that the knife might in some way be connected to Eanflaed's death.

"Where have you been?" Heafa asked, the moment Winfrith stepped through the door. "Olwen's been looking out for you since mid-morning. I've sent her to draw water to give her something else to think about."

"I'm sorry. I went to Chilton. I left early so as not to wake you."

Heafa put down the barrel she had been scraping with a birch twig. "Chilton? What on earth did you go there for? You were lucky to get away without losing the clothes off your back."

"Well I'm back safe enough so there's no harm done. I just wanted a word with Beornhelm, Aethelnoth's wife."

Heafa looked alarmed, glancing across to where Flaedda was hanging birch twigs coated with yeast from the used barrels onto the rafters. She motioned to Winfrith move further away, clearly not wanting Flaedda to hear anything that might be said about Aethelnoth or his wife.

"You haven't been fool enough to tell her, have you?"

"Who?"

"Beornhelm of course…about Flaedda."

"No, Heafa, of course not. She doesn't suspect anything."

"That woman would suspect a saint," Heafa said. "She wouldn't trust her own mother."

"She's reason to be grateful to me. Not so long ago I took her and her children in on a freezing night in Cheddar. I fed them and warmed them up so they were fit enough to walk back to Frome. She was actually almost friendly. Took me out of the hamlet to see the views across the marshes towards the sea."

Heafa frowned. "Doesn't sound like her at all. She'll be up to something. By the time we've washed the yeast off those twigs, she'll be down here after something. What was it you asked her, if it wasn't about Flaedda?"

Winfrith hesitated, undecided about how much to reveal. "I didn't have a plan. It's just that Beornhelm's arrival in Cheddar came at the same time a young girl, Ourdilic, disappeared. Then you told me she was not far away when Eanflaed drowned. It's probably just chance…"

"You think she killed them both then," Heafa said, raising her voice enough for Flaedda to look up from scraping out another barrel. "She's capable of it," she whispered, gesturing to Flaedda to get on with her work, "but even she'd have to have a reason. What had they done to anger her?"

"Nothing," Winfrith said, "probably nothing. She probably had nothing to do with either of their deaths. She'd give any woman she caught looking at her husband the sharp end of her tongue, but I don't suppose she'd go as far as killing them."

"So this girl who disappeared and the woman who drowned, Eanflaed I think you said, were Aethelnoth's…"

Heafa paused in mid-sentence and turned to stare hard at Flaedda. Winfrith followed her gaze, thinking perhaps the girl was paying too little attention to her task but she looked to be still busy at it.

"Why didn't I see it before?" Heafa said. "I should have guessed when you told me the woman's name. I always thought Flaedda's mother couldn't be a weaver or a pig minder. Why bother to hush it up if it had been so? The names are the same aren't they? This Eanflaed of yours was Flaedda's mother. No wonder Beornhelm hated her and Aethelnoth…"

"Wait a minute, Heafa…slow down," Winfrith hissed. "We don't know that and you don't want Flaedda to hear this. We'll never know now unless Aethelnoth admits it."

"He might admit it. If Eanflaed's dead the truth can't hurt her now."

"He won't though, even if it's true. He wouldn't risk Beornhelm finding out."

Heafa did not look convinced. Winfrith herself had her own doubts about Beornhelm. It was Aethelnoth's wife who'd told her Eanflaed's reputation was that of a faithless wife. Given her mistrust of her own husband, it was hard to believe she hadn't suspected Aethelnoth of trying his luck with a handsome woman like Eanflaed.

"Unless Beornhelm already knew and attacked Eanflaed on the Sweet Way."

"He still wouldn't admit to fathering Flaedda," Winfrith insisted. "Nor, if his wife had anything to do with Eanflaed's death, would he want it known. Hardly good for an ealdorman's reputation if his wife's branded a murderess."

"What about Eanflaed's husband then? He would surely know if his wife once bore another man's child. Why not ask him?"

"Because he dislikes me enough already, without me suggesting he's been cuckolded."

"Then I could ask him. He's still here with Alfred, I suppose?"

Before Winfrith could reply there was a thump on the door. It creaked open an inch or two and Olwen called through the gap.

"Someone open the door. I can't put these down."

Heafa looked across at Flaedda, but the girl had already started towards the door without her mother's bidding. She eased it open and Olwen made her way cautiously inside, two almost full buckets of water swinging gently from the pole across her shoulders. She lowered them carefully to the ground, breathing a sigh of relief before beginning to slowly massage her shoulders. Only then did she catch sight of Winfrith and a broad smile spread across her face.

"You're back. I was worried when I woke to see your bed empty."

"I'm sorry, Olwen. I didn't mean to frighten you. I was out walking."

"She went to Chilton, would you believe?" Heafa said, ignoring Winfrith's warning look. "Asking questions about that woman who drowned."

"Eanflaed? Did you learn anything?" Olwen asked.

"Nothing that explains how she died."

"But good reasons for asking the woman's husband a few questions," Heafa said, giving a meaningful nod towards Flaedda.

"I think you'd better leave that to me," Winfrith said. "He does at least know me. I'll just have to be very careful what I say."

Heafa considered this for a moment. Eventually she nodded her agreement. She leaned closer to Winfrith, lowering her voice again. "As long as you tell me what you find out. Don't forget it's me who's clothed and fed the girl all these years."

And had the use of an unpaid servant, Winfrith said to herself. Heafa rested a hand on Winfrith's sleeve, whispering, "Tell him a few shillings towards the girl's keep wouldn't go amiss."

"Let's see if he'll even to speak to me first. If he flies into a rage at the sight of my face, I don't think asking him for money will be very wise. He's well-known for his quick temper."

"Perhaps it was him who…you know…saw off the woman. Found out about her goings on. That would answer all your questions."

"Heafa, don't forget the man's a thegn. He's not a Shapwick ploughman. You can't just accuse a man like that of drowning his wife. Anyway, I think we've talked enough. Flaedda is giving us very suspicious looks. I'll speak to Beorhtric and come and tell you if I find out anything useful."

"Well, just make sure you're not next," Heafa said, heading back down the room to where Flaedda had suddenly resumed vigorously scrubbing out another barrel.

20

Winfrith woke early the next morning, though not early enough to slip out of the house unnoticed. Her arm had stiffened up overnight and a dark bruise had spread from her wrist to just above her elbow. If she did annoy Beorhtric by asking awkward questions about his wife she'd not be well placed to defend herself if he threatened to harm her. It wouldn't stop her though. As soon as she could get away she would go looking for him.

Flaedda was busy stacking bundles of kindling under the wall benches nearest the fire and Heafa cutting up roots to go in soup. No-one took much notice of Olwen as she rolled off her sleeping platform and headed swiftly for the door. It was only when she cried out in surprise that they all turned to look at her. The door was open wide enough for her to pass through but she had halted in the doorway and was reaching up to release something hanging down from the lintel.

She turned back into the room, holding out her hand to reveal a small cloth bundle.

"Who put that there?" Heafa demanded. "It wasn't there last night. Not you, Flaedda…expecting me to walk into it as soon as I went outside?"

Flaedda shook her head, though Winfrith thought she saw the trace of a smile on the girl's face.

"What do you think it is?" Olwen said. "It feels as though there's something inside."

"Then open it," Heafa said. "No need to keep us all waiting."

Winfrith, Heafa and Flaedda gathered round Olwen as she pulled the knotted thread around the neck of the bundle apart and drew out a smaller cloth bag, placing it carefully on the table. As she did so, something small fell out, rolling beneath Winfrith's feet. It took her a moment to retrieve it but when she held out her palm the sight drew gasps of surprise from Heafa and Olwen. A small oval glittered brightly as it caught a rare shaft of sunlight angling through the half-open door.

"It's a crystal," Olwen said, almost dropping the stone in her excitement. "It's beautiful. I've never seen anything like it, except perhaps on Ourdilic's morning gift."

"What's inside the bag?" Heafa said. "There could be more in there."

Olwen seemed unable to take her eyes off the crystal and Winfrith gently loosened the bag from her grasp and felt inside it. Whatever it contained was loosely wrapped in something which felt very soft. Winfrith tugged at it, curious about the hard shape she could feel within it. She barely looked at the strip of white silk she drew out and Heafa snatched it away, tracing her fingers along it as if considering what it might be worth. Winfrith reached inside the bag again, touching first the handle then the cold metal blade of a small knife. She carefully withdrew it from the bag, by which time both Heafa and Olwen had seen enough of its first two treasures to be eager to see what the third would be.

"Look, there are flowers on the handle," Olwen said. "Who'd leave something like that? It's beautifully made, isn't it?"

"It doesn't matter who it is," Heafa said. "They left it at my door. They must have meant me to have it."

Winfrith turned the knife over in her hand, pretending to study it…as if there might be some sign of who it belonged to. She didn't need to of course. She'd seen the knife only the previous evening. Its owner then had looked very unwilling to part with it, despite his companions' scorn. The question was, how had the knife got from Aethelwold to this bundle left tied to Heafa's door and, more than that, what had been the purpose of leaving it there? One thing she was sure of. The bundle was not intended for Heafa, though it might be wise to let her believe it had been.

"You must be curious though," Winfrith said. "Perhaps you have an admirer." She looked at Olwen, expecting at least a smile, but the girl had lost interest in the knife. Instead she had picked up the length of white silk, turning it over in her hand as if she expected to find something concealed in it. It was enough to set Winfrith's heart pounding and the image she had fought so hard to erase from her mind was suddenly back. She was below the cliffs of Cheddar again, standing among dark trees, wanting not to believe she was seeing the white silk sleeves and the frail twisted body of Ourdilic beneath her. She brushed a sleeve across her brow and took a deep breath, certain now that the bundle was meant as a warning.

"At my age?" Heafa said, seemingly unaware of Winfrith's discomfort. "One husband was enough. The last thing I need is another."

Olwen finally laid the silk down again and looked up at Winfrith. A tear slipped from the corner of her eye and she brushed it angrily away. "It reminds me of Ourdilic," she said. "She loved silk."

Winfrith said nothing, laying the knife down alongside the silk and the crystal and trying to decide what the three objects together might mean. Two of them could point to Ourdilic, though the crystal might not be from her morning gift and in any case the aestel had disappeared after Ourdilic's death, possibly taken by Eanflaed. The knife was Aethelwold's so perhaps someone was trying to suggest he'd been responsible for the two women's deaths. If they were, it was hardly a clear message. Neither woman had been stabbed.

The silence finally woke Heafa up to the fact that both Winfrith and Olwen were troubled by the items on the table. "What's the matter with you two?" she said, reaching out to touch the knife handle. "It's not often gifts like these appear out of nowhere."

"Just wondering who put them there," Winfrith said quickly. "I expect Olwen's wondering if she's the one who has an admirer. She's a good-looking girl after all."

Heafa made a great show of looking Olwen up and down. "I suppose a man with a taste for pale-skinned girls without much flesh on them might look kindly on her. So, who's been casting longing looks at you, Olwen? There can't be anyone shy enough to leave gifts without saying who they're from."

Olwen glanced briefly at the items on the bench but before she could say anything Winfrith intervened. "She's a good-looking girl but still young…and she's more sense than to encourage anyone who's too shy to speak. We should keep these and return them once we know who left them here. Don't you think so, Olwen?"

"Wait a minute," Heafa said. "They were left at my door…"

"And everyone knows Olwen lodges here," Winfrith said, "and that she's often the first to step outside in the morning. Alfred's thegns are more likely to favour a young girl than us two widows."

Heafa scowled. "I was handsome enough at her age…turned a few heads back then."

"I'm not surprised," Winfrith replied, smiling. "And perhaps no-one will admit to leaving these little treasures. In that case I'm sure Olwen won't mind you having your pick of them."

"Won't mind? Who says…" Heafa paused, clearly changing her mind about what she was going to say. "Well, let's get on and ask. The sooner we know, the sooner we can decide what to do with them."

"We should start with the knife," Olwen said. "Anyone who's seen it will probably remember it. One crystal and one piece of silk looks much like another, at least at first glance."

"You're right," Winfrith said, "the handle's quite unusual." She tried unsuccessfully to call to mind the faces of the three drunken thegns she'd seen with Aethelwold. All she could think of was that one had been very tall with fair hair. No doubt all three would still be sleeping off the effects of too much ale but there might be some gain in trying to question them before their heads had cleared.

"We can take it to Ceolfa's two old long houses. It's where most of Alfred's thegns are lodged. One of them's bound to have seen it before," Heafa said, reaching behind her to where a woolen cloak hung on a hook.

"Once it disappeared inside one of those houses, you'd never see it again," Winfrith said. "Being thegns, they'd probably accuse you of stealing it as well. We need to be cleverer than that."

"How? They can't say it's theirs if they don't see it."

"There is another way, Heafa. One or two of the thegns here knew my husband. He fought alongside them as their equal. They might be persuaded to say if they've seen the knife without questioning where I got it. Let me try that first. If it doesn't work, we'll think again."

Heafa's disappointment was plain but she reluctantly agreed so that an hour or so later Winfrith found herself heading outside in search of Aethelwold's companions of the previous afternoon.

As she approached the two long houses Heafa had described, Winfrith couldn't help but smile. For once good fortune had put the one man she was looking for in her way. Rising behind the nearest house was a small hill capped by moss-covered rocks.

Sitting astride one of them, looking out towards Westhay, was Aethelwold's fair-haired companion from the previous evening.

"I thought you'd be sleeping off the ale," she called up to him.

He turned his head, rubbing his eyes as if unsure who had disturbed him. "Should be," he said, watching as Winfrith climbed the slope towards him. "Cuthbert's idea of a jest. Give me the early morning watch. I wasn't the only one the worse for wear."

He turned back to look downhill towards where the boards of the walkway snaked away into the marsh. Two figures with water buckets laboured their way up the hill but otherwise the track was deserted.

"Maybe you'll drink less ale next time," Winfrith said. "You seemed to be barely able to walk when I saw you yesterday."

The thegn looked surprised. He stared at Winfrith, clearly struggling to remember. "There's not a lot else to do here," he said eventually, brushing his hands through his hair. "We should be fighting Danes. Running away's for women."

"Like Aethelwold you mean? You seemed to think his little knife should belong to a woman yesterday."

The thegn thought for a moment, then smiled. "Poor Aethelwold. Likes everyone to think he's brave as a king's son should be. We all know he's a coward...easy to pick on. He won't fight back."

"The knife did look well-made. I wonder where he got it from."

"Not from any woman I know. He can hardly speak in their presence, never mind earn gifts from them."

"Perhaps someone dropped it on the way here and he picked it up."

The thegn adjusted his position so that he faced Winfrith. "Not you though? Or are you hoping to claim it as your own?"

Winfrith shook her head. "It's not mine, but I did wonder what Aethelwold would do with it...especially after you and your friends had ridiculed him so much for having it."

"He'll get rid of it. Sell it if he can find a fool with shillings to spare. You could make him an offer if you're so keen to have it."

Winfrith pretended to consider the possibility. It wasn't such a bad idea. Aethelwold knew she'd seen the knife and if he thought there was profit in it he might he might reveal what he'd done with it...always assuming he hadn't left the bundle outside Heafa's house himself.

A shout from the doorway of the nearer of the long houses made them both turn their heads. "Watch the path, not the woman. That's what you're there for."

"Get yourself up here, Beorhtric," the tall thegn shouted back. "My turn for a sleep now. Leave me up here all day, some of them," he muttered, half-heartedly waving Beorhtric towards them.

Winfrith watched as Beorhtric sauntered outside, stretching his arms and looking slowly around him. He bent down to adjust his shoes, then made a great show of brushing bits from his jerkin. Finally he began to make his way slowly up the slope.

"Good to see you're doing something useful, Winfrith," he said, taking the tall thegn's place on the mossy stone. "It makes a change from interfering. Watching an empty track for hours does get very dull without company."

"I'll go if my presence bothers you."

To Winfrith's surprise Beorhtric caught hold of her sleeve. "Stay. Any company's better than none." He studied the path down the hill and the beginning of the walkway, appearing to think company did not require talk. Winfrith allowed the silence to continue for a little while before asking gently,

"Are you missing Eanflaed? Life must feel empty without her."

"What would you know about it?" he asked fiercely, though his anger sounded more tired than threatening. He stared grimly back at the long houses. "It was sudden. She should have had more years yet, even if they'd only been filled with more complaints."

"I couldn't believe it when I saw her," Winfrith said. "The water was so shallow. She should have been able to get out easily."

"But she didn't and she's beyond help now. She wasn't a child…to have her hand held all the way."

"Perhaps she didn't want to get out. That's what folk are saying."

Beorhtric sighed. "All I know is she didn't want to be here. Who could blame her? Surrounded by swamp, stuck in a damp, pokey barn and not a decent meal to be had…who'd choose to dwell in this hole?"

"It's not easy, I know. My husband was killed a year after we met. I was angry that someone had taken him away from me."

"No-one took Eanflaed," Beorhtric said, grinding his heels into the soft turf. "She fell, banged her head and drowned. That's all there is to it."

"So she hadn't any enemies?"

He shook his head. "She had a sharp tongue sometimes, but men don't usually drown someone over a few cross words. You're too fond of looking for riddles where there are none. It was just unfortunate. Not her fate to live longer."

"What about Aethelwold? There's no love lost between you and him."

"What's he got to do with it?" Beorhtric's voice rose almost to a shout and Winfrith raised her hands apologetically.

"I wasn't suggesting anything…really." She paused. "I suppose I've just been thinking about Ourdilic. I know you didn't like her, but she didn't deserve to die so young either."

"She's not missed…nothing from Cornwall would be."

Winfrith decided against reminding him that Eanflaed had been born there too. "She would have been married to the nephew of the king of Wessex if she'd lived."

"They deserved each other. What's it got to do with Eanflaed anyway?"

"I don't know. Maybe nothing. Two young women brought together by a betrothal …two unexpected deaths. It just seems strange, that's all."

Winfrith watched Beorhtric's face, looking for a reaction, but it showed no emotion.

"Aethelwold never looked very sure he wanted Ourdilic as his wife."

"Why would he? He's few enough friends as it is, and the ones he's got only follow him because he's the king's nephew. He'd likely have lost those too if he'd taken a Cornish wife."

"Perhaps he changed his mind about marrying her," Winfrith said, choosing her words carefully. "It would have been difficult to find a way out of it once he'd agreed it in front of Alfred."

Unexpectedly Beorhtric laughed. "What are you saying? That Aethelwold decided to silence her? He wouldn't have the nerve. And what other mad ideas have you got? Since you keep hinting my wife's death was suspicious too, do think he killed her as well? What possible reason could he have for doing that?"

Winfrith took her time answering. "None that I know of. Had they ever argued?"

Beorhtric shook his head. "Not unless you call her wishing him good day and him not answering an argument. She'd better things to do."

"She can't have found it easy…this sort of life. I should know. Women trailing round after an exhausted army, never settling anywhere, uncertain where the next food, bed or heathen attack is coming from. There's little pleasure in it."

"She rarely stopped complaining about it, if you must know. Couldn't wait to get back to the comforts of a king's palace. But a wife's duty is to be with her husband…that's what I kept telling her."

"And now she's gone for good," Winfrith said softly. "She's made her last complaint. At least you're free of that now."

Beorhtric stood up, taking a few steps forward and staring down the path. Shielding his eyes against the low sun, he spent a few moments scanning the approaches to the settlement. "Why did I marry her? I suppose that's what you're thinking. Would I have done it if I hadn't been alone and a long way from home? I knew she'd have me of course. She was just like your friend Ourdilic…eager to escape Cornwall and become someone more important. The truth is I took her knowing all that. And if we argued a lot, we were still man and wife. I didn't wish her dead."

He stood still with his back to Winfrith and, though she couldn't see his face, he sounded as though he meant what he said. At that moment it would have been easy to rule out any chance of him having harmed his wife had it not been for the fact that she'd witnessed his temper directed at Eanflaed more than once.

"And you're sure there's no-one else who might have wished her dead? Perhaps there were enemies her family had made in Cornwall…just like Ourdilic's father."

Beorhtric turned sharply, scowling. "Her father never killed any hostages as far as I know. Besides she hadn't always lived with him. She once told me she'd been sent to live with an older sister for several years. Strangely enough not far from here…Chilton."

The name startled Winfrith. Chilton…just three miles from Shapwick…three miles from where Flaedda now lived. Suddenly the idea that Eanflaed might have been Flaedda's mother was not so far-fetched after all. Yet she could hardly ask Beorhtric outright if his wife had borne a bastard child by Aethelnoth.

"She never talked much about her past when she was with Ourdilic," Winfrith said. "She certainly never mentioned Chilton. Strangely enough I went there yesterday. The shire ealdorman, Aethelnoth, has a house there. Not that he was at home. I did speak to his wife though. I'd met here before in Cheddar, just before Ourdilic died."

Beorhtric returned to his seat on the stone. "Beornhelm? Now there is a woman you could argue with. She could pick a fight with a straw bale. No wonder her husband disappears from time to time."

"He can't be an easy man to be married to. They say round here he's fathered more than one bastard."

Beorhtric seemed to find this amusing and he offered Winfrith a rare smile. "You said you'd spoken to Beornhelm. You must have seen why he'd look for company elsewhere. What possessed him to choose the woman in the first place is beyond me."

"He seems to have chosen a few wives of other men since," Winfrith said, watching Beorhtric's face carefully. There was surely a flash of doubt there before he forced a laugh, shrugging his shoulders and spreading his arms wide.

"What man in his position wouldn't? It's only to be expected."

"So it's fine as long as it's not your wife?"

"If a man can't keep his own wife in check then perhaps he deserves it. Eanflaed wouldn't have so much as looked at him as long as I was about."

But perhaps before you even set eyes on her, Winfrith thought, as a young girl in Chilton she might have caught Aethelnoth's eye and, just maybe, Flaedda had been the result. It raised two immediate questions. How likely was it and had Beorhtric, despite his putting on a convincing show of ignorance, somehow found out? She was still trying to think of a safe way of prolonging the conversation when Cuthbert emerged from the long house and shouted up to Beorhtric.

"Eyes on the track, Beorhtric. You're not up there to gossip."

Beorhtric glared down at him but thought better of an angry reply. Instead he turned to Winfrith.

"You live in his household in quieter times, don't you? Don't know how you stand it. Treats everyone like servants…thegns and ceorls alike. You'd better go. He'll only stand there staring if you don't."

It was an unsatisfactory end to what had been a surprisingly revealing meeting. Winfrith stood up and smiled down at Beorhtric. She hadn't got the definite answer Heafa would expect but the knowledge that Eanflaed had stayed in Chilton increased the chances of establishing whether she'd been Flaedda's mother.

"Thank you for the company," she said. "I hope you're back in front of the fire soon."

He gave a brief nod, swiftly resuming his watch, and Winfrith began to walk down towards where Cuthbert was now leaning casually against the hall doorpost.

21

As she descended the hill, Winfrith thought rapidly about what to say to Cuthbert. He was no more likely to take her concerns about Eanflaed's death seriously than Beorhtric had been. Yet as the widow of one of his loyal thegns and a useful member of his household at Easton he would usually listen to what she had to say. His value to Alfred was clear from the hours he spent training the inexperienced to fight and ensuring that weapons were in good order. It meant he both heard things Winfrith was unable to and could raise concerns with the king himself. He wouldn't be easily persuaded someone had killed twice, but she could at least give him something to think about.

"Distracting the watchman now?" Cuthbert said as she joined him. "I hope he hasn't missed a heathen raiding party."

"There can't have been more than one old woman on the hill since daylight," Winfrith answered, smiling. "I was just asking him about Eanflaed, that's all. I thought he might have been finding it hard…to be without her, I mean."

"And is he? He hasn't looked upset. No more than usual, anyway."

"He's not showing it, I agree, but in his eyes that would look like a sign of weakness. I don't think he and Eanflaed were very happy together."

"Not hoping to take her place, are you?" Cuthbert asked, raising his eyebrows in mock surprise. "You'd be sorely missed at Easton. The place would be in chaos."

"Of course not. He's far too bad-tempered for me."

"And you do like your own way…" He was obviously enjoying himself and would certainly have added more if two thegns hadn't appeared in the doorway behind him. One of them Winfrith recognized as Raedberht and the other, a lanky, gap-toothed youth, she took a few moments to place. Suddenly it came to her. This was Aeshwyn, son of Cuthbert's steward at Easton. Both men carried well-filled saddle bags over their shoulders, as if they were not intending to return to Shapwick that night. Raedberht nodded to Winfrith and tapped Cuthbert's shoulder.

"Time we were going," he said. "We've near enough a day's march ahead of us."

"Where are you off to?" Winfrith asked, not really expecting to be told. "Does it mean we all need to get ready to depart?"

"In a day or two perhaps," Cuthbert said. "Alfred is just being careful. We'll go west towards Pawlet. The ground's high enough to see right across the marshes to the sea."

"Not that there'll be any Danes there," Raedberht said, stepping outside. "They won't go far from the hearth until it's warmer. They certainly won't risk getting a soaking in the marshes."

It suddenly occurred to Winfrith that she might go with them. The long walk might encourage talk, especially about their fellow thegns. They'd take some persuading though. She sighed. "I haven't seen the sea since I was a girl. My father took me on his cart, down the river to Hamwic. I was so excited, hearing the seamen shouting strange words as they unloaded their ships. I'd love to see it again."

"Your father wouldn't have encouraged it," Cuthbert said. "He'd have said you were better off staying at home and mending his clothes or stirring his soup."

"But as you well know he's been dead a long time and I haven't mended any clothes for anyone but myself for years."

"She's not coming with us, is she?" Aeshwyn asked, following Raedberht outside.

"She's just dreaming," Cuthbert said. He took Winfrith's arm, steering her away from his two companions until they were out of earshot. "You can't. The ridge we're heading for is a good nine miles away…and the same distance back. There are hard climbs and steep descents and Alfred expects us back in good time. We can't have you holding us up. Your sight of the sea will have to wait until another day."

Winfrith glanced back to where Raedberht and Aeshwyn waited. "Why should I be any slower than those two? Aeshwyn looks nothing more than skin and bones and he and Raedberht have both got heavy bags to carry. You're not a young man either. I doubt if I'd be any slower than the rest of you."

Cuthbert followed her gaze, taking his time to answer. "You'd be better company than either of them…one full of himself; the other tongue-tied. I suppose there's no harm in taking you along but we can't afford to be waiting for you to catch up."

"You won't have to," Winfrith said, smiling. "I'll just let Olwen know. We'll pass the house on the way."

"I must be getting old," Cuthbert grumbled as Winfrith turned to go, "letting an interfering woman have her own way."

They passed quickly over the brow of the hill above Shapwick, descending down a stony, willow-lined track. They moved in single file, Raedberht at the front and Aeshwyn bringing up the rear. The ground underfoot was uneven but Raedberht was setting a fast pace and several times Winfrith almost stumbled. Already her bruised arm was beginning to ache but she urged herself on, determined to deliver on her promise to keep up with the others. Cuthbert, at any rate, seemed not to notice her discomfort. Indeed he seemed to be enjoying the change of scene, pointing out landmarks as they went.

"We follow this ridge, the Polden Ridge, right to the end," he said, as they passed through another small cluster of rickety houses flanking the track. Pawlet's right at the end of the ridge. The River Parrett runs below the hill it stands on, pointing the way towards the sea."

Winfrith refrained from testing his good mood with questions about Eanflaed. There would be time enough for that on the return journey. Besides, she needed to keep her mind on moving faster than her limbs and lungs were telling her was a comfortable pace. She breathed a deep sigh of relief when they finally topped a low hill to see Pawlet and the end of the ridge ahead of them. The hamlet had no more than seven or eight thatched roofs but it clearly made a perfect vantage point. There were views into the far distance in almost every direction. North west, across a grey expanse of mud flats, stretched a glassy strip of sea while further west, on the far side of the River Parrett, the ancient hill fort of Countisbury rose up above the marshes. To the north only the dark outline of Brent Knoll disturbed the straight horizon.

Cuthbert stopped a little way short of the first house, calling out to Raedberht, "We'll stop here. Food and a short rest, then we'll study what there is to see more closely and question the folk who live here."

Winfrith made herself as comfortable as she could, sitting with her back against a stone and gently massaging her aching hip. Cuthbert remained standing, turning slowly until he had studied every possible approach. By now it was well past midday and from time to time the sun pierced the pale clouds, sending broad shafts of light slanting down onto the distant water.

"No sign of any heathens," Cuthbert said, taking a seat alongside Winfrith, "though we can't see behind Countisbury. We'll take a look from there before we go back."

Raedberht and Aeshwyn sat a little further down the track, their feet dangling over a rocky ledge. A saddle bag lay between them and they were already making short work of hunks of flat bread and what looked like the remains of a duck carcase.

"Greedy pair," Cuthbert said. "There's plenty though…enough for two days. You must be ready to eat after walking all morning."

"In a minute. First I wanted to tell you something…something that happened in Shapwick."

"Important enough to keep us from food?"

"Yes. Someone left a message in Heafa's doorway. It was obviously meant for me."

"What do you mean, a message? No-one in Shapwick can write."

Winfrith smiled. "It wasn't writing…that would have been easier to track down. It was a small bundle containing a crystal from Ourdilic's morning gift, a strip from the dress she was wearing when she went over the cliff and a small knife belonging to Aethelwold. I think someone is trying to warn me to stop asking questions about how Ourdilic died."

Cuthbert sighed. "It doesn't sound like much of a threat. More like an old village woman trying to cast a spell. At least you haven't turned into a toad yet."

Winfrith forced herself to take several long, slow breaths before replying. "That's not all. I walked to Chilton yesterday. On my way back someone tried to kill me. They had blocked the path and felled a tree as I stood trying to see a way through. The trunk just missed my head but trapped my arm." She pulled up her sleeve, holding her scratched and bruised arm in front of his face. "There…look at that. Someone was hoping that was my head."

"She giving you trouble, Cuthbert?" Raedberht called up to them. "Told you this was no job for a woman."

Cuthbert ignored him. "Isn't it more likely the tree feller just didn't see you? It would be a very uncertain way of trying to kill someone."

"Perhaps they didn't want to be seen."

"But you said you were in amongst the trees. Anyone attacking you wouldn't have been seen anyway."

"I know it's hard to believe," Winfrith said, sensing that Cuthbert's patience was running out or perhaps that hunger was getting the better of him. "It's just that when you put the message, the tree, the attempt to drown me, and the odd things about both Ourdilic's and Eanflaed's deaths together…it doesn't look like chance, does it?"

Cuthbert placed his palms on the ground, readying himself to get up. "Even if I thought all this was sinister, Winfrith, who would go to such lengths? Who among us has the time to think up, let alone carry out, murders and attempted murders that all look like accidents? I can't think of anyone, can you?"

"I'd seen Aethelwold with the same knife the day before. Maybe it was him trying to warn me off."

Cuthbert laughed, loud enough for Raedberht to nudge Aeshwyn and say something which made the young thegn smile. "Why? Because he'd done away with Ourdilic and Eanflaed…his betrothed and another thegn's wife? It sounds far too ruthless for Aethelwold."

"Someone else then," Winfrith insisted. "Beorhtric or Aethelnoth maybe."

"Why stop at those two?" Cuthbert said, getting to his feet. "Why not me…or old Mildred…or even King Alfred himself?"

"Because those two don't like women. Beorhtric hit his wife and Aethelnoth thinks he can take any woman he sets eyes on."

Cuthbert studied Winfrith's face for a few moments before answering. "They live hard lives, both of them. They're not patient men either. But I'd think long and hard before telling anyone else either is a woman-killer. You'd need witnesses to swear oaths they'd seen them do it before accusing them and we both know there aren't any. In the meantime, just in case you're right and someone is trying to silence you, I'd suggest you keep some company around you. Despite your habit of stirring up trouble I'd rather not lose you too. And now we'd better get moving or it'll be too dark to see anything at all from Countisbury…unless you'd rather wait here. It's a steep climb."

Winfrith stretched out her legs. Already her aching hip was beginning to stiffen. "I'll come with you. It's only going to get cooler sitting here, and I'd like to see the view anyway."

Cuthbert nodded. "As long as you can keep up. We can't wait."

From Pawlet the climb up to the old hill fort didn't look too hard but as they started to ascend Winfrith began to wonder if she'd made the right choice. There was no clear path and sheep had cropped the grass back almost to the roots. There were not even any rocks or bushes to use as hand holds. Once Winfrith's feet slid away from underneath her and she was forced to advance on hands and knees until she felt secure enough to stand again. She kept her eyes fixed on the ground ahead, searching out anything which might offer a secure foothold. Despite her care she fell again, feeling herself begin to slide downhill until a hand caught at her skirt.

"In need of a helping hand? It's a long way down from here. We wouldn't want to lose you, would we?" The voice was Raedberht's and he shifted his grip from her skirt to her arm, clearly amused at Winfrith's difficulties.

"I can manage," she said, brushing his arm away and raising her head to try and see how much further it was to the summit. The highest point was obscured by an uneven line of earth ramparts, now no more than fifty paces above them and seeming to form an unclimbable barrier. Yet it wasn't that which made her point upwards in surprise. Peering over the ramparts, clearly outlined against the pale sky, were six faces watching their approach with interest. Alongside each one a long spear shaft, the head pointing downhill, rested on the earth bank. Cuthbert and Aeshwyn, a few paces above Winfrith and Raedberht, had stopped and were looking up at the faces on the ramparts, clearly just as surprised to find the old fort occupied. It was Cuthbert who eventually broke the silence, calling out a greeting.

"Good day. My name is Cuthbert…from the house of King Alfred of Wessex. Who is it holds his fort of Countisbury?"

There was a brief discussion along the ramparts before one of the men called back. His deep voice carried well but the words were hard to make out and he had to repeat them before they made sense to the Saxons below.

"Odda's men…from Devon. Watching for heathen ships."

"Odda, ealdorman of Devon?" Cuthbert called back. "He's with you?"

One of the spear carriers nodded, waiting silently as Cuthbert began climbing towards them. Aeshwyn, Winfrith and Raedberht followed, heading towards a narrow gap in the ramparts, lined with blocks of red stone. As they passed through it they saw Cuthbert standing just inside the ramparts and a tall, broad-shouldered man in a flowing russet cloak striding swiftly towards him from the top of the hill. He spread his arms wide in greeting, the cloak catching in the breeze. A hooked nose and deep-set eyes added to the impression of a huge hawk descending on them.

"That must be Odda," Winfrith whispered, though Raedberht and Aeshwyn had clearly already guessed as much.

"Welcome to Countisbury," Odda said, shaking Cuthbert's hand. "You've come from Alfred, I hear. A long journey?"

"Not so far," Cuthbert said. "Alfred is in Shapwick…half a day's brisk walk."

"And what brings him so far from the heart of Wessex? Even the old folk here have never set eyes on him before."

"What brings him here is the same reason your men say you're here for…heathens. There are too many Danes circling Wessex and too many exhausted men defending it. We need to build up our strength ready to fight again in the spring. Coming west allows us to train more men to fight with less risk of facing a surprise heathen attack."

"I wouldn't be too sure of that," Odda said. "The reason we're here is that villagers along the coast are claiming to have seen as many as twenty long boats passing. There's been no sign of them for three days but that doesn't mean they've gone home."

"Twenty? Are you sure? That could be four or five hundred men."

Odda shrugged. "Maybe. Villagers love telling tales and at each telling the numbers grow. Even so, we don't intend to be caught out, so if there are twenty ships, someone will report seeing them again before long. I've got two hundred men of my own on the hilltop, all of them itching for battle. I promise you heathens won't find it easy to pillage Devon. We'll camp here for a day or two, keeping a sea watch but ready to march if Danish landings are reported nearby. You're welcome to join us." He glanced briefly at Winfrith. "Three more men in the shield wall…and help in the kitchen perhaps."

Winfrith scowled at him but Cuthbert was quick to take up the offer. "We'll stay a day or two. If there is a fresh heathen army landing here Alfred will want to know all about it."

There was little or no shelter inside the ramparts and once the light began to go only half a dozen fires to offer any warmth. Odda's men had claimed all the room closest to the flames and, while they showed a passing interest in the new arrivals, they showed no sign of surrendering their places. Winfrith tried to make herself comfortable in the lee of the ramparts, but the ground was dry and stony enough to make the likelihood of sleep seem small. She gathered a few handfuls of spiky grass, spreading it out over any stones she couldn't move. She lay awake for a long time, watching the fires die down and the shouts and laughter of Offa's men give way to snores. She must have slept eventually because when she opened her eyes there was just enough light in the sky to make out the dark outline of the hilltop. She got stiffly to her feet, stretching her arms above her head and trying to shake the cold from her limbs. She reached out to feel the earth rampart and began to edge her way along it, gradually restoring some feeling to her numb fingers and toes. From the inside the banks had been raised to the height of a man's shoulder so that, had it been lighter, Winfrith might just have seen over the top by standing on tiptoe.

It wasn't long before she felt the smooth stone blocks lining the narrow entrance to the fort. She stopped to listen, expecting that Odda would have posted guards in case of unexpected night-time raids. She waited a moment before easing herself through the gap in the wall, but no voice rang out to challenge her. Either no guards had been set to watch or they had deserted their post for some reason. She had a fleeting thought that they might be lying close by with their throats cut but dismissed it once she'd hastily searched the ground on either side of the entrance. She was about to turn back inside when she caught a sudden whiff of woodsmoke and a burst of flame leapt up from a spot a little further along the ramparts. For a moment she thought she must have been right about the guards being taken by surprise. Danes were under the ramparts, planning to break through. But then, why would they stop to light a fire? And when she looked more carefully, as the fire flared up again, she saw that one of the faces lit up by it was Raedberht's.

22

Winfrith stepped swiftly out of sight, easing herself back through the narrow gap in the ramparts. She wasn't quite sure why. Raedberht probably had a perfectly good reason for being outside the ramparts and it was certainly cold enough to justify lighting a fire. She could even have gone and joined him, taking the opportunity of working some warmth into her fingers and toes. He wasn't much liked among Alfred's thegns of course. Some were still ready to accuse him of treachery, of being a step away from joining his uncle Wulfhere and Guthrum. Whether that was true or not, he hadn't gone yet and Alfred obviously trusted him enough to send him on missions like this.

Winfrith began to make her way back to where she'd tried to sleep. A few streaks of grey were beginning to appear above the hills to the east, enough to suggest that others would soon be stirring and to raise the chances of finding something to eat. She soon discovered there was not much to be had. Odda supervised the doling out of pieces of stale, flat bread and small lumps of pale cheese which had long since lost any flavour. Several leather bottles of ale were passed around, each man gulping down as much as he could before it was snatched away by his neighbour. Winfrith had managed to squeeze herself in next to Cuthbert in a circle of perhaps twenty men. By the time an ale bottle was finally handed to her it was streaked with spilt ale and, judging by its weight, not far short of empty. She managed a few mouthfuls but the contents were as thick as soup and left a sour taste in her mouth. At least they would pass one or two fresh springs on their way back to Shapwick.

Perhaps Cuthbert was thinking the same. He cleared his throat, loudly enough to get the attention of all the seated men, including Odda to his left.

"Thank you for the food and ale, Odda. I know it's in short supply. The three of us will set off back to Shapwick shortly. Alfred will be glad to hear news of his ealdorman in Devon."

"Tell him you found us well," Odda replied. "We continue to defend our lands and people against heathen raids…without any help. It's a great drain on our men and our food supplies. Tell Alfred have haven't much more to give."

"He values your loyalty above all else," Cuthbert said. "Not all parts of Wessex have been so true to him." As he said these words Winfrith thought she saw him glance towards Raedberht, now back inside the ramparts and sitting with Aeshwyn, but it might have been no more than chance that had made him pick out Wulfhere's nephew.

Odda raised his arm and in a sweeping motion included all his men in what he was about to say. "We have our way of speaking, our customs and our crafts…different from you men of Wintanceaster…but we're Saxons not Danes. There are no heathens here. We answer to Alfred not Guthrum."

"The king will be glad to hear it," Cuthbert said and looked set to add his own words of gratitude when he was interrupted by a raucous yell from the ramparts. All heads turned to look. One of Odda's men had dropped his spear and was pointing excitedly at something beyond the ramparts. Several of the men in the circle scrambled to their feet and began running down the hill, leaving Cuthbert, Odda and Winfrith to follow at a more leisurely pace.

The sight which met their eyes once they had climbed the flat stones set into the walls was enough to silence all who saw it. A line of ships had already made its way along the river below and the first of them was now coming alongside the wooden jetty at the foot of the hill. The four houses beyond the jetty looked deserted and no-one emerged as the first ship began to disembark. Winfrith counted twenty men stepping ashore, and a further twenty-two ships waiting behind. The first band began immediately to fan out around the base of the hill, staring up at the ramparts.

There was hardly time to question how the ships seen off the coast and which Odda's men had come to look for had managed to arrive at Countisbury unseen. If guards had been posted, they had been either blind or asleep. The second ship was quick to take its place alongside the jetty. It carried fewer men and they were clearly struggling to lift a long pole from the floor of the ship. Their shouts drifted up to the ramparts as they heaved it onto the banks, lifted the narrower end into the sky and drove the base into the soft ground near the water's edge. A strip of red cloth tied to the top fluttered briefly in the breeze before falling still again. It had only offered the briefest sight of its full length but Winfrith had no doubt she had recognized the black shape at its heart.

"That was the raven, wasn't it? The banner woven by the daughters of Ragnar Lothbrok." Everyone knew the story. The banner was planted in the ground before battle. If the wind lifted it, victory would follow.

"It could have been," Cuthbert said, keeping his gaze fixed on it. "Keep the thought to yourself for now. No-one else seems to have eyes as sharp as yours."

"It's probably just an old wives' tale anyway," Winfrith said without sounding quite convinced. Whether it was the raven banner or not it was obvious Odda's men had been caught out and that they were considerably outnumbered by the Danes below. The steep hill and the ramparts might offer some protection but any thoughts of flight or returning to Shapwick were clearly out of the question.

Whatever this Danish army had in mind they seemed in no hurry. Winfrith watched as they unloaded the boats and set about lighting fires and making themselves comfortable. Cuthbert kept her company while Odda went off to deploy his forces around the ramparts, returning with a surprisingly satisfied look on his face.

"They'll have been at sea four or five days," he said, climbing up beside Winfrith and Cuthbert, "and they won't know how many of us there are. They won't be in any hurry to attack."

"They've managed to surprise us once, getting this close without us noticing," Cuthbert said. "Let's hope your men are better prepared if they do."

"Already done," Offa said, clearly irritated. "A man placed every twenty paces around the ramparts and twenty or more armed and ready to hold the entrance. They'll keep their eyes open this time. I'll personally kick downhill any man who fails to spot a heathen even a flea's jump from the bottom of the hill."

Cuthbert looked right and left along the ramparts. "It's not an easy place to attack. They don't look to have sent large numbers around the back of the hill. You'd think they already know there's only one way into the fort."

"They can afford to wait," Offa said. "We'll run out of food and water in a few days."

Cuthbert nodded and the two men watched the comings and goings at the foot of the hill in silence. From time to time one of Odda's men brought him news from other sections of the ramparts but none of it suggested any immediate threat. Cuthbert however grew increasingly restless, occasionally stepping down from his vantage point to walk briskly around the hilltop. Finally his patience seemed to run out and he summoned Odda to join him, just far enough from the men posted along the ramparts to be out of earshot. Sensing he had reached a decision about what they should do, Winfrith went to join them. Odda looked as if he might protest but Cuthbert was quick to wave it away.

"No harm in her hearing. She won't repeat anything," he said. Odda spread his arms, the long sleeves falling almost to the ground, and then folded them across his chest, as if to show he bore no responsibility for what was to come.

"We can't just wait in the hope they'll go away," Cuthbert said. "We must act now, before they've got their land legs. Take them by surprise, like they did us."

"And how would we do that? They'd see us coming the moment we set foot outside."

"Not if it was dark," Cuthbert said.

Odda laughed. "And break our necks? The heathens wouldn't need to put up a fight if we all went headlong down that hill."

"That's true, but look at them now. The more the light begins to fade, the more they're beginning to gather round the fires. There are bits of shelter going up too. If you look over the ramparts at the back of the hill they've passed round it but left very few men there. They're not expecting anyone to descend on that side."

"That's because no-one would," Odda insisted. "There's no gap in the ramparts, no path and it's steeper even than this side."

"But not impossible. We could let ourselves down the ramparts on a rope. There's a sheep track which slants across the hillside. I've marked the place where it passes under the ramparts. It's narrow but with care a man…or a woman…might get safely down it."

"In the dark, without making a sound?" Odda said. "My men have bigger feet than any sheep I've ever seen. We'd find several hundred Danes waiting for as at the bottom."

"I don't think so, especially if we were able to distract the main force down there."

"That wouldn't be easy, with us stuck up here and unable to move."

"There is something that would grab their attention," Winfrith said. "Something that would really make them worry."

"They don't look as though they've a care in the world," Odda said. "Hard to see from up here how anything could change that. Nothing short of a flood would shift them."

"We don't need them to move," Cuthbert said, "just to be busy enough with something by the river to forget the back of the hill altogether."

"And what do you suggest? Sending them down some sides of beef and a barrel of ale?"

Cuthbert smiled. "That might work, if we had any, but I was thinking of something else...something Winfrith spotted."

"The banner," Winfrith said, unable to hide her excitement. "That's what I was going to say. The raven banner. They've planted it by the river, away from the fires. If it flutters they think it means a victory. But what if someone were to creep down in the dark and take it? That would put their camp into turmoil."

Odda's face suggested he thought this idea even madder than Cuthbert's sheep track. "And are you offering to go? You don't think heathens might object to someone stealing their banner?"

"Well if Devon men haven't the courage to try, I think Wessex men might be made of sterner stuff. I'll speak to the men who came with me. One of them might be persuaded it's our best chance of escape."

Odda nodded towards the men lining the ramparts. "They're brave enough, but they're not fools. They'll take on any heathen army but walking into a Danish camp alone is a waste of a man's life."

"Only if they're caught. It will be dark soon. Leave me to think of a way it could be done. A bit of fear and panic down there could only help us get away unnoticed."

Odda sighed but raised no further objection. He turned away, shouting at his men to keep their eyes open as he went. Cuthbert watched him, deep in thought while Winfrith turned over in her mind what he'd said. He'd only come with two others, Raedberht and Aeshwyn, and the latter was surely too afraid of his own shadow to be sent to steal the banner. Cuthbert hadn't suggested going himself, which left only Raedberht. Would he be persuaded to take on such a dangerous task? And if he was, could he be relied on to make a success of it? Winfrith knew the answer to neither question and Cuthbert was clearly in no mood to discuss the idea any further.

"What happens now?" she asked.

"Don't sleep tonight," Cuthbert said. "Be ready to climb the ramparts. Find Aeshwyn and get hold of a good length of rope if you can find one. Wait on the far side of the hill, as near opposite to the fort entrance as you can. I'm going to speak to Odda again. He'll have to decide whether he wants his men to come with us."

Despite darkness having fallen it was soon clear that Odda had decided that Cuthbert's plan, however foolish, was preferable to waiting in the fort until food and drink ran out. As Winfrith looked for Aeshwyn she came across several clusters of Devon men gathered round fires discussing how they could best descend the back of the hill noiselessly. Belt buckles, cloak fastenings and rings might have to be taken off and spears and shields held well clear of each other. Shoes were being tested for grip and for sound, though no-one seemed to have thought of the difficulty of not being able to see where they were going or who was ahead of them.

Aeshwyn proved easier to find than a good length of rope. He sat a little way apart from the ring of Devon men circling a modest fire. A saddle bag rested on either side of him.

"Raedberht's left you to carry both of those?" Winfrith said, joining him.

"He said he'd be back, but that was ages ago. I'm not carrying both if we have to leave in a hurry."

"He can't have gone far, can he?"

Aeshwyn shrugged. "Don't know. He just disappeared."

"I'll help you carry them over to where we're meant to be crossing the ramparts. He can pick it up on his way out of here." Aeshwyn seemed happy to move, once Winfrith had asked the men round the fire for rope.

"The woman wants to hang herself," a voice called out.

"She must have seen your face," another replied. Once the laughter had died down it was clear there was no rope to be had. Climbing the ramparts and dropping down on the outside was not going to be simple, especially when any noise might alert any Danes below.

It was long past the middle of the night by the time Odda and Cuthbert began to direct the exit from Countisbury. Two thegns were lifted up onto the ramparts and knotted strips of blanket used to lower one of them down the far side. No-one spoke but each scrape of a foot or grunt of effort set everyone listening for sounds of heathens waiting at the foot of the hill. Winfrith counted thirty men over the ramparts before Cuthbert signaled that she and Aeshwyn should go next. There was still no sign of Raedberht but in any case it was obvious both saddlebags would have to be left if Aeshwyn was to reach the top of the rampart. Winfrith followed, her fingers scrabbling for the top as Cuthbert hoisted her upwards. An unseen hand grasped her wrist, pulling her up and thrusting the knotted blanket into her hand. Barely pausing the hand guided her forward and she felt her feet fall away and her body slide rapidly downwards until her feet slammed into hard ground. She had hardly regained her balance when she felt the blanket tugged from her grasp and her arm catch Aeshwyn's shoulder as he struggled to his feet.

She held herself still, listening for any sound that might hint at danger, but there was nothing, not even a breeze ruffling the grass or the hoot of an owl. And despite the dark, Offa's men already on their way down might not have been there for all the sound they were making. Perhaps Cuthbert's plan was going to work after all. Even more encouraging than the silence was the sheep path itself. It was narrow, but Winfrith soon discovered the ridge of grass on either side of it was high enough to guide her feet. It meant progress was slow, little more than a shuffle, but it lessened the fear of falling. Not being able to see the drop helped too. She found it easy to imagine there was no more than a gentle slope on either side of her. Now and then she heard the soft footfall of Aeshwyn ahead of her. But for that she could have believed she was alone.

The longer they descended without any sound of a challenge, the more Winfrith relaxed. She began to think about Raedberht. Had he really agreed to attempt the theft of the raven banner? If he'd succeeded, or if he'd been caught in the attempt, it might explain why Offa's men, who must be close to the foot of the hill by now, hadn't encountered any heathens guarding the back of the fort. They'd be glad of an excuse to return to the fires along the river and by the time Winfrith felt her feet emerge onto flat ground it was clear that they had done exactly that. Offa's men, growing in numbers every minute, were so sure the area to either side of the sheep track was deserted that whispered conversations soon grew into excited chatter. It was only when Odda's voice cut through the dark that silence fell again.

"Listen to me," he called out. "The night's not done yet. We can teach the heathens a few things about surprises. They believe we're sleeping behind the ramparts. They won't have weapons to hand. Anyone awake at first light will see the dozen men left to show themselves above the ramparts. The last thing they'll expect is the men of Devon coming at them from the riverbank. We've found our way downhill in the dark. Surrounding the heathen camp should be easier, as long as we keep just as silent. The time for noise will be as your spears are thrust home. We'll show them then what the men of Devon are made of."

Several cheers rang out, quickly silenced by Odda, and Winfrith felt men brushing past her in their eagerness to join their ealdorman. One however hung back by her side and, once they were no longer surrounded, she heard Aeshwyn say softly enough not to be overheard, "We should wait here. This is a battle for Odda's men." She couldn't blame him for wanting to stay out of it and she was grateful for the company. No doubt his time for risking his life in the face of a line of Danish axes would come all too soon.

"We should," she said. "There's not much we could do."

23

Much of the night had already gone but the few remaining hours before dawn passed unbearably slowly. It was too cold to stay still for long and Winfrith and Aeshwyn began slowly making their way around the base of the hill, listening out all the time for the noise of battle. The sounds when they came were sudden, piercing the night air despite appearing still some way off. Though the sky was turning grey to the east, they could see nothing of the attack. There was no doubt it had begun. They halted, listening to the confused shouts, the screams of pain, and the cracks and thuds of violent blows being carried towards them. The noise of battle quickly died away as as it grew lighter dark columns of smoke began to rise beyond the hill. Either the attack had been resisted and fires were being lit or the Danes had been put to flight and their ships and possessions set alight. There was no sign of Offa's men fleeing which was encouraging. With the river ahead of them they'd surely come this way if they'd been driven back.

"Time to take a look?" Winfrith said to Aeshwyn. "It sounds all over."

"What if Odda's men have been cut down?" Aeshwyn said. "They'd kill us too."

"Only if they see us. They won't be looking out for a woman and an unarmed boy if they've just slaughtered the best of Devon's fighting men."

"I'm not a boy," Aeshwyn said. "I just don't see…"

"Then don't behave like one," Winfrith said, cutting him short. "I want to know what's happened even if you don't."

Winfrith set off towards where a track bent round the hill, sure that the heathen landing site and the river would be visible from there. A line of young willow trees led away from the corner of the hill and she made her way carefully along it, feeling the marshy ground cling to her shoes. She hoped that the thin upright branches would provide some cover while at the same time allowing her a good view of the heathen camp. She'd been close to fighting before of course, and heard many accounts of it from her much-missed husband, but the sight that met her eyes as she parted the branches still made her catch her breath.

From the river's edge to the muddy gully just the other side of the willow trees the ground was littered with Danish bodies, some close enough to make out their faces. A few lay neatly, as if at rest, but most were twisted into shapes they could never have held in life. Some stared wide-eyed into the sky while others buried their faces in the grass, as if ashamed. Most bore gashes where flesh was visible or dark bloodstains on their tunics but it was a snapped arm, the whiteness of bone clearly visible, which finally made Winfrith turn her head away.

She had seen thegns returning from battle before, including her own husband Leofranc, and she had known the long wait, hoping he had lived and would return whole, and the grief when she heard he'd been among the hostages killed at Wareham. What she was looking at was no doubt a great victory but at that moment she felt no joy in it. It was the only way to save Wessex, she was sure, and the Danes showed no mercy whenever they gained the upper hand. Even so, what lay before her were perhaps two hundred men who had died in pain, far from home and she would somehow have to summon the will to walk through them to find out if Cuthbert had come through this slaughter unscathed.

Winfrith held her head high, only glancing down when she sensed a body might lie in her way. She could see Odda's men now, mustered along the river bank. A few showed signs of wounds, lying flat on the grass while others applied makeshift bandages, and most bore the marks of heathen blood on their jerkins. As far as Winfrith could see the Danes had been taken by surprise and overwhelmed, and yet Offa's men seemed oddly quiet…as if this had not been a victory at all.

As she drew nearer Wifrith saw that the smoke she'd seen earlier did indeed come from timbers broken up from several of the Danish ships and from time to time heathen shields, axes and items of clothing were being hurled into the flames. Most of these Devon men gave Winfrith little more than a passing glance. Perhaps it was too soon to be talking about what they had just witnessed or maybe they were simply exhausted. It wasn't until she caught sight of Cuthbert, moving among them with a quiet word here and there, that she risked asking exactly what had happened.

"Look around you," he said, drawing her to one side. "It's what happens when you drop your guard. At sea for weeks, grateful to feel your feet on hard ground, thinking your enemy asleep above you, crowding into tents, drinking to forget you're far from home. It was easy to set tents alight and cut down heathens still half asleep and choking with the smoke. They didn't have a chance. No brave death facing a shield wall for them."

"You sound sorry for them," Winfrith said.

He shook his head. "Not sorry…they'd have done the same to us given the chance. Just that there's no pride to be drawn from it."

He turned to survey the results of the night's work and a grim smile spread across his face. "At least the raven banner won't flutter in victory again." The pole lay on the river bank, the base submerged in the water. Tattered remnants of red cloth still clung to the top where the banner had been ripped away. Winfrith went to take a closer look. "Burnt and the ashes thrown in the river," Cuthbert said, following her.

"And did your plan to get Raedberht to steal it work?"

"No need. The tents were alight before they had any idea we were here."

"What will you do now? Return to Shapwick?"

Cuthbert nodded. "Once I've seen Odda's men count and bury the bodies. Alfred will want to know the number of heathen dead. Somehow he'll make sure Guthrum knows the force he was expecting to join him has been slaughtered."

It did not take long for news of the night's attack to spread. Around mid-morning, while Odda's men were busy digging a huge hole in the heavy, cloying soil and bailing out the water which swiftly collected in the bottom, a small group of horsemen appeared on the far side of the river. Winfrith was surprised and not a little irritated when she saw that Aethelnoth was one of them. Yet perhaps it was to be expected that the ealdorman of Somerset would want to know of any threats to his shire. Winfrith watched him stand impatiently on the far river bank, shouting for someone to send a boat over. No-one seemed in any great hurry to oblige and it was only when Odda himself recognized a fellow ealdorman that a boat was sent to ferry him across. Aethelnoth stepped out of the boat in the shallows and splashed his way ashore, striding up to Odda and enclosing him in a tight embrace.

"A fine sight," Aethelnoth said, stepping back and watching as Odda's men began to drag bodies towards the hole they had dug. "Best place for a heathen, under a few shovelfuls of earth. Somerset folk will thank you for a good night's work."

"That's who they have to thank," Odda said, extending an arm towards his men. "They came by night without a sound and cut down the Danes exactly as we had planned. They've Cuthbert to thank too. It was his idea."

Aethelnoth glanced over at Cuthbert, but made no move to greet him. "We're known for our good sense, us Wessex men. I heard Alfred's band were still in Shapwick."

"We keep an eye out for trouble," Cuthbert said. "We don't hide at the first sign of it."

Athelnoth glared back at him, but his face gradually relaxed into a grin. "You would if you were married to Beornhelm. Live to fight another day…it's the only way with a woman like that."

"And the needs of your king are forgotten in the meantime?"

"Not at all. I know where he is and I know who crosses these lands better than anyone. How else would I be here so soon?"

Cuthbert shrugged. "After the fighting's over…that's what your fellow thegns will say."

Aethelnoth took Odda's arm. "They don't understand how we are in the west, do they? Wait till they've spent a winter on the marshes. They'll see why you need friends who can find their way about, track down food and warn of enemies. Alfred will learn the worth of his Somerset ealdorman then."

Aethelnoth looked as though he intended to lead Odda towards the mass grave being prepared for the heathens but as he turned he caught sight of Winfrith.

"You here too? Can't keep away from thegns, can you? Or have you got a taste for attacking heathens now?"

"I'd attack anyone who threatened me…even you…if you remember."

Aethelnoth laughed, though his stare made it plain he was not amused.

"Then it must be Cuthbert who's brought you along for protection. He's not as youthful as he was."

Cuthbert ignored the jibe and for once Winfrith decided it might be wise to do the same. Now that Aethelnoth had turned up again she would seize the chance to watch him closely and, if an opportunity arose, do her best to press him about the pregnancies of Ourdilic and Eanflaed and the fatherhood of Flaedda.

The burials were almost finished. Winfrith sat watching the turgid, brown water of the Parret sliding past. Offa's men were gathering in the lee of the hill, perhaps preparing to return into Devon. As she watched she saw Cuthbert exchange a few words with Aethelnoth, before coming over to speak to her.

"Seems my words to Aethelnoth have hit home," he said. "He's offered to ride with us to Shapwick and make his peace with Alfred. You and I can take two of the horses he came with and he'll return with them later. One of Offa's men will row us across shortly."

"What about Aeshwyn and Raedberht?"

"Aeshwyn can walk. There's nothing to carry. As for Raedberht, he seems to have
disappeared for the moment but I'm sure he's capable of finding his own way back."

The oarsman appeared quite promptly, accompanied by Odda himself.

"Have a safe journey," he said, taking Cuthbert's hand in his own. "We'll be on our way west ourselves very soon. Tell Alfred he should be proud of the men of Devon. They'll never run from heathens."

If Aethelnoth, approaching them now he saw the boatman was ready, heard this he showed no sign, ignoring Odda as he climbed into the boat.

"I'll make sure he knows," Cuthbert said. "I'm sure it won't be the last time he needs your help."

Winfrith leaned back against the side of the boat, suddenly very tired. She glanced back at the freshly turned mound of earth covering the dead heathens. Their cries echoing in the dark and their twisted bodies at first light were still fresh in her mind and she trailed a hand in the icy water, willing them to fade away. She caught Aethelnoth's eye, watching her, but he quickly looked away, pointing to the horses on the river bank ahead.

"Good mounts," he said to Cuthbert. "They'll have us in Shapwick in no time."

His judgment was right about that. They cantered across the short causeway to Pawlet and were soon climbing up to the ridge beyond. At the top the track widened and Aethelnoth urged his horse forward, alongside Winfrith.

"I meant you no harm," he said, smiling, "in Cheddar. I thought you had the same thought in mind…"

"I didn't," Winfrith replied sharply, glancing round to see Cuthbert following some fifty paces behind them. "And you knew it. You just thought any woman was yours for the taking."

"And you showed it wasn't so…painfully enough to stop me trying again."

"And turn your attention elsewhere I suppose? You make a habit of it. That's what they say in Shapwick."

Aethelnoth's horse threw his head back, drawing a curse and a sharp pull of the reins from his rider. "Do they really? Even my horse can't believe it. Who in Shapwick finds me interesting enough to gossip about? Old women I suppose?"

"Not so old…your wife, Beornhelm, for one. She clearly thinks you aren't to be trusted near other women."

Aethelnoth laughed, too loud to suggest he was amused. "You've met her then? She'd accuse a deaf, blind, limbless man washed up on a deserted island of some sin or other."

"So she doesn't have any cause to mistrust you then?"

"Beornhelm's no different from any woman. She's got a suspicious mind. No woman who knew she was my wife would look long at me for fear they'd soon be running for their lives."

Winfrith looked over her shoulder again, checking that Cuthbert was within hailing distance. "Ourdilic looked at you…but she never got the chance to run for her life. Someone made sure of that."

Aethelnoth shot a quick glance backwards, as if it had only just occurred to him that they might be overheard. "What are you suggesting…that Beornhelm pushed her off that cliff? You can't think that. She might make threats now and again but it's her tongue people fear not her strength."

"Are you sure she didn't? She was looking for you in Cheddar. Maybe she heard the rumours about you and Ourdilic."

"That was nothing," Aethelnoth said, keeping his voice down. "She was just a girl."

"A good reason for not leading her on."

"She didn't need any leading on. She knew what she was doing."

"She was just a girl," Winfrith insisted, her temper rising despite her intention to tread carefully with Aethelnoth. "You forced yourself on her."

"So what if I did? She was old enough to marry. And in any case there wasn't any need for force. She planned it all, getting herself lost. It could have been any thegn sent to look for her."

"You weren't sent to get her with child."

"Who says she was? Only Ourdilic herself and no-one believed half the tales she came out with. The only truth is that I shouldn't have had anything to do with her. She was obviously trouble."

"She was a child…and a child among strangers too. She'd hardly lie about being pregnant either. She was betrothed to the king's nephew. Being with child would have put an end to that. Besides, she showed all the signs of being pregnant."

Aethelnoth rode on in silence for a few moments, staring ahead along the ridge. "She was cunning enough to put on the signs. She liked to be the centre of attention."

"I don't think she was pretending. You must have been worried that Beornhelm might get to hear of it. Perhaps it suited you to have Ourdilic silenced."

"And now it's me you think sent her over the cliff?"

Winfrith took a deep breath. "Someone did…and you had a reason."

Aethelnoth threw back his head. "God's bones. Don't you women ever give up? The girl got lost. I know she did. I saw her that night. But I'd no more push her off a cliff than drink goat's piss."

"You saw her? The night she died? Why didn't you say so?"

"And have people thinking I'd gone to meet her? Or worse, thinking I'd harmed her, just like you seem to."

"Then how did you come to see her if you hadn't planned to meet? It was long after dark when she went out."

"By chance. I was coming to Cheddar…late at night to stop Beornhelm following me there. She'd got it into her head I was up to something."

"With another woman? Ourdilic perhaps?"

"Who knows what she was thinking? I didn't ask. I certainly wasn't looking for Ourdilic and I'd almost reached Cheddar when I heard someone ahead of me, clearly in a foul temper and completely lost."

"And it just happened to be Ourdilic, the girl who claimed you'd made her pregnant?"

Aethelnoth nodded, as if he thought Winfrith must understand now. "It was. I don't know which of us was more surprised. I dismounted and tried to offer her a ride back but before I could get the words out she flew into a rage. She began screaming, shouting, kicking and punching…there was no controlling her. It was all I could do to keep her at arm's length. She wouldn't stop and I began to think sooner or later someone might hear."

"So you decided to silence her?"

Aethelnoth pulled hard on his reins, bringing his mount to a sudden stop. "I've spent long enough satisfying your curiosity. God knows why. I did not kill the girl, however annoying she'd become. I pointed her in the right direction, remounted and left her to find her own way back. And that's all that happened. You'd be wise to look elsewhere if you can't rid yourself of the thought that Ourdilic was murdered."

"Everything all right?" Cuthbert called.

Winfrith looked round, grateful that he had begun to close the distance between them. "And where would you suggest I look?" she said softly to Aethelnoth. "Did you see or hear anyone else as you passed through the gorge?"

"No-one," he replied, before looking back towards the approaching Cuthbert and calling out to him. "Everything's fine. Just stopped to make sure you hadn't lost your way. Alfred wouldn't forgive us for losing one of his thegns."

24

If Aethelnoth wasn't exactly warmly welcomed back in Shapwick, Winfrith could see that there was some relief among Alfred's thegns that his Somerset men would again be at their disposal. He was quick to dismiss any hint that he had deserted them at Cheddar, arguing that someone needed to go ahead to smooth their journey west. Alfred chose not to remind him he had left no explanation for his sudden departure, calling for cups of ale for the travelers before they told what they had seen at Countisbury.

Cuthbert's description of the dawn slaughter of heathens made Winfrith uneasy. She found it hard to stop her mind straying to the twisted bodies, the ugly wounds and the bloodstains seeping into the soil. Each detail of the battle scene fired up Alfred's thegns, filling the air with cheers and threats of how they'd inflict the same devastation on Guthrum's men. She knew she ought to be sharing their joy. The Danes had treacherously murdered her own husband, Leofranc, after all. Yet some of the dead faces she had glimpsed had been hardly more than boys…little older than Ourdilic and perhaps that was why she was struggling to accept what she'd seen as a victory.

Being reminded of Ourdilic made her look towards Aethelnoth. He stood beside Cuthbert, saying little but nodding from time to time to confirm details of what they had both witnessed. He'd taken no part in it himself, Winfrith knew, but he avoided having to mention that he'd only appeared some hours after the killing was done. Not that anyone would accuse him of cowardice. Thegns didn't become ealdormen without being able to stand up for themselves. The question in her mind was not his courage, but whether he'd only stumbled across Ourdilic by chance or whether he'd arranged a meeting in order to silence her for good.

"So none escaped," Cuthbert was saying. "One or two of the wounded tried to cross the river but they were quickly swept downstream. I doubt if any of them had the strength to pull themselves out."

"You did well," Alfred replied, "you and Odda. You'll be well rewarded once we've dealt with Guthrum as well. It was a bold plan and will be talked of for years to come. And you're back safely, though without Raedberht I see. You say he set out to destroy the raven banner and dishearten the heathens, but he's not returned with you. Not dead, I hope?"

"He wouldn't be much missed," Aethelnoth said, drawing a reproving look from Alfred.

"Still breathing the last time I saw him. He'll have a good story to tell about his part in surprising the Danes. He's probably stopped somewhere on his way back to spread the good news."

"Gone off to see his Uncle Wulfhere more likely," a voice shouted. "In search of a warm fire and a full plate of food."

"And his friend Guthrum," someone else added.

Alfred held up his hand for quiet. "Let's wait until he's back before we condemn him. And don't forget he risked his life going after the raven banner."

"Which no-one saw him cut down," Aethelnoth said. "And if he did, why would he then disappear?"

"A woman perhaps?" Cuthbert said.

"There's only Pawlet and Chilton on the way back here and I didn't see a woman in either with a full set of teeth or skin that didn't look like leather."

Cuthbert laughed. "Such women make a good audience. Half Chilton will believe he slew the Danes single-handed by now."

"We'll be heading that way shortly," Alfred said. "It won't take long to put them right."

It was time to move on. Shortly after first light Winfrith and Olwen took their leave of Heafa who embraced them both warmly, sad to see them go. Flaedda seemed to have made herself scarce though Winfrith was sure that when she looked back to wave she caught a glimpse of her face in the doorway. They climbed the Polden ridge, making for Chilton, and even though Alfred was still keeping their final destination to himself Winfrith found it comforting to be following a familiar path. It was only when they descended into woodland and they passed stacks of recently felled wood that she became more on edge. The grey bulk of a boulder, half blocking the path, came suddenly into view and caused her to stop. She looked up into the trees, listening hard for the sounds of an axe biting into a trunk but the only sounds were Alfred's men ahead of her dragging their feet through dead leaves. She became aware of Olwen looking back, curious as to why she'd halted, and hurried to join her. As they edged their way past the boulder Winfrith's heart began racing as she heard something thud to the ground somewhere in among the trees. She was sure she saw branches move and there were definitely shuffling sounds as if someone was trying to follow their progress without being seen. She gripped Olwen's arm.

"Did you hear that? Someone's in there."

Olwen looked surprised. "A pig, I expect...rooting out some breakfast."

They both stood listening until Aethelnoth and two others appeared round the boulder and they heard whatever had been in the trees hurry away.

"Keep moving," Aethelnoth said, gently pushing Winfrith forward. "There'll be food and a cup of ale in Chilton once we're out of the wood."

Aethelnoth quickly overtook them and hurried on ahead. Winfrith guessed it wasn't just the promise of ale he had in mind. He'd want to be sure what kind of mood Boernhelm was in before showing himself in Chilton. Arriving in the company of Winfrith and Olwen would certainly have done nothing to sweeten her temper. By the time they stepped out of the trees and into the close-knit circle of houses it was clear Aethelnoth need not have worried. There was no sign of Beornhelm and a skinny girl whose grubby skirt looked in need of repair was already ladelling soup from a large pot. Winfrith accepted a bowlful and ate without much enthusiasm. The greasy liquid was tepid and the tough green leaves more plentiful than the few scraps of eel. Despite that the pot was soon empty and Alfred began urging his men to their feet again.

Winfrith made her way along the wall of the nearest house, bending down to gather up discarded bowls and cups, intending to save the skinny girl a little work. As she straightened up something thudded into her back. She turned sharply but whoever had thrown it had already disappeared down the narrow gap between the houses. She looked down, unsure what she would see but relieved to feel she'd suffered no harm from it. The missile was black and glossy, perhaps the length of her forearm, with a length of twine knotted tightly around it. She turned it over with her foot, revealing the black beak and shaggy throat of a dead raven. But it wasn't the bird itself which set her heart racing but the faded enamel clasp pinned to its breast. It had once been red but the colour had faded and it was marked by several chips and scratches. Yet despite the damage and the rusty bent pin which held it in place Winfrith recognized it straight away and knew that whoever had thrown it must have take it from the small wooden box of keepsakes she always carried. The clasp had been her mother's, one of the few things she still had to remember her by, and she had last looked at it in Cheddar. But who would have done such a thing? And why go to the trouble of pinning it to a dead raven? Before she could come up wih any answers Olwen, seeing her studying the ground, called across to her.

"What's the matter? Have you lost something?"

Winfrith nodded. "Something I didn't know I'd lost has unexpectedly turned up again. It gave me a shock. My mother's clasp…come and see."

"What's it doing pinned to a dead bird?" Olwen asked, screwing up her face.

"Someone trying to scare me off, I expect. Just like the package hung in Heafa's doorway."

"Who'd do something like that…and why now?"

Winfrith thought for a moment. "Someone I've upset recently, I suppose…and someone who had the chance to look in my keepsake box either in Cheddar or since. Whoever it was didn't intend to be seen."

"It's a raven, isn't it?" Olwen said, bending down to look more closely. "Like the Danish banner at Countisbury."

Winfrith reached down and unpinned the clasp, trying unsuccessfully to avoid brushing the glossy feathers. "It looks like it…though what the Danes have got to do with anyone I've upset I don't know."

"You went to see Beornhelm, didn't you? You said she was a bit strange."

Winfrith nudged the dead bird with her foot into a patch of longer grass. "It could have been her, I suppose. She came into the house at Cheddar and might have taken the clasp then. If she knows her husband is back with Alfred she might have meant it as a warning to keep away from him. Not that I'd want anything to do with him," she added quickly.

"Perhaps she killed Ourdilic and Eanflaed for the same reason...to stop Aethelnoth chasing after them," Olwen said.

"She wasn't far away from either of them when they died. I don't know whether she'd go to those lengths though."

"It's not the first time someone's tried to scare us. There was the giant outside the house in Cheddar and then Aethelwold's knife and the bit of Ourdilic's dress outside Heafa's house."

"And the setting me adrift in the river and the tree that nearly cut me in half," Winfrith said, racking her brain for something that might suggest the same hand was behind all the attempts.

"Maybe Beornhelm had help. She wasn't there when we crossed the river and I can't see her chopping down a tree. It was Aethelnoth who found you after that don't forget."

Winfrith stared at the clasp again before slipping it into her pocket and taking Olwen's arm. "We'd better get going or we'll be left behind. Don't say anything about this for the moment. Beornhelm's not here in Chilton or she'd have greeted her husband but she usually comes looking for him if she thinks he's up to something. Once she knows he's rejoined Alfred she'll probably turn up again sooner or later. Let's wait and see if she's surprised to find us still with him too."

Olwen and Winfrith were almost the last of Alfred's followers to leave Chilton and the three thegns bringing up the rear hurried them along, anxious not to be left too far behind. Keeping up the fast pace left little energy for talk and Winfrith turned her mind to considering whether Aethelnoth and Beornhelm, who appeared to be at each other's throats most of the time, might be acting together to frighten her off and perhaps commit murder. They were not often together long enough to hatch a plan requiring such detail and timing, though their appearances seemed to coincide with the warnings and the deaths. Was it possible both were involved without being aware of what the other was up to? Winfrith sighed. The more she learned, the further away from answers she seemed to get. Aethelnoth's admission he'd spoken to Ourdilic the night she died felt the closest she'd come to discovering what happened, but she was at a loss to know how to establish whether he'd done more than talk to her.

A bend in the track brought the main group of Alfred's thegns into view and put an to Winfrith's musing. They had paused to rest, dumping bags and weapons across the track while they sat along the grass bank which flanked it. A leather bottle of ale was being passed along the row and as Winfrith came nearer she could hear Aethelnoth retelling the story of how the Danes were slaughtered at Countisbury and the raven banner destroyed. She noticed Beorhtric was among those listening, though Cuthbert and Alfred stood a little way off. A tall thegn with a fair wispy beard, clearly puzzled by something Aethelnoth had said, interrupted him.

"Cuthbert said it was Devon men who did the killing. It wasn't, was it? They wouldn't have the courage. Run away from a rabbit, I heard."

Aethelnoth glanced round to see who was listening. "It was dark still. Cuthbert wouldn't have seen everything. Odda's men needed a Wessex heart to spur them on."

"And that Wessex heart was yours?" Winfrith said, stopping in front of him.

Aethelnoth was clearly taken aback. He had surely seen her coming, but wrongly assumed she'd pay no attention to talk of battle. "What would you know about it? I didn't see you carrying a spear into the battle."

"Maybe, but from what I saw of Odda's men, they didn't need to call on much help from anyone else."

"All talk," Beorhtric said, gesturing Winfrith away. "I've travelled in the west. Folk there smile in your face while they're picking your pocket. As for fighting, I'd lay six of them on the ground with a hand tied behind my back."

This drew enough laughter to attract Alfred's attention and he called to them to begin readying themselves to move on. Reluctantly men began to pick up their loads and gather round their king who raised an arm for silence.

"We've still a long march ahead of us but we've much to keep our spirits up too. News of the deaths at Countisbury will be on its way to Guthrum. He won't get the reinforcements he was hoping for. The raven banner will never flutter in the wind again, predicting victory. Keep that uppermost in your minds as we prepare to see out the winter and build up our strength. Aethelnoth has rejoined us and his Somerset force can be summoned when we need them. We may seem few in number, but our hearts are strong."

Despite the damp, chilly air and the journey ahead, Alfred's words were enough to raise a few cheers and shouts of encouragement before they started to move off again.

25

The high spirits did not last long. Though Alfred looked confident they were heading for a safe destination he was still unwilling to name it and every extra mile across the flat marshy moors drew grumbles from the more outspoken of his thegns. In the early afternoon he led them onto a track he said was known as the Grey Lake Fosse. It wound its way across Sedgemoor, protected from flooding by earth banks hiding the marshes on either side from view. It was hard to see what progress they were making until the dark outline of barren-looking hill came into view.

Winfrith heard voices raised in excitement a little way ahead and the news soon came back along the line that this was Barrow Mump and they would be stopping where the River Tone wound its way round it. Alfred had promised their efforts in coming so far with him would be rewarded with a celebration too. Waterfowl were plentiful along the river and Aethelnoth, as ealdorman of the shire, would see that houses on the river bank would welcome them.

"As long as we don't stay too long," Olwen said. "Mind you, I couldn't walk much further."

"You're still getting on with it," Winfrith said, smiling. "Think what Ourdilic would have been like."

"She'd have found a horse from somewhere, or coaxed some thegn into carrying her… or turned old Milred off the mule given to him in Chilton."

It was an amusing picture, but a reminder to Winfrith too that she'd got no closer to finding Ourdilic's killer.

"Every journey has its end…this one, your life, my life. Ourdilic's journey was shorter than most but before mine's done I'll do everything to find out why. Once we've settled wherever Alfred's taking us it'll be easier to get on with it."

There were no more than half a dozen houses perched along the river bank, all of them small and appearing to offer little protection against the worst of winter weather. Their occupants watched from their doorways as Alfred's men set about building a fire and skewering the waterfowl and fish that Aethelnoth had exacted from these riverside dwellers. Alfred's promised celebration began with the uncovering of a barrel of honey-sweetened ale from among his supply bags and Olwen fetched Winfrith a generous cupful before it all disappeared down thegns' throats. They found a rickety bench propped against the side of a house and moved it to where they had a good view of the fire without being in the way of any of the more boisterous celebrations. Cuthbert saw to it that they didn't miss out on the freshly roasted fowl and fish which lasted little longer than the time it took to cook.

Whether it was the pleasure of fresh food, the limited supply of ale or the slackening off of the breeze, the evening appeared to be passing with few signs of trouble. Winfrith and Olwen exchanged few words, listening to the rise and fall of voices and the soft lapping of the river against its banks. Towards the end of the evening a few voices grew louder and the occasional curse rang out but it looked nothing serious and a number of thegns appeared to have already been tired enough to fall asleep lying round the fire.

"A few headaches in the morning," she said to Olwen, nodding towards the sleepers. "They'll be in want of feverfew to dull the pain."

"Ivy berries…that's supposed to cure drunkenness."

Winfrith laughed. "That's probably because they make you ill enough to want nothing at all in your belly, never mind ale."

They lapsed back into silence again and Winfrith began to pass the time composing a riddle. She got as far as *I have red tongues, taking many shapes but with little substance* and *I serve masters well who treat me with care* and was trying to find a way of hiding the obvious answer when a violent argument suddenly erupted among the thegns around the fire. Winfrith couldn't see exactly who was involved, though this hardly mattered since she quickly identified the two raised voices. That one was Beorhtric came as no surprise. He was short-tempered enough to argue with a saint. The other getting angry was Aethelnoth and Winfrith knew he was not one to back down from an argument. The rest of the thegns still awake fell silent and the words exchanged carried clearly to where Winfrith and Olwen sat.

"Watch who you're stepping on, pig."

"Stepped in pig shit, did I?"

"Slept with it, more like…that ugly sow of a wife you've got." There was some rough laughter and Winfrith saw one or two shapes, lit by the glow of the fire, rising to their feet.

"At least I've still got mine. What happened to Eanflaed? Got tired of your foul mouth, did she? Or maybe she found someone who could pleasure her better…"

There were brief sounds of a scuffle before the two were pulled apart. The intervention was no doubt enough to prevent serious injury but it didn't stop Beorhtric continuing to hurl threats at Aethelnoth.

"As if you'd know how. None but young girls will lie with you and then they have to be forced. Still, if they complain afterwards you can always push them off a cliff."

"Watch your mouth, Beorhtric, unless you want it filled with a fence post. If it's Ourdilic you're thinking of, we all know who'd like to rid us of everything Cornish. Is that why you got rid of Eanflaed too?"

There were further sounds of a struggle before Beorhtric was restrained. "I'd rid us of the likes of you too. Not so different, are they…Cornish scum and Somerset plough-boys? Sleep with their mothers and sisters for a cup of ale. Little wonder you lusted after a wrinkled goat like Beornhelm and a child barely off her mother's breast."

This time there was no separating them. Winfrith saw sparks fly as two flailing bodies crashed to the ground. A confusion of cries and shouts rang out as arms reached out to drag them clear of the fire. Perhaps it was the shock of the flames or possibly the reek of singed cloth, but both Beorhtric and Aethelnoth were silent for a moment. Winfrith got up from the bench and advanced towards the fire, arriving in time to see Alfred and Cuthbert push the knot of thegns aside and stand over the two fighters.

"Get up," Alfred said, clearly displeased but containing his anger for the moment. "Save your strength for fighting Danes. Dislike each other if you will, but remember you both serve me. Fight again in my presence and you'll be rewarded with what you deserve…nothing."

He watched as the two men got to their feet, brushing themselves down. Winfrith tried to make out their expressions but neither man looked up and the flickering firelight made it hard to tell whether anger, shame or disdain was uppermost in their minds… annoying because she was desperate to see what effect the accusations about Ourdilic and Eanflaed had made on them. One thing was certain. Both men considered the other capable of murder and that at least gave her something to work on once this incident had been put behind them.

"You're an ealdorman, Aethelnoth, appointed by me," Alfred said. "Land and wealth came with that. It can be as easily taken away as given. And you've been rewarded for your service, Beorhtric. You're both men I'd want around me in a shield wall. Remember who you are before you think of pricking each other's anger again."

He turned away, disappearing into the shadows. "Some are easily roused," Aethelnoth muttered. "As for rewards, he should try getting rents or fighting men in Somerset. He won't find anyone can do it better." Beorhtric looked after Alfred, as if he'd something to add of his own but decided on nothing more than a shake of the head and a final glare at Aethelwold before joining those sitting round the fire.

"Come and sit with Milred and me," Cuthbert said, taking Winfrith's arm. "He's in a talkative mood and he finds me a dull audience."

Someone had found Milred a chair and he sat between the fire and the river's edge, a thick blanket draped across his knees. His head was bent forward and his hands fidgeted in his lap but he looked up and smiled when he heard Cuthbert and Winfrith draw near.

"Ah, you're back, Cuthbert…and Winfrith too. There's room for two." He motioned them towards two flat stones, set into the river bank, passing Winfrith a half-filled cup of ale. "We were talking of Easter I think, Cuthbert."

"Not something to look forward to," Cuthbert said, "more folk reminding us of our sins and wanting payment for them."

"And very good for you too," Milred replied, laughing. "I'm sure even you've transgressed now and again. It wasn't that I was thinking of though."

"What put you in mind of Easter, Milred?" Winfrith asked.

"I think it was just the state we find ourselves in. Everything seemed lost. The king was in hiding and his kingdom at the mercy of Guthrum and then, out of the blue, Odda and his men appeared and wiped out a whole heathen force and belief is back. Suddenly we feel Alfred can save us."

"I'm not sure his bishops would like to hear you put it like that. Mind you, if Alfred was the Saviour, Guthrum would make a very good Devil."

Milred couldn't help chuckling but held up a bony hand in protest. "I didn't mean to stretch the comparison that far. After all it would make old Aethelwulf, Alfred's father, God himself and we all know he was far from that."

"If by some small chance he is and he's listening to us, he's sure to send us a downpour hard enough to douse that fire," Cuthbert said, "though Alfred, as his son, should have enough powers to summon it back to life."

Milred rubbed his hands vigorously together. "I suppose I'll be the one setting out on the donkey tomorrow. I hope a better fate awaits me than the rider in the Easter story. "But enough of that," he added hastily. "We're none of us likely to be mistaken for gods."

"Unless it's the god of chatter," Winfrith said, giving Milred an affectionate pat on the shoulder. "If I was one I think I'd settle for being the god of sleep myself."

"Then it's fortunate there are no priests, monks, bishops or men like Alfred and his father to overhear us," he replied, taking her hand, "otherwise we should all be castigated as blasphemers and heretics."

"We'll be crossing the river onto the marshes tomorrow," Cuthbert said, staring away into the dark. "Then we will be in a Godless land. We won't be troubled by too many holy men there."

Patches of sedge, arrowgrass, valerian and black rushes dotted the surface of the marsh, concealing any obvious way through it. Winfrith joined the watchers on the river bank as Aethelnoth shouted across to the other side and almost immediately three long flat-bottomed boats emerged from reed beds and were punted slowly across the water by three stocky pole-handlers who could easily have been brothers. Alfred had clearly been expected though little was exchanged in the way of greeting and in no time Winfrith found herself at the front of one of the punts, nosing its way back across the river and into the marsh.

The boat was low in the water and it was difficult to see far but as soon as they left the river Winfrith felt she was entering a different world, a gloomy place of mists and shadows with few striking features to mark the way. The dull surface of the water revealed nothing but reflections of the massing clouds above. All around her gurgling, squelching sounds echoed each other, with no obvious source. Tortuous streams, seeming to join and divide at will, disappeared behind reeds and rushes, and from time to time the boat broke through into black pools, heavy scents of rotting leaves and roots drifting up from their depths. It seemed impossible that anyone could avoid losing their way. Winfrith glanced towards the swarthy pole-handler trying to read in his face a sign that he knew where he was heading, but his distant look gave nothing away. He simply lifted, planted, and pushed the pole in a steady rhythm, ignoring the complaints of those caught in the occasional spray.

The oppressiveness of the place seemed to cast a shadow over them all, so that before long even the most talkative fell silent and the regular sound of the pole slapping against the water induced, in Winfrith at least, a fresh feeling of drowsiness. Several times she was brought suddenly awake by the prow of the boat ploughing into a tangle of weeds underwater or grazing another thick bed of reeds. On the third or fourth occasion someone shouted a question at the boatman and she looked back just in time to see him nod his head towards something ahead of them. She sat up straighter, straining to see what he might have been looking at, but she was too low down to make out anything other than a murky channel of water flanked by dry, wind-blown sedge. Perhaps the sky ahead, just above the horizon, looked darker but it was probably no more than another threatening storm cloud. She thought no more of it, content to get what rest the boat's rough plank floor would allow, until, looking up again, she saw that now they were closer the dark patch of sky had taken on a more solid form. Spiky tree trunks, some thicker than a man's waist; others no bigger than broom handles, sprouted up from the marsh in a long ragged line. They bore no leaves and the branches, blackened by rain, gave the shore on which they stood a grim, forbidding feel. As far as Winfrith could see, anyone who set eyes on this spot for the first time would hardly be encouraged to take a closer look. If they'd any sense they'd turn back and search out a more welcoming place.

Despite its unappealing look it soon became clear that this grim hump rising above the marsh was where the boatman was heading. He eased the boat into a gap in the trees and the boat rocked as Alfred made his way unsteadily to his side, eager to be the first to step ashore.

"Remember this moment," he said, clutching at a passing branch to still the boat and turning to face his followers. It was not hard to see the uncertainty, resentment even, among them but he spoke with conviction in spite of it. "This is Aethelney…which was kind to me as a child and will be again. We shall be like these alders, living in land and water, being cut back and returning stronger, forming defences that no-one will find easy to breach. When we meet Guthrum again he will find us better prepared than he could ever imagine."

Alfred's thegns showed little sign that they were persuaded, watching him as he splashed his way onto dry land and pushed his way into the trees. He quickly disappeared from view with only the occasional snap of branches indicating his presence. No-one seemed in a hurry to follow and only when Aethelnoth assured them Aethelney was a much more desirable place inside the trees than outside did others begin to disembark and follow.

It did not take Winfrith long to decide that Aethelnoth had exaggerated the merits of Aethelney. Tucked away from the prying eyes of Danish raiders it might be, but it had few comforts to offer. While others started work on shelters, she and Olwen made a full circuit of the island, following the dense alder-brake which lined its edges. They were swiftly back where they had begun and at no point had they been out of sight of the cluster of grey rocks which marked the highest point. It wasn't strictly true to call it an island of course. They had passed a gap in the trees in the south west corner through which they could see a rickety causeway leading out across the marsh. A closer look showed the swampy ground on either side to be so choked with reeds and rushes that even the shallowest boat would struggle to get through it and anyone on foot would surely soon either lose their way or drown. Already several of Alfred's men were busy inspecting the causeway and pointing out where repairs would be needed. Aside from the boat which had brought them here and since departed again, this appeared to be their only way on and off Athelney.

"Looks as though we'll be as hard to feed as we'll be hard to find," Winfrith said as she and Olwen made their way back. Yet there were one or two more encouraging signs as well. They startled a small deer among the alders and heard the occasional calls of wildfowl somewhere out on the marshes. A few shelters put up by hunters remained on the higher ground though these looked too flimsy to keep out the worst of the winter winds and too small to sleep more than half a dozen men. Yet any comfort they could take from the presence of meat was short-lived. They had come across neither spring nor well and the alder branches which were gathered and piled up in a shallow dip protected from the wind produced a smoky, slow-burning fire which gave off little warmth.

"Well at least we've got no more walking to do," Olwen said.

"And time to watch and listen," Winfrith said. "It won't take long for thegns to tire of this place and it doesn't look as though they can go far. Perhaps someone's tongue will be loosened."

"About Eanflaed and Ourdilic you mean?"

Winfrith nodded. "Whoever killed them won't easily be able to put it out of their mind…especially being stuck here with little to do. Keep your eyes and ears open. We're unlikely to get a better chance to catch someone out."

26

Gradually life on Athelney settled into some kind of pattern. Winfrith and Olwen occupied themselves with weaving fresh branches into the walls and roof of the shelter they'd been allotted and stuffing moss and dry grass into any remaining gaps. Cuthbert spent much of his time supervising the building of ditches and stockades inside the alders though, as he complained to Winfrith, his work force was for ever disappearing to answer calls from Alfred. It was impossible not to be aware of the constant comings and goings across the causeway towards East Lyng. No sooner had one band of thegns set off than another rode in and Alfred, Milred and the three ealdormen seemed always to be deep in conversations from which others were carefully excluded. Food proved more plentiful than might have been expected even if the stubborn fires they managed to get going took an age to cook any meat hung over them and the taste of the flesh was often too smoky to enjoy.

If Winfrith was hoping to tempt Aethelwold, Aethelnoth or Beorhtric into saying more about either Ourdilic or Eanflaed she was given few opportunities. The eldorman of Somerset was often required to make contact with other local settlements while Aethelwold and Beorhtric rarely left the company of their companions. Unexpectedly it was through Olwen and her resumed friendship with Aethelhelm that she first learned something new. The young thegn had taken to joining them in the late afternoon, sitting outside the shelter with Olwen while Winfrith retired inside where she could hear them talking without intruding on their obvious desire to be alone.

One evening, four or five days after their arrival on Athelney, Winfrith sat in her usual place just inside the door trying not very successfully to twist lengths of willow into something resembling a basket. Olwen and Aethelhelm had fallen silent and she was just thinking she ought to put her head around the door and check all was well when she heard Aethelwold call out a greeting.

"Good day to you, little brother. Taking it easy while the rest of us work, I see." He made a great fuss of brushing dust and wood shavings from his tunic, before glancing down at Olwen. "Isn't she a bit young…even for you?"

"As old as Ourdilic, and you were set to marry her. What happened? Afraid your friends would laugh at you?"

Winfrith edged nearer the door, eager not to miss a word of Aethelwold's reply.

"What would you know about girls or women?" he said, his voice rising almost to a screech. Even without being able to see him Winfrith could tell he clearly riled. "They don't tell you everything, as you'll soon learn. I'd watch that one if I were you or you'll be trapped in her web before you know it."

"He won't come to any harm from me. A pity the same can't be said for Ourdilic." Winfrith, despite a concern Olwen might push Aethelnoth too far, smiled. The girl had spirit…not so different from the way she'd been herself at that age. "It's not girls who don't tell everything," Olwen continued. "It's the men who harm them. They never admit it."

"I've got nothing to admit," Aethelwold snapped. "And anyway, what if I did change my mind? Ourdilic was no saint. Maybe she wouldn't have made a good wife after all."

"Fortunate for you that she died then. It saved you the embarrassment of having to take back your betrothal promise."

Winfrith put down her half-finished basket, ready to step swiftly outside if the talk got any more heated. There was a short delay before Aethelwold replied and, when he did, he sounded to have calmed down.

"I don't know what happened to Ourdilic. She wandered off on her own. It wasn't the first time. If anyone had it in for her it was Beorhtric not me. He blamed the Cornish for his brother's death at Wareham and Ourdilic made no effort to hide the fact she came from Cornwall and was proud of it. It made Beorhtric furious every time she said a word about it. Try asking him how she finished up dead, though I'd learn to defend yourself better before you do or you might end up the same way."

"Are you saying you know Beorhtric killed her?" Aethelhelm asked.

Aethelwold laughed. "Little brother, you have much to learn. If I did know such a thing I'd hardly tell all and sundry. But there's nothing to tell. It was an accident. That's what everyone believes.

Why make enemies by pointing the finger at me or Beorhtric or anyone else?"

"Because if someone did kill her, they shouldn't get away with it," Winfrith said, emerging from the shelter. "And don't forget Eanflaed's death was straight away said to be an accident, despite the wound she had before she went in the water."

Aethelwold stared at Winfrith for a moment. "So it's you who's been putting ideas into my brother's head, is it? I ought to have known. You might have been a thegn's wife once but Leofranc's long gone. Maybe it's time you stopped meddling where you don't belong."

"Leofranc's got nothing to do with it," Winfrith said, suddenly angry. "Just because a man has enough money or kills enough heathens to be rewarded with land and the king's gratitude, it doesn't mean he's free to murder women and not pay for it."

Aethelwold shrugged his shoulders. "Well, brother, if you're willing to listen to this woman, don't blame me if you land yourself in trouble with Beorhtric. He won't take kindly to being accused of killing his wife."

"Winfrith doesn't tell me what to think," Aethelhelm said. "She…"

He got no further before he was interrupted by a shout from the palisade some fifty paces down the hill.

"Aethelwold, where's the ale?" Two figures appeared from behind it, both carrying axes, and began to climb the slope towards them.

"Well you've been warned," Aethelwold said and headed off to join his fellow thegns. As soon as he was out of earshot, Olwen pointed at his retreating back.

"He's keeping something back," she said. "He used to watch Ourdilic wherever she went…couldn't take his eyes off her. Now he's trying to make it sound as if he thought no better of her than thegns like Beorhtric did. He must have found out about…"

"Not now, Olwen," Winfrith said. "Aethelhelm doesn't need to know that."

Olwen looked as though she was ready to argue but Aethelhelm unexpectedly came to Winfrith's aid. "It doesn't matter," he said. "I know my brother's got plenty of faults so I don't need to hear more examples of them."

Olwen seemed satisfied with this but still clearly had not finished. "All that talk about Beorhtric and Wareham…why did he bring that up if not to turn attention away from himself?"

"You don't really think my brother killed anyone, do you?" Aethelhelm sounded genuinely concerned and Winfrith noticed Olwen shift her position so that, briefly, her hand brushed his. "He's not easy to get along with…awkward and shy one minute; rude and argumentative the next…but that doesn't make him a murderer."

"Nobody's saying he is," Olwen said. "But if he didn't, he's acting as though he knows more about it than he's admitting. Otherwise, why was he so sure Beorhtric knows something?"

"Maybe I could try," Aethelhelm said, looking earnestly at Olwen. "He said I know nothing about women. I could ask his advice…ask him what went wrong with Ourdilic. He thinks enough of himself to be flattered if I seek his help."

Olwen grabbed his hand and then let it go at once, shooting a guilty look towards Winfrith. "That would be perfect. You could see what he knows about Eanflead too."

Winfrith laughed. "You be careful. He may be your brother but he's hardly taken good care of you since you joined us. We've already rescued you once if you remember."

"That won't happen again, I promise. And I will be careful…but if my brother did have anything to do with Ourdilic and Eanflaed dying, I'd like to know as much as you two obviously do."

Winfrith saw little of Aethelhelm in the following days. She and Olwen did their best to keep themselves occupied despite the confined space of Athelney. Olwen picked a flattish oval of wood, discarded at the start of the East Lyng causeway, and Winfrith spent a morning sitting on the grass outside the shelter doing her best to scratch holes around its edge. A pile of willow rods, cut to an even length, lay beside her and she was determined that by the end of the day at least the framework of a basket would be in place. It was not proving as easy as she had expected and she was concentrating so hard that she failed to notice Aethelwold approaching until he spoke.

"Aethelnoth says you're hard to please," he said, glancing behind him as if to check whether he was being watched. Winfrith followed the direction of his look towards the pale wood of the newly-built stockade. If anyone was watching, they were well hidden.

"Then he speaks the truth for once," she replied, resuming her efforts with a needle she wished was sharper.

"A king's nephew could do it, couldn't he? His interest would be worth a smile at least..." Winfrith looked up at him. This was strange, even for Aethelwold. She might have expected some approaches from thegns, given that she and Olwen and a pair of older women from East Lyng who came to cook were the only women among thirty or so men, but Aethelwold was well-known for his awkwardness in speaking to women. At least it would not be too difficult to put him off.

"Aethelhelm only has eyes only for Olwen. You've seen that yourself."

His cheeks reddened but he forced himself to go on. "You well know I didn't mean him. The little..." Whatever name he was about to give his younger brother, at the last minute he seemed to think better of it and stood in front of Winfrith, shifting uneasily from one foot to the other. What might have been annoying suddenly made her smile. He was not afraid of someone watching...he thought they were. Someone had put him up to this. No doubt bored with Athelney, digging ditches and building palisades, some thegn had thought it amusing to wager that Aethelwold wouldn't dare to try and win her favour. Well, if that was the idea she would play along with it, for a while anyway. If he thought there was even a slim chance of winning his bet, that might be enough to further loosen his tongue.

"I knew what you meant." She smiled up at Aethelwold and he looked quickly away. "There is one way you could please me."

He shot her a nervous glance and cleared his throat. "What's that?"

"By telling me something. You said if I want to know what happened to Ourdilic and Eanflaed I should ask Beorhtric. Why did he hate the girl so much? I was supposed to be protecting her so you can see why her dying like that still troubles me. I just don't understand it. She wasn't responsible for what happened to Beorhtric's brother at Wareham, was she?"

"No-one trusts the Cornish. Why would Beorhtric be any different?"

Winfrith pushed the basket base to one side and patted the ground next to her.

"Sit down. Your friends won't miss you for a while yet." He glanced furtively towards the palisade again, before lowering himself awkwardly onto the grass, sitting stiffly and keeping an arm's length away from Winfrith.

"I'm not just being nosey," she said, once he had settled, "and it's not just because I feel guilty about not looking after Ourdilic. You probably know my husband, Leofranc, was also one of the hostages killed at Wareham. He was always a good servant of your uncle, our king. So you see I'm bound to be curious about anything that happened back then. If it made Beorhtric hate the Cornish so much, why did he take Eanflaed as his wife? She was from Cornwall, wasn't she?"

Aethelwold did not reply. He tugged at a loose thread in his jerkin and Winfrith resisted the urge to press him for an answer. He flicked the loose thread into the grass and then, to her surprise, began to speak.

"Look as though we are getting on well. A smile perhaps? Then I'll tell you something, but don't say you heard it from me." Winfrith smiled and briefly stroked his arm as if something he'd said pleased her. Aethelwold looked far from comfortable but he kept his word, speaking so softly Winfrith took a moment to realize what he was saying.

"It's about Wareham. Eanflaed was there when Beorhtric's brother Brigmund was killed."

"But she can't have been. All the hostages were killed. Why would Guthrum have let her go free?"

"Ourdilic said at that time Eanflaed was betrothed to Brigmund. That's why she was there…with him. Beorhtric married her as a way of honouring his older brother."

"Ourdilic told you this? She never so much as hinted at it to me…not even when Alfred sent Eanflaed to prepare her for her betrothal to you. Are you sure she wasn't spinning you a yarn?"

Aethelwold shrugged. "It's what she told me." He shifted his position, disturbing Winfrith's pile of willow rods and hastily scooping them back into an untidy heap.

"But even if it's true, I don't see how Ourdilic came to hear of it. Eanflaed wouldn't have told her. As far as I could see they strongly disliked each other. Perhaps Ourdilic made it up because Saxon thegns were always accusing her father of helping Guthrum so she tried to suggest Eanflaed was no better. She must have thought that if she could persuade you it was true, you'd spread the story among other thegns."

Aethelwold blew out a long breath of air. "I wasn't sure if she was lying so I asked her how she knew. It wasn't Eanflaed who told her. She was there at Wareham herself and witnessed everything. That's what she said anyway."

"That's nonsense," Winfrith said, all thought of satisfying anyone watching Aethelwold with her gone for the moment. "She'd have said something. She knew my husband was there and that I'd have given anything to hear more of his last days. She would have told me she'd been there."

"Not if she was sworn to secrecy. She and Eanflaed were both allowed to leave. Don't ask me why. She wouldn't say. She just insisted it couldn't be spoken of and that she'd be happy if she never saw Eanflaed again."

Winfrith studied his face, looking for signs of uneasiness but if anything he seemed to be gaining in confidence. Perhaps he felt his wager was almost won. Winfrith gave him the benefit of another smile.

"She would have been very young," she said. "No more than ten. Children imagine things sometimes."

Aethelwold shrugged again. "She seemed to remember it well enough."

"What about Beorhtric then? Why did you tell Olwen to ask him about how Ourdilic and Eanflaed died? Was it something to do with both of them having been at Wareham?"

There was a sudden cracking sound from somewhere behind the palisade, a branch snapping perhaps, followed by a muffled curse. Aethelwold looked up, startled, but no faces appeared and everything fell silent again.

"Ignore them," Winfrith said. "They've seen all they need to. So what was it Ourdilic said about Beorhtric?"

"Nothing," Aethelwold said. "But think about it. Those two were allowed to leave Wareham while his brother was killed. If he found out, after taking Eanflaed as his wife, that they'd been there or maybe what they'd done to be let free, he might have been very angry with them both."

If it was true that both Eanflaed and Ourdilic had been in Wareham, how had they got out? Winfrith was sure Ourdilic herself had never given any hint of having been there, neither had Eanflaed. But why keep quiet about it? Whatever they had agreed to, would Guthrum really have let them go?

"Is that why you changed your mind about your betrothal to Ourdilic? Something to do with her being at Wareham?"

"No…nothing to do with that." The question clearly unsettled him and Winfrith decided now was the time to press him harder.

"What then? Something changed your mind. If it wasn't the death of the hostages…"

"It wasn't. I've told you."

"But you watched her all the time, hung on her words, admired her…"

"Until she…"

"Until she what? She was only a girl. What could she do to harm a grown man like you?"

"Got pregnant! That's what…and not by me, if that's what you're thinking. Now do you understand why I no longer wanted her as a wife?"

Aethelwold stared at Winfrith, his eyes wide with shock. He hadn't meant to tell her and in other circumstances she might have felt sorry for him, but now she needed to think fast. At first she had thought only Olwen and she knew of the pregnancy but by telling Aethelwold Ourdilic had surely given him a strong reason to silence her. Marrying a Cornish girl would have won him few friends among Saxon thegns; being cuckolded by her would have made him a laughing stock. She'd heard Raedberht taunting him with it.

"I'm sorry," Winfrith said. "You can't have been expecting that. How did you find out?" She thought for a moment he was going to clam up but once he began to explain he sounded relieved to be telling what had happened.

"It was the night she died. I went to look for her, along the gorge, and I heard her shouting at someone. Thinking she was in danger, I stamped out my torch so I could get closer with out being seen, but it wasn't what I was expecting." He stopped, clearing his throat and pressing his clenched knuckles against his cheeks.

"You heard something?"

"They were arguing," Aethelwold said, struggling to get the words out. "She was yelling, telling him he'd got her with child and he'd have to take her away with him."

"Who...who was she telling, Aethelwold?"

"Aethelnoth of course. Who else? The randy goat. He swore the child wasn't his...swore she was lying, but she kept on at him. He started to threaten her so I called out. I didn't think he'd heard me at first but by the time I found the path again and caught up with Ourdilic he had gone. She wanted to go after him but I stopped her."

"You must have been furious, hearing what she'd accused him of."

He nodded sadly. "I hardly knew what I was doing. I cursed her. I cursed Aethelnoth. I told her never to set foot in Cheddar again. I..." He paused, unable to go on.

"Did you hit her? Maybe she fell against a rock. Is that what happened?"

Aethelwold jerked his head round to face Winfrith. "No...no, I wouldn't. Never." He shook his head vigorously. "I was angry but it was Aethelnoth I'd like to have killed. I was going to go after him but she grabbed at my clothes and wouldn't be shaken off. She said I'd never catch him. She was right of course. It was dark and he knew every bit of the shire."

"So if you didn't harm her, why didn't you get her to safety? She was only a girl and clearly upset."

"I don't know. I wasn't thinking straight. Ourdilic swore the pregnancy wasn't her fault. Aethelnoth had forced himself on her. She was pleading with me to forgive her but all I could think about was her grinning on the back of Aethelnoth's horse. I pushed her away and went after him."

"Even though you'd no hope of catching him?"

He nodded. "He'd only have laughed if I had. I'd be no match for him if it came to a fight."

"So you just left Ourdilic?"

"I thought she'd go back the way she came. It wasn't that far to Cheddar."

"But she didn't, did she? Someone led her up to the cliff top and forced her off it. She wouldn't have found her way alone."

"I wouldn't have tried in the dark either," Aethelwold said. "The only person who knows the ground well enough is Aethelnoth. Perhaps he came back later."

"But you said you didn't meet him."

"He might have heard me coming. I made enough noise, blundering about in the dark. He could have stepped off the path and waited for me to pass."

"And Ourdilic wasn't where you left her when you finally decided to return?"

He shook his head. "Not as far as I could tell. I called her name but there was no answer."

Winfrith pulled at a blade of grass, considering how much of Aethelwold's story she believed. "You must have had a shock the next morning…discovering Ourdilic was dead. Why didn't you say anything about her argument with Aethelnoth?"

He looked Winfrith in the face again, his eyebrows raised. "How could I? You think I wanted everyone to know she was pregnant with his child?"

"It wasn't her fault," Wifrith said, her anger rising. "You thought it possible Aethelnoth had come back and killed her and you said nothing just because you feared a little mockery from your worthless companions? If you didn't kill her yourself, you left her to die."

Aethelwold glanced anxiously towards the palisade. Winfrith's raised voice must have carried far enough to tell anyone still watching they were no longer on friendly terms.

"I told you, I didn't kill her. She was so mad she probably went off without any idea where she was heading…just lost her way. I should have seen her safely back to Cheddar but I was angry at what she'd done. She'd made a fool of me, even if she hadn't meant to. I'm sorry now…I really am."

"Too late for that now. So Aethelnoth could have come back…but you thought Beorhtric could have harmed her too. Something to do with Wareham and his brother Brigmund?"

"I didn't say he'd kill her," Aethelwold protested. "I only repeated what Ourdilic told me. She was always telling stories about how important she was. I doubt if half of them were true."

Winfrith had to agree with that. Was it likely Ourdilic had only imagined being at Wareham and that Eanflaed had been betrothed first to Brigmund? It was possible. She might have felt Aethelwold would be impressed by what she claimed to know and perhaps by her escape from Guthrum's clutches too. There was one person who would either confirm or deny the tale about Brigmund of course. Finding out would be simple if the man who could tell her was anyone but Beorhtric.

A face appeared briefly above the palisade before ducking out of sight again. Winfrith rested a hand on Aethelwold's shoulder. "You've done enough to satisfy your friend down there. You've pleased me by answering my questions, but you can't please me any more unless you know who caused Ourdilic's death and probably Eanflaed's too. Time you went and collected your winnings before I get cross again."

Aethelwold got to his feet and looked around, as if unsure which direction to take. He took a couple of steps downhill towards the palisade, but then turned suddenly and began to walk briskly to the gap in the trees marking the start of East Lyng causeway.

27

Olwen stirred, muttering something in her sleep. Winfrith listened as her steady breathing quickly resumed and wondered if it had been Aethelhelm's name on the girl's lips. She pulled the thin blanket tighter under her chin, wishing she could sleep as well as the young. Despite their best efforts to make the shelter weather-proof, it was still a far from comfortable place to spend a night. There was no room for even the smallest of fires and the slightest breeze made the brushwood walls tremble.

It wasn't just discomfort keeping her awake of course. Ever since Aethelwold had mentioned it she hadn't been able to get Wareham and the death of the hostages out of her mind. It was hard to imagine Ourdilic and Eanflaed there and even harder to believe they'd been allowed to leave. Thinking about it brought back her own bitter memories of her mother being dragged out of the house and her own feeble efforts to stop it. She ran a finger down the scar on her cheek, a constant reminder of how heathens looked on Saxon women and children. She had lost a husband too, one she'd barely had time to get to know. It was natural to feel angry at Guthrum's treachery but what had happened couldn't be changed. Beorhtric had good reason to resent his brother's death but that hadn't stopped him marrying Eanflaed. Had he turned against her for some other reason…something he had discovered much more recently?

A scraping noise outside interrupted Winfrith's thoughts but she quickly dismissed it. Athelney had more than its fair share of small creatures scratching about in the night. It occurred to her that no-one ever spoke of Brigmund apart from Beorhtric. He had never come to Easton in King Aethelred's time and Winfrith had never seen him in her time following Cuthbert and the king' thegns. It was unusual, especially in the long winter evenings, for thegns not to sit talking of feats of arms, battles, wounds and the loss of friends yet she'd never heard Brigmund's name. She was sure her husband Wiglaf had never mentioned him either so, if it was rare for him to be part of the king's close circle, how had he ended up a hostage in Wareham?

She had no answer to that, except that perhaps the presence there of both Brigmund and Eanflaed, betrothed to each other according to Ourdilic, held the key. Had one of them gone there, knowing the other was held captive? Had Guthrum used Eanflaed to lure Brigmund there and, if he had, what was his purpose? The trouble was Winfrith knew very little about Brigmund and certainly nothing which might suggest why he could have been valuable to Guthrum. Could Eanflaed and Ourdilic have been promised freedom in return for luring Brigmund to Wareham? Had that been the reason, once he learned of it, for Beorhtric venting his anger against Eanflaed? She sighed, picturing how Cuthbert would laugh off such a tale and tell her not to mistake dreams for reality.

Winfrith turned over, trying hard not to nudge the sleeping Olwen. She would have to find a way to get Beorhtric to talk about his brother though it would be far from easy. Even leaving aside his unpredictable temper, he was rarely to be seen. Increasingly, small groups of Alfred's thegns set off along the East Lyng causeway, sometimes staying away from Aethelney for several days. No-one talked openly of the purpose of such journeys but they often returned with new faces, swelling the numbers already crowding onto the island. Most were assigned to Cuthbert's care, to be taught the skills they'd need for a spring campaign against the Danes. Payment for the deaths of Ourdilic and Eanflaed was the last thing on the minds of almost everyone around her but Winfrith took a deep breath and whispered into the darkness, "They won't be forgotten as easily as that, just because they're not thegns. Their lives were worth something. They won't be dismissed as easily as stamping on a troublesome fly."

Olwen stirred in her sleep, perhaps hearing Winfrith but more probably because of the scrape of a footstep somewhere outside. Whoever it was paused before swiftly moving on. It wasn't unusual to hear thegns up and about in the night, too many cups of ale in most cases, and Winfrith turned onto her back, hunching her shoulders in the vain hope of finding a more comfortable position. It wasn't hard to see why only summer hunters had favoured a life on Athelney.

Sleep must have come eventually because Winfrith woke with a start. She peered into the darkness, sure something must have disturbed her but she could hear nothing except the light rustle of straw as Olwen stirred.

"Are you awake?" she whispered. "Did you hear something?" Olwen didn't reply, slipping quickly back into the regular breathing of deep sleep. Winfrith stretched out her legs, trying to ease the stiffness out of them. She moved cautiously, hoping to avoid knocking against either Olwen or the flimsy brushwood of the shelter. She was drawing up her knees again, thinking she had managed it successfully, when she felt something move against her leg. At first she thought Olwen must be waking after all and she edged back, trying to put a little more space between them. Yet a moment or two later the pressure against her leg began again. She could feel it through the blanket, nudging her ankle and then moving along her calf. Several fears flashed through her mind…a rat, a dog, a drunken thegn…and then she felt it slide along her thigh and she rolled away, kicking at it and calling out as she collided with Olwen.

"Snake…there's a snake in here." Somehow Winfrith scrambled outside, dragging Olwen after her. Her ankle began to itch and she rubbed it furiously, pulling the sock down and trying to make out any marks on the skin. It was still too dark to see and she shut her eyes, certain that at any moment the pain would strike and her flesh would begin to swell. Olwen clung to her sleeve, shivering and still only half awake, watching wide-eyed as half a dozen men, alerted by Winfrith's shout, came running as if they feared Athelney was under attack.

"What happened?" the first to arrive demanded.

"Inside the shelter…there's a snake in there."

"Are you sure? Sure you didn't dream it?"

"How would it have got here?" another voice asked. "This is an island."

"Look for yourself if you don't believe me," Winfrith said. "It was definitely there. I felt it."

Someone sniggered in the darkness. "Mine feels like a snake…"

"Shut up, Caedric, and go and fetch a torch. We might as well look now we're here."

They stood uneasily in the darkness until he returned and one of the men held the brushwood which served as the shelter entrance aside while Caedric ducked his head and went in.

"Nothing," he said. "See." Several heads craned forward to look, almost colliding with Caedric as he suddenly backed out. He lifted the torch, lighting up the faces of the watchers, and pointed excitedly towards the dark interior.

"No..she's right. It's there, coiled up in the corner. You can't mistake the marks of an adder. Lucky it didn't bite." Winfrith felt for her ankle again but the itch had gone and there was no sign of swelling.

By now the commotion had drawn a few more light sleepers out of their shelters, curious to know what the fuss was about. Caedric checked his boots were tightly fastened and, arming himself with a thick branch, re-entered the shelter. The thud of several heavy blows sounded from inside before he emerged, torch in one hand and the dead adder triumphantly held aloft in the other. As he swung the torch around for all the watchers to get a look Winfrith had just enough time to notice Beorhtric among them and although it was no more than a brief glimpse she could have sworn he was smiling.

Caedric flung the dead adder into the darkness and the gathering swiftly broke up. Winfrith and Olwen went reluctantly back inside, nervous despite having seen the snake disposed of.

"Who put it there?" Olwen asked, as soon as they had checked any nook or cranny which might hide another snake. "Adders sleep in winter, don't they?"

"I wish I knew," Winfrith answered. "It's not the first time someone's tried to scare us."

"You mean the giant? Surely that was meant for Ourdilic?"

"I thought it was at the time, but I'm not so sure now. There was the knife and the cloth from Ourdilic's dress hung outside Heafa's house. And that's not the only thing. There was the dead raven with my mother's clasp pinned to it, hung across our path on the way back from Countisbury."

"This is different though," Olwen said. "Those were just messages…warnings maybe. That snake could have killed one of us. And you're forgetting someone cutting you loose in the river and the time they tried to land a tree on you. Someone wants you dead."

Winfrith reached for Olwen's hand. "It means they're frightened and the only reason I can think of for that is they're worried I'm getting closer to exposing them as a murderer."

"But aren't you afraid? They might succeed next time."

Winfrith squeezed Olwen's hand. "They haven't yet…and I can't give up now. If they get away with killing Ourdilic and Eanflaed, they'll think any woman who gets in their way can just be got rid of."

Olwen was silent for a moment. "So who do you think it is?" she said suddenly. "Beorhtric…or Aethelwold…or Aethelnoth even?"

"I don't know, Olwen. I've thought each one of them must be guilty until something made me turn to one of the others. I even thought Beornhelm might have left the warnings, so I'm still not sure. It must be one of them though."

"They made Ourdilic's and Eanflaed's deaths look like accidents, didn't they? That shows it's the same person who tried to drown you and then crush you under a tree and now get a poisonous snake to bite you. It's someone very clever."

Winfrith managed a laugh. "Except they seem to have lost the ability to carry it off. That's three failures in a row now. The strain must be getting to them. Perhaps they'll get careless."

"You will watch out though, won't you?"

Before Winfrith could answer there was a polite cough outside.

"Are you still awake? No-one hurt?" a soft voice enquired.

Winfrith sat up and pulled back the brushwood blocking the shelter entrance. Dawn was still some way off but she could just make out a crouching figure four or five paces away. It wasn't until he spoke again that she recognized the speaker as Alfred.

"You're not hurt?" he repeated.

"No, not at all…just a bit startled," Winfrith replied, echoing his quiet tones.

"I'm glad," Alfred said, hesitating before going on. "It can't be easy for the two of you, stuck here with little to do, especially when everyone else is occupied with preparing to surprise Guthrum."

"We're coping well enough," Winfrith said. "No-one takes much notice of us."

Alfred levered himself upright. "I want it to stay that way. Leave questions about Ourdilic to Cuthbert. If there's anything still to discover about how she died, he'll report it to me. As for Eanflaed, I hear you've been questioning how she died too. That can only lead to arguments, maybe violence even, among my thegns and that's the last thing we need at the moment."

"But if someone killed them, surely they should pay? Your own laws say as much."

"If they did, they will, but it seems unlikely and in any case now is not the time. I need every man who can carry a spear and shield thinking of nothing but defeating the Danes."

Winfrith knew she was expected to bow to Alfred's wishes but she felt angry and frustrated and in the near darkness he seemed no more a king than any other shadowy figure.

"So when will the right time be? We've been fighting heathens for years."

Alfred leaned forward and Winfrith felt his sleeve brush her face. "When I choose it, Winfrith. Cuthbert and Milred both say you're a clever woman who has been very useful to them. I applaud you for that, but if you continue to stir up trouble among my thegns you'll be exercising your cleverness somewhere a long way from Athelney. Is that clear?"

"It is," Winfrith said, making no attempt to hide her reluctance.

"Then I'll wish you goodnight."

Winfrith knew she would not get back to sleep. She lay with her face close to a tiny gap in the brushwood and watched the sky slowly get lighter. As soon as she saw one or two thegns up and about she crept quietly out of the shelter, sure that some at least would be keen to recount the events of the night to anyone who hadn't heard about them. There was always a faint hope that whoever had put the adder there might give himself away somehow.

Unsurprisingly Caedric was the first to draw an audience. Winfrith spotted him outside a brushwood shelter, greeting three thegns as they emerged yawning and stretching. She hurried to join them, hoping that her part in the night's events would make her presence welcome. He wasted little time in launching into his tale, pausing only when three more thegns, one of them Beorhtric, appeared from a neighbouring shelter.

"I was telling these fellows," he continued, "I didn't see it at first. No-one else was willing to go in of course..."

"Because you had the torch," one of the listeners said. "Not much point in us looking for a snake in the dark. It scared you enough anyway."

"It did not," Caedric said, glaring at his accuser. "It was me went back in and killed it. You can't deny that."

"Caedric defeats a sleeping snake," the thegn replied. "A noble victory..."

"It was good of him to help," Winfrith said, "and it wasn't asleep. It moved. We could easily have been bitten."

"You see," Caedric said, grinning. "It was me took the risk, not you, Haestan."

Haestan, a heavily built man whose thinning hair and narrow eyes made him look older than most of Alfred's thegns raised his eyes skywards. "Caedric the hero saves us yet again. What I'd like to know how it got there." He turned to Winfrith. "It wasn't there when your shelter went up?"

She glanced at Beorhtric as she prepared to answer. "Which means someone must have put it there, don't you think?" If Beorhtric thought the question was directed at him he chose not to answer it and his expression gave nothing away.

"Then someone has a strange idea of a jest or else they really don't like you," Haestan said. "There's a story going round that Aethelwold, the worse for wear from too much ale, took a wager that he could win your favour. Was he mad when you sent him packing ...or perhaps you didn't?"

"We talked politely for long enough for his friends to think he had made a reasonable attempt. He left me quite pleased with himself."

Haestan grinned at the other thegns. "But expecting more later perhaps?"

"Certainly not. I told him I'd talk...nothing more. Perhaps someone was worried he might have told me something they wanted kept quiet."

"Like what?" Beorhtric said, suddenly interested.

Winfrith did her best to look unsure, despite Beorhtric's sharp tone suggesting he found the thought of Aethelwold revealing something worrying. "Oh, I don't know. Something about how they look or what they're afraid of. Something about a woman…maybe something about his betrothed, Ourdilic…the girl who died."

"Not much worth repeating about her," Beorhtric said. "He had a fortunate escape there."

"None of you liked her," Winfrith said, trying to keep the anger out of her voice. "I know she came from Cornwall but that isn't a sin, is it? She might have thought highly of herself but then so do most of you. There must be another reason why most of you hated her so much. Athelwold hinted at it."

"He couldn't stand folk laughing at him," Beorhtric said, looking to the others for support. "Wanting to marry a Cornish girl who thought she ought to be queen of Wessex. Most of us told him he was a fool. Whatever nonsense he told you was his way of saying he knew better than us…and you're a fool if you believed it."

"You don't know what it was he told me." Winfrith paused, on the verge of revealing Ourdilic's possible presence at Wareham. Would Beorhtric say more in front of other thegns or in private? It would be difficult to get him alone and unwise if he was responsible for two deaths. Safer to do it now perhaps. "He sounded convincing. There might have been some truth in it."

"So what was the other reason for disliking the girl he'd found?" Haesten said. "It's not as if we needed any more. You must have seen the way she thought she was above us all."

"Most of us suspected her father was partly responsible for what happened to our hostages at Wareham," Winfrith said, choosing her words carefully, "including me. My husband was one of those murdered by Guthrum and I know Beorhtric lost his brother Brigmund too. Everyone said Ourdilic's father had helped the Danes but no-one survived to say how. She was Cornish and so she must be as treacherous as we think her father was. That's what we all thought."

"And Aethelwold told you something different?" Beorhtric said. "I told you he's a fool."

"He told me, and it was Ourdilic who had told him, that she had also been at Wareham and, not only that, but Eanflaed, Beorhtric's wife had been there too."

Most of the listeners greeted this with scornful laughter but Beorhtric was clearly angry. "What? He said my wife had been in Wareham? Utter nonsense. Wait till I get hold of the idiot. I'll throttle him. He's gone too far this time."

He looked set to go and carry out his threat immediately but Haesten held him back. "Wait a minute. Let's hear the rest of what the woman has to say. We could do with a good story to cheer us all up. Go on, Winfrith, so what did he say the two of them were doing there – knitting jerkins for Guthrum?"

"He didn't know. Ourdilic didn't say. He just thought if it was true and anyone else found out they'd been there it would have turned you all against them both."

"If Ourdilic's father was there, she could have been with him," Haesten said, "but what on earth would Beorhtric's wife have been doing there? They'd hardly have let her go if she had been."

"I told you," Beorhtric said, pushing Haesten out of his way, "Aethelwold is losing his wits. He'll tell you he's queen of Mercia next. If he says Eanflaed was in Wareham to me I'll make sure he chokes on the words."

As he strode away towards the shelters on higher ground, Caedric called after him, "Ask him about the adder. Perhaps he's mad enough to have put that there too."

"Any mention of Brigmund makes him angry," Haesten said, staring after Beorhtric. "Seems he'd always looked up to his big brother. Hard to see why. He never appeared on the battlefield."

"Does he ever talk about Brigmund?" Winfrith asked. "You know…how much land he had, where they were raised, whether he had a wife and children…"

"You sound uncommonly curious about Beorhtric's family," Haesten said, grinning. "Why's that, I wonder? Perhaps you think he'll be looking to take another wife now Eanflead's dead. Yourself, perhaps?"

"Not me," Winfrith said hastily. "Too much of a temper to suit me. It's nothing like that. It's that I heard a rumour about Brigmund too and I wondered if there was any truth in it."

Haesten shook his head in disbelief but it was a fair-haired thegn Winfrith didn't know who spoke. "Not another of Aethelwold's tales. Alfred will be appointing him royal scop soon. What was it this time…Aethelwold had single-handedly fought off fifty Danes in trying to rescue Brigmund?"

"No, nothing so obviously untrue," Winfrith replied. "I heard that Brigmund had been betrothed to Eanflaed which could explain how she came to be in Wareham and then after he was killed Beorhtric later agreed to take Eanflaed as his bride in order to honour his brother."

"Now that does sound an interesting story," Haesten said. "There's only one problem with it. All the hostages held at Wareham were slaughtered by that evil bastard, Guthrum. If Eanflaed had been there with Brigmund, she'd hardly have been let go. She was a good-looking woman after all."

"The only reason I could think of for freeing her was if she could have been exchanged for a more valuable thegn, someone wealthy enough to command a high ransom."

Haestan rested a friendly hand on Winfrith's shoulder. "See, friends, this is how a good story is made. Aethelwold has a dream and tells Winfrith here. She takes it as truth and adds some nonsense of her own and repeats it to us. By the time Alfred hears the story Brigmund will be the Bishop of Sherbourne and Eanflaed the Abbess of Romsey."

Winfrith pushed his hand away, ignoring the scornful laughter his words encouraged. "You're probably right. It does sound far-fetched, but the only person who could confirm or deny it is Beorhtric since the others who could have been in Wareham are all dead. That's why I was interested in whether he'd ever said anything about his family."

"Well, I'd be careful if you're thinking of asking the man himself," Haestan said, "especially if you're going to suggest Eanflaed did something bad to secure her escape. He won't like that one bit."

Once it became clear Winfrith had nothing more to tell, Haesten and the others drifted off in search of food. She was about to follow them when she saw Beorhtric returning. Either he had not found Aethelwold or their exchange had been brief. Whichever was the case he approached her purposefully, leaving little doubt he had not calmed down and meant to have further words with her. She glanced swiftly around her, relieved to note several men up and about and within hailing distance.

"You sure you heard that story from Aethelwold?" he demanded, stopping just a couple of paces in front of Winfrith. She held her ground, refusing to be intimidated.

"That's what I said. Ourdilic told him and he repeated it to me."

"That damned girl…still causing trouble even after she's dead."

"It shouldn't trouble you if it's just a story, should it? There's no other witness who says your wife was in Wareham, or that she was betrothed to Brigmund."

"Not a single one. People talk, that's all. Some aren't happy if they're not spreading lies." He stared hard at Winfrith, making it clear he thought her one of them.

"I haven't told anyone before this morning. And you heard me. I didn't say it was true, just that what Ourdilic claimed was surprising. I never denied she was capable of making up the whole story."

He leaned forward so that Winfrith could feel the heat of his breath on her cheeks. "So if you didn't tell anyone before today, how did that stinking goat Aethelnoth get to hear of it?"

"Do you mean Aethelnoth…ealdorman of Somerset?"

"You heard me." He spat the words out and Winfrith wiped a sleeve across her face before gently reaching out to ease him a pace further away.

"If Aethelnoth knows he didn't hear it from me," Winfrith said softly. "So does that mean you'd already heard gossip about Eanflaed being in Wareham before today?"

Beorhtric frowned, but allowed the space between them to remain. "I didn't believe it. He was drunk…we both were. I remember saying it was easy to bed young girls like Ourdilic, harder to persuade grown women. He said something about being able to lie with Eanflaed if he had a mind to do it. I put a knife to his throat and said I'd kill him if he tried. That's when he said she wasn't worth it and came out with that horse shit about Eanflaed and Wareham. If I'd believed it I'd have slit his throat there and then, ealdorman or not."

"So you didn't marry Eanflaed to honour your dead brother?"

"How could I? I wasn't aware then she'd ever met him and I've still no reason to think she did. Besides, Brigmund would have told me if he'd planned to marry."

Winfrith watched his eyes as he spoke. There was no trace of doubt or hesitation in them, though perhaps that only meant he was a good liar. "It's strange that Brigmund himself was in Wareham too, isn't it?" she asked. "Haestan was saying he wasn't usually to be found among the king's fighting bands."

Beorhtric shook his head. "I don't know what he was doing there, only that his body was among those of the other hostages. He was fond of money, my brother. The only things likely to have taken him to Dorset were wool, meat or grain. He might not have carried a spear well but he knew the best price to buy and the best price to sell."

"So he'd have made a valuable hostage if Guthrum had known his whereabouts?"

"Except that the treacherous bastard heathen slaughtered them all so they were worth nothing in the end."

"The other hostages were captured attempting to raid Wareham, weren't they? Maybe someone betrayed Brigmund's presence in Dorset to try and save their own skin."

Beorhtric gave a dismissive shake of the head. "Thegns, all of them. Used to fighting shoulder to shoulder where your life depends on the men either side of you. They'd never trade lives with heathens."

"Then perhaps someone else gave him away?" Winfrith glanced to her right, checking there were still other men in view. "If Eanflaed and Ourdilic were there…and gave Guthrum a good reason to let them go…"

"One of them might have told Guthrum where to find him?" Far from being angry, Beorhtric appeared to give the idea serious consideration. "Even supposing they were there, it's unlikely. I doubt if either of them had ever seen Brigmund, never mind knowing where he might be. I wouldn't have trusted Ourdilic with my brother's life but Eanflaed wouldn't have given him away. I'm sure of it."

"It all happened before you met her. She probably wouldn't have known he was your brother."

Beorhtric waved his arm asif sweeping the suggestion aside. "Forget this story about Eanflaed being in Wareham. If she and Ourdilic had been there and somehow managed to escape together, they'd have had much in common, but you and I know that's not so. When Alfred insisted Eanflaed advise Ourdilic in preparing for her betrothal at Cheddar you could see they loathed each other. They behaved like women who'd never met before and had no wish to spend a moment in each other's company."

Winfrith nodded. There was no denying it and yet much of what she thought she knew about Ourdilic and Eanflaed was proving to be some way from the whole truth. "You're right…they did. I suppose they wouldn't have wanted anyone to know they'd been there, especially if they'd done something they were ashamed of in order to be spared. They might have agreed to do or say nothing that could betray their shared knowledge of what happened."

Beorhtric took a deep breath, his patience clearly wearing thin. "You're like a dog with a bone. Eanflaed wasn't in Wareham. She'd have told me. Even if she had been, you don't think Guthrum would have let her go, whatever she did, do you? Twelve hostages, all good men, ought to have been exchanged. The bastard cut their throats. Is that a man who would have let a shapely woman like Eanflaed go? It's impossible. Find something better to do than repeating lies. I'm warning you. You'll regret it if you don't take heed."

Before Winfrith could reply he pushed past her, knocking against her shoulder, and set off downhill towards the palisade. She watched him go, pleased that he'd answered her questions but unsure how much she'd actually learnt. One thing he'd said was interesting though. Aethelwold wasn't the only person who knew Ourdilic's tale about Wareham. Aethelnoth had goaded Beorhtric with it too, so where had he heard the story? If it had been from Ourdilic, the girl who had been carrying his unborn child, might she have confided more to him than she had to Aethelwold? Winfrith smiled. Aside from Olwen no-one was willing or eager to help her find out how Ourdilic and Eanflaed had died, but despite the lack of help, bit by bit, details were beginning to slip out. A picture was building in her mind. Surely it wouldn't be long before the identity of the killer would appear clearly within it?

28

Alfred might have warned that any questions about Ourdilic's death should be asked by Cuthbert but there was little sign that the thegn was doing much about it. Winfrith caught sight of him several times in the days after the snake had disturbed her sleep but he had always been too busy to talk. The general mood among Alfred's thegns seemed to have lifted, as if they sensed their time on Aethelney would soon be over. Fearing that if they were right she would lose her chance of getting someone admit they had killed Ourdilic and Eanflaed, Winfrith went in search of Cuthbert determined to remind him of the responsibility Alfred had put on him.

She eventually tracked him down at the start of the causeway, explaining rather impatiently to two burly Somerset ceorls who should be allowed off the island.

"They can promise you what they like…duck, goose, fish…but they don't pass unless the king says so. Understand?" The men nodded. "And if I find you've ignored this, I'll promise you something…no food of any sort for three days and cleaning the cesspits twice a day. Got it?" They nodded again, moving slowly back to take up their positions a short way along the boardwalk. Cuthbert turned away, then stopped abruptly, clearly surprised to come face to face with Winfrith.

"Winfrith, must you creep up behind me? Haven't I got enough on my hands without you jumping out at me?"

"I didn't. You'd have heard me if you hadn't been shouting."

Cuthbert glanced towards the two Somerset men. "Thick skulls, both of them. Takes a lot of noise to get through and even then it doesn't always reach whatever's inside. What are you after anyway? You never seek me out unless there's something."

"It's about Ourdilic…and Eanflaed."

Cuthbert took Winfrith's arm, guiding her further away from the curious glances of the two men on the causeway.

"You were told to let it go, by Alfred himself. He's not going to stand for anyone distracting his thegns from the campaign ahead. He's said I should think about sending you back to Easton."

"Too late, isn't it? You've just told that pair no-one's to be allowed off the island."

Cuthbert laughed. "I'm sure the king could order an exception to be made in your case."

"They'll have to drag me away. I'm still not giving up trying to expose whoever killed them."

Cuthbert shook his head, though the smile did not quite disappear from his face. "You might find your bed free of snakes at Easton. That would be a gain."

They had emerged from the alder trees and straight away saw a crowd beginning to gather around the grey stones at the top of the rise. Others appeared from shelter entrances and from behind the palisade and started to make their way uphill. Winfrith stopped, watching them.

"Someone put that snake there," she said, as Cuthbert half-turned, waiting for her. "Probably the same person who sent other warnings to try and scare me off. It shows I'm getting closer to whoever killed Ourdilic and Eanflaed. That's what I came to tell you. There really could be reasons why someone wanted both of them silenced."

Cuthbert sighed. "I thought Alfred warned you to leave all that well alone?"

"He did, but he also said you were the thegn who would deal with it."

"Perhaps he did but now is not the right moment." Cuthbert pointed towards the gathering crowd. "Alfred has summoned everyone up there this morning. He's let it be known he's got important things to say and I don't intend to miss it."

Just for a moment Winfrith got it into her head that Alfred was about to denounce a murderer but she immediately dismissed the idea. It was far more likely to be something to sustain the better mood among his thegns. A feast or a raid on the heathens…either would be of far more interest to them than finding Ourdilic's killer or paying wergild. Whatever he had in mind Cuthbert was intent on hearing it and Winfrith fell into step beside him, hoping that Alfred was not about to thwart her efforts for good.

As they neared the small outcrops of pale rock which circled the high ground they caught up with Milred, moving slowly with the aid of a stick.

"Can I help?" Winfrith asked.

The old man smiled but shook his head. "I'd rather Alfred had chosen to speak outside my shelter door, but I'll get up there in time. Don't want to miss this. I just hope Alfred takes my advice. Not too much Boethius...most of this lot have ale-pots for brains. Not you of course, Cuthbert."

"Kind of you, Milred," Cuthbert replied, laughing, "sometimes I doubt I've got any at all. We'll walk with you and stand together. When we get to the long words and the deep thoughts you can explain to us what Alfred really means."

Alfred selected his spot carefully, choosing a flat rock high enough that he could be seen by everyone but not so high that he would appear like a man apart. He looked pale and drawn but he stood upright, his back straight, his feet planted firmly and his arms spread wide to welcome all those who stood before him. Anyone could see that he was not the biggest of men...some of his thegns were half a foot taller...and yet at this moment he seemed able to hold them all in his power. It was easy to see why he had been chosen to succeed Aethelwulf as king, despite some voices in the witan putting forward the claims of Aethelwulf's young sons, Aethelwold and Aethelhelm. Most eyes were on him now as he raised his arms aloft, making sure he had everyone's full attention before he spoke. Winfrith glanced around the gathering. It had to be nearly fifty strong, though Alfred's voice would have carried to four times that many.

"Out of adversity comes good," he announced, pausing to let the words sink in.

"Keep it simple," Milred muttered, barely loud enough for Winfrith to hear.

"Take a good look at me," Alfred went on. "What do you see?"

"The King of Wessex," someone in the crowd called out.

"Used to be," another added and was greeted by one or two uncertain laughs.

"You may well laugh," Alfred answered him, unconcerned. "My cloak's threadbare, my shoes are muddy and my beard uncombed. I could easily be mistaken for one of you. A stranger might think I had nothing...no land, no wealth, no gifts to offer. Yet they'd be wrong. Few things are as they seem on the surface. There's always a sun behind black clouds. Milred warned me against repeating the wisdom of Boethius to you but I'll just remind you of one thing he says. He tells us nothing, not even the worst and direst of misfortunes, is miserable unless we think it so. And whatever you have been thinking since we came here, the time will soon be right for the sun to break through the clouds again."

Winfrith noticed several faces looking up, as if they expected sunlight to pierce the murky greyness overhead. Alfred smiled.

"It won't be long coming. And while we've been waiting hardship has left us stronger. Coming here hasn't been easy but you've all shown your loyalty and it will be rewarded."

This was met with murmurs of approval and Milred leaned over to whisper in Winfrith's ear. "A few hides of land occupied by Danes won't satisfy them."

"Of course that feels still a long way off," Alfred continued. "We all look like men who have fallen on hard times, but better that than to be like Nero, arrayed in splendid clothes and all manner of gems but beneath it a heart full of vice and sin. Beneath your rough clothes lie courage, loyalty and the determination to restore Wessex to its former glory. And what is in our hearts is our true self, not the way we look to others."

"Except for Caerlac," someone at the back called out, "he really is as mean as he looks." There was some laughter at this and Alfred waited patiently for it to die down, happy to keep his audience in good humour.

"We've had some arguments of course. It's to be expected, but now's the time to put them all behind us. In the coming days unity must hold if our fortunes are to change and, providing it does, what can we achieve?"

"Kill that bastard, Guthrum," an impatient voice shouted.

"Why not?" Alfred said, his voice rising above the shouts of agreement. "Nothing ever stays the same. Guthrum can lose land and wealth just as fast as he gained it. Remember too that fine clothes and precious gems are only earthly trappings. Courage, loyalty and faith in God count for far more in the life to come..."

Milred, who had been standing patiently just below Alfred, now leaned forward and raised his arm to catch his king's attention. He said something inaudible and Alfred flashed him the briefest of smiles.

"My trusted friend Milred thinks most of you have your minds set on living this life before you contemplate the next one. He's right, of course. What we do now, today, tomorrow, in the days that follow…that's going to decide our future. But one day we shall all stand before God and we must be able to recall these times with pride. That's so, is it not?"

There were enough nods and murmurs of assent to suggest most agreed but few hoped it would happen soon.

"We shall have to fight…we know that. But strength of arms alone won't be enough. My father always said if we spread our boat's sail we are at the mercy of the wind. What he meant was that we must believe we can win if we are to overcome the forces we face. It's why I've called you together now. The time to decide our fate once and for all is almost upon us. You will all share it, whatever kind of man you are. Looking around me it's obvious no two men are exactly the same. Some seek gold; others a good child-bearing wife; some would be landowners, ealdormen, kings even; a few of you even thirst for the knowledge to be found in books. Most of you rightly expect to be rewarded for your courage and loyalty. There is only one way your king can deliver that to you. You must forget your differences. Arguments, jealousies, suspicions, rivalries…they must all be forgotten until Guthrum is defeated. We must all fix our eyes on that and that alone."

Winfrith glanced around the circle of faces, many of them clearly lifted by the direction Alfred's words had taken, and saw her hopes of finding Ourdilic's killer fading. She wanted to shout out in protest but no-one would have heeded her and in any case her words would probably have been drowned out by the eager calls to put an end to Guthrum.

"A Saxon spear in his gut would do it," someone shouted.

"Perhaps," Alfred said, smiling as he spread his arms wide and waited for the noise to die down, "but others would take his place. Being here in Athelney is a reminder of what we're all missing…home, kin, fireside, the hills and valleys of Hampshire, Wiltshire, Dorset, Berkshire, the heart of Wessex. It's not just a dead Guthrum we want, but a land free of heathens."

There were more calls for Guthrum's head and again Alfred was forced to wait for silence to return. "It is almost time to go home. You have all endured a hard winter in these fens and marshes. It has been wet, cold and has lacked the comforts of your own hearths and, those who have them, the company of your wives and children. I see some of you grow restless, but I shall not be long now. Winter is almost gone. The days are growing longer. At home seeds will have been planted and the first lambs will be starting to appear. It means my ealdormen can summon the men of Somerset, Wiltshire and Hampshire to join us. We will meet them three days from now at Egbert's Stone. They will be our muscle and sinew. But you men before me...you are our heart and life-blood. Without you we could not have come this far. I thank you all for your faith in me. I know that with you all around me we shall carry the day and drive the heathens from the lands that are ours."

Alfred raised his right arm, fist clenched, high in the air and a chorus of cheers and shouts greeted what most took to be the end of Alfred's speech. It was with some difficulty that he managed to make himself heard to add a final warning.

"Friends...listen...one more thing before you go. Guthrum must not hear of our plans. If he has watchers in the hills, they must not see us out on the causeway. They mustn't think we are preparing for battle. Until we leave for Egbert's Stone in three days, no-one is to leave the island, not even for the chance of a fish or a fowl. I have placed guards at the start of the causeway with orders to stop anyone, even me. That's all. I really have finished now. May God grant us a happy return to the country, to the peace and to the friendship we once had."

Winfrith heard Milred mutter "Amen to that" as Alfred stepped carefully off the white stone, leaving his thegns chattering excitedly about Egbert's Stone and the days ahead.

"Ourdilic and Eanflaed won't be going home," Winfrith said softly, but neither Milred nor Cuthbert appeared to hear her.

Winfrith turned away towards the shelter, feeling none of the excitement of Alfred's thegns. Three more days and they would all be gone from Athelney. In the meantime their heads would be full of spears to be sharpened, shields to be toughened, buckles to be polished and tales of how many Danes they meant to kill. The hardships of the island would be forgotten and the memory of the loss of two young women's lives would cease to trouble even the guilty. It wasn't that she didn't long to return to her former life.

Cuthbert's estate at Easton offered order, comfort, good food and warmth. It would be blissful to see it again and know that each new day didn't threaten a fresh raid or an urgent flight. Yet even as the thought occurred to her, Winfrith knew she was incapable of going back without making one last effort to bring whoever had killed Ourdilic and Eanflaed to account. She quickened her pace. Only three days remained in which to do it.

29

 Winfrith sighed. She was getting older. Not so long ago the knowedge that she had only three days to find an answer would have sent her rushing to Cuthbert, Beorhtric, Aethelwold or Aethelnoth…anyone she thought might be hiding something…demanding to know what they were keeping from her. Yet now all she wanted was to find a quiet spot and try to straighten out what she already knew. It was easier said than done in the close confines of Athelney, especially now that Alfred had put guards at the entrance to the causeway. She made her way aimlessly towards the gap in the palisade from where thegns had watched Aethelwold's efforts to befriend her.

 The gap was narrow, barely wide enough to squeeze through, and on the far side a small patch of ground had been trodden flat. A dense thicket of alders surrounded it and the stale smell of the cesspit hung in the air. Winfrith pushed her way in among the branches, hoping to find somewhere to sit in peace. Keeping the palisade to her right she worked her way forward. The black, wiry branches could be parted but had an unpleasant habit of springing back unexpectedly. She covered her face with her hands but found it hard to escape occasional stinging blows to her legs and body. Conditions underfoot were no better. Several times her feet slid off slippery coverings of moss into the muddy gullies which ran between the trees.

 The going showed no sign of getting easier and Winfrith was about to turn back when several broken branches ahead of her caught her eye. It was perhaps not particularly unusual, except that the exposed wood was pale enough, almost white, to suggest the damage had been caused very recently. It could easily be the work of a deer or a goat, always supposing such an animal foolish enough to stray onto Athelney, but equally it might show someone had come this way before Winfrith. She edged through the intervening undergrowth and was only a few paces away from the first broken branch when her feet suddenly gave way. As she fell she heard the wild squawking and frantic beating of wings of a startled water fowl. The frightened bird flapped its way clear of the trees, leaving Winfrith breathing a sigh of relief. The dense branches of the alders had cushioned her fall and apart from a scratched cheek she seemed to have come to no harm. As far as she could make out she had landed on a rare strip of flat grass and just ahead of her, past the first snapped branch, ran a narrow creek, no more than twenty paces long and sheltered at the end by a curtain of trailing willows. Grasping a sturdy-looking branch she pulled herself up and edged her way closer to the bank. At some point not too long ago someone had cut down the trees along both sides of the water and stacked the dead branches waist-high against the palisade.

She listened for a moment but the only sounds were the occasional rustle of dead leaves lifted on the wind and the lapping of water somewhere beyond the fringe of willows. She chose a comfortable spot to sit, her back against a smooth trunk and her feet dangling above the creek, and began to take stock of what she knew. The deaths of Ourdilic and Eanflaed had not been accidents. She was sure of that. Both deaths had been made to look like accidents, as had her own narrow escapes in the river, under the fallen tree and with the adder. That surely meant the same hand had been at work each time. That simple fact must hold the key. Who had a powerful reason for wanting to silence both Ourdilic and Eanflaed?

Winfrith thought about the girl and the woman. What linked them? They both hailed from Cornwall. Ourdilic was about to be betrothed to the king's nephew, Aethelwold, and Eanflaed was asked by Alfred to help prepare her for it. Ourdilic had received a jeweled morning gift fom the king which Eanflaed had admired before it disappeared. Then, last but not least, according to Aethelwold, Ourdilic had told him that both she and Eanflaed had been at Wareham before the Saxon hostages were killed but for some unkown reason the Danish king, Guthrum, had freed them.

A sudden gust of wind shook the willow branches at the mouth of the creek, briefly parting them and sending light ripples along the surface of the creek. The brief glimpse of the marsh was enough to plant an idea in Winfrith's head that someone had cleared the banks of the creek so that a small boat could be rowed through the hanging willows. Anyone wanting to slip in and out of Athelney unseen would have found it useful. She shook her head. Interesting as the thought was, it didn't get her any nearer to naming the killer.

One thing at a time, she told herself. Take Wareham, for example. If the story was true, why were they allowed to go free? She could think of only two explanations. They might have offered to lie with Danish jarls in return for freedom. It seemed improbable. What was to stop heathens taking them by force? They had killed the hostages after all. And why would they have let go afterwards? It was much more likely that they had something else to offer. One thought Winfrith had considered was that it might have been something to do with Brigmund's presence at Wareham. Beorhtric's brother was not a fighter and had no reason to be there. Aethelwold had suggested Brigmund and Eanflaed had been betrothed, though there was no way of confirming such a story. He said he'd heard his from Ourdilic and no-one could press her about it now. Even so, the story left Winfrith wondering if Eanflaed might have betrayed Brigmund's whereabouts to the Danes. A wealthy trader, dealing in grain among other things, might have been worth the freedom of two women. If there was any truth in the Wareham story it surely pointed to Beorhtric as the killer, especially if he had discovered his wife had betrayed his brother. The only problem with it as an explanation was that Beorhtric strongly denied Eanflaed had ever been in Wareham.

So, if the heart of the puzzle did not lie in Wareham, what else did she have? Winfrith shifted her position, disturbing a shower of tiny stones which pinged into the water. There was the matter of Ourdilic's pregnancy and the possibility that Flaedda was Eanflaed's child, conceived when she was little more than a girl herself. Flaedda had been born in Chilton, not far from Aethelnoth's home, and the Somerset ealdorman was paying for her upkeep. It seemed likely he had also fathered Ourdilic's unborn child. It wasn't unheard of for thegns to father bastards, or even for them to admit the fact. Ordinarily they would shrug their shoulders and pay an agreed number of shillings to the girl's kin. The only difference Winrith could see in this case was that Aethelnoth was married to a fearsome woman like Beornhelm. Might he have twice committed murder to stop his wife learning he'd got two women pregnant or could she have found out and taken her own revenge on the women concerned?

It was difficult to know what to make of Beornhelm. She had dragged her children all the way to Cheddar for no better reason than to keep an eye on Aethelnoth. She'd not been far from Shapwick when Eanflaed died either. Winrith couldn't see who could have told her about Ourdilic's pregnancy though she'd had many years to hear the story of Flaedda's arrival in a neighbouring village with enough funds to feed and clothe her. It was rare to hear of women committing murder but Winrith was sure Beornhelm had the strength to overpower Ourdilic and Eanflaed. The warnings – the giant Bolster, her mother's brooch and the dead raven – did feel more like the work of Beornhelm, well known for her persistence in old beliefs. If Beornhelm did know of the two pregnancies it would certainly account for Aethelnoth taking so much care to avoid her.

A small spider began working its way across Winrith's skirt and she brushed it away, frustrated that she had not narrowed down the possibilities at all. There was still Aethelwold to consider as well. He had known Ourdilic was with child. He was angry and perhaps feared humiliation if it became known that Aethelnoth was the father. He admitted meeting Ourdilic on the night she died. Had he lied about her being still alive when he left her? It was quite possible to see him panic at the thought of his fellow thegns, already scornful of his betrothal to a Cornish girl no-one liked, mocking him but less easy to imagine Ourdilic being unable to frighten him off. There was Eanflaed to think of too. Winrith could think of no reason why Aethelwold would have wanted her dead. He generally seemed to dread the company of women and would surely not have sought out the wife of a short-tempered thegn like Beorhtric.

Winrith closed her eyes. Had she missed something obvious? Considering possible killers didn't seem to be getting her anywhere, so she turned her mind to the victims again. What did they have in common apart from possibly having been at Wareham? They had both been born in Cornwall, in itself enough to make them unreliable in the eyes of most Saxons. Travellers told of monsters, devils and midnight rites…sacrificing children even. Much of it was probably made up to show the traveler as fearless but most of Alfred's thegns believed there was good reason to mistrust the Cornish. Many even said that Ourdilic's father, Drumgarth, had drowned on his way to help the Danes rather than in trying to escape from them. The thought led her back to Beorhtric again. Despite taking a Cornish wife he still seemed to harbour more resentment than most against her people. Yet it was hard to see why he would have waited so long if it was merely his hatred for Cornwall which had driven him to kill.

She shifted her position, feeling chillier and rubbing the feeling back into her calves. What had sitting quietly and organizing her thoughts really achieved? A damp backside certainly…otherwise little more than to confirm four possible suspects with three days to narrow the number to one. She levered herself back on her feet, stooping slightly to keep her hair clear of the branches overhead. She looked again at the stack of branches heaped against the palisade. It struck her that whoever had built it had done so with great care. The wood had not been flung haphazardly but had been neatly stacked, as if someone had been determined that wind or passing animals would not disturb it. There might be any number of reasons for wishing that but before she had lifted the first branch, close to the water's edge, Winfrith was convinced something must be hidden there. With mounting excitement she dragged away the top layers of wood until the curved planks of a small boat began to appear. Once she had exposed the rest of it, she saw that there was a length of rope and a roughly carved oar lying along the bottom and on top of those a small bundle of cloth, carelessly tied as though it had been stowed in haste.

The moment Winfrith had it in her hands she was sure she knew what it contained, even if she couldn't think how it had got there. She pulled feverishly at the string around it until it came away and she was left looking down at Ourdilic's morning gift, the jeweled aestel given to her by Alfred. She turned it over in her hand, hardly believing what she held there. The light under the trees was dim and the jewel might be in need of a polish, but the pale enamel face was the same and the crystals around it glittered faintly as she turned it from side to side. There couldn't be any doubt it was the same jewel which had disappeared from the house in Cheddar immediately after Ourdilic's death. She and Olwen had thought Eanflaed must have taken it, though Winfrith had found no trace of it near where Eanflaed's body had been found. That opened up a further possibility though, one which might help solve everything. Had Eanflaed's killer found the aestel on her, or perhaps even known she was carrying it? If that was so, they must have brought it here and hidden it in the boat, perhaps planning to escape with it. Somewhere there would be rich buyers for such a beautiful thing.

Winfrith cast her eyes over the aestel again. It was far too valuable to be abandoned. Whoever had hidden it here would surely be back for it and everyone who had come to Athelney from Cheddar would be leaving in three days. She folded the cloth back round the aestel and loosely knotted the string before returning it to the the bottom of the boat. A quick search of the boat and the ground alongside it offered no hint as to who had put it there and so she set about piling brushwood over it again. Worried that she might be disturbed before she had finished, she heaped the branches without the neat arrangement in which she'd found them but at least the boat and its contents were out of sight.

Taking a last quick look about her she pushed her way back into the alders, her mind racing. Should she tell Alfred? He'd be delighted to have the aestel back, but he'd made it very clear that at this moment preparing to do battle with Guthrum was his only concern. The same was true for Cuthbert and while Milred would listen his days of helping to catch murderers were long past. She slowed down a little, aware that in her haste thin branches had several times sprung back in her face. Once she was sure she had almost reached the gap in the palisade she halted, coming to a decision. She would keep the discovery of the aestel to herself for a day or day. The shelter she and Olwen occupied allowed a clear view down to the gap. No-one would be surprised to see them sitting outside, sewing or basket-making. It would be easy to keep an eye on anyone passing beyond the palisade. There would be plenty of them of course, given the absence of cesspits on Athelney, but most would remain no longer than it took to empty bladder or bowels. Anyone lingering for any length of time must surely be heading for the creek.

Her satisfaction with this plan did not last long and Winfrith cursed herself for rushing. Not for the first time she hadn't thought far enough ahead. If she tried to follow whoever had taken the aestel it would be impossible to keep close without being heard. Even if she armed herself the dense alders would make standing up to a thegn trained for battle a dangerous matter, especially someone who had already shown no scruple about killing two women. And as if that was not problem enough, there was nothing to stop her prey getting into the boat and rowing away across the marsh. At least there was one thing which would put a stop to that. Once again Winfrith began pushing her way back towards the creek. If the aestel was no longer in the bottom of the boat, that would make escaping from Athelney far less worthwhile.

Winfrith was breathing heavily by the time she had uncovered the boat again and removed the aestel. It would be too risky to return to Aethelney with it but there looked to be no shortage of hiding places at the foot of the trees where there were many holes among the twisted, blackened roots. Her only fear was that one looked much like another. Finally she settled on one a little way back from the creek, just deep enough to take the wrapped aestel without any of the cloth showing. She scratched a tiny mark into the bark of the tree and, blowing out a long breath of air, set off again in the direction she had come.

Olwen and Winfrith sat outside the shelter, nipping the tender shoots from a pile of nettles and dropping them into a pot of water. Aethelhelm had left them a cup of goat's milk and a handful of barley, promising to return later to share some soup with them. Winfrith kept a careful eye on the palisade, though the longer she watched the less sure she felt about who planned to keep the aestel. The thing that troubled her most was how the boat had come to be hidden in the creek. No-one among Alfred's men could have arrived with it, so either an earlier visitor had abandoned it there or someone from outside Athelney had arrived in it, perhaps alerted to the presence of the morning gift by whoever had taken it.

Each time anyone disappeared through the gap Winfrith counted the moments until they returned. She glanced up at the sky, hoping that the build up of grey cloud did not mean heavy enough rain drive them back inside.

"You're very interested in Alfred's thegns this afternoon," Olwen said, the hint of a smile visible at the corners of her mouth. "You always chided Ourdilic and me whenever we chanced to look in their direction."

"I'm sure you deserved it," Winfrith said, laughing.

"Is there one you like the look of?"

"No, there isn't, Olwen. I was merely curious. I suppose it's the thought of battle that's making them nervous." Winfrith nodded towards the back of a disappearing thegn. "That's Gifmund's third visit since midday."

"Perhaps he ate the bread they brought from Cheddar. It's not fit for pigs by now. And look...Beorhtric's following him. Maybe he ate some too."

Winfrith looked to where Olwen was pointing. It was true. Beorhtric was also making his way towards the gap, though from from a different direction. He was approaching along the inside of the palisade and Winfrith wondered briefly whether he might have been checking for any other places where he could pass through it.

"Did he drown Eanflaed?" Olwen asked, taking Winfrith by surprise.

"What?"

"His wife...do you think Beorhtric held her under the water?"

"What makes you say that, Olwen? We don't know it was him."

"He's got a temper...and I know he hated Ourdilic. We agreed the same person was behind both deaths and the threats to you."

Winfrith tossed the last of the nettle leaves into the pot and put a reassuring arm around Olwen's shoulder. "We did...and it could be him. We'll watch and wait. If he doesn't reappear by the time the soup's cooked we'll know something other than an upset stomach is keeping him."

They watched in silence as two more thegns came and went and Gifmund trudged up the hill looking very pale as he passed close by them. "Why don't you get a fire going?" Winfrith said, trying to sound calm. "I'm sure Aethelhelm will want his soup hot when he comes back. I'll keep an eye out for Beorhtric."

The mention of Aethelhelm had the desired effect. Olwen sprang to her feet and carried the pot inside, leaving Winfrith free to walk unobserved towards the palisade. If Beorhtric was not still within hailing distance, there was surely a good chance he had gone to check on the aestel.

30

Winfrith stepped cautiously through the gap in the palisade, relieved to find no-one waiting for her on the far side. The narrow, rank-smelling avenue leading down to the water's edge was deserted. She listened for any sound of Beorhtric and, hearing nothing, pushed her way into the thickets of alder, looking out for the broken branches which marked the way she had last taken. The going was no easier than before and, to make matters worse, a stirring among the branches suggested the wind was rising. Now and again in the gaps overhead she caught glimpses of dark clouds chasing each other across the sky. A few spots of rain splashed icily against her cheek.

Catching her foot against a root, Winfrith paused for a moment. In her haste she hadn't thought to arm herself with any kind of weapon. The thin, bendy alder branches would be fine for weaving hurdles but of no use in fighting off an angry thegn. She couldn't be far away from the creek by now but the noise of the wind in the trees was making it impossible to hear anyone ahead of her. At least Beorhtric, if he had headed for the creek, would probably not be expecting her. A sudden gust whipped up a shower of dead leaves, sending them racing past her and making her turn sharply, afraid she was being followed. There was no-one behind her but the thought was enough to spur her on and she set off again through the dense alders.

The creek seemed further than Winfrith remembered and she was beginning to think she must somehow have missed it when she stumbled forward out of the trees and onto the strip of grass which bordered it. It wasn't the quiet arrival she had planned as she grabbed the nearest branch to stop herself sliding into the water. Had Beorhtric been waiting for her he couldn't have failed to hear her coming, but she was relieved to see the creek was deserted. Everything looked much the same as on her previous visit, though when she looked more closely it appeared someone had uncovered the corner of the boat, very close to where the aestel had been stowed. It was surely unlikely that wind or animals had disturbed the pile of branches just in that one place? It must mean the thief had returned and found the aestel gone. She'd not passed anyone returning to the gap in the palisade, so perhaps they were still here, somewhere in the trees, looking for other hiding places.

The urge to check that the aestel was safely concealed where she had left it was strong but Winfrith resisted the temptation, just in case Beorhtric or someone else was watching her. The rain was getting heavier now and even above the noise of the wind she could hear occasional distant rumbles of thunder. It was time to go back. If it was Beorhtric who had acquired the aestel from Eanflaed he would be furious at having lost it again. Rather than coming face to face with him here among the trees it made more sense to return to the open ground around the shelter and watch for his mood and manner when he reappeared.

Once she set off Winfrith began to relax. Even the thought of the draughty, cramped shelter began to feel appealing and she upped her pace, less careful now of the occasional branch springing back and stinging her hands and face. There was no longer any need for caution. She would soon be clear of the trees and the sound of branches thrashing about in the wind would drown any noise she made. Cursing her own stupidity, she sensed a sudden movement behind her and felt course sacking thrown over her face and pulled tight, jerking her head backwards. She tried to swing her arms back to push her attacker away but overbalanced. She flung out an arm to break her fall, feeling it twist under her as she hit the ground. Before she could cry out or remove the sack she felt her attacker's knee slam into her back and the foul-tasting cloth pressed harder against her mouth. A searing pain gripped her shoulder and spread along her arm and the knee pressing into her back pinned her down, preventing any move to try and ease the pain.

"Where's the aestel?" a harsh voice, close to her ear, demanded. For a moment Winfrith was too angry to think about who it belonged to. How was she supposed to answer anyway with her shoulder in agony and her mouth full of sacking? What kind of fool thought it possible? It should have been Beorhtric. That was who she'd followed through the gap, wasn't it? The voice was familiar…but it wasn't his. She'd heard it before, and quite recently too, but she couldn't put a name to it.

She tried again to free her shoulder from the weight bearing down on it, crying out at the burning pain. Straight away a hand gripped her neck and her face was pressed into the ground, leaving her fighting for breath.

"Make one more sound and I'll rip this arm right off. You'll have something to scream about then. Now, tell me what you've done with the aestel or I'll start feeding bits of you to the eels." Winfrith felt her arm tugged away from her side and bit hard into the sackcloth to stop herself crying out again. Then a hand grabbed a fistful of her hair, using it to pull her head just clear of the ground. "Now, where is it? Either it's in my hand before I'm much older or there'll be another accident. A shame if harm befell your young friend, Olwen."

"Leave her alone." The words sounded muffled and Winfrith felt the cloth being pulled out of her mouth and away from her eyes. She sucked at her teeth, spitting grit and hair into the grass. "It's nothing to do with her. I'll find it if you get off me."

"Make sure you do, without making a sound or looking behind you. You'll suffer the same fate as Eanflaed if you try anything. Understand?"

"You're welcome to the aestel. It's brought no good to anyone who's had it. It's no use to you. What can you do with something so recognizable?"

"Just get it."

Winfrith felt the weight lifted from her back and she was pulled roughly to her feet, wincing as the movement set fresh waves of pain through her shoulder and down her arm. The instinct to look behind her was strong but her attacker bunched her hair in his fist, holding it tightly enough to prevent her turning her head.

"What does it matter if I see you? You'll have to get away from here if you want to keep the aestel. That's what the boat's for, isn't it?"

"You'll see. Just get moving, while you've still got limbs to move. There's a sharpened blade a hair's breadth away from your neck. You'll get more than a scar if you look round."

Winfrith rubbed her eyes taking a moment to get her bearings.

"Which way?" the harsh voice demanded, not Beorhtric's…but not Aethelwold's or Aethelnoth's either, unless they were disguising it. Someone she'd met before though. She stretched her shoulder and straight away regretted it. A burning needle pressed in right to the bone could not have felt worse. And that wasn't all.

As soon as she took a step forward the bones in her lower back felt as though they were try to rearrange themselves. One thing was certain, making a run for it was out of the question, at least for the time being.

"It's not far," she said, gritting her teeth as she felt herself pushed forward, "but I don't need the helping hand. I'll only fall." The man behind her grunted but said nothing and Winfrith heard him follow as she nudged her way into the trees. "It's through here. I scratched a mark in the tree." She briefly considered leading him back towards the gap in the palisade but he was unlikely to be taken in by that. He was close enough behind her to catch hold of her cloak from time to time and once, when she stopped, she felt the cold tip of the threatened blade against her neck and his hoarse whisper in her ear,

"Keep moving. You said not far."

"It's not…only all these trees look the same." The knife blade pricked her neck and she moved on hurriedly, relieved to find that the marked tree almost immediately appeared ahead of her and that the hole beneath it remained above water. She pointed to the opening, reluctant at the last moment to retrieve the aestel itself. The man behind her had surely killed for it and now it seemed she was simply handing it back to him. She was still racking her brain for something she could do to make his task more difficult when he pushed past her and knelt down to reach into the hole. For a second she had an unhindered view of the back of his head, the perfect position from which to strike him senseless, but she could lift only one arm and had no weapon to hand and the chance was quickly gone. He stood upright again, pulling eagerly at the muddy cloth until the jewel was exposed.

In his haste to reclaim the aestel he seemed to have forgotten his desire to hide his face from Winfrith. The jewel's spell lasted only a moment. He thrust it into a deep pocket, looking up at Winfrith as if seeing her for the first time. She knew him at once: tall, fair, broad-shouldered and with the kind of wide eyes and unblemished skin that had drawn admiring looks from girls like Ourdilic and Olwen. Raedberht wasn't popular among Alfred's thegns though. His uncle Wulfhere, once ealdorman of Wiltshire and a trusted supporter of Alfred, had gone over to Guthrum in Chippenham. What was he doing here in Athelney? After the slaughter of the

Danes at Countisbury he'd gone in search of the raven banner, hadn't he? They'd expected him back and when he hadn't appeared most said he'd probably gone to join his uncle. Whatever the reason for his presence, he clearly meant to leave with the aestel and she was the only one in a position to delay him. She had to try and get him talking…at least that would give her time to think.

"That was the king's gift to his nephew's bride-to-be," she said. "If Alfred learns you stole it, you'll lose everything."

"Who's going to tell him?" Raedberht said, patting his pocket. "Not you. You hid it away rather than returning it. So who's the thief now?"

"I didn't keep it for my own sake. Someone took it from Eanflaed when she drowned. I wanted to know who."

Raedberht trod down the disturbed earth around the hole and glanced around him, checking he'd left no sign of their presence. "Who'll believe that? It was Ourdilic's and she was housed with you. It's far more likely you took a liking to it. That's what they'll say." Satisfied he had left no trace, he advanced towards Winfrith, making sure that she saw the knife he still carried. "Time we went. Do just what I tell you and I might even let you live." Winfrith nodded. "Now, turn around and head back to the creek."

Her shoulder hurt with each footfall but Winfrith determined she would not show it. Raedberht's sudden appearance had confused her, and she was still struggling to make it fit with what she already knew. She knew she was in danger, especially if Raedberht had killed Ourdilic and Eanflaed. It wouldn't be wise to provoke him, yet if she said nothing now he might never be seen in Wessex again.

"It hasn't brought good fortune to anyone, that aestel," she said, parting the last tangle of branches before emerging onto the banks of the creek. "Neither Ourdilic nor Eanflaed had it for long. And it looks like someone helped both of them to their deaths."

She heard a coarse laugh behind her. "They won't be much missed…either of them," Raedberht said. "A Cornish brat and an ice-cold wife. You won't hear Aethelwold or Beorhtric complaining."

"Ourdilic would have grown up and Eanflaed might have got away from her bad-tempered bully of a husband. They had a right to a full life."

Winfrith felt the knife blade scratch the back of her neck and Raedberht leaned his other arm over her painful shoulder, pointing towards the boat. "You talk too much. Start moving the brushwood off the boat. We're going on a little journey."

"Why? Where? You don't need me." Winfrith stood still, trying not to show her alarm, but a firm hand in the small of her back pushed her forward.

"Never mind. Just do as you're told or you'll be joining the souls of those women you're so interested in."

Winfrith glanced at the palisade. Could she get there before Raedberht could stop her and shout for help? Probably not. There were branches, tree roots, brushwood and the creek itself in the way and even if she reached the palisade there was no certainty anyone on the other side would hear her. Reluctantly she headed for the boat.

"You could just go, couldn't you?" she said, grimacing in pain as she bent to begin clearing the branches away. "You've got the aestel. You don't need me."

"And have you go running to Alfred? Most of his thegns wouldn't realize their own mother had gone missing. We'll be long gone by the time anyone asks after me."

"At least one person will want to know where I've gone though. Olwen will be worried if I'm not back soon."

Raedberht considered this for a moment before coming to join Winfrith and speed up the removal of the last of the pile of branches. "Then we'd better get moving. Who knows? You might be safer with me. You've upset enough folk here with all your questions and it's a very small band of men to do battle with Guthrum. Chippenham is the place to be right now. Now, into the boat with you."

"But you're a Saxon," Winfrith protested as she cautiously placed one foot into the boat. "Guthrum's a heathen…an enemy. You'd betray your friends to join him?"

Raedberht waited until Winfrith was seated and steadied the rocking boat before joining her. "I haven't a friend among them, not since my uncle left us. He knew what he was doing. He sips

Frankish wine and dines on roast pig while Alfred's thegns live on nettle soup with nothing more than a few sticks to keep out the mud, wind and rain. Tell me, which sounds the better life?"

"It won't always be like that," Winfrith said, as Raedberht used the oar to lever the boat away from the bank and into the trailing willows. "You heard Alfred. He has plans to gather more men and take Guthrum by surprise." Even as she said it, Winfrith realized the Raedberht had more than selling the aestel in mind.

Raedberht laughed. "Yes, three days from now at Egbert's Stone...the great meeting of loyal Saxons. It will hardly come as a surprise to Guthrum. He'll have received news of the plan before then."

Raedberht had made sure Winfrith sat facing him at the front end of the boat from where he could keep an eye on her and row at the same time. She bent her head as they pushed their way through the trailing willows and out onto the surrounding marshes. Despite being out in the open it was not much lighter. Grey clouds were building up overhead and they were barely clear of the trees when a flash of lightning lit up the sky to the west and a faint rumble of thunder echoed across the water.

Winfrith felt the boat surge forward with each powerful pull of the oar. Raedberht was clearly intent on putting as much distance as possible between himself and Athelney as swiftly as he could. He had confessed to being a thief, had not denied being a murderer and seemed to be about to add treachery to his list of crimes. There was little she could do about the first two, especially with an injured shoulder and the handle of a knife visible above his belt, but could she delay his arrival in Chippenham...at least long enough for the news of the meeting at Egbert's Stone to reach Guthrum after it had already taken place? If she could find a way of stopping him getting there at all, even better. If he reached Chippenham and, like his uncle, threw his support behind the Danes, there would never be any wergild paid for the deaths of Ourdilic and Eanflaed and she wasn't going to give up seeking that, however uninterested anyone else might be.

Winfrith cast her eye around the bottom of the boat in the forlorn hope that a weapon of some sort might present itself. There was no chance of overpowering him and even less of talking him out of what he intended. All she could see was a short length of grimy rope and what looked like a worn-out shoe. Neither would be much use against a knife or a swinging oar. Raedberht followed her gaze. He opened his mouth to speak but was seized by a fresh bout of coughing…harsh, throaty barks which shook the boat and left him thumping a fist against his chest as if that might relieve the discomfort. He made several efforts at clearing his throat before spitting the results over the side.

"Don't try anything. Just be glad you're leaving such a foul place. Unfit for humans. Think of this as your best hope of staying alive." Raedberht resumed paddling, more steadily now, and Winfrith watched behind him as the dark line of alders marking Athelney's shore vanished in the gloom. The clumps of reed and sedge on either side of them were denser now, blocking the few islands of higher ground from view and leaving nothing to take bearings from.

"Hard to see the way now," Winfrith said, glancing over her shoulder. "Easy to get lost."

"Then you'd better keep your mouth shut," Raedberht replied hoarsely, "unless you want to end up as another heap of bones at the bottom of a swamp."

"Like Eanflaed, you mean…if I hadn't stumbled on her body?"

Raedberht let the oar trail in the water for a moment and a grim smile spread across his face. "Just like poor Eanflaed. Shows what a dangerous place the marsh can be, doesn't it?" He stared hard at Winfrith, challenging her to contradict him, but she kept silent, sure that he wouldn't hesitate to see she suffered the same fate if she got in the way of his plan to join his uncle. "So we'd better make haste towards setting our feet on firm ground again."

"Was it you who forced Eanflaed under the water? So you could take the aestel? And pushed Ourdilic off the cliff so you could come back and steal it? Except someone, Eanflaed probably, beat you to it?"

Raedberht patted the front of his jerkin, reassuring himself the aestel was still safely tucked away inside it. It crossed Winfrith's mind that if it were somehow to go missing again, that would be the perfect way to delay him. Perhaps he meant to impress Guthrum by making a gift of it and so ease his arrival among his former enemies. Not that parting him from it would be easy, especially if she continued to provoke him.

"Accidents, both of them…carelessness. Ask anyone." He sounded less angry than Winfrith had expected, not that that made him innocent in her eyes. "The dead can't hold on to earthly things, so the aestel has fallen into my hands now. I'm told the writing around the edge says 'Alfred had me made'. That makes it worth much more to Guthrum than to any Saxon. It will show he has Alfred in his hand."

There were many things Winfrith wanted to say but she forced herself to hold back. Somehow she had to find a way of making Raedberht more relaxed…perhaps confident enough to take a rest at some point and, if she was lucky, even to fall asleep. Satisfied that she had nothing more to say, he took up the oar again and began to row. Occasional heavy drops of rain spattered against boat and spread neat round marks on their clothes. The claps of thunder sounded to be edging closer and another streak of lightning briefly lit up the sky. A rising wind whipped up the surface of the water and the rain rapidly grew heavier. Winfrith narrowed her eyes as the rain stung her face and began to seep into her clothes. She heard Raedberht curse as another bout of coughing gripped him. By now she could scarcely make him out which must mean he could no longer see where they were going. This was swiftly confirmed as Winfrith felt the boat thump into something solid and tip alarmingly over to one side. A patch of dead reeds caught on her sleeve as they juddered to a halt. Winfrith was thrown backwards, vaguely aware of an angry shout and a heavy splash as the boat rolled on its side and she was tipped out, not into water but against firm ground. Before she could make sense of what had happened a searing pain in her shoulder, as if someone was trying to rip away her arm away, took hold, leaving her fighting for breath and desperately afraid she was about to pass out.

31

Winfrith rolled slowly onto her back, taking the weight off her shoulder. The boat lay on its side, half out of the water. She couldn't see or hear Raedberht but if he had gone into the water he wouldn't be long dragging himself out. He couldn't be far away but there was a chance he might not be able to make out the boat straight away through the driving rain. Winfrith clutched the edge of the boat, meaning to use it to help her stand, but it shifted under her weight, enough to dislodge something from beneath the back seat. Winfrith crawled towards it, thinking it must be the length of rope or the old shoe. The shoe was there, sinking slowly into the water but it was something else, nestling in the reeds at the water's edge, that caught Winfrith's eye. The small bundle, wrapped in familiar cloth, had to be Ourdilic's morning gift. The collision must have shaken it free from Raedberht's jerkin. Winfrith reached for it. There was no time to dwell on her good fortune because she could hear sounds of someone thrashing about in the water. Either Raedberht thought that was where he'd dropped the aestel or he was finding his way back to the boat.

Winfrith remained on hands and knees, hoping she couldn't be seen as she pushed the cloth bundle deep into her pocket. She knew she ought to move but her clothes were sodden and a continuous trickle of water into her eyes made it hard to make out what lay around her. The boat might have hit a stretch of raised ground but she could just as easily be on an island no more than ten paces across. Raedberht might appear out of the gloom at any moment, knife in hand. She got painfully to her feet and stepped away from the boat and into the reed bed. Her feet sank into cloying mud and each step felt as though hidden hands were clutching at her ankles, dragging her back. She lifted her good arm to shield her eyes against the wind and rain but an angry shout made her look back. A black shape, like some monster from the depths, was dragging itself, coughing and spluttering, from the water.

There was no time to worry about what lay ahead. Gritting her teeth against the pain in her shoulder and weight of her cold, sodden clothes, Winfrith ploughed on through the reeds, expecting

Raedberht to appear behind her at any moment. With each step her legs felt heavier but she refused to look back. She mumbled Ourdilic's name to herself in an effort to drive herself forward but she knew she was beginning to tire. The constant drumming of the rain shut out any other sound now so that perhaps she would feel Raedberht's knife in her back before she heard him. The thought spurred her on, fighting to keep her balance as the reeds gave way to tussocks of wiry grass. It was still hard going and impossible to see the way ahead. Perhaps a fall was inevitable but Winfrith still felt a surge of anger as her foot caught something and she plunged forward, throwing out her good arm to break the fall. For a brief moment she couldn't work out what had happened…icy cold water everywhere and a sensation of drifting smoothly forward before her head rose up into fresh air. She was afloat, her skirt billowing out around her and her feet searching in vain for a secure foothold.

Her first instinct was to go back but she swiftly checked it. Raedberht would not be far behind. She kicked her legs and waved her good arm, satisfied that she had not forgotten her father's teaching. A child brought up on a riverbank needed to be able to get to the bank if they ever fell in. Easy enough if it wasn't in spate. There didn't feel to be any current here but Winfrith knew she could not stay in the water long. She could paddle her way forward but her heavy clothes dragged in the water and each stroke set off a burning pain in her shoulder. It was impossible to tell how far away the next stretch of land might be and already her skin felt numb with cold. The image of mile after mile of open water came into her head and the thought she might just sink exhausted below the surface. She blinked the water out of her eyes and forced herself to kick harder. She called Raedberht's name but if there was any reply it was drowned by the noise of whining wind and spattering rain.

A thick black line, just above the water, suddenly appeared out of nowhere. As she closed in on it, the dark line took on the shape of a bank of blackened stones. The water grew shallower and she felt her feet brush a clump of weed. She struggled to stand, swallowing a mouthful of brackish water as relief and excitement got the better of her. The stones were smooth and coated with dark lichen, too slippery to walk up. Winfrith was forced to crawl on hands and knees, cursing each time she lost her grip. Once she reached the top she shook herself but with little effect. The wet clothes clung to her and though the rain had abated a little it was still falling steadily.

She looked back across the grey surface of the water. There were several dark patches in the distance but it was impossible to tell whether any of them was where she had entered the water. She cheered herself with the thought that there was no sign of Raedberht and that either he couldn't swim or had baulked at the idea of plunging into unknown waters. He would probably get the boat moving again before long, especially if he decided Winfrith had the aestel. The thought made her reach for her pocket but her fingers missed the opening. She gently lifted the sodden folds of her skirt, hoping to avoid using the painful arm, but saw only a loose strip of cloth hanging where the pocket had been. She urgently patted her side, from the hip down to the knee, and around her back, hoping the aestel had caught somewhere else but already sure it now lay somewhere on the bottom of the grey, murky water between her and Raedberht's boat. She kicked the ground, cursing her own foolishness and hoping that Raedberht believed she still had the morning gift. It was the only thing that might stop him hurrying on to Chippenham and out of her reach for good.

A shout made her look up. One of the dark patches was moving, throwing up showers of water as it drew nearer. Driving shafts of rain still lashed the surface, blurring the outlines, but Winfrith had no doubt it was Raedberht. He had recovered the boat and had clearly already spotted her. She glanced quickly to left and right, deciding the stone causeway looked more even to the right. She set off – half running, half walking – along a very narrow track. With only one good arm balancing was far from easy but at least the many hoof prints suggested the causeway must lead somewhere. If Raedberht did catch up with her she had nothing to defend herself with but a few stones and perhaps her best hope was that darkness would fall before he succeeded.

The causeway seemed to go on for ever and yet, every time Winfrith looked back, she could see no sign of her pursuer. The wet clothes chafed against her legs and as she began to tire as each gust of wind threatened to tip her into the water. Finally the stones gave way to trampled mud and the path broadened out into a broad circle of level ground. The rain was slackening off now, its noise replaced by the sound of fast-running water. Ahead of her, across the open space, Winfrith could just make out a low wall and an unevenly thatched roof, one moment lit up by the leaping flame of a fire and the next disappearing into the shadows again. She hurried towards it, arriving just in time to see a woman's pale, oval face appear in the doorway of a low house. The woman said something Winfrith couldn't make out and a man stepped past her, ushering her back inside. He was shorter than Winfrith but his barrel chest and thick forearms hinted at strength. He stared at her from beneath bushy, black eyebrows as if the arrival of a visitor was a rare event.

"I need help," she said hastily, glancing back towards the causeway.

"What are you doing here?" he said, his voice unexpectedly soft. "And on a night like this? No roads pass this way."

"There's no time to explain. A man's pursuing me with a knife. He's out to kill me. Will you help?"

The man studied her face for a moment before stepping aside and waving Winfrith into the house. "Over there," he said, pointing to a dark corner and then turning to the woman. "Throw some blankets over her, Aerith. Then keep your mouth shut. I'll do the talking."

Winfrith felt the man take her elbow and guide her across the room and then push her down to the floor. She bit her lip to stop herself crying out as her bad shoulder bumped against the wall. Straight away she felt rough wool blankets thrown on top of her and she covered her nose until the feeling she might sneeze had passed. All she could do now was lie still and hope her presence would not be betrayed. Poor folk might be easily persuaded to give her up. It might only take the threat of a knife or the offer of a shilling. Then again poor folk had few reasons to trust thegns. She hoped that in this case they didn't like the look of Raedberht. A hoarse shout from somewhere outside suggested she would not be long in finding out.

"Which way did she go...a woman...scar on her face?"

It sounded as though the old man was in no hurry to reply. He cleared his throat and Winfrith imagined him looking suspiciously at the newcomer.

"What woman? Few come this way...specially not in this weather."

"Not blind are you? You must have seen her. Dripping wet…in a hurry."

There was another pause. Perhaps the old man was shaking his head. She smiled to herself when he finally answered. "My eyes are good enough to see you and a woman passing this way would be better to look on. Not something I'd have missed."

"What's inside? If you're hiding her you'll regret it."

"My wife. Take a look if you'd like. She's not much to look at these days."

Winfrith held her breath, but there was no sign that Raedberht had taken up the old man's invitation. When he spoke again he sounded convinced she had somehow given him the slip.

"She's a cunning fox. Must have stayed out of sight somehow. She's stolen something of mine but she won't get far with it. What food have you got? I've a long journey ahead."

"Nothing in the house, but if you follow the river a mile that way there's a fish trap. It's not been emptied for two days. Take what you find there."

"A mile you say? And you've a fire going. I'll be back to roast the fish. Watch for the girl with the scar while I'm gone and keep her here if you see her. It's a jewel belonging to the king she stole. You'll be well rewarded if you catch her."

The old man didn't answer and Winfrith assumed Raedberht had set off in search of fish. Even so, she stayed where she was, hoping the mention of a reward had not made the man or his wife have second thoughts. She shivered and the thought of cooking fish reminded her she'd had nothing to eat or drink since morning. The sight of skins, held over glowing embers, turning crisp and brown and the scent of the flesh as it cooked would do much to put the pain, cold and damp out of her mind. Yet she'd have to leave this place before Raedberht returned and the old man was clearly of the same mind. She felt the blankets being lifted away and a hand helping her to her feet.

"He's gone…but he won't be away long."

"Thank you," Winfrith said, her eyes slowly adjusting to the shadowy room, "for not giving me away. He offered you money."

The old man chuckled. "And would we ever see it? He hadn't the look of an honest fellow. If you have got something of his, you'd better not be here when he gets back."

Winfrith was about to deny the theft but stopped herself. She wanted Raedberht to think she still had the aestel and he had promised to return. If she said she had lost it somewhere in the marsh she might lose track of him.

"I didn't steal it and it doesn't belong to him," she said. "It was a morning gift from the king to a friend of mine. She's…she's gone on a journey and I'm keeping it safe."

"Whatever you say," the old man said, looking towards his wife. "We won't say anything but you should be going. You need to cross the river. I can row you over and he won't follow easily that way."

The wife sighed. She grabbed a broom which had been leaning against the wall and began vigorously sweeping the corner where Winfrith had been lying under the blankets.

"I'm not worried if he follows me," Winfrith said. "He might give you a few shillings if you tell him later which way I went."

"When that old fool has already denied seeing you?" the old woman said, glaring at her husband. "It would get him a beating at the very least. You said the fellow carried a knife and meant to kill you. Why should we risk our own lives?"

"Take no notice of her," the old man said. "She doesn't mean it. Let's go, before it's dark. From the other bank it's only a short walk to Othery. My sister lives there. She'll direct you to the track across the grey lakes. From there you can cross the hills to Shapwick. I'll find some strong ale for this fellow to have with his fish. He won't want to go any further until morning by which time you'll be well on your way."

The mention of Shapwick set Winfrith thinking. Not only did it mean Heafa's warm, comfortable house, it was also the start of the Sweet Way and the best route over the marshes to Westhay. Anyone heading for Chippenham would be sure to go that way.

"I don't know how to thank you. You risked a lot hiding me and I don't even know your name."

"Pudding brain," the woman muttered but her husband ignored her.

"Cenhelm," he said, "and she's Aerith. We don't have much, as you can see, but we wouldn't take his money if he offered it. He won't follow you because of anything we've said."

"It's good of you," Winfrith said, "but if I can get as far as Shapwick I'd be happy if he came after me. If I had a few hours start I could prepare an uncomfortable welcome for him."

Cenhelm looked unconvinced and Aerith stared at her as if she was mad. "Are you sure about that?" he said. "He doesn't look the sort to be frightened easily."

"He's not," Winfrith said, moving towards the door, "but he won't be expecting any danger in Shapwick. We lodged there on King Alfred's journey west."

"Why not just stay out of his way? You've got the morning gift."

"Because I think he killed twice for it...a woman and a young girl. I promised I'd make someone pay for it. I want to hear him admit what he did."

Cenhelm puffed out his cheeks, blowing out a long breath of air. "Well you're either very brave or else foolhardy...one or the other. Either way it looks as though your mind's made up." He reached for a thick coat, hanging next to the door, before turning to his wife. "I won't be long. If the fellow's back before me, fill him a cup of ale and skewer the fish...and don't tell him anything."

"But if he's still here in the morning, you can let slip that a fisherman stopped at your door and said he'd spoken to me earlier and directed me towards Shapwick. I'd said I was heading for the house of my friend Heafa."

"I'm not as daft as he is," Aerith said. "No-one passes this way. He'd guess you were here and that old fool lied about it."

"Never mind her," Cenhelm said, ushering Winfrith out of the door. "I'll find a way of letting him know. I might claim this Heafa is another of my sisters and suggest he can be sure of a meal and a good bed if he calls on her."

Winfrith stepped outside, circling the fire and following the sound of Cenhelm's heavy tread. Straight away stiffness in her calves and thighs slowed her down but at least it had stopped raining and it was not a long walk to the river bank and Cenhelm's boat. Only when she began to climb unsteadily into it did she realize her shoulder would still complain if she tried to put weight on it.

"Steady," Cenhelm warned as the boat rocked violently. "You don't want saving from a knife only to drown."

A night in a hut no bigger than a hen coop ought to have had little appeal. A constant wind howled outside, threatening at times to lift off the flimsy-looking roof, and no-one had bothered to pick out the stones from the earth floor. Despite these drawbacks, Winfrith was grateful for any sort of shelter and while her own clothes were drying out Cenhelm's sister had found her a thick woollen dress which at least hinted at warmth.

She slept fitfully, troubled by a dream that Olwen had tried to follow her onto the marsh and had become trapped in the mud. She kept calling out to the girl to turn back but each time her words were lost in the wind. Her attempts to go back and help Olwen woke her and it took a few moments before she remembered where she was. The sense of panic stayed with her and it took some effort to shrug it off. Gradually she calmed down, telling herself Olwen was far too sensible to set off alone across the marshes. Besides, she would have no way of knowing where Winfrith had gone. She would be worried though and Winfrith pushed open the door of the hut, looking for signs of first light. The sooner she could get to Shapwick, the sooner she could prepare for Raedberht's likely pursuit of her. If she was lucky, there might be someone there who would carry a message back to Athelney too.

It was still dark outside, but Winfrith was at least able to stand and stretch her stiff and aching limbs. Gentle movements of her shoulder suggested it was still sore but that walking would not be as painful as it had been the day before. Cenhelm's sister said Shapwick was half a day away so she ought to be able to reach Heafa's house before noon. That would give her most of the afternoon to get ready for Raedberht, assuming that the promise of fish and ale had persuaded him to stay overnight with Cenhelm. She would not find much help in Shapwick. Most of the young men had either joined Aethelnoth's Somerset fyrd or else spent their days in search of fish and wildfowl. On the other hand her stay there meant she was familiar with all its corners, alleys, ditches, and streams. Raedberht had seen her running away in fear. He would not be expecting an attack, not that she had the slightest idea how she might overpower him. She looked east, just about persuaded there was a hint of grey beginning to show. She would be walking very soon and that would give her time to think...three hours to come up with something to force a confession from Raedberht.

32

By mid morning Winfrith was crossing the last stretch of marsh before the Polden ridge. She had not found the walking easy but the thought of Heafa's house with its promise of food and a warm fire spurred her on. A twisting line of sticks marked the firm ground but she soon found she needed to watch her footing in places where the markers had blown down or sunk into mud. For a while the grey line of hills standing between her and Shapwick seemed to get no nearer and she looked back anxiously across the marsh, half expecting to see Raedberht. It would be maddening to be caught so close to Heafa, even if she hadn't yet thought of a way of getting the truth from Raedberht when she got there. Despite her fears, there was no sign of anyone following and, massaging some feeling back into her aching shoulder, she set off again.

It was such a relief to top the ridge and see the rooftops of Shapwick below. Winfrith stumbled, almost falling, in her eagerness to descend as far as the passage through the holly trees leading to Heafa's door. She forced herself to slow down. One painful shoulder was enough. The door was flung open the moment she knocked and she winced as Heafa enclosed her in a tight embrace.

"Winfrith...you're back. I knew we'd see you again. I said so, didn't I, Flaedda?" The girl, who was sitting by the hearth, was slowly stirring a pot from which the smell of herbs filled the room. She looked up and smiled but said nothing. "They say Alfred's been hiding out in the marshes," Heafa said, releasing Winfrith and ushering her inside. "From the look of you, it's not been a comfortable stay. Looks as though some clean, dry clothes wouldn't go amiss."

"Thank you, Heafa, but that can wait. A bit of whatever's in that pot would be welcome but there's something else..."

"I knew it," Heafa said. She gestured to her daughter to fill a bowl of soup. "As soon as I saw you. You're worn out and you've hurt your arm. What happened?"

"I think the man who killed Ourdilic and Eanflaed is on his way here." Heafa glanced across at Flaedda and Winfrith had to quickly think back, reminding herself she'd already shared with Heafa her idea that perhaps, when she was young, Eanflaed could have given birth to Flaedda.

"You know who it was?" Heafa demanded. "Beorhtric, I suppose...with that temper of his?"

"No, not him," Winfrith replied, lowering her voice. "It wasn't anyone I'd suspected. Not Beorhtric, Aethelnoth or Aethelwold."

"Who then? Who else would do such a thing?"

"It's Raedberht, ealdorman Wulfhere's nephew."

Heafa's eyes widened in surprise. "You mean the uncle who sits at Guthrum's table?"

"Yes, him. How did you know his uncle went over to the heathens?"

A satisfied smile spread across Heafa's face. "Simple...the Sweet Way. Everyone travelling from west to north uses it and they all pause in Shapwick. There's never any shortage of news and gossip here."

"Well Raedberht will soon be another. He's on his way to join his uncle in Chippenham but he'll be looking out for me as he goes. He knows I think he killed Ourdilic and Eanflaed. He'd welcome the chance to keep that quiet. That's not all either. He thinks I stole Ourdilic's morning gift from him. He wants it back, maybe to impress Guthrum. So you see, I need to be ready for him when he gets here."

Heafa nodded. "One thing I don't understand though...why would Raedberht kill Eanflead and Ourdilic?"

"That's what I mean to get out of him," Winfrith said, taking the offered bowl of soup and chunk of hard bread from Flaedda. "The jewel Alfred gave Ourdilic is beautiful but would he have killed twice for it? I don't know. What I thought was, if I can find a way of taking him captive I might be able to wring the truth out of him. Sounds easy when you say it, doesn't it?"

Heafa thought for a moment. "And I don't suppose he's puny enough for two women to wrestle to the ground." Suddenly her face lit up. "Of course...the storm drain. That would be just the thing." Heafa leaned back in triumph, as if everything was settled. Winfrith smiled, aware she would have to allow Heafa her moment of pleasure if she was going to get a prompt explanation.

"How would a storm drain help? Raedberht won't fear that."

"Not if he knew it was there," Heafa said, "but he's not born and bred round here. He won't know how flood water used to rush down the tunnel between the holly trees leading to this house. Years ago a drain was cut. Gradually floodwater running off the hills dug a deeper channel so it became impossible to cross into Shapwick from here whenever there was heavy rain. A solid plank bridge was built and it slowly got so overgrown you wouldn't know it was there now. After another channel was dug to divert water into a pond deep enough to draw from, the gully underneath the planks was blocked off with heavy stones."

"How will that catch Raedberht out, if it's all hidden from view and folk have crossed it safely for years?"

"Because…obviously…because," Heafa replied, stumbling over her words in her excitement, "we'll dig up the planks and replace them with twigs and thin branches. It's gloomy along there and a thegn in a hurry won't be taking great care about where he puts his feet."

"But surely he'll just climb out again?"

"It's a big drop. He probably won't be in a state to climb anything. And if he does, then we'll just have to wait behind the door armed with the heaviest cooking pots."

Heafa's confidence was catching. Looking at her was enough to make Winfrith think the idea was not so unlikely, yet there were risks and perhaps it was not right to involve Heafa.

"He wouldn't hesitate to kill both of us, you know. Flaedda too. You don't have to get mixed up in this."

Heafa glanced across at her daughter but the girl appeared to be staring at the hearth, paying them no attention. Even so, Heafa leaned close to Winfrith's ear and answered in a whisper.

"I have my reasons. Men like this Raedberht think the lives of girls and young women are worth nothing. They should be taught how wrong they are. And then there's Eanflaed of course. It was you put the idea in my head that she could have been Flaedda's mother. If she was, then I've as good a reason as you for seeing Raedberht pays for his misdeeds."

"Does she know your suspicions?" Winfrith asked, nodding towards Flaedda.

Heafa shook her head. "I don't think so. She seems in a world of her own much of the time. She listens when folk talk about

Eanflaed's death but then everyone here was curious about it. It's not every day a thegn's wife is drowned on our doorstep."

"I don't want her to get hurt either," Winfrith said.

"She'll be fine," Heafa replied. "I'll send her to turn away curious neigbours from the mouth of the tunnel. We don't want them falling into the trap before Raedberht gets here. If he's already on his way we ought to make a start on uncovering the old planks which cross the drain."

Uncovering the heavy planks proved much harder work than Heafa had implied it would be. Winfrith's left shoulder and arm were still too painful to use and Heafa could find nothing better than a light three-pronged fork with which to clear the layer of earth and weeds which had spread over them. While Heafa feverishly scaped this away, Winfrith used her feet to kick the loose soil out of sight under the trees. It soon became clear that the planks would be too heavy for Winfrith to lift so Flaedda was summoned to help while Winfrith kept watch for any sign of Raedberht's approach. By the time Flaedda returned to relieve her, the planks had been dragged into the trees and a network of light branches had been laid in their place. She smiled at Heafa. No-one in a hurry would spot anything unusual.

"I've tied that strip of cloth," Heafa said, pointing to a low branch at the side of the path, "so that we'll knew exactly where the drain is. That way we'll avoid falling into it ourselves. There's a small gap in the trees on the left, just where you're standing. If you squeeze into that, you can push your way past the trap and get to this side."

"And you're sure he can't get out?"

"Not a hope. It's solid rock at the bottom. He'll be lucky to survive the fall...not that he deserves to."

Winfrith studied the carefully arranged branches for a moment. It all seemed too simple. Would Raedberht really come marching towards Heafa's front door and end up down there, at her mercy?

"He might not even come," she said.

"Well we're ready if he does," Heafa said. "Flaedda can act the innocent when she wants to. She'll sit out there quite happily and she'll give nothing away if Raedberht asks for my house. She'll point the way the same as if he was a frequent visitor."

"We'd better get inside then. We can use the time sorting out which are the heaviest of your cooking pots."

"I'll leave the door open," Heafa said, grinning. "That way we'll be able to hear him scream as he falls."

Winfrith found it impossible to stay in the house for long. Each moment that passed convinced her more that Raedberht wouldn't come…that telling Guthrum about the gathering of Alfred's forces at Egbert's Stone was more important to him than hunting for Winfrith and the aestel. Several times she returned to the covered storm drain, until finally she suggested to Heafa that she would feel less on edge if she found a hiding place from where she could see anyone approaching. The thorns caught in her clothes as she squeezed through the outer branches of one of the tallest holly trees and into a gloomy cave-like space which circled the gnarled trunk. Crisp, dead leaves crackled under her feet and above her head a startled bird flapped noisily away. She waited until she was sure there were no sounds on the path before gently parting the branches to make sure she could see where the trap had been laid. She soon found that waiting without Heafa's constant chatter only left her dwelling on other worries. What if a deer made its way along the tunnel and fell through the loose branches? What if Raedberht forced Flaedda to lead him right to Heafa's door? This last fear was interrupted by the sound of footsteps on the path but when Winfrith cautiously peered through a gap in the branches she saw it was only Heafa, no doubt equally impatient to see what was happening.

"I thought I heard something," she said in a loud whisper, once Winfrith had shown herself. "Footsteps perhaps?"

"I haven't seen anyone," Winfrith whispered back.

"Maybe I should go and see that Flaedda's all right."

"Let's wait just a bit longer. We can't look for Flaedda without putting the plank over the drain again and if Raedberht came he'd use it to cross. Go back to the house, just for a while longer."

Heafa turned back with obvious reluctance, looking frequently over her shoulder as she went. Winfrith settled down to listen again. Somewhere beyond the trees a dog began barking, keeping up a steady complaint until an angry shout put a sudden end to it. The space under the tree was cramped and the effort of bending her head to look out was making her neck and shoulders ache. She decided to move closer to the trap, both for a better view and in the hope she'd be able to stretch out stiff muscles. As she crouched to pass under the low branches her hood caught and she twisted her head, trying to shake off what it had become tangled in. She whirled round, sighing with irritation, only to come face to face not with expected prickly holly pulling at her hood but with the bunched fist of a grinning Raedberht holding it tightly in a firm grip.

"Thought you'd slip like an eel out of my hands, did you? No such luck for you. Perhaps the same fate though…gutted, skinned and roasted. How would you like that?"

"Hard to make that look like an accident," Winfrith said, struggling in vain to free herself.

"Not so hard," Raedberht said, forcing her to the ground. "Houses catch fire. Hard to say what a roasted eel has suffered before it's burnt. So I think you'd better take me to the aestel you stole, don't you? The sullen girl back there says this path leads to the house you're lodged in, so let's go and get it before I'm tempted to start on the gutting."

"It's not there," Winfrith said, gritting her teeth as her painful shoulder scraped against the tree trunk. She felt Raedberht relax his grip to get her on her feet but instead she rolled away onto the path. The fresh branches laid over the drain were only a few paces away but Raedberht crashed his way out of the trees and was standing over her before she could get any closer. Even if she'd succeeded it was hard to see how she'd get him to step on the trap without the risk of being dragged in with him.

"Get up," he said, glaring down at her, his knife pointing towards her throat. "Enough games. Give me the aestel and I'll think about leaving you in peace."

It was an offer Winfrith might have accepted if she'd still had the aestel. He might fall into the drain in his eagerness to be on his way, although he'd avoided it on his approach by leaving the path. Somehow she must have given her hiding place away. Without the morning gift she daren't take him back to the house and risk his anger when he found it wasn't there. She shifted her hips, edging a little closer to the trap, and saw the knife blade flash past her face, nicking her cheek so that a drop of blood tricked down her face.

She clapped her hand to the cut and for a moment she was a child again, staring up at the Dane who had dragged her mother away and left her with a scarred face.

"The jewel's not worth dying for," Raedberht said, reaching for her hood and trying to drag her to her feet. "Now…to the house or do you want me to cut deeper?"

"It's not there," Winfrith said, taking a deep breath and allowing herself to be lifted. "I lost it…when I went into the water and had to swim. It wasn't in my pocket when I got out. You'll have to go back if you want to find it."

"Do you think I'm a fool? No woman would lose such a jewel. You think I'm going to waste time wading about in mud and water? Where is it? Tell me or your life is going to be shorter than you'd expected."

"Alright…alright…I didn't lose it. It's in…in the village. I buried it in a grain sack." Winfrith pointed back down the path, hoping he hadn't seen the uncertainty in her face. She felt a hand push her forward. Her leading foot was one long stride away from the freshly laid branches. One more and she would plunge through them onto the rock below. She halted, bracing herself for the expected nudge from behind, hoping she could twist to one side at the last moment but a sudden shout from the far side of the trap made Raedberht stop too.

"Here." Flaedda had clearly left her post and had come just far enough down the tunnel to be seen. She had shouted just the single word and Winfrith could make no sense of until she saw the girl hold up a hand in which she held something small. It was impossible to make out what it was but Raedberht drew his own conclusions. As Flaedda turned and began to run he pushed his way past Winfrith, intent on giving chase. There was a sharp crack of a breaking branch and an angry yell as the ground under his feet gave way and he vanished from sight. A heavy thud was followed by the clatter of falling stones, an anguished groan and then silence. Winfrith stared at the gaping hole, her heart racing. If Raedberht thought he could climb out, he was being very quiet about it. She edged slowly closer and peered down into the drain. The sides looked reassuring smooth with no footholds and a slippery green slime covered much of them. At first she couldn't see Raedberht at all but as her eyes began to adjust to the near darkness below she started to make out lighter patches suggesting sand or gravel, and hunched against one wall, the unmistakable shape of a body, clutching itself as if to offer some comfort.

"Are you alive?" Winfrith called, feeling a little foolish. Her words echoed around the walls of the drain and she was about to repeat them when the dark shape shifted slightly, emitting a painful groan.

"Get me out of here," Raedberht growled, slowly forcing out each word, "unless you want to hang."

"I doubt if I could even if I wanted to. It looks impossible and you look in no state to do it on your own."

Raedberht tried shifting again but a sharp cry of pain suggested he wouldn't get far. He looked up, though it was hard to make out the expression on his face. "My ankles are smashed. They need binding. Fetch help or I'll break every bone in your body when I get out of here." For all his efforts to sound threatening, Winfrith was sure there was a hint of fear in his voice too. Enough to make him admit his crimes? She'd find out soon enough.

"That's a good enough reason to leave you there," Winfrith said. "No-one comes this way so I wouldn't bother shouting. I can only just hear you from here so cries for help certainly won't carry to Shapwick."

"Damn you…damn you to hell. I'll get out somehow and, when I do, you'll wish you'd never set eyes on me. I'll make you suffer…" His voice trailed off and Winfrith waited a few moments before replying.

"Suffering's what Eanflaed and Ourdilic did, and what you're about to share. Once the planks go back over the top you'll be in total darkness down there. No food, no drink… how long do you think you'll last? It could be ten years before they're lifted again. You'll be nothing more than a heap of bones. Anyone coming across them will think you're some unknown traveler who met with an accident. That would be a fair exchange, wouldn't it…dying just like those you killed?"

Winfrith paused, waiting for him to deny the accusation.

"You can't kill a thegn. My uncle will see you hang." He was breathing heavily and the words came more slowly. Yet perhaps he was not quite ready to confess in a way that would satisfy

Winfrith. For that she needed a witness and Heafa was the only one she could trust to back up her story afterwards.

"He's in Chippenham," she said. "Who's going to tell him you're here?"

"What good will leaving me here do you? You can have the aestel, if you want it. I won't stay around to accuse you of stealing it."

"It's lost. I told you. And in any case I never wanted it for myself. I thought it would lead me to Ourdilic's killer and it has, hasn't it?"

A sharp cry suggested Raedberht was still finding any movement painful, yet he was managing to choose his words carefully. "So if it's not that cursed morning gift you want, what is it? You can't let me die down here. You'll rot in hell yourself. What do you want?"

"I want a confession that you killed Ourdilic and Eanflaed, made before Alfred's witan, and full wergild payments made on behalf of both of them. Their lives must have been worth more that at least."

A hoarse laugh, followed by a spluttering cough and a curse echoed round the walls of the drain. Twice Raedberht almost choked on his words before he was able to give an audible reply.

"Go back to Alfred…to Athelney? You must be mad. I'm off to join my uncle. That's where the future of Wessex lies. Even if Alfed's dim-witted council decided wergild should be paid, what difference would a hundred shillings make to two dead women? No-one will think any better of them."

"Whatever anyone thought of them, they didn't deserve to be killed. If we killed everyone we didn't like, you'd have been dead long ago. You threatened me with a knife. Why would I want to save you now?"

"Because you'll hang if you don't."

Winfrith leaned a little further over the hole, hoping that Raedberht could make out her face. "It's taking you a long time to understand. Perhaps your injuries have dulled your brain. You'll be dead in three or four days. This drain will be covered over with solid planks. No-one will ever know you've been here. The Saxons on Athelney will assume you went to join your uncle. I'm going to eat now…a large bowl of hot pottage and a few cups of ale. A warm fire too. I'll come back with witnesses I trust. You can either tell the truth about what happened to Ourdilic and Eanflaed or I'll leave you there for good."

Winfrith waited a moment, giving him a chance to take up her offer, before turning back towards Heafa's door. As she stepped away from the trap she heard Raedberht's rasping voice, already sounding weaker.

"Wait! You can't do this. It's madness. No-one will believe I killed them." Winfrith smiled to herself. He sounded to be edging closer to a confession. A couple more hours in pain and near darkness ought to make him ready.

33

It was a relief to feel the warmth from Heafa's fire and to get some hot food inside her. Winfrith closed her eyes for a moment, enjoying the the sensation that her long search for the truth was near its end. Heafa was equally excited, swearing that she would remember every single word Raedberht might say and would repeat it word for word before the king himself. Winfrith doubted she could do so without adding a fair few words of her own but was grateful for the support.

"We should go back now," Heafa said, snatching away Winfrith's bowl as soon as she had emptied it. "The two of us must be able to scare the truth out of him."

"There's no hurry. The longer he waits, the more he'll suffer and the more frightened he'll get. Besides, I was thinking Flaedda should be with us too. Three witnesses are always more believable than two."

Heafa's eyes widened. "Flaedda? What use would she be? She never listens and as for speaking up as a witness, she'd be too timid even to open her mouth."

"You might be surprised," Winfrith said. "She might not say much and she likes to stay in the background but I think she takes in more than you think."

Heafa shrugged. "Well, if you think it's worth it, I'll go and collect her while you're finishing that cup of ale. We'll meet you by the storm drain."

"Watch where you're going," Winfrith called as Heafa headed outside. "You don't want to be joining Raedberht."

Heafa and Flaedda were crouched over one of the heavy planks when Winfrith returned to the storm drain, one at either end, clearly intent on moving it closer to the the gaping hole. Heafa looked up as she heard Winfrith approaching.

"He's not saying much," she said. "This ought to make him change his mind."

"Get me out of here," Raedberht called as Winfrith peered over the edge of the hole. His voice sounded weaker but he was still clearly defiant. She nodded towards Heafa.

"It's worth a try. See what awaits you, Raedberht. Talk or this could be the last time you see daylight."

Raedberht shifted onto his back as Heafa and Flaedda began to edge the plank into position. He cursed loudly as a shower of loose earth was scattered over him.

"One more and a bit of covering over and no-one will know there was anyone here," Winfrith said, hardly able to make out Raedberht at all now. "Take a last look at this world and remember Hell waits for murderers." She kicked a few more loose stones into the hole.

"Wait…wait. How do I know you'll get me out?"

"You don't know," Winfrith said, "but it's your only hope. Once we have our story, told before witnesses, we'll take it to Alfred. I'll tell folk here about your fall. Someone will probably come to your aid, as long as you promise to reward them."

Raedberht was silent long enough for Heafa to begin shifting the second plank. "See what it's like in utter darkness," she called. "Black as Hell itself."

He waited until a corner of the second plank began to overlap the remaining gap.

"Alright…alright…stop. I'll tell you."

Winfrith signaled to Heafa and Flaedda to join her, she hoped close enough to the edge of the drain for Raedberht to be able to make out their outlines. "Right, we're listening. Make sure it's the truth this time."

"They could have been accidents, both of them," he began wearily. "One was fool enough to run off in the dark; the other stepped off a sound causeway into a treacherous marsh. They'd probably have died anyway."

"But you made sure they did," Winfrith said.

"I didn't set out to. I was just trying to delay Aethelnoth. If he hadn't got his Somerset fyrd together, that would have been good news to take to my uncle. It was mere chance that I followed Aethelwold looking for that wretched girl. I heard them arguing, about Aethelnoth and her being pregnant. Not much of a surprise. Aethelnoth could never keep his hands off girls. Then Aethelwold stormed off leaving the girl alone. It was too good a chance to miss. If the girl vanished, Aethelnoth would have to face some awkward questions."

"So you threw her over a cliff? How brave."

They heard Raedberht clear his throat but he said nothing.

"Why would anyone accuse Aethelnoth?" Winfrith said. "Everyone assumed it was an accident."

"I'd have spread the story of him fathering Ourdilic's child. It would have kept him out of Cheddar for a few days, especially if he knew his wife was coming there."

"You took her life just to delay Alfred's preparations for a day or two?"

"I'd have let her wander further off, but she started kicking and screaming, trying to turn back. I didn't mean to push her..." He fell silent again. Heafa leaned closer to Winfrith, whispering in her ear.

"Liar...don't believe a word."

"What about Eanflaed?" Winfrith said. "You didn't mean her to drown either?"

Flaedda edged closer to the drain, near enough for Heafa to throw out a protective arm, and the girl shot her an angry look.

"Another of Aethelnoth's conquests...when she was just a girl. Byrtnoth might have saved me the trouble if he'd known."

"So why kill her? She'd done you no harm."

"She had that cursed jewel. She was hiding it before getting to Shapwick. I was curious about why she'd leave the causeway so I followed her and saw where she'd left it. I'd just retrieved it when for some reason she came back. She tried to snatch it from me and fell backwards. She must have caught her head on a rock. There was nothing I could do. She wouldn't have lasted long with a wound like that."

"You left her to drown," Heafa called down to him. "Just for a pretty bit of gold. We should leave you here to starve. See if you take it so lightly then."

"You promised to get me out." Raedberht was beginning to sound desperate now. "It wasn't just for the jewel. There was gossip about her in Shapwick...that she'd borne Aethelnoth's child. What with Ourdilic's pregnancy and Eanflaed possibly having a secret child, Aethelnoth would have good reason to steer clear of Shapwick if they both died suddenly. He'd be no use to Alfred then. And that's it. I've told you everything now. Go and get the help you promised."

"That makes you a traitor as well as a murderer and a thief," Heafa said, spitting out the words. "Shame there are no Saxon thegns here. I know what sort of help they'd give you if they heard what you've done…help to separate your limbs from the rest of you."

"We made a bargain," Winfrith said hastily. "We'll let someone know you're here once we've worked out the swiftest way to get your story to the king. In the meantime don't waste your breath shouting. There's no-one to hear."

She stepped back from the drain edge, catching hold of Heafa's sleeve and pulling her away before she could say any more.

"Leave him. Let him worry about his fate while we decide what to do. We all need to agree exactly what he said if anyone's going to believe us." Heafa took a couple of steps towards the house, obviously reluctant to leave Raedberht. Winfrith glanced behind her, assuming Flaedda would follow but the girl slipped into the holly trees, reappearing on the far side of the storm drain and heading off towards Shapwick.

"Flaedda, wait," Winfrith called after her.

"Leave her," Heafa said. "She'll wander about for a while and be back when she's ready…probably when all the hard work's been done."

Back inside the smoky warmth of Heafa's house, she and Winfrith pulled stools closer to the hearth. Heafa pulled a wrinkled strip of dried fish in two, handing Winfrith the smaller piece.

"He doesn't deserve to live," she said, gnawing at the fish, "whether he meant to kill them or not."

"Perhaps, but he can't pay for what he's done if he's dead," Winfrith said.

"Nor if he's supping ale with Guthrum in Chippenham."

"No, but his uncle had land and houses. When Alfred returns there will be Wulfhere's estate to divide."

Heafa nodded and resumed chewing at the dried fish. "Well he did admit he'd killed them. I'll swear to that if we get the chance."

"I'm still not sure he told the truth about why. There must have been easier ways of holding up Alfred's plans."

"Perhaps he just wanted the aestel. If Alfred had it made specially the heathens might have valued it highly."

"I'm fairly sure Eanflaed stole it after Ourdilic died," Winfrith said, shifting an unchewable lump of fish into her cheek. "She could hardly take her eyes off it whenever Ourdilic showed it off. Something else puzzles me though. Raedberht must also have tried to make me meet with an accident. I told you about almost drowning and about someone cutting a tree so it fell on me. If he was out to create discord and delay among Alfred's thegns, you'd think he'd be happy I was raising suspicions about Aethelnoth, Aethelwold and Byrtnoth. I never had any idea he was responsible. Why didn't he let me go on stirring up trouble?"

Heafa carefully picked a fishbone from her teeth. "Maybe someone else took a dislike to you too…or else Raedberht thought you were cleverer than you are. He imagined you'd already guessed what he'd done."

"I suppose so, though I don't know how he'd have got that idea. His name had never entered my head. Who knows? Perhaps it was just wanted the aestel and delaying Alfred was an afterthought. Ourdilic had lived with Olwen and I. He might have thought it was me and not Eanflaed who had taken the jewel."

Heafa took a noisy slurp of ale from a cup beside her before passing it to Winfrith. "Well it won't be up to us to give his reasons. We'll just have to swear oaths that we heard him admit to struggling with them both in a way that led to their deaths. You can count on me and Flaedda will say what she's told to."

"It might not be so easy," Winfrith said. "If the witan knows how the confession was got they might say Raedberht made it just to escape from the drain. We don't have the aestel to show it was stolen and our other oath-swearer Flaedda seems to have disappeared."

"Then we'll just have to persuade them. We can't do much about the aestel but we could start by looking for Flaedda. She won't have gone far."

Heafa and Winfrith set off again towards the storm drain.

"I've brought the rest of this half-chewed fish," Heafa said, holding it up. "The smell of food ought to loosen his tongue."

As they drew nearer there was still no sign of Flaedda but something else made Winfrith stop and catch hold of Heafa's sleeve.

"Look. One of the planks has been dragged back over the drain. Raedberht must have got out."

Heafa pushed past her. "He couldn't have…not without help. Someone must have been here." Winfrith caught up with Heafa and they advanced to the edge of the drain together.

"Probably some nosy neighbour heard him groaning. Probably run off to tell everyone there's a devil lurking in the holly trees. They won't be back in a hurry."

"It's hard to tell," Winfrith said, staring down into the hole. "That dark shape against the wall…that's him, isn't it?"

"You there, Raedberht?" Heafa shouted. "Hungry yet?" She waved the chewed lump of fish over the hole, clearly enjoying herself.

Winfrith squatted as near the edge as she dared, peering down at the dark shapes below. "It's not moving. Perhaps that's not him."

"Lost your tongue, Raedberht?" Heafa called, loud enough for his name to echo around the drain walls. "Might be your last chance to beg for mercy so you'd better speak up now or we'll have to leave you here for good."

"He can't." Winfrith scrambled to her feet, knocking Heafa backwards. They both scanned the trees alongside the drain where the words seemed to have come from. The voice had sounded throaty, as if the words had not come easily, just like a wounded half-starved man might sound. A slight movement among the holly branches caught Winfrith's eye. She clenched her fists, sure that they were about to be confronted by Raedberht. She glanced down, hoping to spot a stout stick or a heavy stone, but by the time she looked up again Flaedda was standing in the middle of the path.

"God's bones, girl, what are you about? Trying to scare us to death? And what do you mean 'he can't'? What nonsense are you talking now?"

"He can't answer you," the girl said calmly. Despite the shock of Flaedda's sudden appearance, Winfrith couldn't help smiling. For once Heafa's scolding seemed to be having no effect.

"Why not?" Heafa demanded. "What would you know about it?"

"I was coming back to the house so I looked to see he was still there. I think he was trying to climb. He must have fallen and hit his head. It made a dreadful noise."

"You heard him fall?" Winfrith asked, studying the girl's face.

Flaedda nodded, looking no more concerned than if she'd heard a pigeon calling. "I shouted down to see if he was alright but there was no answer. He must be dead."

"It'd serve him right," Heafa said, "and even if I was twenty years younger I wouldn't offer to go down there and see if he's still breathing."

"He's not moving…even if you kick stones down there."

Heafa stared at the girl and Winfrith wondered if the same thought had crossed both their minds. Had Flaedda dropped something heavier than a few loose pebbles? Was the dreadful noise she'd heard the sound of solid rock being rolled into the drain and falling on the defenceless Raedberht? The thought raised more questions than it answered, not least whether or not Raedberht was still alive. They should find that out before wondering whether Flaedda had worked out Eanflead was her mother and Raedberht had murdered her.

"How can you tell that, you foolish girl?" Heafa said, staring down into the drain. "There's barely enough light to see anything."

"Not if you pull that plank away. You can see him lying flat."

Heafa and Winfrith each took an end of the plank and dragged it away from the hole. It was true a little more light was admitted but it took Winfrith several moments to pick out the dark shape Flaedda had seen. It did look something like a body spread-eagled on the floor, except that one arm was not flung out wide, as you might expect if he had fallen back from the wall, but seemed to be curled around his head, as if defending it from a hail of missiles.

"If that's him," Heafa said, "he won't be climbing any walls again. Not in this life anyway. Even if we wanted to, we'd never get him out now."

They walked back to the house in silence. Even Heafa was lost in thought. Winfrith stole occasional glances at Flaedda, searching for signs that the girl was tense but her expression gave nothing away. Once inside Flaedda picked up some darning and retired to a corner.

"Some devil must have taken pity on him," Heafa said, finally breaking the silence. "Decided to finish him off rather than let him slowly starve."

"He can't have tried to climb," Winfrith said, "but Flaedda was sure she heard him fall. You don't think…" She nodded across to where the girl sat in the shadows.

Heafa shook her head. "Not a chance. Lives in a world of her own. She'll have forgotten there was a storm drain by tomorrow morning."

Winfrith nodded. Perhaps it was best forgotten. It seemed fairly certain that Raedberht was dead and that was probably no more than he deserved. If Heafa was wrong and, as Winfrith suspected, Flaedda took in a great deal more than she showed, there was nothing to be gained by pursuing it. Killing a thegn was a hanging offence and no amount of protesting innocence was likely to save someone like Flaedda. In fact it would be best if all the details of Raedberht's end were forgotten. After all, if Flaedda hadn't hastened his end, Winfrith herself and Heafa had caused his death and she had no wish to have to explain that to Alfred's witan.

"We should set both those planks back in place," Heafa said eventually. "Spring's not far off. They'll be overgrown again in no time."

34

Winfrith sat on the well-worn step leading up to the Sweet Way. It was only a few weeks since she had set off from this very spot to go in search of Eanflaed yet already the memory of that day was fading. Neither her death nor Ourdilic's had stood in the way of Alfred's plans to revive the fortunes of his kingdom. So was she right in thinking that the aestel had been what had spurred Raedberht to kill? It was strange that Ourdilic had seemed to care so little for the jewel itself, wanting it not for the gold or the bright stones but only for what a morning gift stood for…a marriage to the king's nephew. Eanflaed on the other hand had been unable to hide her desire for it, casting longing eyes whenever Ourdilic took it out. Not that Winfrith blamed her. It was easy to belittle earthly treasures if you had never had the slightest hope of owning any, but anyone who had held something as dazzling as the aestel in their hand would understand how easy it was to be bewitched by it. And now the shining gold and sparkling stones lay somewhere at the bottom of the vast stretch of marsh between where Winfrith sat and Athelney. It was probably the best place for it. The aestel had brought no joy to anyone who'd possessed it.

Alfred's band of loyal followers would soon be passing on their way to Egbert's Stone. Would they be surprised to find her here in Shapwick and, of more concern, would there be awkward questions about why she and Raedberht had disappeared from Athelney at the same time? He at least was in no position to warn Guthrum of Alfred's intentions though Winfrith had still not decided whether his fate should remain secret. Best perhaps to reveal only how he had taken her hostage and how she had managed to escape. Should she say he had stolen the aestel too? That would lead to further questions about where he'd got it from and she would have to either lie or name Eanflaed as a thief too. She cursed her indecision. She did want people to know what Raedberht had done, but she was determined no suspicion should fall on Heafa and Flaedda, the only two other witnesses to his confession. There had to be some way it could be safely done.

She looked up the hill towards the rooftops of Shapwick. A small group of women had gathered outside, keeping a watchful eye on the ridge above them. One or two had husbands and sons among Aethelnoth's Somerset fyrd and were hoping to catch a glimpse of them. Winfrith was looking forward to seeing Milred and Cuthbert and especially Olwen. She'd given little thought to the girl in the upheaval of the last few days. Her sudden disappearance from Athelney must have caused the girl considerable anxiety and it would be good to be able to set her mind at rest. She was turning over in her mind how much she should tell Olwen about Raedberht's last hours when she heard a shout from the watching women. One of them was pointing up the hill to where half a dozen figures had appeared above the skyline and were descending slowly towards them.

By the time Winfrith had joined Heafa on the path above the village, the line of men heading towards them had grown. As they came nearer Winfrith thought she recognized Aethelwold's red hair and the stocky figure of Beorhtric among them, but of Milred, Cuthbert and Olwen there was as yet no sign.

"I don't want to be seen…not yet," Winfrith said to Heafa, "not till I've spoken to Milred and Cuthbert."

Heafa looked surprised but for once realized the need to act promptly. She nodded towards the nearest doorway. "Go in there. Gilda's friendly enough. She won't mind. No-one up there will have recognized you if you're quick about it."

Winfrith stood in the shadow of Gilfa's doorway, keeping an eye on the new arrivals as they filed past. Most were too weary to look in her direction, more intent on finding a place to set down their various burdens and go in search of food and ale. She saw Alfred pass, along with a group of men she was sure hadn't been at Athelney. Gradually the gaps between new arrivals became longer until the path into Shapwick was deserted. What had happened to Cuthbert, Milred and Olwen? Surely the first two at least were too important to leave behind? She fought back the fear that something terrible had happened to Olwen, keeping her eyes fixed on the empty path.

She was on the verge of heading uphill to look for the three of them, when two more figures appeared over the ridge. One, a slight figure, was surely Olwen while the other, taller but laboring under a heavy burden, she hoped was Cuthbert. She slipped out of the doorway and headed up to meet them, expecting at any moment to hear shouts of recognition from behind her but none came. The meeting, half way between the village and the ridge, left Winfrith unsure whether to laugh or cry. She and Olwen clung together, unable to speak, while over the girl's shoulder Winfrith saw that Cuthbert's burden had frail hands and spindly legs and was the cause of loud complaints.

"A wonder all horses don't have short tempers," he said, lowering Milred to the ground. "This old fellow feels as though he ate an ox for breakfast."

"I said I'd walk," Milred said, "but you wouldn't hear of it." He sounded weary and a little confused, and Winfrith was sure he hadn't yet recognized her. Before she had a chance to greet him Olwen detached herself from Winfrith's embrace, holding her at arm's length and studying her face. "I thought I'd never see you again. I was sure something bad had happened…like Eanflaed…and Ourdilic…"

"It's alright," Winfrith said, smiling. "You can't get rid of me that easily."

"What happened?"

"Yes, what have you been up to?" Cuthbert asked, rubbing some feeling back into his shoulders. "We've had to manage without being questioned morning, noon and night."

"He doesn't mean it," Milred said, his eyes lighting up as they settled on Winfrith. "We were all concerned. No-one had any idea where you'd gone."

"It's a long story, best told over some food and ale. You all look much in need of both. Heafa has some soup bubbling away and we can exchange news in peace there."

"Not too long a story," Cuthbert warned. "We won't be stopping long."

"Raedberht forced me to go with him. He held a knife to my throat." Most of the soup was finished and now Cuthbert, Milred and Olwen sat round the hearth, eager to hear Winfrith's account of leaving Athelney.

"Surely Raedberht meant to join his uncle in Chippenham?" Cuthbert said. "Why would he take you with him? Unless, of course, a lonely man…"

"Nothing like that," Winfrith answered hastily, "not at all. Perhaps he meant to use me as a hostage, in case Alfred sent thegns after him. He was prepared to reveal Alfred's plans to assemble a force at Egbert's Stone to Guthrum. I suppose he thought he'd be pursued."

"We looked along the causeway and the track beyond but we didn't see any sign of him."

"Because he…we…left by boat," Winfrith said. "That's how I managed to get away from him. The boat turned over and he couldn't swim."

"You mean the poor fellow drowned?" Milred asked.

"Nothing poor about him," Cuthbert said. "No-one would reach out a hand to save a drowning traitor…any more than they would a drowning heathen."

"But you can't swim either, can you?" Olwen asked. "You nearly drowned when the rope broke crossing the river."

Winfrith hesitated. There was a chance here to explain away Raedberht's death without mentioning either the aestel or the storm drain. It was what she'd decided was the safest course and yet the innocent concern on Olwen's face was pulling her in the opposite direction. It would leave the deaths of Eanflaed and Ourdilic remembered simply as two unfortunate accidents, no different from what must have befallen Raedberht. She and Heafa and perhaps Flaedda would know that Raedberht had paid for two murders with his own life, but no-one else would. Could she live with that?

"You can't have forgotten. We all saw it."

"Of course, Olwen, I'm sorry. I was thinking back…to when I was a child. We lived by the river. My father made his living going up and down it to Hamwic. He taught us to swim, but we were never to go near the water after heavy rain."

"Good advice," Cuthbert said. "Easy to be swept away. So Raedberht ended up in a watery grave. We must make sure his uncle Wulfhere knows. If everything goes to plan he might be joining his nephew there soon."

"He didn't drown," Winfrith said, aware all eyes, including Heafa's and Flaedda's, were on her. "He managed to get back in the boat. He came after me and an old couple helped me hide until he'd gone."

Milred patted her arm. "So thankfully you're safe. He'll be well on his way to Chippenham by now."

"Er, no…he's not. He's here…in Shapwick."

"What? What's he doing here?" Cuthbert leaned forward, as if he was on the point of getting to his feet.

"Wait…it's alright," Winfrith said. "You won't find him…not alive anyway. He fell… into a storm drain. Must have hit his head. It's too deep to get him out."

Cuthbert gave her a searching look. Perhaps it seemed an unlikely accident to have befallen someone like Raedberht but Milred had no such difficulty, smiling happily at Winfrith.

"Well it's wonderful to find you safe and well. I always had my doubts about Raedberht but Alfred was loth to loose a good fighter."

"Where is this place Raedberht fell into? Alfred will want to know if he's dead," Cuthbert said.

"It's covered over now, with overgrown planks. No-one will ever know Raedberht's body is down there."

"You're sure no-one else knows?"

"Only Heafa and Flaedda, but they'll never say anything."

"Of course we won't. Do we look like fools?" Heafa called across the room from the corner where she was idly stirring the remnants of the soup. Winfrith smiled. Heafa had been so quiet she had almost forgotten she was there and yet there was clearly nothing wrong with her hearing. Cuthbert looked far from convinced she wouldn't repeat what she knew the moment they'd left but said nothing. After all, there was little he could do about it.

"We should probably leave things as they are," Milred said. "Raedberht had chosen to desert his king and side with heathens. No-one will want to mark his death. Leave him where he is, I say."

"There's more," Winfrith said uncertainly, knowing that she couldn't simply leave matters like that. "He had Ourdilic's morning gift with him when he left Athelney. He thought it would make a favorable impression if he presented it to Guthrum. I was sure he'd taken it from Eanflaed. When I accused him of killing them both to get it he admitted it. He was a murderer as well as a traitor and a thief."

Cuthbert sighed. "Not that again, Winfrith. And why Raedberht? You've already accused Aethelwold, Beorhtric and Aethelnoth. Who's next? Milred or me perhaps?"

"Of course not…and just because I was wrong before, it doesn't mean I'm wrong this time. Besides, he said he killed them both. He didn't mean to but that's what happened. People ought to know what he did. Ourdilic and Eanflaed didn't deserve to die like that and no-one should hold anyone but Raedberht responsible."

Winfrith glared at Cuthbert, prepared to argue for as long as it took to make him see. Milred laid a gentle arm on her shoulder. "Raedberht's dead. He can't be punished for anything he did now. If you persist in calling him a murderer, his kin won't leave you in peace. Wulfhere might sit in Chippenham with Guthrum but he still has many in Wessex who owe him favours."

Winfrith brushed his arm aside. "So just forget it…because his uncle was once an ealdorman? Ourdilic and Eanflaed don't matter? They were women. They came from Cornwall. If Raedberht can't pay, his kin should."

Milred nodded. "You're right. Sadly, it's not a perfect world we live in. Getting Raedberht's kin to pay wergild without credible oath-takers to back up your story will be nigh impossible, but we shouldn't abandon the idea without trying. Let me speak to Alfred, though now may not exactly be the best time. We head for Egbert's Stone as soon as everyone's fed and rested. Once we're there, I'll tell him the matter should be raised when his witan next meets."

"Thank you," Winfrith said, clasping his hands in hers. "I'm sorry I spoke harshly. Your help means a lot to me."

"Then let's hope it does some good. In the meantime, perhaps Heafa can find us another cup of ale."

It was easy to see why Alfred had chosen Egbert's Stone as a meeting place. A tree-encircled glade was dominated by a bulging granite boulder which looked as though it had sat there for a thousand years. As they waited Milred entertained Winfrith and Cuthbert with tales of how once crowds had been drawn here to watch the sacrifice of sheep and goats to the old gods. Some folk said that at dawn it was still possible to make out the places where the blood had flowed down the stone. Such practices would be loudly condemned now of course, though Alfred would be hoping for similarly large crowds. The fyrds of Hampshire, Wiltshire and Somerset had all been summoned, though, despite the months of planning for this day, no-one was sure how many men would answer the call. Those who had followed Alfred from Athelney had wandered a little uneasily into the centre of the glade. The king, looking pale and careworn, had gathered them around him, preparing to offer words of encouragement. Yet before he was able to speak one of his thegns gave a shout and pointedly excitedly towards the edge of the glade where the early morning sun cast the longest shadows. The powerful figure of Aethelnoth had emerged from under the trees and, as they watched, others stepped forward from the shade in two and threes, then small groups and finally in such numbers that they stood three or four deep in places. From somewhere among them a shout of 'Death to all heathens' rang out and others quickly took up the cry. The chant continued long enough to force Alfred to climb the stone and hold up his arms before quiet was sufficiently restored for him to make himself heard.

"Welcome," he began, his voice wavering a little. "It does my heart good to see you all here, and in such good spirits. The looks on your faces make the winter months hiding in the marshes and living on scraps seem worth the hardship. Not so long ago we all feared Wessex was lost. We were about to lose not just our kingdom, but our crops, our beasts, our houses, our pots, our knives, our gold…everything we held dear. Some, like my old friend Wulfhere, had given up hope and gone to join Guthrum. Others had taken to the hills and a few, no more than thirty and all here before me now, followed me loyally into the marshes so that we could begin preparing for this day."

Shouts and cheers greeted these words, echoing around the glade until Alfred again held up his hand for silence.

"We took care to ensure Guthrum was supplied with news of course. He was led to believe the few of us that were left were starving…that there was no fight left in us. Wessex was his for the taking. How surprised he will be when he's suddenly faced by a rampaging horde of mighty Saxons, determined to drive him from Wessex for good."

"Just as well there's no Raedberht to warn him," Winfrith shouted in Milred's ear as the chants of 'Death to the heathens' rose up again.

"Something to remind the witan of," Milred replied. "Nothing they hate more than a traitor."

The noise grew as shields were beaten with spears and new arrivals added their voices to the chant. If Alfred had meant to say more there was little chance of being heard. Besides, there was clearly no need to lift spirits any further. Everyone present, except perhaps Winfrith, Olwen and Milred, looked eager to be gone. Olwen leaned closer to Winfrith.

"I'm glad it was Ourdilic's morning gift and not you that ended up at the bottom of the marsh. I really thought you'd shared Ourdilic and Eanflaed's fate."

"It's not so easy to get rid of me," Winfrith answered, smiling, "as you've found out yourself. Someone needs to keep an eye on you."

Olwen laughed. "It's you needs watching. Always upsetting the rich and powerful."

"The wisdom of the young, eh? You might be right. In fact, if you ever see me poking my nose into something like this again, tie me to a doorpost and don't set me free until someone else has righted it."

It was quieter now as the crowd began to thin out. Cuthbert had clearly heard Winfrith's last instruction to Olwen.

"You might live longer," he said, "and save us all having to defend your endless awkward questions."

Winfrith didn't reply. He was probably right. She wouldn't mind an end to long marches, scarce food, inadequate shelter and threats to life and limb. She'd happily settle for a peaceful estate, a comfortable bed, food on the table and the older and wiser Olwen for companionship…for now at any rate. Until the next injustice came along…

Printed in Great Britain
by Amazon.co.uk, Ltd.,
Marston Gate.